NICHOLAS CARTER

KING'S MEN CROW

THE SHADOW ON THE CROWN

Book 3

PAN BOOKS

First published 1997 by Macmillan

This edition published 1998 by Pan Books
an imprint of Macmillan Publishers Ltd
25 Eccleston Place, London SW1W 9NF
and Basingstoke

Associated companies throughout the world

ISBN 0 330 33862 5

1 3 5 7 9 8 6 4 2

A CIP catalogue record for this book is available from
the British Library.

Typeset by SetSystems Ltd, Saffron Walden, Essex
Printed and bound in Great Britain by
Mackays of Chatham plc, Chatham, Kent

DRAMATIS PERSONAE

King Charles I.
Prince Rupert of the Rhine, his nephew.
Prince Maurice, Rupert's younger brother.
Charles, Prince of Wales; James, Duke of York:
His Majesty's sons.
Dr William Chillingworth, mathematician and inventor.
James Stuart, Duke of Richmond, a friend of
Prince Rupert's.
Mary Villiers, Duchess of Richmond, a very good friend of
Prince Rupert's.
Lucius Cary, Viscount Falkland, His Majesty's Secretary
of State.
Patrick Ruthven, Earl of Brentford, commander of His
Majesty's forces before Gloucester.
Sir Jacob Astley, commander of Royalist foot.
Sir John Byron, commander of Royalist cavalry.

Sir Edward Massey, Governor of Gloucester for
the Parliament.
Robert Devereux, Earl of Essex, principal
Parliamentarian warlord.
Captain Lieutenant James Harcus, officer, Earl of
Stamford's regiment, attached to the Gloucester garrison.

UNMENTIONED IN HISTORY

Parliamentarian:

William Sparrow, former officer of militia and cavalry
cornet, now captain, Mercer's regiment of foot.
Lieutenant Colonel Tobias Fulke, a gallant but elderly
gentleman, acting commander of Mercer's regiment
of foot.
Henry Mercer, cheesemonger and colonel.
Colston Muffet, sergeant, serving with Mercer's regiment
of foot.
Hereward Gillingfeather, an agitator, William Butcher,
sharpshooter, Caleb Cruickshank, pikeman, Stephen
Talbot, Rodney Sark, and John Jewell, enthusiastic new
recruits to Mercer's regiment of foot.
Ella and John Clamp, citizen defenders of Gloucester.
Nicodemus Burke, a boy, garrison runner.
Thomas Minter, Robin Fry, musketeers, Earl of
Stamford's regiment.
Mordecai Pitt, serving in the militia.
Alderman Simon Layton, a Gloucestershire magnate.
Samuel Jackson, his overseer.
Handy Michael, Elgar Maynard, Randall Planter,
his labourers.
Gallen Fey, captain of Parliament's ship *Conqueror*.

Royalist:

Sir Gilbert Morrison, disgraced MP, former colonel of
militia, wool merchant and turncoat, governor-in-waiting
of the Royal Westward Society of Oceanic Venturers.
Captain Jamie Morrison, his son, recuperating from
battle vapours.

Bella Margueritte Morrison, Sir Gilbert's
energetic daughter.
Anthony St John Dyle, Lord Clavincale, Royalist
entrepreneur and magnate, Bella's fiancé.
Mary Keziah Pitt, Bella's maid and confidante, William
Sparrow's sweetheart.
Master Algernon Starling, clerk to Sir Gilbert.
Captain Hugo Telling, disgraced officer of horse, Prince
Maurice's regiment, now captain to Morrison's regiment
of foot.
Benjamin Hazell, cornet to Prince Rupert's lifeguard
of horse.
Alexander Gull, his manservant.
Colonel Michael Slaughter, an officer recently returned
from service in Ireland.
Captain Shea, his second in command.
Colonel Nybb, mercenary and freebooter, acting
commander of Morrison's regiment of foot.
Zachary, Eli, and Jeremiah Pitt, serving in Morrison's
regiment of foot, or in Morrison's household in Chipping
Marleward, Somerset.
Elder Sergeant Cully Oates, one of Morrison's
veteran troops.
Ross 'Roy' Dunblane, Laird of Tullymallock, Scots
Royalist lord.
Rory George Dunblane of Candlewood, his father, a
Royalist lord.
Margaret, Lady Ramsay, widow of the Royalist squire Sir
Marmaduke Ramsay.
Anneliese Ramsay, her daughter.
Findlay, their gamekeeper and sharpshooter, serving as
sergeant major to Morrison's regiment of foot.
Matilda Dawkins, a Royalist camp follower.

Gideon Pike, a messenger.
Sergeant Joshua Lawton, dragoon.
Captain Andrew Malvern, commander of the guard.

'Your God Waller hath forsaken you, Essex is beaten like a dog. Yield to the King's Mercy.'

Royalist warning message fired by bow and arrow into the besieged city of Gloucester, August 1643.

PART ONE

CAVALIER SUMMER

Bristol Taking,
Exeter Shaking,
Gloucester Quaking.

Royalist rhyme

MUCH HINDON, ON THE GLOUCESTERSHIRE–WILTSHIRE BORDER

11 AUGUST 1643

The canny ringleaders worked their will through the scowling mob like maggots through a ripe cheese, insulating themselves from the apoplectic colonel's hawk-eyed stare behind wavering ranks of muttering men. His rasping bark knocked the guts from the unfortunates pressed up in the front rank quicker than a bellyful of chainshot, and undermined the uncertain rabble packed in behind them.

But their colonel's exasperated challenges failed to silence the whispers at the back, to still the sly, shuffling, shiftless insinuations of the hidden old hands – Michael Slaughter's renegade veterans.

Elder sergeants and scarred corporals pierced by their commander's pale-eyed gaze looked away, studied the battered steeple rising crookedly from the squat Saxon church across the square. Ragged waifs in greasy buff coats examined the waxy filth under their fingernails rather than endure his hateful glare.

But not a man jack of them moved.

'Slaughter's foot, have a care,' Captain Shea warbled, red-faced and as nervous as a new colt before the angry mob of men. 'Advance, *advance* your pikes and muskets!' he ordered.

The thickets of battle-grimed weapons bristled like

3

reeds in a breeze, but their surly owners remained where
they were, leaning wearily on their pikes as if they were at
the end of a long day's march, not being ordered off on
one. The musketeers' charges clinked on their worn bandoliers as they shuffled in sympathy with their comrades-
in-arms.

Michael Slaughter strode along the front rank, his feral
breath hanging in threatening clouds about his pale face.
They drew away from him as if he had the plague, a
buboed victim rising from the lime pit to ensnare their
souls.

'I thought it was King's men they'd sent me to lead, not
a pack of damned rebels,' Slaughter snarled, spittle spotting his wax-encrusted buff coat. 'Who says they won't
march?' he demanded, voice as harsh as a raven's in the
misty morning.

Long years of campaigning on the Continent – and
more recently in Ireland – had mangled his accent and
clipped the corners from his vowels. The scowling pack
gathered in the village square despised his dialect as much
as his manner, found his stern and vigorous command
almost unbearable after long months of easier service.

Who did he think he was ordering about, the damned
bogtrotter?

'Well?' Slaughter roared. His chilling challenge sparked
another epidemic of boot shuffling, another blind surge
of whispering from the sly soldiers at the back.

'We won't serve any Irish!' came an answering call from
the obscurity of the rearguard, a mass of smeared faces
peering over their comrades' shoulders.

Michael Slaughter squinted in at them as if he was a
gamekeeper out after a copseful of poachers. He gazed at
their resentful faces, turned away beneath steaming felt

4

hats, dew-jewelled morion helmets. He thought the shout had come from the wagon lines, stalled beside the abandoned inn on the far side of the trampled village green.

He couldn't even remember the name of the place. So much had happened so quickly since he had been sent down from Oxford to take command of these swineherds they had dared call a regiment. The former colonel, John Sparkes, had succumbed to the fevers which had decimated the training depot, weeded out the weediest of their weedy new recruits. Slaughter had inherited a sickly, surly mob, ill-disposed to marching, let alone fighting. God only knew how these wretched shits would act under fire.

He had been instructed to assume command and complete the march to Gloucester, to bring the newly raised regiment into the King's camp before the hastily erected walls of the old market town. They were ten miles short, a day's march from their triumphant monarch's mighty encampment. Ten miles short of the war which had been simmering and spluttering up and down the country for the past twelve months.

They could hear the dull thump of the guns clearly enough, but instead of marching on through the night to join King Charles' irresistible army they had dawdled and dwindled, running off into the woods as soon as the new colonel's back was turned.

'Ye're all fools,' Slaughter growled. 'I'm a Midlands man, as well you know.'

The surly pack knew no such thing.

He was fresh off the boat from Ireland, the Devil's own doorstep, who, why, and where he had served too complicated a matter for their campfire deliberations.

If he'd come from Ireland he must be Irish. Irish or not he was no better than the rest of the murdering Papist heathens who'd slaughtered men, women, and children during the notorious rebellions and constant bloodletting which the news-sheets had been breathlessly reporting for the past two years. Scenes of rape and slaughter luridly reproduced in crude but effective woodcuts, in endless pages of badly set type.

The wild rumours were puffed up like a paper galleon and blown into every port along the coast along with the pale-faced refugees, the pitifully few survivors of the holocaust. The scandalous stories were repeated around a thousand towns, passed like the pox from camp to camp, army to army, horrifying soldier and civilian alike. Even those readers hardened by reports of the atrocities on the Continent blanched at the descriptions of the abominations being committed in Ireland.

The heathen mobs had roasted children on spits before their gagging parents and gorged themselves on the scorched flesh. Given half a chance they would be scrambling on their leather boats and paddling like demons for England's shores, eating their kinfolk too!

A dozen armies roamed like rabid wolves over the ravaged countryside, Scots and Irish, Loyalists and Confederate, in the name of the King or Parliament, Catholic or Covenanter. Each regiment, each band divided upon itself, sub-let for the ceaseless slaughter.

To the four hundred ragged-arsed recruits on Much Hindon green, far from home under their stiff and unfamiliar new colours, Michael Slaughter's service was proof enough of his guilt, his vile complicity in the barbaric genocide across the water.

''E's Nottingham born and bred, I'll vouch for the colonel,' Captain Shea said stoutly, seconding the pale and silent commander who was pacing before them like an expectant father outside the midwife's hut.

The mob stood still, breathing as one. A big, stinking bear rousing itself from a long and arduous hibernation.

Nottingham, York, Newcastle.

The defiant scarecrows had no more grasp of their divided country's northern geography than the noisy rooks cawing in the churchyard elms. These were raw-boned country boys from the south-west, driven like cattle from one poorly armed militia to another, ruffians who didn't know who they served or particularly care. Bewildered herdsmen from the Wiltshire and Berkshire downs, poor tenants' sons from down the Fosseway, a scattering of turncoat Welsh who had served in half a dozen regiments already and never won a fight yet. Most of them had followed the drum – and the promise of a shilling or two – into the regiment that summer. A few dozen more had been pressed into service from the doss-pits and alehouses along the way, along with an equal number of turncoats captured on Roundway a few weeks previously. Half a hundred had already deserted, made off while the old colonel lay puking and dying and shedding his scaly skin in his tent. Another fifty more slipped off over the dewy fields while Michael Slaughter toured the pestilent camp counting heads.

Now the remnant looked ready to bolt, to join the scramble for the hedges and ditches, to desert their sovereign in his hour of need before Gloucester's Puritan walls.

If the King could take the city he would hold the key to Wales and the west, control all the territory from Cornwall into the south Midlands. His Royalist armies had whipped

Essex and destroyed William Waller's army on the slopes above Devizes, and then hurried west to wrestle Bristol from its Parliamentary overlords.

If Charles could finish the triumphant summer by taking Gloucester the war would be halfway won.

''E may be from Nottingen, but 'im's still Oirish,' a well-concealed wag bawled back.

'I've been fighting the Irish Confederates for eighteen months,' Slaughter snapped, unable to prevent himself from being drawn into an unseemly slanging match with his troops. Bickering like a corporal with his scum-pissing crew.

'Who dares suggest I'm one of them? Stand forth!' Slaughter yelled.

Captain Shea nervously tracked his commander, laying about the muttering ranks with his greasy gauntlet. 'Stand aside! Have a care!'

Shea's furious shouts seemed to send a frisson of anger through the thickets of pikes and blunt undergrowth of musketeers, further undermining the regiment's question-able loyalty. A bow-legged old veteran shoved the captain out of the honeycombed ranks.

'Watch it, Shea boy, or we'll be after you too, mind,' the veteran leered through the gaps in his black teeth.

'Cully Oates, you drunken oaf, any more of that clatter and you'll be running the gauntlet!' Shea snarled back.

The elder sergeant stood his ground, the regiment coagulating behind him like a bloody scab.

'Mutiny, would you, you feckless dogs?' Slaughter roared, thrusting the muttering mob back.

'Feckless yourself, you Irish butcher!'

'We'll not serve any Papist, King's commission or no!'

'Away with the bastard!'

8

'Do him in!'

Michael Slaughter spluttered with rage, wrenched his sword from its scabbard. The mob, propelled forward by the clever men at the back, closed in and pinned his arms to his sides so he thrashed in impotent fury. A brass-bound musket butt caught Shea behind his red ear and he jumped back, screaming. 'Hands off me, you scum!'

'Tie him up!'

'Hang the bugger!'

The angry crowd lurched and rippled, closing in like a greasy knotted noose about their screaming victims, lifting them like sacks of meal towards the elms beyond the churchyard wall.

The excited, shrieking mob froze in its tracks as the pistol shot cracked the air, sent the cawing rooks tumbling from their treetops. They peered over their shoulders like startled hares, completely oblivious of the horsemen who had trotted up. The narrow street leading between the leaning hovels was blocked by a phalanx of horsemen, a solid wedge of steaming horses and bedraggled Cavaliers.

Prince Rupert's dreaded cavalry, the scourge of every field.

Officers squatted over their saddles, armed to the teeth, watching the mutiny with beady eyed intent. A roly-poly red-faced colonel swallowed nervously, clearly relieved to be in the company of his rather more formidable major. A trollish bandit on a broken-backed chestnut cob, half a dozen callow youths pressing in beside him. Pasty-faced dandies from Oxford, a handful of the many hundreds of young bucks who had flocked to the King's colours. Their gaudy cornet hung limp on its battered standard, a splash of colour for the miserable town.

The mob paused, wondering. A whole regiment of

sword-rattling horsemen packed in behind them, no doubt. They'd be cut up like fat calves in this damned square.

The bully who had fired one of his assortment of pistols spurred his steaming horse forward, worked his way into the milling mutineers with impudent disdain.

'What's about, mineers?' he called, his outlandish accent even more startling than his peculiarly cut doublet and faded breeches. The baggy outfit looked as if it had been washed out under a thousand German downpours, the gaudy colours faded like old battle flags. The mutineers squinted at the newcomer, a ragged bear of a man in a rusty Polish helmet, the nose-guard crooked like an eagle's beak.

A war-band captain, a hugely experienced officer fresh from the endless German wars. An expert with death.

'And who might you be?' one of the perplexed ringleaders wanted to know. The boar-nosed giant grinned, his teeth glinting like sawn-off tusks under his barred helmet.

'Ah, mineers, my name's Nybb,' he called casually. 'And these brave boys behind me, they's my regiment. Now I reckon you'd best leave off mauling yer man there, don't you, now?'

The mob melted away like fat on a grate, depositing their stricken officers in a snarling heap beneath Nybb's steaming cob.

'That's better, boys. Nice and friendly, like. We dussn't want nay trouble now,' he assured them.

He lied.

BY
THE PIED HORSE,

HIGH HOLBORN, LONDON

The four of them had hauled their captain into the gloomy capital on a makeshift litter of broken pike-shafts lashed together with lengths of worn leather belt. The hastily improvised stretcher had broken down several times, depositing the unfortunate invalid into the potholed road on more than one occasion.

William Sparrow was oblivious to the upsets. He had missed the greater part of the hundred and thirty mile march, lost in a sweat-soaked nightmare of feverish imaginings. He had stumbled out of Bristol with the rest of the lost city's beaten garrison, but succumbed to the suppurating wound in his forearm as the dwindling column had approached Marlborough. His comrades carried him the rest of the way, suspended between them as he trembled and barked in his drooling delirium. Billy Butcher reacted to the captain's pitiful groaning with weary complaints of his own, eyeing the refuse-cluttered ditches along their way as if he was prospecting for a likely gravepit.

''E's cracked up as an ol' 'orse,' the Peckham dyer's apprentice complained to his equally exhausted sergeant. 'Can't see why we're botherin'.'

Colston Muffet, the grey-headed veteran, eyed him, lip curling contemptuously from his streaked teeth.

'We'll carry him back, dead or alive come to that,' he

11

rasped, hauling his corner of the stretcher higher and tilting the groaning passenger against his heavily bandaged right arm. Sparrow rolled his head, his mouth gasping the chill air.

'I'll not leave him, not after the *Purse*,' Muffet vowed.

'Me neither, not after the *Purse*,' Caleb Cruickshank repeated dumbly.

Butcher rolled his eyes as the slow-witted youngster struggling along behind him added his twopennyworth.

'Curse that captain to the deepest pits of purgatory,' Hereward Gillingfeather added from the far side of the stretcher. 'Throwing us overboard like so many sprats. Meaning no offence to you, boy,' he told Caleb gruffly, his blue eyes burning bright.

They tramped along in silence for a while, lost in their own gloomy reflections. A few short weeks before, and already their dreadful experiences seemed like somebody else's memories.

Sparrow had been caught with the Londoners on Roundway Down, rounded up like so many sheep as Sir William Waller's carefully cherished army fell apart like a paper tiger, swallowed up whole by the gleeful Royalist cavalry. They expected to be marched east to the Royalist gaols in Oxford, but had been among a hundred and six able-bodied men picked out for a longer, even more desperate march. South, to the Royalist-held Dorset coast.

Unknown to them, they had been selected by an ambitious and greedy Royalist lordling, anxious to make his name and fortune in the King's cause. If he could engage in a spot of freelance business of his own, so much the better. Anthony St John Dyle – Lord Clavincale, no less – had many contacts at the Spanish court, and had arranged to deliver a company of sound men for service in

Flanders. They had been marched into a hostile fishing village deep in Royalist territory, and loaded on board the *Messalina's Purse*, sleekest of all the King's privateers, which was running amok in the Channel, supporting the King's troubled cause in return for gold. The privateers operated out of Dunkirk, preying on Parliamentary merchantmen and running arms and supplies to the King's beleaguered forces.

Sparrow and his companions had been bound for Antwerp, cannon fodder for the hard-pressed Spanish tercios fighting for their lives in the Netherlands against the growing power of the French.

Fate took a hand before they had gone ten miles. Fate in the shape of a Parliamentarian man-of-war, a hundred-gun leviathan which ploughed through the teeth of a howling gale to pursue the unwary pirate vessel.

Caleb, the captain's dim-witted son, had been aloft, crouched in the foretop as the wind picked at his eyeballs, chilled his bones, and paralysed what little sense he had been born with. His furious father had cut and run, leaving a fiendish trail in his wake. He ordered a dozen of the spewing prisoners on deck, and had each one of them thrown overboard, reckoning the enemy captain might halt the chase to pick up his pitiful victims. His own flesh and blood fared no better, sharing their fate like a bag of refuse from the ship's galley.

Luckily for the drowning Roundheads and the unlucky boy, the skipper of Parliament's ship *Conqueror* rated their lives higher than his fleeing prize, and hauled half a dozen frozen survivors to safety.

William Sparrow, a strong swimmer since his boyhood in Bristol's busy docklands, saved the elder sergeant from drowning, hauling the old veteran into one of the ship's boats before slipping under the wild waves. Sparrow was saved by the horrified lieutenant in the prow, who ducked under the freezing spray to catch hold of the drowning man's drenched jacket.

The blue-skinned swimmers had been wrapped in blankets and warmed with hot grog, but had barely recovered their wits before the *Conqueror* arrived at her destination: the closely besieged port of Bristol, held for the Parliament by Nathaniel Fiennes and a couple of thousand highly unreliable troops.

The wretched survivors had been glad enough to go ashore with the landing party, taking powder and stores to the hard-pressed garrison. They were just in time to lend a hand on the walls as Prince Rupert's massively superior infantry brigades stormed the city from three sides. But the Prince's bawling troops were halted in their tracks all along the burning wall, hurled back in bloody confusion from the defiant forts.

Hundreds were slaughtered, more took to their heels despite Prince Rupert's furious attempts to rally them.

All except for Colonel Washington's dragoons, who took cover in dead ground between the forts on the north wall. The bewildered attackers probed the mysteriously deserted defences in front of them, hurried over the wall, and tore a breach for the fresh forces hurrying up behind them. The triumphant Royalists swarmed into the maze of burning streets near Park Row, sweeping Nathaniel Fiennes' small reserve out of their way and hurrying to occupy key points in the smoke-clogged city. The spirited and successful defence crumpled, the defenders haemorrhaging from the walls like blood from a mortal wound.

Long Col's battered squad had joined the desperate Roundhead rearguard on the Christmas Steps, a steep and

14

narrow short cut to the centre of the city. The King's men were hurled back twice, but their weight of numbers forced the passage at last and allowed the attackers to fan out towards the docks and the beleaguered castle. By the morning it was all over.

Bristol had been dearly bought, and the angry Royalists, cheated of their chance to plunder the city by the terms of the capitulation, had turned their frustration on the miserable prisoners as they shuffled out of Lawford's Gate.

The survivors were jeered as they marched out, and walked into an equally hostile reception as they made their way back to London, harangued and heckled by the country folk every step of the way. Many of the West Country men slipped away, having had a bellyful of war. Dozens more succumbed to their injuries, gangrenous arms and legs foul smelling and swollen, stinking stomach wounds and split skulls. The fighting on Bristol's walls had seen the worst carnage of the war so far, and many of its victims were rolled into the duckweed ditches which ran along their tortured route home. Shallow pits were dug each dawn at their improvised camps, swallowing up the night's crop of corpses.

Long Col remained at William's side, sharing what little food they had managed to obtain along the way. The captain, cut through the forearm by a Cavalier swordsman not far from the Christmas Steps, went from bad to worse, screaming and howling in his sweaty delirium. The deep cut went bad, seeping watery blood and evil-smelling pus into the grubby bandage Long Col had torn from the sleeve of his shirt. Billy Butcher wrinkled his nose in disgust as he watched the veteran sergeant tend the wounded man, lifting the grubby dressing from the captain's arm with infinite care.

''E'll 'ave to 'ave it orf,' Butcher commented.

Muffet eyed the belligerent apprentice warningly. 'Mr Fulke's promised he'll see the surgeons in London,' he growled, losing patience with the thick-skinned sniper. The colonel endorsed Muffet's prognosis as he made his cheerful way up and down the scattered packs of his rapidly dwindling command. He paused, looked down at the big man on the litter, noting the captain's waxy skin, the beaded sweat on his cold brow.

'I'll have Jacobs take a look at him, aye, and all the rest of you wounded,' Colonel Fulke called for the benefit of the exhausted survivors, huddled around their meagre campfires.

'A good hot meal and a flagon of ale for every man, as soon as we get to London,' he encouraged.

'And what about pay?'

'Aye, what about our arrears?'

'Home!'

An all too familiar chorus from the gloomy, dispirited encampment. Fulke straightened up with difficulty, his wild mop of snow-white hair filthy now, plastered to his careworn skull like a drenched goat. Sweat, blood, and mortar dust clouded his robustly healthy cheeks, giving him a ghoulish pallor to match that of his men.

The dreary column tramped on, shuffling along the dusty, potholed road: mile after mile of unceasing torment under the pitiless stare of the hostile country folk. They seemed to regard the ragged remnant as the sole cause of all their misfortunes, blamed the country's predicament on the sallow scarecrows who merely wanted to get home. The country folk shouted insults, denied food and water, and pelted the hungry mobs with stones and refuse. Tobias

Fulke was an officer, and as such he had been allowed to keep his sword when Bristol had fallen. The game old bird sallied out with it, driving the unwashed rabble away from his defenceless men.

'Get back to your homes, you fornicating scum, or I'll bring Waller's cavalry back to this damned burgh tomorrow and put the lot of you to the sword!' he barked, striding into the packed mob as if he commanded a thousand elite horsemen.

Fulke refused to be defeated. He cajoled and cheered, helped the wounded and regaled the waverers with tales of his dreadful experiences in the German wars. 'If you think this was bad, you should have seen Magdeburg,' he would say, clicking his tongue and nodding his tireless white head.

Despite his best efforts, the tattered regiments evaporated day by day, less than a thousand men reaching the dubious sanctuary of the capital. The gloomy Londoners gaped as they shuffled in like whipped curs. All they lacked were the chains of their captivity, a deficiency which the triumphant King would no doubt remedy all too soon.

The defeated officers rode ahead of their men to face the angry, frightened questions of their fellows in the House. The garrison commander, Nathaniel Fiennes, was made an immediate scapegoat, blamed by his Parliamentary colleagues for surrendering the second city of the land so soon. His former friends ordered an immediate inquiry into his conduct of the defence, accusing him of cravenly selling the city to the enemy. Fiennes, stung by his accusers, blamed the disaster on Sir William Waller, claiming he had drained men from the garrison for the field army he had subsequently lost on Roundway. If they were going to try him for cowardice, what about William the Conqueror?

Nathaniel Fiennes' exhausted lieutenants retired to their own headquarters to begin the thankless task of rebuilding their decimated regiments. Tobias Fulke set up his base at the Pied Horse in High Holborn, and set about his assignment with his usual good cheer. He had less than fifty men left, but they needed board and lodging until the army sorted out what to do with them. Fulke, typically, agreed to meet the bill from his own somewhat straitened resources.

'You can pay me back when the Commissariat office catches up with you,' he joked to the unarmed rabble.

'What about our pay?'

'Home, home!'

True to his word, Fulke ordered his personal physician to tend the few wounded who had survived the evil march east. Mr Neremiah Jacobs bathed the wounded captain's forearm, drained the vile fluid from the raw muscle beneath the yellow flesh. Bathed and bandaged, and fortified by Goodwife Jacobs' steaming possets, Sparrow recovered slowly but surely, and was sitting up and talking with his comrades by the end of the week. He shook his bearded head in wonder at Long Col's description of the agonizing journey.

'Ah, you were better off out of it, mate.'

'Good job you fell in with us, Will. The other buggers would have dumped you in the nearest ditch and good bliddy riddance,' Butcher chortled.

Long Col scowled at him. 'Good job he fell in with us?'

18

he asked. 'He wouldn't have gotten far if it had been up to you, you damned jackdaw.'

'I niver said a word,' Butcher replied indignantly.

Gillingfeather, their agitator and fire-and-brimstone soldier of God's fortune, shook his head. He had been unusually tight-lipped during the hellish march, but seemed to rediscover his tongue back in his home town.

'Work it out for yourselves, lads,' he said wonderingly. 'Forty days and forty nights we've been at it. Forty days and nights in the wilderness,' he went on, piously. 'Tried and tested at every turn. Ah, boys,' he said, rolling his bright eyes towards the smoky eaves of the crowded pub, 'Our Father sought us out and found us worthy.'

Sparrow sank back on his sickbed, on the verge of a serious relapse. Billy Butcher sniggered into his dirty fist.

'Ah, you can smile, Billy Butcher, but he saved you too,' Gillingfeather scolded him. 'He saved us all, to fight the good fight,' he said, warming to his theme and pacing the tiny garret in delighted agitation. The dapper little fighter turned on his worn heels and pointed a trembling finger at Sparrow.

'You survived your trial, your trial was our trial,' he reasoned.

'We'll all be on trial all right, if the King comes,' Butcher said sulkily.

'Waller gone, Bristol lost, that fat bastard Essex squatting on his arse.' Colston Muffet shook his head, stroked his stubbled chin.

'The King had his chance after Etch-Hill,' he said meditatively. 'He hasn't the men left to take the capital, no matter what else he gets his mitts on.'

'The Lord shall smite the serpents who serve that Papist

19

hound, He shall rise and . . .' Gillingfeather worked himself up into a genocidal rage, striding about the gloomy garret as if he was addressing the entire Roundhead army. Long Col got to his feet and held the smaller man back by his twitching shoulders.

'I think we'd better let Cap'n Sparrow rest a while now, Gilly,' he said encouragingly. 'He's had enough excitement for one day.'

William slumped back on his damp pillows, gave an indulgent yawn.

He'd had enough bloody excitement to last him a lifetime.

Three days after his unconscious arrival in the capital, William took his first tentative steps around the crowded, noisy inn. Over a hundred men were crowded into the lopsided building, smoking, drinking, waiting. Officers went to and fro counting heads, stepping over the legs of the truculent warriors stretched out on the narrow landings.

Tobias Fulke pushed his way through to the snug, nodded indulgently at the pack of soldiers busy watching a one-eyed musketeer deal the greasy cards. His arrival sparked an immediate outcry from the disgruntled (and penniless) players.

'Yes, yes, you'll get your money,' Fulke snapped testily, irritated by their constant catechism. 'Home home, pay pay.' He scowled at the idle soldiery, knowing full well half of them would be off the moment they had received a penny of their long-awaited arrears. 'They're sending the Commissariat officers down this very afternoon,' he told them.

'About bloody time and all!'

William Sparrow queued with the rest, holding on to his heavily bandaged arm and blinking back waves of exhaustion which threatened to overwhelm him. He hadn't fully recovered from his ordeal, and if he fell to the floor in the middle of this damned mob he never would either.

The dirty soldiers packed into the passage barging and shoving each other, lining the snug in feverish expectation as the unsmiling paymaster eased his black broadclothed bulk behind one of the Pied Horse's well-worn gaming tables, and calmly set up his stall in front of the staring troopers. The commissioner took off his hat, rubbed some dirt from the wide brim, and set it down alongside the bound chest he had carried in with him. He kept the box at his elbow, resting his thick cheesy fingers on the bound lid while his clerk settled himself on the stool beside him, and unrolled a bewildering assortment of rolls and lists. As well as his pasty-faced assistant Master Pritchard had brought along a couple of trusted captains from the Earl of Essex's lifeguard, and had also invited Colonel Fulke to sit in on the interesting discussions ahead. The russet-coated cavalrymen eyed the unwashed rabble with contempt, as if Parliament had decreed they were to pay the men from their own pockets. Master Pritchard gathered the precious chest to him and gingerly opened the lid, as if it were a treasure trove for his eyes only. He worked his pale hand into the box, bringing out a fistful of coins, and stacked them in neat towers next to his enormous leather-bound ledger. Tobias Fulke sat beside the leering paymaster, to keep an eye on his men and provide testimonials as to their services if and when necessary. Master Pritchard coughed loudly, heralding the start of the historic transaction. His overworked assistant bent over the ledger, recording every name in large black letters, and the amount they had received in the next margin. Every now and then he scanned his payroll lists to ensure the claimant had served as he suggested.

'Colston Muffet, Elder Sergeant, Merrick's foot, sir!' Long Col had been one of the first to enlist in the city of London regiment which had been raised the previous year for the Earl of Essex's fledgeling army. He hadn't been home to Greenwich since. 'I was at Chewton, sir, then Lansdown, Rowde Ford, and Roundway with Waller.'

'Sir William,' Pritchard corrected him, punctilious to the end.

Long Col nodded. 'We were captured on Roundway with the rest of 'em and shipped off west and put on a boat for Flanders—'

'Yes, yes, we don't need your life story, man!' Pritchard interrupted. 'Just give us the dates of your service or we'll be here all day!'

The clerk located Muffet's name on one of the muster rolls, added his name to the ledger.

'Captured, eh? Not served since?'

'I was saying, sir, we got shipped to Bristol on the *Conqueror*—'

'Really? Gallen Fey's ship? Good friend of mine, old Gallen,' Pritchard went on.

'So we were there for the storming,' Muffet continued, patient as a rock before the red-faced commissioner.

Tobias Fulke nodded soberly. 'And damned glad we were to see him, and all his men,' he volunteered.

The commissioner scribbled something in the ledger, and lifted the lid of the precious box. Every eye in the inn was glued to the magical contents.

'Half now, the rest will be payable in three weeks' time,' Pritchard growled.

There was a murmur of dismay around the packed inn.

'Anybody signing on for further service will be entitled to an extra two shillings, payable immediately,' he called over the tumult.

'Further service? We've served enough!'

'Pay up, you old bugger!'

'We've earned it, aye, and more!'

Fulke climbed to his feet, calming the more belligerent philanthropists.

'We fought and we died for that money, it's ours by rights!'

Pritchard hunched over his chest like a protective hen. 'Parliament will pay every man for every moment of his service as and when funds become available,' he snapped. 'In the meantime, in consideration of the desperate straits in which we find ourselves, anybody signing up with Henry Mercer's regiment will receive two shillings bounty with all other monies being paid in three weeks' time.'

'Henry Mercer? Cheesemonger Mercer?'

'Has been commissioned to raise a regiment of men for the Earl of Essex's army. Your Colonel Fulke here has already agreed to command in the field.'

Fulke nodded encouragingly. 'There we are, lads, all together again, what d'you say?'

The inn fell silent.

Colston Muffet, who made a point never to make any unwarranted advertisement of his political or religious views, gazed around the packed room, nodded his grey head wearily.

'Aye, sign me up,' he said slowly.

Pritchard's clerk completed the entry beside his name

and the commissioner released a small advance guard from his jealously hoarded pile of coins.

'Name?'

'William Sparrow of Chipping Marleward. Captain.'

Pritchard eyed the hollow-cheeked officer, who was propping himself up against the table with difficulty, left hand clutching his injured arm.

'Captain?'

'Aye. Field promotion. He did sterling work on Bristol's walls,' Fulke agreed.

'And how long have you served?'

'I joined Morrison's militia back in July. Then I joined McNabb's cavalry as cornet the day before Lansdown. I also fought at Rowde Ford and Roundway, I got captured...'

'And voyaged to the Americas, no doubt. Wait a moment, young man. Morrison's militia? Sir Gilbert Morrison?'

William nodded glumly. They had heard of him, then.

'Are you aware there is a warrant out for his arrest?'

William was well aware of the warrant. His former colonel and mentor had raised a regiment from the Somerset hills near his home, but promptly left them in the lurch taking the pay for six hundred men with him. He had deserted to the enemy before his ragged-arsed militia had heard one shot fired in anger. William's dubious commission wasn't worth the paper it was written on, which was why he had joined the cavalry. Surely they had heard of Archibald McNabb? A great one for filling out forms, old Archie. William wondered where the red-haired Scot had got to.

'I signed up in good faith, whether he was a turncoat or no,' he argued wearily.

Pritchard frowned. 'We've no record of his blasted regiment,' he snapped. 'McNabb, you say?'

'Major in Waller's horse.'

'Ah yes, that McNabb. Made you a cornet, did he? On or about July the fifth?'

William nodded.

'Then what?'

'I got captured on Roundway.'

'On July the thirteenth. That's one week's pay as cornet. Next!'

William blinked, hardly able to believe his ears. One week's pay? 'I served at Bristol!' he declared.

Fulke nodded. 'Aye, he served all right. I made him captain the morning we marched out,' the gallant old gentleman confirmed.

'Two weeks' half-pay as captain,' Pritchard dictated to the busy clerk. 'We don't pay men to sit around on ships or wander about the country,' he observed waspishly, peering over William's slumped shoulder.

'I've been in arms since June,' he spluttered, hardly able to maintain the one-sided and clearly hopeless argument.

'Here's your money, take it or leave it,' Pritchard snarled.

'An extra two shillings for signing on, eh?' he asked.

'Aye, come on, lad, no hard feelings now, eh? You did well on Bristol's walls, we'll do well again, together, what d'you say?'

'Sign me on,' William said wearily. What choice did he have? He had no home, and no work, now that Bristol had fallen and the countryside round about had been invaded by the enemy. All he had was war, and he was little enough use at that. He stood to one side, and watched the clerk record his name on the fresh new muster list. Twenty minutes later, Gillingfeather, Butcher, and Cruickshank's names had been added to the growing column.

'Cheesemonger Mercer, eh?' Muffet asked, shaking his head in disbelief as they made their way past the queue of men into the courtyard of the overcrowded inn.

'Home from home for you boys,' one of the orange-sashed cavalrymen sneered. 'You're all off to Gloucester!'

'At the double and all,' his grinning companion guffawed.

'Gloucester at the double . . . double Gloucester, get it? Ah ha ha ha!'

MUCH HINDON CHURCH

N ight had crept up on the village like a thief, worked its dark fingers through the dripping woods behind the churchyard and jemmied the darkness between the ancient tombstones. The crooked slabs, eaten up with spongy mosses and damp lichens, were cropped and grazed by the horses picketed along the drystone wall. The animals stretched their necks over the tottering obstacle and stripped the growths from every tomb and broken memorial within reach, revealing the names of the long-dead villagers. Clouds of gnats rose and fell from the steaming beasts as they swished their tails in the cool twilight, completely oblivious to their nervous and agitated masters.

Michael Slaughter's mutinous crew were shoaled together in the middle of the village green, clustered around a dozen watchfires, watching their backs. The Cavalier horsemen who had ruined their play that morning had continued to patrol the deserted village, trotting up the main street and off down the narrow lane beside the church into the brooding wood beyond. They would complete a circuit of the plantation and circle back to the other end of the village through the tangle of allotments and vegetable gardens at the back of the poorer hovels, ensuring the surly foot soldiers remained where they were, so many mackerel meshed by a roving steel net. Slaughter's men might have made it to the temporary sanctuary of the wood, but they wouldn't have gotten far trying to outrun a horseman over the sticky clay furrows beyond.

There were plenty more newcomers camped just over the field, commanded by a former gamekeeper who could shoot the wedding tackle from a house mouse at a hundred yards – according to that bloated sack of a colonel who had arrived to nip their bad-tempered mutiny in the bud. Slaughter's accusers had retired to the green for the night, huddled together to reconsider their ill-conceived actions.

Cully Oates stamped his worn boots in the middle of the nervous rabble, and spread his palms over the flickering flames. His belly was rumbling the same as the rest, their provisions having run out the day before. The regiment had fallen on the village like a plague of locusts, snatching up squawking pullets and tugging root vegetables from the villagers' neatly worked plots. But Mr High and Mighty Whoreson Slaughter had put an end to that, threatening to flog any man caught looting. Little wonder the men had turned sour on him. What good were four hundred blasted skillingtons to the King's cause?

'By God, look at 'em.' Oates spat into the hissing flames, nodding at the patrolling horsemen on their steaming horses. 'Don't those candle-wasting bloats ever give up? Up and down all bliddy day never givin' folk a bit of peace! Get off and milk it, you bliddy whores' melts,' he called as the young Cavalier captain guided his horse along the perimeter of the surly encampment.

The callow youth looked up gloomily, but hunched himself back down into his new buff coat like a nervous turtle. Cully Oates shook his head.

'That's right, sir, give the beast a breather,' he advised

as the youngster, apparently satisfied with his reconnais-
sance, swung his horse towards the picket line along the
church wall and dismounted with a heavy, heartfelt sigh.

'Fuck my old boots, what a set of sprats. They better not
get saucy around me, I can tell yer,' the gruff old veteran
promised, winking at his distracted neighbours. Two strapping pikemen, Monmouth caps pulled down over their
bushy black hair, eyed the strange horsemen as if they
were so many centaurs.

'What's the matter with you two pricks? Ain't yer seen a
bliddy 'orse afore? Don't they 'ave 'em down your way,
then?'

Zachary and Eli Pitt, many miles from home and cut off
from their old friends in Chipping Marleward's simple-
minded militia, shook their heads mournfully. Rounded
up with the rest of Sir William Waller's army on Roundway
Down, they had volunteered for service with the King's
forces rather than face an uncertain future in one of
Oxford's notorious gaols. Now, these few short weeks later,
their future seemed equally grim. They had no idea where
they were, where they were going, or who they were
supposed to be fighting at the other end – let alone why.
Their most pressing concern was the all too real possibility
of running into their younger brother Mordecai, who as
far as they knew was still fighting for the Roundheads.
What if they were thrown in together, firing and banging
and piking their own flesh and blood? The bewildered
brothers shivered miserably, shuffling closer to the muttering veteran as if he was a buff-coated mother hen.

'What d'you reckon they'll do to us then, Cully? For
making sport with the colonel, like?'

'Well, they haven't hung us up yet, so count yer
blessings,' the old soldier said gamely, kicking up the fire

with the toe of his broken-down boot. 'They'll cuss us out as usual, but it'll be matey this and old pal that when they wants their fightin' done for 'em, mark my words.'

The villagers had shut themselves up like brick and mortar crabs, lampless hermits closed down in their precious shells. There was hardly a light to be seen behind the shuttered windows along Much Hindon's dreary main street, as if the fearful citizens imagined they could make the invaders disappear into the night if they held their breath long enough. Not all the panic-stricken population had managed to lock the Royalist rogues out of their homes, however. The wandering horsemen who had caused such a stir that afternoon had requisitioned Mr Rice's fine timbered house overlooking the green, forcing the lawyer and his young family to abandon their own hearth and take refuge in the scullery. The frail, prematurely aged solicitor squatted by the grate munching a piece of cheese as his servants hurried in and out of the best room with trays of provisions for their uninvited guests.

Mr Rice looked up as the back door opened and a morose young man in riding boots and a threadbare coat stepped in and snatched off his hat. The youth cast one gloomy look at the lawyer and his frightened family, and nodded his careworn head.

'They're through there, are they?' he asked flatly, wiping his boots on the rush mat.

'Aye. Help yourself,' Rice invited sourly.

The buggers would need no second invitation. All he could do was sit tight and pray they would leave in the morning. Free quarter was a terrible burden for the country folk throughout the land. It could also be extremely nerve-racking, especially if one had established a reputation for strong views towards any particular party. Mr Rice, cursed by a thoughtful and deeply pacific nature, had seen the trouble the King was bringing on himself and wished to God he had been blessed with wiser counsels, but he could not condone rebellion, and had used what little authority he had in the village to try and keep his more headstrong neighbours from over-hasty decisions. He understood well enough the best option now was to give the soldiers what they wanted, and try and keep the best plate out of sight.

The downcast youth nodded as if it was his own home being invaded, and strode through the parlour to the oak-panelled splendour of the main room. They had banked the fire up high with several buckets of coals (all too scarce with the trouble up north and all) and half a dozen logs they had sent the lawyer's eldest son to fetch from the outhouse: the fierce heat had penetrated their damp coats, which were steaming gently on the backs of their chairs.

Sir Gilbert Morrison looked up from his armchair beside the fire as the young cavalryman closed the latch on the fearful family in the parlour. 'Ah, there you are, Hugo lad. All quiet?'

Hugo Telling nodded miserably. 'They fell for it, like you said,' he reported. 'We kept riding around them, they thought there were hundreds of us.'

'Capital! A stratagem worthy of the great Wallenstein himself, wouldn't you say?' the merchant turned warrior enquired. Michael Slaughter, squatting uncomfortably on the settle opposite, snorted into his damp russet moustache.

Major Nybb grinned like a hungry bear, nodding his head as he recalled his days fighting alongside the great Czech adventurer.

'Ah, mineers, old Albrecht,' he reminisced in his peculiar camp dialect, the lingua franca of the mercenary armies which had ranged all over Germany for the past twenty years. The monstrously mutilated mother tongue of a generation of warriors who had known nothing but war, and could not under any circumstances contemplate peace.

Hugo wasn't listening.

He gazed gloomily at the unlikely allies, wondered for the hundredth time how they had ever talked him into signing up for their Machiavellian manoeuvrings. None of them got up in the morning without a crafty peek under the covers to make sure their toes weren't whispering secrets. They must have known he was no use as a spy, that he was far too transparent for their steel-eyed intrigues. He wore his heart on his sleeve, always had and always would. He sighed heavily. The despondent youth knew he had been easy meat for the crafty merchant. Hugo could have cut him to ribbons in thirty seconds if it had been a test of arms rather than brains, but the wily old bugger had preyed on his mind, fed like a leech on Hugo's brimming reservoir of personal grievances.

He knew he had been duped, roped into their bizarre schemes like a newly broken colt, but the knowledge only served to fan the raging fires of his self-disgust. He was a useless fool, robbed of his rank and robbed of his honour. He should have stayed at home, playing in the gardens of the old rectory at Wainbridge with his spaniels or riding around the orchard on his plump little pony. A weak, sickly boy tormented by his bigger brothers and his father's all too evident disappointment when he had refused to pursue a clerical career. How had he ever imagined he would make a soldier?

Hugo had been half-heartedly studying law at Oxford when the Cavaliers came along and filled his head with dreams of silk and velvet, swords and battle. He had rushed over the quad to enlist in Prince Maurice's regiment of horse (he would have spat on the bare stone flags at the very mention of the name now, but he despised the vile soldiers' habit and allowed himself a small grunt of anger instead), spent a wonderfully bitter winter hunting Round-heads over frosted fields, and had been awarded with the command of a troop of sixty Royalist horsemen for his troubles. Hugo had been happier than he had ever been in his short, barren life.

The summer, though, had brought a marked change in fortunes as well as weather.

He could trace his own personal decline back to that stuffy day in June when he had organized an ambush to relieve a fat Somerset merchant of a wagonload of wool.

Hugo leaned by the dresser, eyed the jolly old buffoon beside the fire. Aye, *that* fat merchant. Sir Gilbert had been strong for the Parliament back then, speculating in wool, milk, meat, and foodstuffs while the warclouds gathered themselves up far to the west. By the time the invading Royalist army under Prince Maurice (drat him) and Sir Ralph Hopton had reached Morrison's highly productive fiefdom in the Mendips, the wily merchant had decided to change sides, and announced his immediate re-enlistment in the King's noble cause.

Before his sudden change of heart, Sir Gilbert had been a formidable and familiar figure around the scattered hill villages, and had enjoyed the dubious assistance of a curly headed rogue called Sparrow (blast *him* to the uttermost pits of hell!) who produced sheaves of lying newsletters and pamphlets to keep the misguided citizens in the dark about Morrison and his precious Parliament's foul, treacherous motives. That swede-brained, ape-armed oaf Sparrow had been hiding in Sir Gilbert's wool wagon when Hugo tried to snatch it, and by a series of unspeakably ungentlemanly tricks managed to ruin his entire, carefully planned enterprise. To add insult to injury Sparrow then wrote about the incident in one of his pestilential news-sheets, making Hugo look a complete fool. *Royal Wool-Gatherer Foiled* indeed!

The headline had burnt into his embarrassed brain like letters of molten lead.

As if he hadn't been humiliated enough by Sparrow's breathtaking insolence, Hugo then endured the mortifying experience of meeting the clumsy soldier in battle on Lansdown. The buffoon had been riding his great wall-eyed piebald cob, a lumbering beast with barely a canter in him. But instead of catching up with the rogue and running him up to the hilt on his sword, the peasants' champion managed to inflict another cowardly blow and unseat his furious attacker. To his eternal shame, Hugo was marched off the ridge a prisoner, jeered by his Roundhead captors, and especially by the overgrown oaf on the stumbling piebald.

He escaped of course, and then, then . . . although God knew he had done nothing to deserve such a run of truly biblical bad fortune, *then*, Hugo had taken his troop of horse to Bristol.

The youth bowed his head at the shocking memory, tears of shame springing into his eyes.

Sir Gilbert looked up from his throne beside the

fireplace, caught the shards of light in the boy's averted eyes.

'By Heaven, lad, what's got into you now?' he called.

Hugo ran the back of his hand over his tortured features, shook his head dismissively. 'It's the fire, it's stinging my eyes,' he explained feebly.

Slaughter glanced at him from his uncomfortable perch on the settle. Nybb muttered something into the tangled rope mat he called a beard. The officers resumed their discussion, ignoring the blubbering boy behind them.

Bristol. Bristol, Hugo mused, determined to run himself through on the bitter, gut-souring memory. He ran the nightmarish events through his head every day, a penance for his disastrously humiliating experience, as if by wallowing in his abject misery he would one day free himself from his dishonour.

He had escaped from the Roundheads by leaping from a barge halfway across the River Avon near Bath, and swam to the bank where he had been rescued by a Royalist cavalry patrol. Hugo eventually returned to his unit suffering from a crippling cold, but returned to duty as the army laid siege to Bristol. Telling's troop had been billeted at nearby Bedminster, but instead of ensuring his men set a proper watch he allowed himself to be persuaded to go to bed and shake off his crippling chills.

That very night Sparrow – whose every martial enterprise God had apparently seen fit to bless as if he was some turnip-brained Alexander – led a daring Roundhead patrol right into their quarters, killing seven of his men and driving off thirty horses.

Hugo, sneezing like the plague, led the pitiful remnants

back to the main Cornish camp on foot, and ran into Prince Maurice, his burly, short-tempered hero. The Prince, already furious with the conduct of the siege, poured all his wrath on the boy, humiliating him in front of the entire army and stripping him of his rank.

Hugo, dying of shame and wracked with chills, wandered the deserted roads until he was picked up by one of Morrison's carts and taken to the merchant's temporary headquarters at Kilmersden Hall, the home of his bitter and detested rival Sir Marmaduke Ramsay, recently slain on Lansdown.

There Hugo was gradually nursed back to gloomy good health, his only occupation trying to fathom out the strange relationship between the wily impostor Sir Gilbert and his somewhat reluctant host Margaret, Lady Ramsay. It appeared the merchant had some kind of financial hold of his rival's widow, the servants whispering that the turncoat merchant was even trying to arrange the marriage of his daft son Jamie to the Ramsays' plain but even-tempered daughter Anneliese.

Young Jamie had fought on Roundway for the Roundheads, and although he hadn't been injured his brain had cracked, leaving him no more than a drooling child, running about the rambling house like a mad March hare while Hugo fretted, swore, and contemplated suicide. Ending it all with a pistol ball to his unworthy temple.

No. Suicide would be the easy way out. He had resolved to face and conquer his disgrace, to swallow his crushed pride. He would serve a penance instead. Drive himself into the very midst of his misery, confront the demon of his dishonour.

And what better way than to abase himself before God

than by falling in with Sir Gilbert, becoming one of his most trusted creatures, the serpent's servant?

By then, Sir Gilbert seemed to have assumed control of the dead squire's estate and ran his household despite the disapproving glances of Ramsay's formerly formidable widow. She was as mortified as young Hugo by the drastic turn of events which had left the unspeakable merchant holding the reins of so many lives.

Sir Gilbert had taken the poor boy under his wing, overseen the whispering servants as he was nursed back to fitness.

'Why, lad, you can't sit moping, not while there's a war on! So this Prince has held you up to complete ridicule and ruined your prospects, my prospects have been ruined more times than I care to count!'

But behind Sir Gilbert's blustering bonhomie Hugo detected a far more sinister intent. He just wished he could work out what it was.

Sir Gilbert Morrison wriggled his stockinged toes, taking a sideways glance at the silly young fool he had enlisted as his captain of horse. The boy was gnawing at his own spleen again, lurking in the shadows like a lovesick monk while he gloated over his self-inflicted woes. He was without doubt the most pliable creature he had ever come across.

The merchant had little by little stoked up the poor boy's hatred and resentment of Prince Maurice, transformed the angry youth into a willing accomplice. The spluttering firebrand might come in very useful in the complex games of cat and mouse being played out at court, the whispering web of intrigues directed against the Prince and, more importantly, his notoriously short-tempered elder brother. The King might be fighting his Parliament, but his court was torn by equally cruel divisions of its own.

Power didn't grow from seed. You couldn't increase your fortune or better your family prospects by sitting at home behind barred doors. He had been furiously active since the beginning of the war, speculating on jittery markets, extending his influence over down-at-heel gentry like the Ramsays. When he had reached the stage that he could do no more he hadn't hesitated to enlist his own children. It was for their own good, after all. He couldn't take his newly made monies with him, could he?

Sir Gilbert Morrison, a grasping, ill-bred tradesman on the outermost fringes of royal favour, had by some remarkably elastic shift of fate (with a little help from his daughter Bella) been admitted into the inner circle of a powerful Royalist lord, Anthony St John Dyle, Lord Clavincale. The family had huge estates in Dorset, and young Clavincale put himself about raising much-needed finances for the King (with no questions asked as to his means or methods).

Clavincale, as well as falling in violent and unrestrained love with his wayward daughter, immediately recognized his prospective father-in-law's moneymaking abilities. Hadn't the resourceful merchant already made three thousand pounds profit from his wartime speculations?

The lovestruck lordling enlisted him as a true and trusted ally in his schemes and intrigues at court. Sir Gilbert, for his part, was eager to marry his tempestuous daughter off to the portly lord as quickly as possible, giving his low-born family powerful claims to rather more noble blood.

Now Clavincale may have been rich and powerful in his own West Country estates, but he lacked connections at the royal court at Oxford. To achieve the favour of the King Sir Gilbert knew only too well one needed to be generous with one's contributions to His Majesty's war chest, and enjoy the favour of either of His Majesty's principal supports: his wife Henrietta Maria or that strutting turkeycock himself, his nephew Prince Rupert.

Sir Gilbert understood at once how the haughty, energetic, and disgustingly dashing Prince would actively despise creatures like Clavincale. Pudgy, spoilt, clever: career courtiers who used their minds before their hands. It was no surprise to Sir Gilbert to learn that the young lordling had been drawn therefore into the opposing party. Into the Queen's circle of admirers, nauseating toadies who influenced the Catholic spitfire to use all her powers of persuasion on the King.

Rupert's party had been at open enmity with the Queen's since the start of the war, with careers made and broken by their malevolent intrigues. Clavincale had begun to enjoy some small favour from the Queen, and Sir Gilbert could imagine why. Henrietta Maria, well versed in bedchamber intrigues, knew the value of a beautiful woman, and his *Bella*, his bright-eyed, low-born, infinitely ambitious little minx of a daughter, could be used as a dart to puncture the mighty Rupert's growing reputation, to confound his friends and besmirch his name.

Sir Gilbert allowed himself a private chuckle. Clavincale imagined the Queen had tacitly agreed to become his patron; in fact she had set her sights on Bella, his far more useful fiancée.

Poor Hugo there had fallen hopelessly in love with the girl when he had met her earlier that summer. She had turned his head with a flick of her chin, left him panting behind her as he recuperated from his wounds up at Kilmersden Hall. Sir Gilbert had even thought for a moment she might elope with the brooding idiot and ruin all his plans!

But as fast as the boy's hopes were lifted she dashed them back down again, and thankfully turned her fly-by-night attentions to Clavincale, who promised to take the girl to Oxford and introduce her to the backbiting but breathtaking royal court. An audience with the Queen? How could a disgraced rector's boy have accomplished such a miracle of social climbing? Hugo had failed, but he, Sir Gilbert Morrison, self-made man, would triumph.

Far from confronting or challenging the overweight lord and his merchant accomplice, Hugo had become their creature, their tool. A sharpened dirk ready to thrust into the despised Prince's back. They had whipped up Telling's thirst for revenge, created a willing weapon in the war against Rupert. Wheels within wheels, plots within plots.

It was now simply a matter of where and when they would draw this dirk of theirs and let the unthinking fool strike their deadly blows. The merchant sipped his brandy and took another sly glance at the brooding youth, as if to assure himself he was still there.

He noted the fluttering movement of his lips beneath his sparse tawny moustache. Talking to himself again – why, this young brat was as cracked up as young Jamie, muttering and ranting in stark silence. The merchant frowned, thought for a moment of his son back at home. Or rather, back at Kilmersden Hall. Young Jamie had been set to marry Anneliese Ramsay, the penniless heiress to the dead squire's mismanaged estate. The merchant had markers from her father for sums way beyond what the widow could meet. She might despise him, but she needs must lose her home if she was to settle her debt. It was either penury and homelessness or marriage, the merger of the two families for ever.

As he had anticipated, Lady Ramsay had taken the easier way out, and reluctantly agreed to the match.

Jamie's bewildered return, though, soured Sir Gilbert's carefully calculated plans. He could hardly insist on the marriage with Jamie standing at the altar bleating like a sheep, could he now? Lady Ramsay was cruelly kind, assuring him his son would mend in time. Just when Sir Gilbert thought his scheme must fall into ruins the young girl herself came to his rescue, taking pity on poor Jamie and insisting she would nurse him back to health. She had already lost her elder brother – mutilated beyond recognition on Edgehill – and meant to replace him in her affections with the blubbering merchant's boy.

Ah well, Sir Gilbert mused. Young Jamie was in good hands now, being nursed night and day by a daft girl who stood to inherit half the hill. Jamie could hardly be expected to return to the wars an idiot, could he? If the boy could recover his wits over the next few months he would be set up for life. If this damned war could be brought to a swift conclusion Sir Gilbert would find himself head of one of the principal merchant houses in the west (and be a lord and all, if Clavincale kept his promise) and everything in the garden would be rosy. His ungrateful children would be wed into powerful, respected old families, and Sir Gilbert would be rich. The backstreet hawker would have transformed himself, aye, just as the country was transforming itself now! Never mind the foolish King or that pistol-happy simpleton Rupert! It was men like him who were coming into their own, creating the wealth the country needed, the mercantile base for expansion overseas. He pondered with delight the boom which would surely follow this damned fighting. The rebuilding, the repairing, the replacing. He would make a mint, once the armies and the generals and the princes had done their bit.

At that moment, Sir Gilbert's future and fortune depended on the end of the war. He had therefore decided to put his not inconsiderable abilities to work in bringing the end of the war about. He had correctly reasoned that if the King could complete his summer conquests by taking Gloucester then Parliament might well be forced to come to terms. How tough could the town be? An old wall and a few frightened Roundheads, a governor who had already been accused of sinister negotiations with the King's party? The siege might well be Sir Gilbert's last chance to earn a name for himself as a commander of men, as Clavincale's principal knight in armour! Sir Gilbert would win his spurs, and his good friend and son-in-law Clavincale would see he was well rewarded.

The smug merchant drank a silent toast to himself, noting his flushed reflection in the borrowed tankard. His close-cropped grey curls glistened with hair oil, gave him a rather slippery appearance which was somewhat offset by his merry blue eyes. The merchant turned warrior looked more like a kindly toymaker than a soldier, round cheeks roasted by the wine and the warmth. As sharp as a needle, though, despite his clownish mannerisms and bottomless store of nonsensical phrases.

By God, he had put one over on this scowling colonel, hadn't he? Bluffing him into thinking he had arrived with several thousand Samaritans? Enforcing his will over four hundred angry soldiers while he and Nybb mustered a bare dozen cavalry and a hundred and fifty ragamuffin foot? Sir Gilbert chortled to himself, eyed the hawk-faced soldier opposite. Slaughter was clearly torn between thanking his hosts for his timely rescue and thrashing about the room demanding the return of his stolen sword. He sat still instead, stiffly formal on the settle in his travel-stained shirt and worn boots. Captain Shea sipped his wine alongside, Morrison noted the officer's dirty hand was shaking like a blushing virgin on her wedding night. Nybb paced the room behind the settle, casting gigantic bearlike shadows on Mr Rice's oak-panelled walls. He had undone his coat to show the paired pistols he had stuck into his belt, and they looked to the merchant like the horned remains of some indigestible feast.

Colonel Slaughter kept a wary eye on the burly bandit. He had met his sort a thousand times before, hard-bitten, professional killers. As tough and resourceful as any of the clan chieftains Slaughter had run across back in Ireland. Nybb was Clavincale's personal bodyguard and enforcer, a useful addition to Sir Gilbert's newly raised regiment. A man to watch.

'They'll be as meek as lambs, once we get to Gloucester,' Slaughter predicted, resuming the debate which had been interrupted by the arrival of the pasty-faced horse boy.

He ran a finger under the collar of his grubby shirt, nodded gruffly. 'All I can do is thank you again, for turning up as you did with all your men,' he said.

Sir Gilbert slapped his pudgy hands against his spread thighs.

'Quite right, old man, no doubt about it,' Morrison agreed. 'They all get niggled now and again. My lot are just as bad. Good troops don't grow from seed, you know.'

Slaughter smiled weakly at the merchant's oft-repeated observations on the supernatural origin of everything from beef stew to the stars. He placed his empty tankard on the table and went to rise.

'I'd best take a turn round the lines. Your horsemen have steadied 'em down, but they'll be off like hares if they get half a chance.'

The merchant frowned. 'Nonsense, old chap, this time of night? Won't hear of it! Young Telling's lads are keeping an eye on your men, don't you worry.'

Slaughter glanced at the moody youth who was still gazing at the fire. He looked more like a sickly infant than a Cavalier commander. He hadn't managed to fathom the strength of Sir Gilbert's formidable force, but his brigade apparently included any number of well-equipped horsemen as well as a regiment of foot who had been left back along the road awhiles. Sir Gilbert had apparently left the bulk of his force on top of the hill, to watch the road west. According to his colourful account of their march, it had been exceedingly lucky for Slaughter that he had decided to come on ahead with the vanguard and find shelter for the night.

'A chap likes his bed at my time of life,' he chortled. 'I've left the rest of the scoundrels sleeping under the hedges. Good job I came on ahead, as it turned out, with your lot turning so truculent,' Sir Gilbert observed breezily.

'They would have come to their senses sooner or later,' Slaughter theorized.

'Once they'd strung us up from the elms out the back,' Shea commented drily.

Slaughter glared at his second-in-command, who immediately turned his attention to the bottom of his tankard. Sir Gilbert shook his head in mock sympathy.

'Damned awkward once they've taken saucy, eh, Nybb?'

'Ye're right, mineer,' Nybb agreed non-committally.

'I'll flog the ringleaders myself,' Slaughter vowed.

Sir Gilbert nodded reassuringly. 'Well, yes, yes, a good flogging can do the trick,' he agreed. 'I hope you don't mind me suggesting another way? I've found it turns a man every time.'

'You have? What's that?' Slaughter enquired, relaxing slightly as the buff-coated buffoon explained his theory of warfare from the comfort of Mr Rice's best armchair.

'A couple of barrels of strong liquor, well watered, of course.' Sir Gilbert Morrison's liquors had been watered enough already, but the thirsty soldiers weren't to know that.

Slaughter's slow smile slipped from his shifty face.

'Strong liquor, you'd give them liquor?' he asked disbelievingly.

'I've taken the liberty of sending for a wagonload from my supply train,' Sir Gilbert explained. 'I'm sure they'll feel different with some fire in their bellies.'

'Fire in their bellies? You might just as well throw oil on a bonfire! These men want a good thrashing, not drink!'

Sir Gilbert looked slightly taken aback at Slaughter's outburst.

'No, no, my dear sir, that won't do at all. Why, I've brought two thousand men up from Bristol and not lost one of 'em! A pint every night keeps 'em bright, is what I always say. Don't I always say so, Nybb?'

Slaughter leapt to his feet, his empty scabbard clattering against the wooden legs of the settle.

'I must absolutely insist, sir, that you refrain from issuing any of *my* men with any liquor!'

Sir Gilbert's jaw dropped. 'Take it steady, my good sir, no need to get uppity!'

'Your pardon, sir, but I've known these men five days – and they are the worst set of scoundrels I've ever come across.'

'I've seen worse, mineer,' Nybb commented.

'Let me try my way, a ration of strong liquor and a couple of flitches of good bacon for their morning fires, you'll see a difference or I'm a Dutchman!'

Slaughter strode forward, glared down at the jolly old gent slumped unconcernedly in the armchair. 'I regret sir, that I must absolutely forbid—'

Sir Gilbert held his hand up.

'I am sorry to have to pull rank, my friend, but I have a commission from Lord Clavincale himself to raise reinforcements to join the King at Gloucester. Now if we hadn't turned up as we did you'd be swinging and your men would be scattered to all points of the compass. In the circumstances,' Sir Gilbert went on soberly, 'I have no choice but to relieve you of your command.'

Slaughter's pale eyes widened in shocked anger. He was about to bawl his reply when he noticed a huge shadow slip across the bare stone grate. He wheeled about to see Nybb bearing down on him. He reached for his sword, but remembered it had been snatched away by his mutineering men. Nybb had thoughtfully retrieved the colonel's weapon, but had neglected to return the notched blade to its bewildered owner. Nybb's thick lips parted from his streaked teeth in a triumphant, humourless grin.

'Lost your pigsticker, mineer? A pretty fix for a *colonel*,' he sneered. Shea looked nervously from the big bandit to

46

his furious chief. Sir Gilbert continued to drink his brandy as if the explosive confrontation was no more than an alehouse brawl.

'What's the meaning of this, what commission are you gabbling about?' Slaughter stuttered.

'A commission from Lord Clavincale, who as you know has been given special responsibility for His Majesty's affairs in the West Country, to take reinforcements to Gloucester with all haste and urgency imaginable.'

'I have a commission from Prince Rupert himself,' Slaughter argued.

The pale youth looked up sharply as if he had taken a sudden interest in their hitherto meaningless debate.

'Prince Rupert, yes, yes, a fine soldier, the King's right-hand man,' Sir Gilbert agreed. 'But I am afraid my commission is completely clear. I am to round up all stragglers and deserters and dispatch them with all urgency to Gloucester. I can show you the order if you wish.'

'I don't want to see any order, I have my own orders!' Slaughter cried.

'And no doubt you have done your best to do your duty,' Sir Gilbert allowed. 'Nobody is blaming you, sir. A mutiny could happen to anybody. Tricky business, rebellion.' Slaughter caught his breath, thinking furiously. Sir Gilbert rambled on as blandly as ever. 'We found your regiment in the act of assassinating its officers and deserting to the hills, isn't that right, Mr Nybb?'

'Right enough, mineer,' Nybb agreed.

'Therefore by the powers invested in me by Anthony St John Dyle, Lord Clavincale, I hereby assume command of said deserters.'

'WHAT?'

'I am taking command of your men, sir, there's no need

to stamp and shout, sir, I am perfectly within my rights as set out in my orders.' He patted his well-tailored doublet conspiratorially.

'This is outrageous. I have orders signed by Prince Rupert himself!'

'Very well and good. But as I have already said, we arrived to find your men about to string you up and take to the hills. I have no choice, given my sacred duty to His Majesty King Charles, but to assume command of your forces and ensure they are marched with all speed to Gloucester.'

Slaughter stared from the cheery merchant to his scowling enforcer, who was patting his worn pistols significantly.

'I will take this up with Prince Rupert the moment we reach Gloucester,' Slaughter vowed.

Sir Gilbert nodded. 'Absolutely within your rights, my dear sir. In fact, I would insist the matter goes through the proper channels.'

Slaughter stopped dead, frantically wondering at the merchant's sinister game. Agreeing to an inquiry before the short-tempered Prince? Volunteering to explain to the headstrong general why his orders had been deliberately countermanded? Was he mad?

'You agree to turn yourself over to a full inquiry the moment we reach Gloucester?'

'It's not a question of turning myself over,' Sir Gilbert corrected him testily. 'We will simply put the facts before the Prince and allow His Highness to review the situation, having taken note of all pertinent submissions, affidavits, and commissions.'

Slaughter swallowed with difficulty. The fat old bloat was as slippery as an eel in a tub of honey.

The callow youth by the dresser was muttering oaths like a penitent in a sacking shirt. 'And I shall insist on an immediate court martial to clear my name, the name his brother was pleased to besmirch for ever!'

'Yes, all right, Hugo lad, there's a time and place for everything,' Sir Gilbert scolded gently.

'And in the meantime I hand over my command to you, is that it?'

'In a nutshell. In the circumstances, I think you've ended the day ahead, don't you?'

The smell of frying bacon sidled out over the camp, drenching what was left of the morning haze with its enticing aroma. The disorderly mob which had been about to string up its own commander a matter of hours before was queuing quietly at the steaming wagon which had arrived in the village that dawn. Cooks in grease-splattered aprons stood on the running-boards cutting chunks of glistening pink meat from the flitches suspended from the canopy, and handing them out to the drooling troops.

Sir Gilbert, Major Nybb, and the scowling Slaughter stood by, watching the men take their bacon and hold up their mugs for their ration of ale, generously dispensed by Elder Sergeant Cully Oates. Nybb had recognized the grizzled old veteran from the German wars, and immediately appointed his kindred spirit as quartermaster.

'That's it, lads, get it down you! Good health and God save the King,' Sir Gilbert called to the admiring mob.

'Huzzah for Sir Gilbert!'

'A Morrison, a Morrison!'

Michael Slaughter rolled his eyes in disgust. Sir Gilbert gave him a broad wink.

'What did I tell you? Commanding troops is like keeping a wife, stick and carrot, old man, stick and carrot!'

Slaughter regarded his transformed troops with supercilious disgust.

'I'm surprised you've food to spare with two thousand men on the hill behind us,' he snarled.

'Two thousand men? Oh, yes, er, those two thousand men.' Sir Gilbert bit his generous lip, winked at that grinning ape Nybb. Michael Slaughter hadn't been the first good man to be hoodwinked by the crafty merchant.

And he wouldn't be the last.

GAUDY GREEN,

The beetroot-cheeked goodwife had hauled the rickety cart well over a mile, balancing the freshly cut load of turfs with one calloused hand as she attempted to steer and shove the unlikely contraption with the other. The narrow streets of top-heavy hovels were crooked and crowded, blocked with heaps of rubble and refuse, as she approached the newly raised wall. The sopping turf had been cut that dawn by a gang of women and old men at Little Mead, the wide water-meadow on the north-western corner of the closely besieged town. The Royalist soldiers in the surrounding trenches could have blazed away and murdered any number of the toiling townsfolk, but seemed content to fire the occasional round at the hastily repaired defences rather than try to obstruct the work itself.

Perhaps the King and all his high and mighty young gentlemen were reluctant even now to spill the blood of their countrymen, Ella Clamp wondered as she straightened up with a wince to wipe her forehead. Her bonnet was soaked with sweat, the oppressive heat and grim labour wearing her out worse than her man when the drink was in him. She peered down the blocked-off lane towards the walls, searched for her family beside the freshly raised palisade. Knots of nervous neighbours were standing about

out of doors to escape the already stifling heat, watching the soldiers and the small army of civilian helpers as they went to and fro on garrison business. She kneaded the small of her damp back through her loosened bodice, and caught sight of her eldest boys scuttling up a ladder to help their father on the broad parapet. By God in Heaven, she'd warned John not to expose the children up there! Keeping the youngsters out of the firing line was a constant nightmare for all Gloucester's parents, rich and poor alike. She shielded her eyes and bit her lip as her sons struggled over the palisade, the wet turfs slung over their backs like green sheepskins.

'John Clamp, for the love of Christ, will you git them boys down 'ere to give Oi 'and?' she bawled, startling her nosy neighbours as they went about their morning chores. They eyed the martial activity warily, as if wishing their houses were further from the dangerously exposed southern corner of the city. Ella had heard the garrison commander had already turned some folk out of their homes, to level their lousy hovels and open up new fields of fire – whatever on God's green earth they were.

Her husband rose from the defences like a badly dressed scarecrow, peering back down the lane at his formidable wife, completely oblivious to the irregular crump of the King's cannons or the frequent sharp pop of a musket from the saps over the walls. John Clamp leaned on his spade, took off his hat, and wiped his face on the greasy brim. He could see his wife waving and bawling down in the street, and could only rejoice he was up there on the palisade safely out of her way.

'There you are, my dove,' he called down as his boys flung their turfs onto his rapidly thickening section of the defences.

'Best get on down now, lads, her'll be cussin' us blind else,' he advised, shooing his eager children from their breathtakingly exciting vantage point. The disappointed boys clambered back down the ladder as Ella manhandled the lopsided barrow on down the lane. John Clamp sat down on the freshly cut sward and fished his pipe from his sopping doublet. He was soon puffing away delightedly, gazing out at the astonishingly altered panorama towards the east. The lush green hills paraded over the horizon, changing colour from right to left as the sun got up. The countryside had been besieged by the fierce summer sun every bit as closely as the King's men crowded about the town. The variously variegated patchwork fields along the slopes of the surrounding hills were deserted; hardly as much as a butterfly seemed to disturb the morning haze. The cattle had long since been herded off to safer pastures, or the reeking slaughter-pens the other side of the tannery. The wild woodland creatures had taken to their holes, the birds of the air had abandoned the meadows and taken to the tops of the trees, as if afraid of the massive explosion of activity further down the basking slopes. John Clamp could see the white-capped camps of their mushroom cities dotted along the horizon, the dirty brown ropes of their diggings reminding him of molehills. He could see their soldiers in their bright white shirts going about their business, the tedium of the siege weighing them down as well as the fearsome summer heat. Their grubby canvas tents and marquees were bathed in sunshine, shining bright like a fleet of sails on an ocean of shimmering green. A rare and beautiful sight to be sure, John thought. Niver seen the like of it, he mused contentedly. Apart from the occasional white cloud and thunderclap shell, the Royalist intruders might have been setting up a summer fair over the meadow there.

Gaudy Green was a broad heath around the south-eastern suburbs of the city. Well, it was a sight gaudier now, the bright flags and pennants of any number of barons, earls, and princes of the blood flapping and fluttering in the light breeze. Complex devices and emblems, the arms of half the divided nation's gentry on show for the quaking rebels to see, no doubt. From his breezy eyrie a hundred yards from the Southgate John could trace the progress of the Royalist saps, complex trenches which criss-crossed the bramble-tangled wilderness on either side of the main road. The Royalist engineers had dug at right angles from Southgate Street, using the houses and tumbledown outbuildings beyond the wall as cover. Looking up over their busy works, John could see the broad brown band of the Severn as it followed a huge meander from the Westgate around the low-lying meadows of Cattle Mead. The flow divided about the island before swinging away on towards the west once more. The neat orchards belonging to Llanthony Priory John could see on the eastern bank of the Severn had been taken over by General Ruthven's brigade of the King's army, but not before the old tower had been demolished to prevent the wily buggers from using it for artillery spotting. Ruthven's men had spent the last few days edging forward from their base around the priory grounds, enveloping the hastily fortified bastion around the Southgate. The freshly repaired defences which had defied them followed the line of Green Dragon Lane, forming a great triangle pointing out along the main road. The new wall had swallowed up the old mason's cottage, the squat medieval building forming a valuable strongpoint in the turf wall. The lower-storey windows had been bricked up but those on the upper floor had been reinforced with sandbags as a vantage point for the defenders.

John was no expert but it was evident the enemy intended to concentrate on the south-eastern corner of the defences. They said Prince Rupert himself had walked the lines, pointing out exactly where the guns should be sited to bring maximum firepower down on the walls. At Gaudy Green he could position batteries to either flank, catching the wedge of wall around the Southgate in a vicious crossfire. To counter the threat the garrison had reinforced the walls with hundreds of gabions – baskets of rubble and earth – and generous swaths of shock-absorbing turf. So far, though, the desultory bombardment had only managed to knock tiles from some of the surrounding houses and topple several chimney stacks to the momentary alarm (and subsequent relief) of the anxious inhabitants. The crumbling stone towers which had been incorporated into the defences took the worst of the punishment, but as fast as Rupert's guns brought down one section of masonry the townsfolk hurried up to plug the gaps with bulging woolsacks. Gloucester's patchwork walls had taken all the mighty Prince could throw at them. The foremost professional soldier in Europe, an expert at engineering, mining, battery fire, and battlefield tactics, had been invited to do his worst by two weak regiments of volunteers and a few thousand determined townsfolk.

John Clamp sucked on his pipe, nodded his head in satisfaction as he thought of the willing citizens out slaving in the sun beside the blue-coated soldiers of the Earl of Stamford's own, or the long-serving musketeers of Henry

Stephen's regiment. The men had been recruited locally, and if they could be relied on for one thing it would be to defend their homes and kinfolk.

Gloucester hadn't been garrisoned by strangers.

John Clamp shielded his eyes and turned his wandering attention on the creeping molehills across the green, the wickerwork emplacements where Prince Rupert had installed his culverins, sakers, and stone-gobbling cannon.

'Are you comin' down to 'elp me, or what?'

John Clamp jumped as Ella's broadside bellow stopped work all down the line. He squirmed over the palisade on his backside, and peered down into the dead-end lane in agitation as a party of officers divided about his red-faced wife, hands on hips as she ordered him down.

Ella Clamp looked round in surprise as one of the young gentleman bent down in front of her, got a grip on the cart handles, and propelled it with a grunt towards her labouring menfolk. The officer was tall and slightly built, wearing a plain but immaculately cut grey suit and a burnished breastplate. His hands, though, were as creased and coarse as her own red paws. No stranger to a bit of graft, then, Ella thought admiringly.

'Why, God bless you, sir, fair done me back in, I reckon,' she said, tucking a strand of greasy brown hair back under her sweat-stained bonnet as she watched the stranger bend his back and steer the precariously loaded cart between the heaps of rubble and dung along the alley. His companions closed in behind him, taking care not to step in the steaming ordure. They glanced at the grinning goodwife as if she was some recently unearthed new species, discovered in the molehill works either side of the new walls. Ella frowned, lifted her sodden skirts, and hurried after the good Samaritan as he wheeled the cart under the ladder and straightened up with a sigh.

'You should get your men to push the barrow, it's far too heavy for you,' the officer scolded her gently, wiping his hands along his breeches. Ella curtsied, taking a crafty peek at the stranger's thin, careworn features and large, soulful eyes.

'Ah, it's nothing I'm not used to, sir,' Ella responded tartly, 'and besides, I've no 'ead for 'ights, sir.'

The officer glanced up the ladder at her undernourished husband, who was now standing, arms akimbo, as if he owned the wall.

'If your man stands there all day he won't have one either,' the officer said concernedly. 'They're not firing cabbages at us, you know.'

John Clamp frowned down at his worryingly flirtatious partner, who was grinning and beaming at the weary officer like a lovesick puppy.

'Oh, don't you go botherin' about me, sir,' John Clamp called. As if to undermine his confident pronouncement there was a sudden rush of sound, as if a broad canvas sail had snapped full in the wind. A piercing whistle heralded the tearing passage of a culverin shot, the red-hot ball trailing a ghostly white comet over the sky. Officers, goodwives, labourers, and soldiers dropped to the floor as the ball sailed into the roof of a nearby hovel, spitefully shattering the haphazard tiling and decapitating the decrepit guttering. Fragments of mossy slate crashed and splintered along the packed alley, knocking an old drab senseless as she ducked out of her hovel with a brimming pail of night slops. One of Ella's boys yelped as a razor-edged sliver cut through his bare shin.

The astonished defenders picked themselves up and dusted themselves off, their mysterious commander pulling out his own handkerchief to dab the boy's cut. Ella Clamp stood over his shoulder, cooing and fussing as he cleaned the wound and tied the cotton triangle around the youngster's leg.

'Din' I tell 'ee to keep out of the way?' she growled as the inspection party resumed their promenade, but not before the tall officer had pressed a shilling into the wounded youngster's dirty hand. A shilling, a whole shilling! Ella, brought back to the earth with a bump by the frightening explosion, prised the coin from the boy's fist and bit down on it. It was as much as she had earned hauling turf that week!

'God bless you, sir!' she yelled at the officer's black-plated back. 'And don't be a stranger!'

Colonel Edward Massey, Governor of Gloucester, paused in the rubble-strewn lane, looked over his shoulder, and waved his white hand.

Ella Clamp would never forget the day, nor the soldier's wide, soulful eyes.

'A gentleman, a very sweet young gentlemen he was,' she reported to her jealous cronies, long after the siege was over and all the soldiers buried and forgotten. 'Looked as if he'd sucked up all our sufferin', those eyes all misty like,' she would remember with a heartfelt sigh.

The object of Goodwife Clamp's fond reminiscences was a twenty-three-year-old engineer, the quietly spoken son of a Cheshire gentleman. He had served with the Dutch on the Continent, and more recently with the English army King Charles sent to punish the Scots for refusing to accept his newly imposed Book of Common Prayer. The Scots wars, a brief but painful dress rehearsal for the full-blown civil conflict, had ended in ignominious failure – the King's hotchpotch of militiamen outmarched, outwitted, and outfought by a Scots army officered almost entirely by experienced soldiers who had learned their trade with the Swedish armies in Germany over the previous two decades.

At the outbreak of war Massey had at first tried to extend his commission with the King's army at York, but on second thoughts had ridden to London, where good officers were in short supply and good wages weren't. Massey had been appointed Lieutenant Colonel to the Earl of Stamford, and assumed the governorship of Gloucester when the earl had left to take command of Roundhead forces in the far west.

Since then, Parliamentary fortunes had gone from bad to worse. The King's forces were rampant in the north, despite the determined efforts of Lord Fairfax and his sober-minded son Sir Thomas. The Earl of Essex's main Roundhead army was largely inactive, ruined by desertion and disease in their widely dispersed quarters in the damp heat of the highly pestilent Thames valley. Sir William Waller, another highly experienced and active soldier for the Parliamentarian cause, had lost his army on Roundway Down a few grim weeks before. The complete removal of his army from the board allowed the Royalist high command to turn their attentions on Bristol, which fell after a bloody, hard-fought siege. Smaller Roundhead garrisons around the west followed suit like ripe plums. The crowing King's men had expected Gloucester to follow suit.

Colonel Massey sighed, turning over the baffling possibilities as he toured the wall with his officers. He was grimly aware of his responsibility, not just to Gloucester

59

but to Parliament's cause. If he couldn't keep Rupert out of the city . . .

The slightly built officer in the sober grey suit picked his way along the busy walls, satisfied at least that the repairs he had ordered were being effected. The majority of the townsfolk seemed eager to help where they could, no doubt encouraged by their strongly Puritan neighbours or friends. If only the city corporation was as cooperative, he thought ruefully. The city aldermen had wanted a local man over them, not some upstart from the north. He had been forced to insist on every scrap of expenditure, explain the spiralling cost of the siege to the doubtful greybeards.

He was happier out here on the walls, well out of the way of their petty cavilling.

He called a halt at Rignall Stile, and nodded to Lieutenant Harcus, a highly excitable young officer who had quickly made a name for himself leading several sorties from the city. Harcus had strung two snapsacks of grenades about his breastplate, and his length of musketeer's match was already smouldering in anticipation.

'All set, Harcus?' Massey called.

'All set, sir,' Harcus agreed with a twitch.

'Your men are rested?' the governor enquired, frowning at the unshaven, red-eyed wretches who made up the sally party. They had only managed to snatch a few hours' sleep since they had been in action the night before. Not even the great Rupert would be anticipating a second sortie on the same length of trenches in less than six hours.

Harcus grinned at him, his strong teeth oddly white against his sooty features. 'We'll convince 'em lightning does strike twice,' he replied, patting his oddly bulging sack.

The governor nodded with satisfaction. Massey knew it

60

was no use blockading himself up behind the partially secured walls while Rupert schemed and plotted his downfall. He would take the fight to him, interfere with every trench and sap and spike every gun he could, worry and tease the enemy forces crouched beyond the walls.

He would make sure this upstart Rupert had an uncomfortable time of it, convince the Prince he had laid siege to a jar of wasps.

Rupert, Rupert, Rupert.

The news-sheets – Roundhead and Cavalier alike – were full of his antics, packed with awestruck descriptions of his supernatural abilities. Half the soldiers believed he could talk with the birds of the air, that he could even change his appearance!

Change his appearance? Massey snorted. He was six foot two! He towered over the majority of the population by more than a foot, how in the name of Heaven was he supposed to disguise himself? As a Teutonic washerwoman? He might well have led a number of successful cavalry charges, scattered the Roundhead horse at Edgehill, but he hadn't reined his men back in until the evening, by which time the battle was honourably drawn. A decent commander would have gathered his triumphant troopers and flung himself on the Earl of Essex's exposed flank, finished the war in an afternoon!

Massey pursed his thin lips. It was no good wishing Rupert, Essex, or anybody else had done things differently. All that mattered was the here and now.

Massey knew full well the Parliamentary cause was in desperate straits.

All the King needed to do to complete the highly successful summer campaign was to take Gloucester, the last Roundhead stronghold in the region. He would then control most of the West Country and Cornwall, and secure communications with his power base in Wales, Cheshire, and the north. All that would be required then would be to tighten the noose around London and the defiant south-east, and strangle the bloody rebellion at its roots.

Everything depended on Gloucester.

The Royalist fortunes depended on Rupert's prompt possession of the town for his uncle, and even Massey had to admit that if the Prince had won his way they would in all probability have taken it by now. Rupert would have thrown all his forces straight at the tumbledown walls and finished the siege in a single bloody afternoon. The headstrong warrior had been overruled by his uncle, however, fearful that such a storm would bring another disastrous crop of casualties. His Majesty had seen ditches full of dead at Bristol, and refused to countenance another butcher's list.

Massey had been alarmed by the alehouse tittle-tattle, which maintained that the Royalist command had hoped to take the city by intrigue, by playing on his own previous loyal service to the crown. His former commander from the Scots wars, Rupert's close friend Colonel William Legge, had sent a personal message to him, urging Massey to remember where his duty lay. But he had put the crafty gossips and muttering aldermen in their place when King Charles had appeared in person before the town on the previous Thursday. He had curtly refused His Majesty's summons to surrender, and vowed that Gloucester would fight on.

Parliament's stuttering fortunes depended on him now. The same age as the renowned Rupert, and every inch as experienced in the intricate arts of siege warfare, the obscure officer would have his chance to set his name alongside the greats.

For him, victory might be the ticket to popular fame, to a higher command with the Parliament, desperately in need of sound leadership.

For the hard-pressed Parliamentary greybeards at White-hall, it was a simple matter of survival.

Nicodemus Burke had to hurry to match his master's long strides, holding a hand to his head to prevent his flamboy-antly feathered hat from flapping off in the stiffening breeze. The colonel led his officers to and fro along the crucial south-eastern sector of the walls, examining the defences, peering into the waterlogged ditches, and scan-ning the enemy artillery positions through a perspective glass. Nicodemus watched the young governor chew his lip and tug nervously on his rather sparse black beard, weigh-ing up which of Prince Rupert's works presented the most serious threat to the defences. Nicodemus, who had been employed as a runner at a firm of solicitors in St Mary's Street, knew his way around the city backwards and blindfolded, from the Pen, an outflung bastion on the north-eastern wall, round to the Alvin Gate and down to the overgrown wasteland of Friar's Orchard.

The red-haired youngster was a little too young to serve with the city volunteer regiments, but found an outlet for his precocious talents at Greyfriars, the old priory Massey had taken over as his headquarters. He graduated from running errands for the officers (which included carrying the occasional surreptitious note to a breathless young lady) to general clerical duties in the command post – largely through the fact that his mop of flaming red hair and freckled features made him stand out so strikingly in the press of eager faces at the priory windows. Nicodemus was a first-rate guide, and could find the quickest routes through the maze of back alleys around the heart of the city, if Colonel Massey or one of his lieutenants needed to get to a far-flung outpost on the surrounding walls. He recently commandeered the governor's map case, a creaking leather portmanteau stuffed with parchment charts and sketches of the works, and the colonel's neatly bound dispatch box, complete with paper, quills, and ink.

After several weeks of feverish activity Nicodemus was widely regarded as an indispensable asset to the city command, not least by himself.

He transferred the bulky cases from his right arm to his left, and caught up with the commander as he arrived at a fortified sally-port a stone's throw from the massive bastion of the Southgate. A party of blue-coated soldiers from Stamford's regiment were standing about or squatting under the walls, leaning on their weapons at smoke. Nicodemus could see muskets, carbines, halberds, and axes. Pikes weren't any use in a hand-to-hand scrap at the bottom of a trench. Nicodemus felt a familiar surge of nervous excitement as he contemplated the calm preparations. He knew it. Another sortie. His friends had been chattering excitedly about the midnight attack on the Royalist lines. Charlie Crabtree maintained a dozen King's men had been put to the sword, Matthew Johns reckoned six.

Either way, Colonel Massey had been unusually active since dawn and had clearly made up his mind to attack the enemy once again, before they could bring their crushing superiority in numbers to bear.

The King had upwards of fifteen thousand men around the city, according to the wide-eyed ensigns back at the headquarters. The defenders had barely two thousand, and a whole circuit of walls to defend. Two days previously the governor had been up in the northern districts, supervising the evacuation of the vineyard over beyond Alney. The outpost had been threatened by the Welshmen closing in over the river, and the men had been needed within the main works. The decision might have been a depressing setback for the townsfolk and garrison if it hadn't been for the antics of the wary Welshmen. They advanced into the abandoned works like so many mice, turned tail and ran back out again when the garrison took a few potshots at them. The spectators safe behind the main walls fell about with laughter, jeered and gesticulated at the despised Welsh, and morale had soared despite the worrying loss of ground.

Nicodemus craned his neck, peered up at the wall. He itched to climb up the ladder and join the men on the parapet, to take a closer look at the arrogant ranks of the King's precious army. He stood by quietly as Colonel Massey held a hurried consultation with that Harcus fellow. A noisy, nervous man with a flaxen moustache and quick, darting eyes. He was nodding his head as if impatient to get on with his assignment. Something was up, all right!

The governor had forgotten him, small and forlorn amongst the pack of armed men, his fiery red hair safely out of sight beneath his gaudy hat. Nicodemus glanced about him, lifted an abandoned axe from beside an empty barrel. Its owner, sharing a pipe of tobacco with a comrade, didn't notice the theft. He was stepping from one boot to the other and mumbling incoherently, blowing wobbling rings of blue smoke up over the wall. His companion was leaning against an immense sack of wool, his mouth hanging open as he gulped the smoke.

'By Heaven now, Tom,' he stammered at last, 'wherever did you get yer weed?'

The armless axeman screwed up his eyes as if he was having difficulty in focusing. 'The usual, out Winchcombe way,' he replied, looking around for his weapon.

'Sally party, have a care!' Colonel Massey completed briefing the captain and marched off to find a vantage point from which to watch the sortie. The red-faced young officer tightened the chin straps of his polished black burgonet, and called his men to attention.

''Ere, Robin, whur d'I put that bliddy axe?'

'Come on, you bloats, get those ladders along here!' Harcus called, his straw moustache bristling above his generous lips. He backed against the wall to make room for the armour-plated pioneers making their overburdened way along the lane. The specially selected men were wearing closed-faced siege helmets, as well as extensive body armour, and were carrying ropes, axes, hammers, and nails instead of personal weapons. Their job was to clear a way for the rest, bridge the muddy moat for the attack group following up behind them. First over the wall, first into the ditch, and first into the enemy trenches, the pioneers received extra pay and a good ration of strong ale.

The storming party stood aside as the small sally-port in the wall was uncovered. Two soldiers hauled the heavily reinforced door open.

Nicodemus, crouching to one side, could smell the stagnant mud and rotting refuse at the bottom of the ditch sidle through the breach. A gust of wind lifted his hat. The first pair of pioneers scrambled through the hatch and hauled the tightly bound siege ladders after them, hand over rung, hand over rung. Their companions followed them out, dropping down with a splash and steadying themselves in the filthy stew as they wrestled the heavy ladder into position, bridging the ditch. Harcus drew his sword, bent down at the sally-port.

'After me, charge!'

The blue-coated soldiers packed through the hatch like rats fleeing a burning grain ship. They scrambled down the greasy wall and scuttled along the wildly bouncing ladders, leapt onto the heaped earth along the far side of the obstacle.

Colonel Massey's portmanteau and papers remained behind, forgotten on an empty barrel.

RIGNALL STILE,

GLOUCESTER

Nicodemus Burke paused at the end of the rickety ladder, bouncing crazily under the combined weight of six shouting soldiers and their assorted side arms. He waited for a moment, blinking in the bright sunlight on the far side of the wall. He felt oddly isolated, venturing beyond the comforting, turf-smothered womb of the defences, as if he had been born into a great whistling wilderness of grass, slag heaps, and brambles. Harcus had already bounded across the ladder, his blue-coated men taking rather more careful steps after him. Three of the soldiers missed their footing altogether and fell into the ditch, where they were being helped up by the pioneers in their heavy, mud-splattered armour.

'Hey, boy! Get back there!'

Nicodemus looked down in surprise at one of the sappers, who was holding the ladder steady with one hand and waving at him with the other. His close-faced helmet had monstrously distorted his angry shout, turned the Gloucester yeoman into a Greek warrior, breathlessly clambering out of the belly of the wooden horse.

'Get on in before you stop one!' the mud-splattered Spartan yelled. Nicodemus needed no further urging. He dashed forward, one, two, three nimble springs taking him over the ladder, out of reach of the cursing pioneer's grasping fingers.

'Oy!' The angry bellow was lost in a sudden spatter of musketry. Red-hot lead wasps bored through the air in every direction as the alerted Royalist guards fired a wild volley at the charging mob. Harcus led them through the diggings, zigzagging between heaps of spoil and rubble as dipping bullets kicked up stones and grit around their boots. Harcus ducked down, the comically bulging snapsacks bouncing against his thighs. Nicodemus caught up with the cursing soldiers bringing up the rear of the pack, their blue coats soaked black with stinking mud. They crawled out of the ditch and hobbled on like jungle natives, tripping over their slippery feet and hunching their heads like turtles into their gaping collars.

'Which way, Tom?'

'Blowed if I know, Robin!'

They careered across the stricken meadow, a yawning no man's land of pits and abandoned trenches, broken tools and heaps of fuming refuse. Nicodemus could see the Royalist sappers, stripped to the waist or flapping their arms in their great baggy shirts as they groped for their weapons. The musketeers guarding the working party were standing above the pits, frantically reloading their weapons. They tipped their powder charges into sooty barrels and groped in their pouches for bullets, ramming the lead peach-pits home with their scouring sticks and feverishly blowing on their smouldering match. It was a bothersome enough manoeuvre at the best of times, and it assumed terrifying complexities when being charged by a mob of bawling, red-faced devils. The blue-coated soldiers seemed to sense the urgency, tearing over the broken ground towards the freshly turned molehills. An officer fired a pistol straight at a bawling blue-coat, who fell away to one side as if he had been kicked by a horse, rolling over and over. Harcus was tugging a grenade from his sack, the match cord fuming between his clenched teeth. The blue-coat musketeers fired at point-blank range, knocking down a handful of enemy sappers, who collapsed into their waterlogged diggings, splashing their wild-eyed comrades with mud and blood. Everybody was bawling, cursing, screaming. Nicodemus was running with them, the heavy axe as light as a feather in his trembling fists. With one last yell the sally party reached the trenches, scrambling up the loosely banked soil and leaping down amongst the terrified sappers. Axes and shovels rose and fell, musket butts thudded into sweat-banded foreheads. A bare-chested Royalist with a tangled red beard brought his axe round in a whistling arc, stopping a gasping Roundhead in his tracks. The growling sapper tried to tug the clay-clogged weapon from his victim's broken ribcage, but was clubbed down by a musketeer before he could straighten up. The Roundhead lay back in the dirt, holding his blood-speckled hands up in mute appeal, his white fingers clawing the air as his lungs gurgled and whistled through his torn coat.

A loud explosion sent up a cloud of dirt and rubble, temporarily deafening the grim-faced fighters. Nicodemus jumped into the trench, steadying himself over a dazed Royalist who was crouched on his hands and knees, spitting strings of blood into the dirty red puddles which had been stamped into the pit by the battle-entranced dancers. The boy stared at the man's matted hair, black and grey strands plastered to his skull. The sapper was retching hopelessly, ribs broken by a blow from a musket. He looked up, his face flushed red and eyes supernaturally bright.

Nicodemus was knocked aside as the last blue-coats leapt down into the ditch, flailing about and screaming like banshees. The sapper crossed his hands over his head and collapsed into the filth as the Roundhead soldiers stamped and kicked him, cursing their victim to the depths of hell. Nicodemus sagged against the wall, sick to his stomach. His fingers fluttered, he dropped the axe to the floor as his ears popped and the screaming started. Harsh, animal screechings which lanced through the poor boy's reeling brain like slivers of ice.

He had imagined proud Cavaliers fencing with russet-sashed Roundheads, gentlemen at arms lunging and parrying at one another like the knights of old.

Instead he found himself in a bear pit of snarling human dogs, barking and snapping and biting and gouging like old soaks in an alley. Punch-drunk vagabonds tearing at one another's eyes.

The stampeding Roundheads had taken the enemy sappers by surprise for the second time in six hours, and weren't about to give up their precious advantage. They clubbed and hacked the last few Royalist fighters into the cold clay works, and charged on down the narrow trench after their friends. Dirt-smeared diggers and sooty musketeers dropped their weapons and scrambled away, hauling themselves out of the death pits and running back towards their main works on Gaudy Green. An officer in a blue suit waved his sword and spread his arms to hold them, but one of the blue-coats took careful aim and put a ball in his gut. The man staggered, sat on his backside with a sigh, hiccuping loudly as he spread his hands over the blood blossoming through his expensive doublet. A blue-coat scrambled out after him, parried the officer's weak sword thrust, and kicked him in the throat. He crouched

71

over his victim, tearing at his pockets and cursing all the while.

Harcus was alternately lighting grenades and lobbing them into the Royalist dugouts, his face smeared with soot, lashes clogged with grit. He frowned, holding the trembling fuse to the black flask clenched in his trembling hand. The mad racket of battle died down suddenly as the blue-coats took cover in the abandoned trench, panting hoarsely as they caught their breath. Across the field, they could hear Royalist officers bawling to their men. To their right they could see the tangled vegetable gardens belonging to the abandoned houses along Southgate Street, the Royalist troops lucky enough to have been billeted indoors hurrying out dragging on their coats. Harcus raised his head, and peered over the back wall of the trench. He could see huddles of enemy soldiers making their way forward behind the main Royalist entrenchment, crouching musketeers advancing cautiously, duck hunters in clay waders.

'Take up all the tools!' he shouted, remembering his orders at last. 'And don't forget their powder!'

Nicodemus swallowed with difficulty, watched the blue-coats pick over the bloody debris littering the abandoned trench. The mud-splattered smokers he had seen earlier had recovered a brace of muskets and were already clambering back up the parapet. Nicodemus blinked, focused on the dying sapper. He was groaning miserably, tiny bubbles of bright blood foaming over his lips and down his smashed nose, mumbling and gasping as he fought to breathe. The man was staring at him, the whites of his eyes swimming with tears.

Harcus cuffed him over the shoulder, rammed a handful of clinking powder horns at him. 'Take these, you little fool!' he roared. Nicodemus grasped the leather straps to his chest as the officer barged past, tugging himself out of the pit on a length of twisted tree root. He turned round on the parapet and held his hand down to the boy, hauling him out of the hole like a frightened rabbit. Another flurry of shots hissed overhead, picking off another blue-coat as he hurried back to the safety of the ditch. Nicodemus copied the officer as he bent down and scuttled away through the devastated works, the angry Royalists hurrying after them. The boy's initial excitement had given way to nausea and disgust, stark fear souring his gut. He thought he was going to be sick as he raced after the fleet-footed lieutenant, the looted powder horns spilling stinking fine-ground powder in his face. He sneezed, blinked his watering eyes as Harcus threw himself down beside the wounded man. The soldier had stopped a ball in the back of his thigh, dark blood staining his waxy half-mast breeches. He was grovelling in the dirt and rubble, propelling himself along on his chest with his right foot. Harcus grabbed hold of his straps and hauled him to his feet, ducked his helmeted head under the man's arm. The blue-coat yelped, hopped along as best he could holding up his bunched breeches with his right hand. Nicodemus grabbed the man's carbine and raced off towards the sanctuary of the defences. The sally party had reached the ladder and were picking their way across holding their weapons out to counterbalance their shaky steps.

Thomas Minter, enthusiastic supporter of the thriving tobacco industry thereabouts, glared at his boots as if he had grown an extra leg, completely confounded by the juddering walkway and apparently unable to cross one foot in front of the other. His companion closed in behind him, barged him in the ribs.

'Get on, you daft bugger, or they'll have us like moles in a trap!' Robin Fry bawled in his ear. The mud-splashed musketeer stumbled forward, his long legs twisting and tangling as he took faster and faster steps and finally lost his balance altogether. The soldier gave one despairing cry and fell arse over tit into the slurry-filled pit. The heavily armoured pioneers crowded about him, anxious to get their brainless charges back inside the safety of the walls. They dragged the cursing soldier to his knees and hauled him up the crumbling bank.

'Tom, it's time you cut down on that Old Rustic you'm been blowin'. It'll be the death of yer yet, boy!' the exasperated pioneer advised, shoving the bewildered musketeer up towards the sally-port. One by one the frantic raiders shoved and squeezed through the narrow doorway, the sappers clambering up the slippery ditch to retrieve their creaking ladder and close the fortified gate behind them.

'Have a care! Hold that gate!' Harcus bawled, hurrying up over the eyesore wilderness with the wounded blue-coat. Nicodemus ran ahead, pulled the end of the ladder back as the startled pioneers looked over their plated shoulders.

The Royalists had regained their trench, and glared in fury at their butchered comrades, their smashed weapons and splintered tools. A score of them took off over the shell-cratered no man's land, loudly intent on hunting down the backstabbing perpetrators. Several paused to aim their muskets at the back markers on their makeshift bridge, their bullets thudding into the turf walls around the desperately ducking heads of their targets. They jumped back in sudden surprise as Roundhead sharpshooters returned their fire from the wall, scattering the pursuit like a flock of pheasants. The Royalists screamed with impotent rage as they watched the enemy pioneers hurry out and shepherd their comrades to safety, and bawled challenges over the battered but defiant defences.

'Come out and fight, you rebel dogs!'

'We'll finish with you yet, Roundheads!'

The delighted defenders looked up, peered over the parapet at their furiously gesticulating enemy. They could have shot them down like sheep, but their killing rage was over, blown out of their heads like the fumes of the previous night's ale.

'Get on, you verminous bloats, you know where we are!'

'Away and shite yourselves, Shagpols! You damned Welshmen!' the Gloucester men called back, antagonizing their old enemies from over the Severn. 'We saw you up at Alney, in and out like a tinker in a cathouse!' There was a roar of raucous laughter from the men and women along the wall.

'You'll not be laughing when we get in there,' a Royalist musketeer promised, leering at the grinning faces along the turf embankment. 'We got into Bristol quick enough!'

'This isn't Bristol, you boar-nosed bandit!' A sooty, bleary eyed blue-coat, exhilarated by their breathless sortie and mightily relieved at his own survival, closed the bitter debate to the general satisfaction of the garrison.

Nicodemus had scrambled up the ladder to watch the Royalists' ignominious retreat. He shouted with laughter, hooted and jeered with the rest, but his heart was pounding and his throat hurt as if he had swallowed a frosted swede. He felt so dizzy and sick and miserable he thought for one desperate moment he might faint away entirely.

Make a fool of himself in front of the scolding goodwives and admiring children who had witnessed his reckless adventure.

Ella Clamp pointed the twitching youngster out to her own wide-eyed offspring, cuffed them about their ears in warning.

'And don't you two candle-wastin' terrors go gettin' any ideas,' she threatened. 'There's fools enough in this damned place wi'out you playing the poltroons!'

Prince Rupert rode into the fuming anthill of partially demolished trenches around the south-eastern corner of the besieged city an hour later, shaking his head as he scanned the lacerated landscape. Muttering country folk in dirty smocks had been ordered in to remove the bodies of his dead sappers, flinging their broken, clay-caulked bodies over their dog carts and wheeling the blood-splattered barrows away over the furrowed ground. Every now and again the scowling drovers would run into a submerged tree stump or lose a wheel into a crumbling puddle, tipping their unlucky loads into the sullen red pools.

'Have a care there, that's my men, not mouldy mutton,' the commander snarled, turning his charger in tight circles as he supervised the removal of the half-naked corpses. The bodies had already been looted and stripped by the Roundheads. Anything the attackers had left had been torn off or cut free by their companions.

Blood was as cheap as watered ale beneath those battered, tumbledown walls.

The Prince sat and fumed while his horse hoofed the puddles, splashing the pack of nervous aides who had reined in, out of breath and out of sorts, a safe distance behind their impetuous overlord. His Majesty's well-favoured cousin Rupert slumped in his saddle for a moment, brooding over the tactical problems being thrown up by this ill-considered (and apparently ill-fated) siege. He knew he had been right all along, of course. An immediate attack from five sides at once, a massive assault on the pathetically patched defences, would have carried the town in an hour. Fifteen thousand men sitting around kicking their heels, up to their necks in dirty water like so many hairy-arsed anglers waiting for a bite.

Well, these Gloucester fish had turned the tables on them, slipping out of the sieve they dared call a wall to snap and pinch at his bogged-down brigades.

Which of the slack-jawed idiots who crowded about His Majesty had dared suggest Massey would surrender the town without a fight? He might have fought in the Scots wars with old Will Legge, but that didn't make the man a Royalist. Massey had been given a job to do and he was doing it, as best he knew how, Rupert thought with a sullen grunt of admiration. He remembered his uncle at their ill-tempered council of war, quietly insistent they could not afford another enormous crop of casualties, not after the carnage under Bristol's walls.

But you couldn't make an omelette without cracking a few eggs. Finish the war before the winter, and the King would save ten thousand lives doomed by the cold and fevers alone. He must keep up the pressure on the rebels up and down the country, go for the jugular.

Rupert blew a gust of cold air down his lean nose.

He should have insisted on an immediate assault, thrown in every regiment, every brigade at the wretched wool-plugged walls.

His uncle had never campaigned before, that was the trouble. War was new to him, a vile, grasping adder which he tried to pat and predict. Stamp on the head and the serpent would die!

He worshipped and honoured his uncle, of course, and would cheerfully have lain down his life in return for the full recovery of his slipping crown, but he had more idea about organizing a ball than fighting a war. He had no idea what it was like to sleep under a hedge and break his fast on a palmful of dirty water and a few ears of unripened corn. King Charles could not (or would not) imagine what a kingdom looked like when the armies had finished with it. Marching to and fro, to and fro across the blighted landscapes, year after year. Eating up the crops and the people like fire-breathing dragons. Rupert had fought in Germany, endured the dragons his own father Frederick, the Winter King of Bohemia, had unleashed upon the world.

Rupert would have unleashed the same dragons on these dozy English, would have been happy to feed every last miserable blabber-mouthed rebel into their sulphurous bellies.

The ill-conceived siege had run awry from the first. Poorly sited trenches, badly positioned batteries, shortages of ammunition.

That very day he had toured the gunpits on the southern side of the city, expecting to find culverins, sakers, and mortars busy reducing the city's makeshift defences to ash. Instead he discovered idle gunners loafing over half-submerged guns, scuttling around their sties like bearded pigs. The fools hadn't even dug their latrines in the correct place! One good blast and half of them would be thrown head over heels into their own shit-pit!

The one encouraging development that day ended,

predictably enough, in dangerous farce. The carters and drovers had finally managed to haul a large mortar into position in one of the badly sited batteries. The toiling crews heaved and pushed and sweated and cursed, and finally manhandled the immense iron pot into position to batter the town to pieces with large-calibre grenades. Rupert stood by, watching with grim fascination as the piece was loaded and fired.

KRABOUF!!!!!!!!!!!!!!!!!!!!!!!!!!!!

The three-inch iron plate cracked like a bad egg, the stubby barrel split open like a frog's belly. They threw themselves to the ground, choked on the boiling cauldron of smoke as the massive detonation rocked the very bones of the earth. It was a miracle the exploding mortar only brained three or four of its unlucky crew.

A few hours later, and his mood had not improved. Rupert sat back on his horse and bit his lip, mortified with impotent fury and chafing at the maddening delays.

'Who was in charge here?' he roared at the pack of quaking toadies whistling and humming behind his back.

'Major Mortlake, your Highness.'

'Where is the damned fool?'

'With Mr Ambrosius, sir, the Italian surgeon. He caught a ball in the stomach.'

'Good,' Rupert snapped. 'It'll teach him to pick his nose in *my* trenches!' he growled. 'Caught napping twice, eh? If he lives I'll cashier the swine!' He tugged at his reins and spurred the mud-splattered charger towards the dark, decapitated mass of Llanthony Priory, half a mile away to the west of the demolished trenches. His tired aides shrugged wearily, and spurred their tired mounts after the furious Prince.

Didn't he ever have an afternoon off?

BY

MATSON HOUSE,

NEAR GLOUCESTER,
14 AUGUST 1643

His Majesty King Charles I had arrived outside the stubbornly held walls of his revolted city on 10 August, brimming with optimism at the head of more than eight thousand well-armed men. But any hopes he might have cherished for a prompt and painless surrender were brusquely dashed that same afternoon. The messengers sent out by the city in response to the King's conciliatory appeal appeared completely unimpressed by his gaudy host, clapping their caps on within thirty yards of their strained but dignified monarch as if he was an itinerant come to sell them brushes. The King's officers and attendants – true servants all – gasped with rage as they noticed the orange ribbons the messengers had worked into their hats, an insolent demonstration of their staggeringly ill-considered allegiance to the opposing party.

The King retired to his new headquarters at nearby Matson House, deeply disappointed by his misguided citizens' refusal to see sense. He had, however, recovered enough of his wandering will-power to countermand his nephew Prince Rupert's loud demands for an immediate storm. He had been sickened by the slaughter beneath Bristol's walls, and would not budge despite Rupert's black-eyed tantrums. They would surround the city, bombard the defences and undermine the walls.

'Most of the men are camping in water-meadows,' Rupert snapped, his long black hair masking his turbulent features as he prodded his finger at the heap of inaccurate maps. The newly completed town walls were sketched in black, the surrounding Royalist dispositions drawn in red ink. Ruthven at Llanthony Priory, six thousand horse and foot at Tredworth, two thousand horse at Walham, Sir Jacob Astley at Barton and Sir William Vasavour's Welsh forces across the Severn at Over. 'The saps are already filling with water, the ground is quite clearly unsuitable for mining,' the Prince concluded.

'We will c–c–continue n–nevertheless,' his uncle insisted, his stammer as usual becoming more pronounced as he became agitated. 'We will p–p–press them at th–three p–points at once. Ma–Massey cannot defend every inch of his l–line.'

Rupert, in a fit of pique, had refused overall control of the operation, preferring an independent command with the widely dispersed and dangerously idle cavalry. Patrick Ruthven, Earl of Brentford and a professional soldier of vast experience, agreed to assume the direction of the siege. His Majesty completed the day's business by issuing a proclamation setting up markets to serve the camps in the forlorn hope that properly supervised trade would prevent the mass of soldiers from pillaging the country folk roundabout. The penalty for molesting anybody on their way to the markets was to be summary execution.

His Majesty would of course be rather more generously provided for than his hungry troops. He had brought along what he fondly imagined to be a suitably spartan court, a household stripped back to the bone by the demands of the campaign. King Charles had his own suite of gowned and slippered gentlemen in waiting, a platoon of manservants and a battalion of secretaries, as well as equerries, tailors, seamstresses, shoemakers, barbers, surgeons, and armourers. He had brought with him clerks, heralds, trumpeters, and a lifeguard of three dozen fully armoured cuirassiers. The squabbling flock had to be housed somewhere, and each draughty loft, corridor, and outhouse had become prime real-estate for the fantastical court. In addition to the King's personal suite there were those of his young sons Charles and James – busy carving their names into the panelling upstairs – as well as his vast retinue of senior officers. Earls, barons, dukes, and knights all required their own swarm of servants, and took as much interest in outdoing one another in the sumptuousness of their quarters as they did in the siege itself. The royal court had attracted a host of precious parasites, with every spare foot of open space or orchard swamped with gaily coloured marquees and pavilions. Servants, squires, maids, and messengers bustled through the overcrowded alleys or got hopelessly lost in the canvas canyons which radiated from the King's headquarters.

Prince Rupert, as usual, had taken a bed at nearby Prinknash Park, although he was rarely in it, his duties taking him from one end of the lines to the other at all times of the day and night. Especially at night.

'Prinknash Park? How very tiresome for him. One almost feels bound to drive out and join him.' Anthony St John Dyle, Lord Clavincale, had no such intention, but he could not resist the opportunity of pouring a little more scorn on the despised German Prince.

Rupert Rupert Rupert.

It was all his scatterbrained fiancée had talked about

since they left Oxford the day before. The coach had been stuck behind convoys of carts, enormous wagons, and massive artillery pieces being hauled by teams of lowing oxen. They had dug enormous ruts in the potholed roads, apparently attempting to backfill their tracks with heaps of steaming dung.

Clavincale's grandly appointed carriage was splashed with their reeking slurry, his immaculately turned out postilions transformed into muck-raking peasants before they had travelled ten miles. God only knew where they would be sleeping that night, at this rate they would reckon a straw-strewn stable to be as good as a sultan's palace.

'We might well find ourselves sharing a tent with Father,' the young woman scowling on the cushions opposite the nobleman observed drily. Clavincale snorted.

'I'd rather share a bed with that heathen Rupert,' he snapped. 'Aye, and that's saying something,' he added.

Bella Margueritte Morrison continued to glare out of the window, gloomily surveying the endless downs and sudden drops along their route. She was just eighteen years of age, a remarkable beauty even among the notable attractions at the royal court in Oxford. She had a mass of soft auburn hair tied up in a rather travel-weary bun, and her fine new gown and jewels reminded her many admirers of a painter who had made unnecessarily fussy additions to an already fine portrait. Her face was at once delicate and resolute, sweetly framed but possessed of a stubbornly held chin. She had the complexion of a gently rubbed rose petal, and a wide, pouting mouth. Darting hazel eyes which could delight one moment and demolish the next. Her hands were white, and her fingers exquisitely tapered.

She crossed her hands in front of her to wrestle with

the plunging neckline of her rich red velvet gown. Anthony had insisted she wear the dress, typical of the low-cut high fashion of the King's court, despite the arduous journey in the cramped coach. Bella had begun to fidget and fret the moment they set out, the whirling dust clouds and fearsome heat exhausting her small store of ladylike decorum. Clavincale's moist eyes glittered as he watched her pulling and tugging at her cleavage, her apricot-down breasts and faintly suggested raspberry nipples heaving in a most satisfactory manner.

'Why not take it off, my dear?' he suggested lewdly, making himself more comfortable in the stubbornly stalled coach.

'Oh, yes, that's typical of you,' she snapped. 'Warning me to mind my Ps and Qs one moment and tweaking my tits like a common polecat the next!'

'There is nothing common about you, my dear,' Clavincale simpered, leaning over the aisle to pat her carelessly twitching knee.

'But plenty of polecat, is that what you mean?' Bella asked, winningly indignant.

'Plenty enough for me,' he winked suggestively. The girl scowled, pleased with the compliment despite the discomfort of the trying journey. She stared out of the window at the massed traffic – carters and drovers in sweat-stained smocks cracking their switches over their oxen, harnessed in tandem to haul the King's culverins. Bella watched the peculiarly rhythmic motion of their bony hindquarters, rising and falling like some kind of clock-work contraption beneath their smooth hides. A miracle of engineering hammered and lashed together by a mad watchmaker. The beasts were smeared with their own slimy slurry, and the cloying reek hung like a foul miasma over the shuffling army.

The musketeers, pikemen, and laughing Cavaliers at the head of the winding snake had already passed by, off to the wars under Gloucester's walls. Clavincale's coach was stuck halfway down the snake's gullet, jammed in with the rest of the army. Gunners and their mates and their ragged-arsed assistants trudged behind their clattering pieces, great creaking cannon with gaping mouths and studded wheels, clogged with the clay torn up from the broken-backed road. With them were miners and pioneers with pick and shovel, field kitchens with smoky stoves and mobile laundries with great oaken tubs full to the brim with slick grey water. Red-armed goodwives balanced as best they could as they wrestled with sodden shifts and shirts, pegging the clothing out along the overloaded canopies of their carts so that they looked from a distant like tiny landbound galleons under full sail. And bringing up the noisome rear shepherds with wandering flocks, tinkers and tradesmen, thieves and looters, tricksters and whores.

Bella had never seen so many people, crowding along the high road like some displaced race of biblical refugees. It was as if the tides of war had lifted them and all their worldly goods, carried the whole filthy flock along on the flood, depositing the weary flotsam and jetsam where it might.

The marching men peered in at the glamorous passenger, whistling and jeering while their womenfolk stared spitefully, making comments behind their hands as this whore of Babylon, this splendid Sheba was carried by in the luxurious – though shit-splattered – coach, the gloating authoress of all their misery.

Lord Clavincale slumped back in his seat, the papers, news-sheets, letters, and dispatches he had been studying strewn over the leather bench beside him.

'Perhaps Father will have saved some room for us, though?' Bella enquired testily. They had finally managed to secure themselves some decent lodgings back in Oxford and here they were on the road again. It was perfect madness, if you asked her. Bella's fiancé pulled at his generous lip as he carried on reading.

'Your father is in the field, my dear. He couldn't save us a space at the bottom of a well!'

'Well, where are we going to sleep? In the coach?'

'Wouldn't be the first time, my angel, needs must when the devil drives. The King's court is at Gloucester, we, therefore, must be at Gloucester,' he said pedantically.

Bella, fast becoming something of an expert on the complex machinations of the turbulent court, was well aware of the vital importance of maintaining the highest possible profile in the royal presence. To be overlooked at court could mean death, the living death of the social outcast. Clavincale had an enviable pedigree and a huge fortune, as well as good connections all over the west and abroad. At Oxford, however, he was just another young buck, richer than most but well known by few. Reputation counted more than ready cash these days and the quickest route to making a name at court was through military prestige: victory in battle or the completion of some perilous sortie. Clavincale, rather delicate and prone to chronic chills despite his well-upholstered frame, preferred to pursue alternative paths to fame and glory.

He had already supervised the confiscation of property belonging to the dispossessed Parliamentarian gentry of the rich territories of the south-west, Dorset, Devon, and Somerset. They had been forced to flee their homes, abandon their farms and mills before the irresistible advance of the Royalist forces. He had organized sales of goods, disposal of property, and collection of horses, weapons, and plate. Clavincale's most lucrative coup, however, was the sale of the mountain of captured Roundhead supplies after the disastrous battle of Roundway Down. He had dispatched several wagonloads of goods to His Majesty's court, worth hundreds of pounds to his desperately bare war chest. Clavincale had not been quite so keen to share in his subsidiary enterprise, however: a complex and completely unauthorized transaction he had worked out with a high-ranking ambassador from the Spanish court. Clavincale had taken it upon himself to relieve His Majesty's gaol at Oxford of a hundred and six Roundhead prisoners, and marched them instead into the far west, to his family's ancient fiefdom on the Dorset–Devon border. He sold the men to the hard-pressed Spanish, who were never overly concerned as to the origins of another boatload of cannon fodder. The freelance operation earned Clavincale a handsome profit, and established the lordling as a major player on the crucial trade routes in and out of the blockaded kingdom.

The Roundheads had another name for the blockade-running captains who brought arms, money, and brandy to the King's forces. They were pirates, impure and simple, to be hanged from the yardarm as soon as their Parliamentary captors reached port.

Clavincale picked at the brittle wax seal of yet another letter, immediately recognizing the stooping-eagle motif belonging to his Spanish associate Count Orlando de

Meola. He unfolded the carefully sealed envelope and scanned the beautifully scripted if somewhat bewildering message.

Sir, Talisman arrived Sceptre a dozen sacks short, blamed shortfall on rebel wind. Kindly remedy deficiency as soon as possible, meantimes return cargo remains with me, your servant always, Conde Orlando Gonzalez de Meola.

Clavincale frowned, chewed at his thumbnail. So his piratical captain Cruickshank (Talisman) had reached his destination of Antwerp (Sceptre) with a dozen of his precious cargo missing, due to the unwanted and unspecified attention of the roving Parliamentary fleet (rebel wind). The nobleman considered the puzzling possibilities. Had they mutinied, jumped ship, or been killed in some desperate boarding action? Perhaps the men had taken a fever and died, they had been coughing like crocks when he toured their makeshift prison in Devizes Castle those few short weeks before. Whatever the outcome, the damned Spaniard was refusing to complete the transaction, retaining the cargo of arms and ammunition they had agreed upon. Clavincale had banked the downpayment, but had reckoned on sending the powder and muskets directly to Oxford, further strengthening his position at court. Without those arms he was just another idle courtier, of little or no use to his hard-pressed majesty. Clavincale rubbed his nose. De Meola was a sly one, all right. Sitting pretty back in the Spanish Netherlands with his muskets. Clavincale had little chance of tracking him down, even if he could have left England. The only course was to write and promise to replace the missing men as soon as possible. Who knows, some of the Gloucester men they would shortly be rounding up might make just as good soldiers serving his friends the Spaniards.

'Is it from Father?' Bella enquired, noting her fiancé's momentary frown.

'No, no, my dear. *This* is from your father.' Clavincale patted a sheaf of grubby dispatches which had been sent on from Oxford after their coach. Bella regarded the casually discarded papers with a sulky pout.

'Well, what does he say?' Bella asked impatiently. 'It's obviously of little interest to you, the time you've spent devouring it.'

Clavincale smiled fondly at her. 'On the contrary, my dear. I never mix business with pleasure, as you know. I have left Sir Gilbert's delightful missive to the very end, relishing the prospect of renewing my acquaintance with your father's sturdy prose.'

Bella scowled, then laughed out loud, leaning over to slap his chubby thigh.

'You monster, mocking him so after all he has done for us. You know he never had time for a proper education. He was too busy . . .'

'Making his fortune, which didn't grow from seed, I'll have you know,' Clavincale mimicked the blustering merchant. Sir Gilbert's wayward daughter froze for a moment as she leaned over, making sure he had digested the mouth-watering view down her gaping cleavage, and then sat back with a provocative sigh. 'And what's all this "all he's done for us" nonsense?'

Bella arched her eyebrows. 'Well, he's let me loose with a notorious rake, for one thing, and allowed you to enjoy my company,' she said, demurely straightening her dress, 'even before we were properly engaged.'

'He only wants the best for you, my dear,' Clavincale responded with a cheeky wink.

In point of fact, Sir Gilbert knew Bella was perfectly well equipped to get the best for herself. As long as the young buck made an honest woman of her soon, he was prepared to overlook the lack of propriety. There was a war on, after all. And fortunes to be made and names to be earned. Noble family names to be spread about among the grafting mercantile classes.

'Well, what does he say?' Bella encouraged, nodding him to continue.

'Let's see,' Clavincale breathed, running his finger under his constricting collar. '"Marched out of Chipping Marleward at the head of several hundred men." Well, three dozen, at least.' Clavincale automatically corrected Sir Gilbert's fanciful figures. '"Reached Bristol and installed Starling back at my headquarters." That rat-infested cavern on Temple Back, does he mean?' Bella glared at him. '"High hopes for renewed trade now that city has rediscovered its allegiance to the crown . . ." de da de da de da . . . "marched east for Oxford but diverted by messenger at Swindon, ordered to Gloucester." He says Nybb and Findlay are already at each other's throats, and young Telling has moped all the way. So much for resurrecting his career!' Clavincale leered.

Bella's bright smile slipped a notch. She had met Hugo at Kilmersden Hall earlier that hectic summer, and immediately fell for the boyish Cavalier's vulnerable good looks and hopelessly indulgent mood swings. But Hugo was more interested in playing farmyard games with his red-headed whore Matilda Dawkins than in paying proper court to her, Bella recalled with a shiver of anger. She snubbed his clumsy advances and trod on his hat for good measure, although she later forgave him and hardly slept a wink when she heard he had been taken prisoner by the Roundheads. She had raced halfway across the country looking for him, only to hear he had escaped once again – and flown straight back to his polecat of a mistress. She hadn't seen or heard from him since his disgrace at Bristol, but still retained a fond memory of the miserable Romeo.

He must have been desperate to sign up with Sir Gilbert, though, pinning what was left of his hopes on glorious service with her father. Bella was no expert but she knew full well the turncoat merchant hadn't exactly set the country alight with a breathtaking display of martial prowess. Hugo was unlikely to achieve the fame he craved serving as her imaginative father's master of horse. Sir Gilbert had needed every man he could lay his hands on for his new regiment. What was it his clerk Starling had called them? A shilling's worth of shadows. A pale, flea-bitten battalion of rickets-riddled vagabonds, gaolbirds, deserters, and drunkards, brought up to strength with beardless farm boys looking for adventure the other side of the hill. The worthless rabble wouldn't have stood their ground against a sackful of rabbits, let alone a psalm-singing Roundhead pikeblock.

To remedy this worrying deficiency Sir Gilbert had enlisted Findlay, whose career as a gamekeeper at Kilmersden Hall had been brought to an all too abrupt end by his master Sir Marmaduke Ramsay's untimely death on Lansdown. An excellent shot (as half his misbegotten new charges could testify), Findlay concentrated on turning the rabble into first-class musketeers. They could make short work of a rank of bottles, but were still not yet ready for battle. Mastering a musket was no passport to victory, the men needed hardening up. Sir Gilbert, recognizing his men lacked a certain warrior instinct, shared his concerns with his would-be son-in-law. Lord Clavincale came up with the ideal solution in the bearlike shape of his bodyguard Nybb. The brawny giant with the outlandish accent had been kicking his heels for months, accompanying the nobleman on his surreptitious missions about the country. He had just returned from the far west, where he had been putting Clavincale's affairs in order (and collecting de Meola's deposit, as it happened) and was eager for some new activity. A commission as lieutenant colonel in Sir Gilbert's regiment would put the fire back in his belly (and of his men).

Bella looked up coldly. She had missed what Clavincale had been saying.

'. . . but he might come in handy, though, God knows the boy hates Maurice almost as much as I do,' the lordling went on carelessly. 'That is . . .'

'Don't you go involving Hugo in your little schemes,' Bella scolded him. 'He's far too transparent for your skulduggery.'

'Skulduggery, my dear? He's a captain in your father's regiment, how can he possibly become embroiled in anything so sinister?' he asked innocently.

Bella frowned, lifting her low-cut neckline an inch as if in veiled warning of further sensory deprivations she could inflict on the grinning aristocrat.

'You leave him out of it, Anthony. He hardly knows his own mind at the moment, let alone yours. He certainly doesn't need you to manipulate his silly grievances.'

'Silly grievances? Cashiered in front of the whole army because he was too ill to mount a proper guard ten miles from the nearest known Roundhead? We've earls and barons who have lost entire armies and yet been allowed to retain their titles,' Clavincale snapped indignantly. 'It's all Rupert's fault, him and his heel-clicking clique. Your Telling was made a scapegoat for their failure, Rupert's and Maurice's.'

'What failure? They captured Bristol the very next day!'

'Not before they had managed to lose half the army! And I hear that if Rupert had gotten his pig-headed way he would have lost the other half storming Gloucester! More bloody glory to that damned House of Palatine!'

'You're just jealous,' Bella cried. 'You wish—' Bella yelped in pain as the corpulent lord suddenly jumped forward and grasped her chin in his pudgy fist.

'I'm not jealous, and I wish for nothing other than His Majesty's speedy return to his capital.' He shook her head hard, tears springing into her flashing eyes. 'And if you know what's good for you, my lady, you will concentrate your wholehearted energies into seconding my efforts on the King's behalf. Rupert and his clumsy brother have more than enough creatures of their own to plead their case,' he snarled, hurling her back in her seat.

Bella stroked her flaring jaw, glaring out of the window while Clavincale resumed his seat and caught his breath, smiled shortly.

'There, my dear. You rouse up my manly spirits and end up fretting. I didn't mean to cause you any hurt, Bella?' He tilted his head, peered at her concernedly. He placed a conciliatory hand on her knee, only to have it shoved away. 'Bella, my love, my angel. You distract me so with your silly outbursts.'

Bella continued to stare out of the window of the coach.

'You know how much I despise those, those Germans!'

he growled. 'Strutting about the country, fighting our battles. There are more ways to serve His Majesty than charging about like a blockhead waving a damned sword.'

Bella continued to glare, her skin changing colour as her moods dipped and swung. Anger, humiliation, pride.

'I'm sorry I hurt you, my love, my dearest heart,' he blurted. 'I promise I'll make it up to you. We'll bring the date forward, how's that? We'll invite the King himself to the wedding!'

'What wedding?' Bella enquired coldly. Clavincale laughed nervously. He decided he had better keep his own counsel for a while, and returned to a most determined study of his bundled correspondence.

She maintained her stony silence all the way to Gloucester, and jumped down from the coach as if she was a prisoner fleeing some vile confinement.

BY

GAUDY GREEN,

GLOUCESTER, 15 AUGUST 1643

The first thing Slaughter's mutinous crew saw on their arrival in the pockmarked outworks surrounding Gloucester was a convoy of wobbly-wheeled dog carts, laden with half-naked corpses. The bodies were smeared in mud, excrement, and congealed blood, some stiff as boards, others flopping raggedly over the splattered planking. Drivers in bloody smocks had tied handkerchiefs about their faces, and were beating their weary teams on through the ploughed lane to a gravepit which had been excavated beside an abandoned orchard on the Barton road.

'Ged on there, boys! Fightin's that way, just follow yu's noses!' a cheery old wagoner called, pointing back the way the caravan of death had come.

Slaughter's men gaped as the burial parties prised the corpses out of the carts and hauled them under the armpits towards the huge brown pit. Their bare heels dragged blunt furrows through the loose soil, parallel lines which were quickly crossed over and crossed out as the wagons were emptied, turned, and led back towards the city.

Elder Sergeant Cully Oates frowned, shaking his tousled head at the depressing spectacle.

'Ah, me beauts, comes to us all. No good frettin' cus there's no preacher man to say a few words over yer.' He trudged on, musket over his shoulder, lifting his montero cap from his rusty grey hair and folding it over his leather bandolier in tribute to the fallen.

Zachary and Eli Pitt immediately snatched off their hats, stared as the burial party completed their morning's work, disposing of the night's crop of corpses. Oates fell in beside the red-faced wagoner, who had eased his buttocks over the bloody running-board of his cart.

'All ours, is it?' the elder sergeant enquired. The merry drover nodded, tugging his handkerchief down and taking a lungful of fresher air.

'Aye. A good dozen a day usually. They'm hurtin' you boys more'n you'm hurtin' them, that's a fact.'

The Pitt brothers exchanged a nervous glance. And what if their younger brother Mordecai was on the wall? They'd be shooting and piking each other, and be cursed to hell for all eternity for it and all.

'They had a pop over at the Kingsholm battery again, but niver got the guns. Got that lot, though, up St Margaret's way,' the driver reported, poking his thumb at the gravepit.

'I'd 'ave thought Princey would have finished with 'em by now. He 'as damn near every place else,' Cully Oates observed, spitting into the trampled ditch beside the road.

'Ah, they're 'ard men before God, strong for the Parl'ment and all. Ain't goin' to fall like Zirin-zester did.'

'Were you there, old-timer? Back in February?'

'I watched 'em march the bleeders out in their drawers! 'Twas a wonder they niver took chills and died!'

The absorbing discussion was cut short by the sight of the scowling regimental officer corps, pulled up on their steaming horses at a busy crossroads. Michael Slaughter glared at his would-be assassins as they trudged past with sloped arms. The men avoided his piercing gaze, but gave a shout for the jolly merchant, Turncoat Morrison, sitting on his grey mare like Gustavus Adolphus himself. The Pitt brothers had served in his original unit, the village militia Morrison raised for service with Parliament. But before they heard a shot fired in anger their brave colonel had fled with all their pay and joined up with the advancing Royalists. Here he was now, waving to his men as they shuffled past laughing down their filthy sleeves at his rumbustious greetings. Mind you, they had turned their coats too. They were no better than the fat merchant, when you got right down to it.

'There you are lads, Zach and Eli!' Sir Gilbert cried, spying his former employees. 'Here's a turn up, all this way from Chipping Marleward, eh?'

'We were wonderin' whether you'd heard from home, sir. Is Mordecai back at all?'

'I heard from your sister he was at Bristol, but that's all,' Sir Gilbert replied as the regiment trooped on past. 'But I expect he's safe enough.'

The Pitt brothers trudged on, brooding over the vicious uncertainty of it all. Fighting wasn't bad, when you got right down to it. They had been at Lansdown and Round-way, and seen bodies aplenty. But the thought they might come across their kin on the opposing party, or even worse, amongst the heaps of dead afterwards, had quite sapped their will.

Colonel Nybb sat astride his massive cob cross just behind the merchant, impatient to get on, with Telling moping on his lighter bay horse just behind him. Michael Slaughter and Captain Shea kept their distance, the disgruntled commander eyeing the blustering usurper with bloodthirsty relish.

'Colonel Nybb can see the men bedded down in their quarters,' he called over the shuffle of feet and dull clanking of the cartwheels. 'You and I can ride for the headquarters, and sort this matter out straight away.'

Sir Gilbert tipped his hat back and regarded the queer fellow on the black charger. 'There's no rush, sir, as you can see, they're as sweet as lambs now, with some food in their bellies!'

That was true enough, at least. They had left Much Hindon in buoyant mood, the ale and bacon warming their hearts and speeding their march. They had been expecting another feast that morning, but the colonel had been forced to tell them the wagons had fallen behind and they would have to make do with double-baked bread and a little ditchwater. The surly regiment could already hear the rumble of guns, and knew they were too close to the besieged city to cause any further trouble. Why, that demon Prince Rupert might be hiding over the next hill, ready to swoop down on the stragglers and cut them to pieces. They hadn't heard the last of the business at the village, either, and woe betide the buggers if Slaughter ever got his hands on them again. He'd flog the lot of them three times a day and laugh while he was doing it. Old Sir Gilbert, he might be a buffoon, but at least he didn't whip 'em.

'I don't give a tinker's cuss what they are. I'll deal with those blackguards when I've got my regiment back!' Slaughter insisted.

Sir Gilbert pursed his generous lips. 'Very well, sir. We'll proceed directly to the headquarters. Maxom House, is it?'

'Matson,' Slaughter corrected.

'Very good. Captain Telling will bring the escort, Colonel Nybb and Captain Shea will remain with the men.'

Slaughter nodded grimly, turning his horse back out onto the potholed road. 'After you, Sir Gilbert,' he breathed. 'It'll be the last time you lead my men,' he promised.

The merchant nodded curtly, momentarily taken aback by this damned Irishman's assurance. Captain Telling, eager for a glimpse of his despised enemy Prince Rupert, waved the small cavalry squadron in behind them. Nine patchwork Cavaliers on matted piebald nags, riding beneath Sir Gilbert's own personal standard. Anneliese Ramsay had sewn it for her dead brother's troop in time for the battle of Edgehill last October. Thomas Ramsay had returned to Kilmersden Hall, the silk pennant draped over the scorched ruin of his face. Sir Gilbert had decided it would make as good an emblem as any for his new troop, and had taken it with him when they had left the week before. The sad relic flapped above the dusty troop as they rode on through the scattered hovels of Barton, passing fields full of tents and queues of shouting soldiers. Long lines of cavalry mounts were picketed along every hedge and ditch, their bored owners taking their ease around their campfires. There were wagons, carts, caravans, and coaches parked in every available yard, the watchful towns-folk going about their business in the unusually packed streets.

The merchant's party followed the line of the outer works around Gaudy Green and back down Southgate Street towards the King's headquarters over at Matson House. Sir Gilbert stared at the brown mass of trenches and saps, of gunpits and batteries. In the distance, he glimpsed the smudged shapes of Gloucester, partially hidden behind sullen columns of smoke. The walls looked like tinker's breeches, the pockmarked grey stone patched with green turf and white woolsacks. Surely the town couldn't hold out against this massive collection of men? Sir Gilbert had never seen so many guns. Thank the Lord he had changed sides when he did!

Nicodemus Burke followed the tiny Royalist troop's cautious progress through Lieutenant Harcus's glass. The boy had climbed up on to the tumbledown tower along from the Southgate to peer at the gradually advancing enemy works. He wondered if the fat man in the bright new buff coat was one of the many great captains who had set themselves against the town. One of the earls, barons, or dukes who had promised their sovereign the town would fall like a ripe plum. The little troop rode out of sight behind the slag heap embankments which had been thrown up along the main road, and Nicodemus swung his glass back to the trenches nearer at hand. The saps bristled with musketeers, he could see their hats bobbing behind the soil-heaped works as they guarded the sweating pioneers. Shovelfuls of earth were flying up into the air as if the enemy had thrown a pack of hounds into their trenches. It was almost comical, watching their antics. But Nicodemus remembered the agonized face of that dying Royalist back in the pit. There was nothing funny about their preparations, or the grimly determined Roundhead death squads which raided the lines every day and every night.

'Well?' Harcus called, ducking his head as he clambered up the crumbling tower and crouched down beside the single grey slab which was all that remained of the medieval battlement. The stone fragment looked like a grey tooth in an old man's gum, but provided a little cover for those brave enough to venture out on the exposed turret.

Nicodemus pointed over the wilderness to the gradually advancing molehill which marked the Royalist works.

'They've doubled the watch, sir. At least two dozen of 'em, and they're blowin' on their match,' Nicodemus reported helpfully.

Harcus frowned. So the King's men had learned their lesson, and had made sure to protect their isolated sappers. Trench raiding would be doubly difficult from now on. But orders were orders. Colonel Massey was right, of course. If they battened down the hatches and waited behind the walls they would be slaughtered by Rupert's massively superior force. Their only chance was to keep him busy, drag out the siege, and wait for relief. Harcus took his glass back, and examined the trenches nearer at hand. The enemy saps had been dug towards the south-eastern corner of the wall which encircled the bulk of the old Friar's Orchard. The neatly laid out fruit trees had been torn and slashed by enemy fire and rotten fruit lay thick in the long grass, food for the furiously rooting pigs the girls drove into the wilderness every morning. If the Royalists could get over the exposed wall there they could tear a breach and allow their horse to pour into the orchard, giving them room to manoeuvre against any counterattack. The lieutenant crawled back away from the pockmarked parapet, and clambered back down the steps to his waiting troops. Nicodemus followed, anxious not to be left out of the action.

The bedraggled blue-coats looked like scarecrows, unshaven and unwashed, their tattered coats and filthy breeches splashed with mud and blood. To the red-haired boy they looked like berserkers, armed to the teeth with muskets and pistols and knives and clubs looted from their enemy. The sally party was standing about the orchard, smoking and coughing as they whiled away their last moments of peace.

'Right, then. They're creeping closer on the left-hand side there. If we don't stop 'em soon they'll be chipping at the wall,' Harcus reported, lifting his sack of grenades from beneath a gnarled tree. The weary soldiers blew pungent tobacco smoke on their match, and fell in behind the fearless officer as he waved them up behind the woolsacked wall. The enemy fire had been increasing in intensity over the last few days as more guns were brought to bear on the exposed corner of the defences. The gaps and breaches had been plugged with gabions, sandbags, and bulging woolsacks, and lined with fresh turf every day. Still the guns roared and rumbled. Nicodemus watched the ever punctual pioneers come trudging along the inner wall, their siege armour rusting rapidly with constant use. Several of the sappers could point out fresh silver streaks in the beaten iron, evidence of near misses from Royalist musket balls. Harcus paused to confer with the engineers, pointing over the wall as he explained his plan.

'You take the sally-port there, make as much noise as you can. Try and get them to open fire while you're in the ditch, that way you can rush 'em while they're reloading. I'll go over the wall when they're looking your way, and give 'em a few of my pies.' He patted the bulging sack. 'That'll take the edge off their day,' he promised.

Nicodemus watched the pioneers gather around the fortified sally-port. Harcus strode back towards the tower, with the boy trailing at his heels.

'You stay back now, you hear?' Harcus halted, looked

down at the red-haired messenger. Nicodemus nodded. He had become a sort of mascot, accompanying the troops up to the walls and waving them off, hurrying out to help them scramble back in. Harcus ruffled his hair, picked one of the grenades from his sack. He climbed up the crumbling tower and crouched down behind the breach overlooking the wall. He waited, peering down at the busy Royalist trenches. Picks and shovels rising and falling, musketeers pacing the waterlogged pits.

Suddenly, he caught a blur of movement out of the corner of his eye, looked round to see the sally-port door hurled back and a frantic sapper tumble out into the refuse-filled ditch. Another and another followed, dragging their battered and mended ladder with them. There was a shout from the alerted Royalists, and an immediate shot. They were on their toes, Harcus thought grimly. He waited another moment and then squeezed out through the breach and onto the wall. He cursed as his sack fell forward, clanking on the battered stone parapet. The strap had caught on a protruding nail as he crawled through the breach, and the tired stitching had given up the ghost, spilling two grenades over the wall and into the slurry. Harcus cursed, made a desperate grasp at the rolling flasks. A musket ball clipped the stonework as he was spotted by an enemy sharpshooter. Nicodemus felt a thrill of terror race through his body and out along his twitching arms. He scrambled out of the breach and ducked down beside the officer as he collected his wares.

'Go back!' Harcus snarled. Nicodemus ducked his head as another shot flew wide. He picked up the last grenades, dropped them into the flap of his shirt. Harcus paused, glared at him, and then jumped over the side into the ditch. Nicodemus peered over the edge, saw him straighten up holding his sack in front of him. Another flurry of shots clipped and pinged off the old stonework, and Nicodemus leapt down into the filth beside the officer. He landed with a splash, hurting his ankle and clawing at the crumbling mud wall of the ditch. Harcus had taken his match and was lighting the end of his first grenade. Thirty yards along the wall, the sally party charged out at the enemy sap, the Royalist soldiers shouting and bawling as they prepared to receive them.

Nicodemus watched Harcus lob the grenade over the lip of the trench.

'That'll give them something to chew on!' he laughed, tugging the pistol from his belt and scrambling up the trench, levering himself up on the broken bag. Nicodemus crouched like a drowned rat in the filthy pit, the iron flasks heavy in his gaping shirt. He was paralysed with fear, terrified that if he raised his head from the trench he would be shot on sight by the alerted Royalists. There was a terrific bang, and a sudden squall of muddy gravel clattered and splashed into the turf-ribbed wall. Nicodemus could hear them screaming and bawling despite the hideous ringing in his ears. He prised himself to his feet and peeped over the filthy rim of the trench.

The smoke stung his eyes but he could see the dim shadows of the soldiers as they grappled on the parapet of the Royalist works, the diggers swinging axes and shovels at the snarling musketeers, swordsmen jabbing and parrying viciously aimed musket butts.

Harcus was lying on his back, hands propped up on his elbows, trembling like a newborn pup's paws. His burgonet had been torn off by the blast he had run straight into, his straw-coloured hair scorched from his crisp black head. His breastplate was dented and scored by flying iron, his jaw practically torn off by a hissing fragment. His boots kicked the air, beat a tattoo against the cloud of drifting smoke which spewed up out of the Royalist dugout. A man in a baggy shirt ran out of the hole clutching at his burning hair. Others, mangled by the grenade, groaned and coughed in the blood-shattered pit. The sally party stared in horror at the body of their chief, shocked by the determined and ferocious resistance which the enemy survivors were putting up. One by one they ducked out of the brawl and doubled back to the wall, the Royalists at their heels. Men grappled in the filth, choked one another or beat each other's brains in with axes and picks, lumps of old stone. Nicodemus dropped back into the ditch, frozen with shock, numb with terror. The sally party scrambled back to the gaping hatch, the pioneers waving them over the rickety bridge. They dragged their wounded with them, smeared in dirt, blinded by the stinging smoke. Nicodemus had taken half a dozen steps towards them, picking his way down the waterlogged ditch, when there was an enormous cheer from the Royalist trench. A dozen and more men had charged out after the intruders, intent on capturing their precious gate in the wall. The sally party threw themselves against the narrow doorway, the pioneers shoving and hauling them through the bottleneck like sacks of wriggling eels.

The Royalists were just ten yards behind now, screaming like banshees in their blood craze. A youthful, fresh-faced ensign led the way with a pistol in either fist, his tawny hair hanging over his pale features. Nicodemus dropped to his knees, the forgotten grenades rolling into the dirt, swallowed up by a billowing wall of dark smoke.

He blinked and retched on the acrid fog, then leaned forward and grasped after the precious grenades. Where were they, for the love of Christ? He lifted the crude iron flasks as if they were black rubies, precious stones spewed from some exploding mine. Stung into action by his friends' frantic screams for help, the ragged intruder hauled himself out of the bloody ditch as the Royalists closed in for the kill, gloating over the last Roundheads stuck beyond the wall. The doomed men turned to face the enraged pursuit, cornered like so many ragged wolves by a circle of enemies. The Royalist ensign lifted his pistols and closed one eye, taking careful aim at the trapped blue-coats.

Nicodemus was frantic with panic, the grenades clutched in his filthy paws. He took a deep breath and scrambled over the rubble-strewn wasteland, hurling himself down beside Harcus. A slim grey snake of smoke was rising from the dying lieutenant's scorched mouth, slinking between the elongated white stumps of his clenched teeth. Nicodemus swallowed the gorge rising in his constricted throat and snatched at the length of burning match Harcus still clutched in his blood-speckled gauntlet. He held the smouldering orange tip to the waxy fuse of the grenade and threw it with all his might at the howling Royalist mob.

The boy hurled himself to the scorched and blasted earth and covered his ears at the immediate, breathtaking crack of iron and fire. He was lifted up and thrown into the Royalist sap by the explosion, a rolling, pulsing ball of flaming shards which tore through the struggling mob like a thunderbolt, slashing and tearing men to heaps of gristle and soot-roasted flesh. The shouting ensign staggered on, firing his pistols and toppling into the ditch with his blue-coat victim. The surviving Royalists picked themselves up and ran for their lives as the Roundhead musketeers crowded up on the walls to save their trapped comrades.

Nicodemus shot out of the open grave, his hands and face smeared with the blood of the dead and dying sappers. He ran in circles through the flying musket balls, attracted by the dim shouts to his left and to his right. Royalist musketeers were waving him out of the way, Roundheads calling him back to the wall. He crouched there between them, lost in the wilderness of tumbled bodies and blood-soaked, trampled, shot-blasted earth, like a rabbit under the unblinking gaze of a hungry stoat.

The pioneer staggered along the trench for him, weighed down by his heavy armour, his boots rising and falling as he stamped through the slurried ditch. The sapper grabbed the boy like a sheaf of mown hay and threw him over his rusty shoulder. Shots thudded into the tired green turf, kicked up stinging grit from the exposed stone as the sapper stumbled back the way he had come, throwing the lad through the hatchway into the arms of his companions. He began to haul himself up the greasy slope of the ditch, his friends holding out their hands to grasp him by his sleeves. A musket ball clipped his iron helmet, sending him sprawling. A bare-headed blue-coat scrambled out of the hole and caught him under the armpits, and was in his turn dragged by his hind legs back through the sally-port.

The sappers hurled the hatch closed, and collapsed, panting, against the bullet-pocked walls. Nicodemus lay staring at the unconcerned sky, blinking at the fleecy clouds through his bitter, soot speckled tears.

Another day under Gloucester's walls, and still no word of their relief.

PART TWO

DOG DAYS AND DOLDRUMS

But for your bug-beare threats so huge and big
If seven score cannons can kill but one pig
We then have cause to fear nothing but sin
Can make a breach to let such rebels in

Roundhead epigram on attempts to
persuade the garrison of Gloucester to yield

MATSON HOUSE,

GLOUCESTER

The velvet-suited terrors were playing an energetic game of tag around what was left of the garden, dashing out between the trees and leaping over the tent pegs, their high-pitched yells a curious counterpoint to the dull rumble and clatter emanating from the busy camp. A couple of red-faced gentleman pensioners from the King's household were pursuing the carefree youngsters, trying to keep them from cutting themselves to pieces or breaking their royal legs. The King's sons were dark-haired, bright-eyed boys, Charles the elder by a year or two, James furiously intent on keeping up with his bigger sibling's rough and tumble games. Charles had seen one real battle already; sitting on a docile pony as the rebels clashed with his father's forces on Edgehill the previous October. A sudden onslaught from the Roundhead reserve had momentarily panicked the Prince's bodyguard, but their obstinate young charge trotted forward regardless, his fierce features contorted with rage as he wound his pistol. His mortified guardians grabbed his bridle and held him back, feverishly seconding His Majesty's determined oath that he 'feared them not'.

'What a fine pair of lads. I was going to say a man's heirs don't grow from seed, but I suppose in a way they do,' Sir Gilbert Morrison reflected, merry eyes twinkling, his flushed features glowing serenely amongst the impatient mob of senior officers gathered near the porch. The peacock-proud throng pulsed and shimmered in the sunlight, the gaily appointed Cavaliers anxiously awaiting their opportunity for an interview with the Royalist high command shut up indoors. Michael Slaughter wore his old soldier's coat and habitual surly scowl as he stood, disdainful as ever, alongside the blustering merchant. He wondered for the umpteenth time whether the bloated turncoat was a simple-minded buffoon or a viciously calculating, supremely plausible brute. As usual his conclusions wavered somewhere between the two.

'Fine lads, aye,' Slaughter allowed, as another party of gossiping Cavalier lords arrived to swell the velvet- and lace-decked rabble outside the house. There were lords and lairds, generals and gentlemen in their best suits and sashes. Their flamboyant headgear reminded Slaughter of a bower full of precious birds of paradise. Swords and spurs clattered and jingled as they stamped about the garden trying to catch the eyes of the artful drones who ran the King's war effort from this cramped hive.

Hugo Telling regarded them balefully, as if each man was a sworn companion of his despised enemy Rupert. He imagined a smirk behind every smile, the rumour of his hopeless disgrace repeated with every careless whisper. Morrison was his usual helpful, encouraging self, taking the boy aside as they waited in the sun-bright yard.

'You're imagining it, boy. And even if they are talking about you, you remember what they say about sticks and stones, don't you? Ignore the scoundrels.'

The officers looked up expectantly as a large gilt coach drawn by six matched dapple-grey horses drew up outside the house with a lively rattle of gravel. Footmen in rich green livery leapt down while the huge wheels were still spinning, hurrying to their positions about the richly appointed vehicle. Before Telling could decipher the complex heraldic devices painted on the side, the door had been thrown open and the eager postilions had crowded forward with a set of steps. They drew back, respectfully bowing their heads as a tall though rather slightly built stranger with a soft reddish-brown moustache ducked out of the coach, turning on the second step to lend a gloved hand to his remarkably handsome wife. For a moment, Telling thought it might be the dreaded Prince himself, come to lord it over his uncle's English subjects, but the newcomer moved with more grace and less menace than the Teutonic knight, clearly a dancer rather than a fighter. The stranger was dressed in an immaculate light-blue suit, trimmed with acres of lawn and lace. He paused on the steps while the red-faced footmen hurried up with armfuls of straw, strewing the husks over the muddy path. Telling turned from the lord to his lady, a stunning, throat-constricting vision of peach-down skin and flashing eyes, as bright as a goldcrest's wing beneath her pearl-framed auburn curls. She threw a light travelling cloak about her shoulders, her small white hand clasping the brooch at her fine neck. Telling's eyes ran this way and that along her exquisitely fluted collarbone, before he finally fixed his drop-jawed stare on her lightly blushing bosom. She lifted her skirts gracefully, and allowed her gallant husband to escort her across the treacherous path, nodding to the admiring gentlemen who had formed an impromptu guard of honour for the fantastical couple. Sir Gilbert snatched off his hat and bowed deeply, Slaughter following suit with the rest of the awestruck officers. The young princes abandoned their game and hurried over with a whoop to greet the new arrivals. The Cavalier swept off his ostrich-plumed hat and shooed the boys towards the house, easily familiar with the heirs to the throne. Telling stared as the woman swept by, searching unsuccessfully for her eyes as she followed her husband after the noisy boys. She had taken his breath away like a cannon shot across the mouth, left the bewildered boy blinking and reeling.

'I thought I'd seen the sun rise once this morning, I was clearly mistaken.'

Telling nodded his head in dumb agreement with Sir Gilbert's heartfelt sentiment. Sir Gilbert's?

'You are too kind, sir. Sir?' The vision paused, acknowledging the merchant's tribute with a modest nod of her pearl-capped head.

Telling closed his eyes. Her voice was like honey being poured into his melting ears.

'Gilbert, ma'am, Gilbert Morrison.' The merchant warbled, nodding and winking as if he had an ants' nest in his breeches. The lady had gone before he could furnish her with any further details about himself or his family. The red-cheeked merchant rolled his eyes at the scowling captain, elbowed him in the ribs in a frustratingly familiar manner.

'By God, I'd have put my Bella against most of the fillies I'd ever seen, but she would have given Cleopatra herself a sleepless night or two!'

Telling fidgeted with annoyance, jealous that he should have to share this newly revealed angel with anybody else – and particularly with the weasel-minded merchant. He was about to leap to the lady's defence when he heard the officers crowding behind him snort with laughter.

'His Grace the Duke of Richmond,' Telling heard one gouty old gentleman whisper to his ill-informed colleague, a short, wiry Highland laird wrapped in a huge blue plaid despite the fierce heat.

'Aye, so that must be the Duchess. They weren't far wrong about her.'

Telling ran his tongue over his teeth. So *that* was the Duchess of Richmond, reputed to be the most beautiful woman in the kingdom. A match even for the remarkable Elizabeth of Bohemia, King Charles' legendarily beautiful sister who had married the Elector Palatine, Frederick, and helped spark the never-ending bloodbaths on the Continent.

If Helen's face launched a thousand ships over the ancient seas, the Winter King's wife had filled ten thousand more with fire, famine, flood, and fever and run them up every river and corpse-choked stream in Germany.

'Rupert's best friend and all, shame,' Telling overheard, ears pricking up like a hound on the scent.

'He wouldn't, though, not him,' the Scot hissed behind his ringed fingers.

'Ah, Ross my boy, you haven't seen him look at her.' The gouty earl rolled his eyes like a lovesick student, an uncomfortably accurate demonstration Telling could imagine only too well.

'They say she's the only woman on God's earth who can turn his head, and married to his only true friend at court. Have you read much of that Shakespeare fellow? It's three times more involved than his most confounded plot.'

'They say he's overrated,' the Scot went on, warming to his theme.

'The Prince?'

'No, this Shakespeare, whatever he calls himself.'

'Well, no matter. The Prince won't lay a finger on her, not while the Duke's a breath in his body, at any rate.'

'He must be made of cold mutton and salmon scales if he can stay away from that one,' the younger man, with the forked beard commented.

'She's lady-in-waiting to the Catholic Spitfire herself. One finger out of place and Henrietta would kick up such a stink her husband the King would have to send Rupert off to your wretched Orkneys!'

'There's nothing wretched about the Orkneys, see you, Richard . . . but I take your point. Still, Rupert wouldn't be the first to . . .' Telling tilted his head but his anonymous informants had drifted away towards the trampled remains of the rose bushes. He would have relished an opportunity to follow the intriguing pair about the garden, but even as clumsy and inexperienced a spy as Telling knew this would have made his immediate detection inevitable.

He stood clenching his fists, his bewildering mind racing in so many directions he could barely blink. Rupert? And *her*?

'Sir Gilbert Masterson, Colonel Michael Slaughter, this way, if you please!'

Telling's brain lurched into gear as a bedraggled clerk in an appalling mauve suit trotted down the passage with a sheaf of documents over his arm, hollering at the peacock pack lurking beside the porch.

The merchant threw up his hands in delight and stood aside as Slaughter strode up to the door behind him. 'After you, sir,' the merchant insisted.

Slaughter leered at the wily old bloat. By God, the turncoat looked like the cat that had gotten the cream, and they hadn't even been shown in yet! What in hell's name had he overlooked? What trump card had the merchant hidden up his sleeve to give him such boundless confidence in the outcome of the inquiry?

Sir Gilbert followed the scowling colonel into the passage, whistling a merry jig.

The secretary in the mauve coat knocked gently and waited for the almost inaudible 'enter' from within.

They were shown into a large, eerily quiet chamber, with oak-panelled walls and a high-timbered ceiling blackened and waxed with years of smoky service. So this was the nerve centre, the headquarters of all His Majesty's forces assembled before Gloucester. The great medieval table had been unceremoniously pushed under the window, stacked with pots and quills and a colourful collection of hats and gloves. Behind the leaded panes they could make out the shadowed shape of a musketeer, pacing back and forth as he kept the more inquisitive soldiers from eavesdropping on the King's counsels. Eight high-backed chairs had been pressed into service to support the enormous heap of papers, dispatches, and charts which arrived with monotonous regularity at the front door. Large studded chests had been dragged into the room, opened like pirate treasure hoards. A detailed map of Gloucester had been tacked up beside the window.

Sir Gilbert bowed low, clutching his hat in his hands as his twinkling eyes adjusted to the gloom.

Prince Rupert was sitting beside the fireplace, watching a middle-aged man in a sober black suit push a model gallows towards the tiled grate. The balding stranger was evidently explaining something of bewildering complexity, because the German Prince didn't even bother looking up to see who had disturbed his uncle's meditations.

The flamboyant duke in the blue suit had helped himself to some wine from the dresser, and was watching the demonstration with an indulgent smile.

'That's all very well, Dr Chillingworth, but I can't for

the life of me see how you'll get it over the ditch,' the Prince – always delighted to study some new aspects of military engineering – observed crossly, his black brows furrowed with concentration.

Sir Gilbert looked from the practical Prince to his rather more esoteric uncle, conversing in an undertone with the doddering Earl of Brentford about the dispositions around Kingsholm. The old earl seemed to be resting his eyes while his sovereign stood by, smoothing his light-brown beard.

A trio of weary staff officers were processing the mountain of correspondence, sorting it into more manageable piles for His Majesty's attention. Lord Falkland, King Charles' morose Secretary of State, looked up from the stack of reports he had balanced on his knees as the nervous visitors stood to attention in the royal presence.

'Ah, yes, Colonel Slaughter,' Falkland remembered, rubbing his inky fingers over his creased temples. 'Something of a mix-up on the road, we understand?'

Rupert looked up for a moment, and then returned his distracted attention to the scientific demonstration in the grate. Slaughter bristled, his mouth dry as chalk, and nodded at the weary bureaucrat.

'Well? We haven't got all day, sir,' Falkland encouraged waspishly. He had a mountain of work to do and was becoming increasingly irritated by the ridiculous squabbles which were being brought before His Majesty every hour of the day. Surely the kingdom had difficulties enough without these fools falling out over who would and would not take orders from whom.

'A simple matter, sir, which needn't detain you for more than a moment,' Sir Gilbert said smoothly, divining

Falkland's mood in an instant. 'I was marching my brigade to Gloucester as ordered, when I happened on Slaughter's troops about to string up their colonel. I ordered my cavalry in to put the fear of God into the rascals, and marched the whole sorry bunch up here this morning.'

Falkland frowned. 'Then where is the difficulty?' He turned to Slaughter, biting his lips raw alongside the grinning merchant.

'He took command of my men, there, he didn't tell you that!' Slaughter snapped.

Prince Rupert straightened up beside the mantelpiece, a towering figure in a bright scarlet suit. He studied the colonel from beneath his bristling black brows.

'Sir Gilbert?' Falkland prompted.

'I did, sir, and I'd do it again! The scoundrels were clearly up to mischief, about to string up poor old Slaughter here, and my orders from Lord Clavincale were particularly clear as to rounding up stragglers and deserters.'

'They weren't deserters!'

'Mutineers, then, assassins, sir, plain as the nose on your face,' Sir Gilbert told them.

His adversary ground his teeth in rage, turned to the bemused Prince. 'Your Highness will remember you sent me to take over Sparkes' regiment of foot at Devizes. I found them in a pretty mood, sir, and they didn't take kindly to my—'

'Starving them to distraction and flogging them into the bargain,' Sir Gilbert interjected.

'The dogs deserved a thrashing!' Slaughter yelled. 'And then this buffoon happens along and bribes them off with liquor! They would have followed the Earl of Essex happily enough, aye, for a bellyful of ale!'

'They didn't follow Essex, they followed me,' Sir Gilbert sniffed. 'They're back at Gaudy Green now, waiting for orders as good as gold!'

Rupert smirked beside the empty fireplace as the drably dressed inventor gathered up his wooden models and let himself out of the room.

'You assumed Colonel Slaughter's command, sir, which I had given him myself?'

'I did, sir.'

'On whose authority?'

'Why, Lord Clavincale's, sir,' Sir Gilbert explained, uncomfortable for once under this German devil's beady-eyed scrutiny.

'I know of no such creature.'

'He has a roving commission from His Majesty himself,' Sir Gilbert said coldly. 'With particular responsibility for the West Country. He gave me my orders before I left Bristol with my reinforcements.'

'Reinforcements? A hundred or so scarecrows and a dozen knackered cavalry . . .'

'Sir! You will be so good as to moderate your language in the presence of His Majesty!' Falkland hissed under his breath. The King continued his one-sided discussion with the old earl, apparently oblivious to the acrimonious debate across the room.

'Your pardon, sir, Your Majesty,' Slaughter bowed, reddening, fighting to control his vicious temper.

'Enough to pull the wool over your rascals' eyes, though,' Sir Gilbert tittered.

Slaughter's wavering control snapped in an instant. He lurched towards the grinning merchant, straight into Prince Rupert's outstretched arm. 'You blackguard!'

'If obeying orders and stopping a mutiny makes me a

blackguard to you, sir, so be it!' Sir Gilbert observed indignantly.

'Gentlemen!' Falkland hissed. They fell silent as the distracted monarch straightened up from his charts and walked quietly into the centre of the room. The King studied the red-faced colonel and his nervously smiling adversary.

'Gentlemen, indeed. I s–s–see no reason for any unpl–pleasantness. Sir Gilbert has delivered the reinforcements as we had requested. As far as I can ... as far as I see the m–matter is s–s–settled.'

'Your Majesty is too kind,' Sir Gilbert bowed. 'And Colonel Slaughter is very welcome to have his men back, if they'll serve him, that is.'

Slaughter clenched his fists. 'They'll serve!'

'Well, they say there's a first time for everything.' Sir Gilbert smiled broadly.

Slaughter went pale, sucked in his colourless cheeks. 'I will persuade them to serve, Your Majesty. With Your Majesty's permission, I will return to my men immediately!'

The King held his small hand up, a delicate gesture which halted the red-faced veteran in mid-salute.

'I believe his Highness Prince Rupert and I should take further counsel before we make our decision as to the correct disposal of your errant troops,' he said gravely.

Slaughter nodded, closing his eyes against the bitter tears of rage bubbling from his fevered brain.

'Although we are pleased to acknowledge Colonel Slaughter was only acting on the express orders of our nephew, we are concerned that his men, having had recourse to open rebellion on one occasion already, cannot be fully trusted to serve him with any degree of resolution again.' He stroked his beard, glanced at the towering figure of his right-hand-man Rupert. 'Gentlemen, I believe we have detained you from your duties long enough.'

Slaughter and the merchant bowed before their monarch and backed out of the room, followed by the busy clerk in the mauve suit.

'Be so kind as to tell Captain Telling we've forwarded his complaint to Prince Maurice's headquarters with the Western Army,' he said briskly, ushering the enemies along the hall towards the bright light flooding in from the garden.

'The man's a rogue, an utter rogue,' Rupert complained, as his uncle settled himself in the easy chair with a heartfelt sigh. 'He's had hundreds of pounds from that *canaille* at Whitehall, and now he means to fleece Your Majesty to better his bargain! My brigade! Slaughter was right all along. He's brought a handful of foot and a few sorry horse, and expects to take command of the entire operation!' Prince Rupert exclaimed. His uncle sighed. 'And he seems to have used them to good effect, if he convinced Slaughter to hand over going on four hundred men,' Charles smiled. 'I feel we ought to be encouraging our senior commanders to use their troops as effectively.' He glanced significantly at the old Earl of Brentford, who was now fast asleep beside the window, the reports lying forgotten in his broad lap.

'Slaughter has been fighting the Irish confederates for two years, Your Majesty. We need men like him to finish this business, not fat owls like Morrison.'

The King pursed his lips, nodded gravely. 'We cannot afford to have two of our commanders at each other's throats,' he agreed, catching his nephew's dark eye for a moment. Rupert was notoriously arrogant, treating many of his fellow officers with utter contempt. He did not suffer fools gladly, and would only ever be overruled by his uncle the King. Rupert snorted in agitation.

'Therefore,' the King went on calmly, 'we will send Slaughter away to help Maurice in the west, and keep Sir Gilbert here, where we can all have an eye on him.'

THE BLACK DOG INN,

NEAR BROCKWORTH,
GLOUCESTERSHIRE,
16 AUGUST 1643

Bella Morrison took a deep breath, calmed her racing mind for a moment, and blew a long sigh into the night air. She had wrapped her cloak about her shoulders and was trying to walk off the dreary dinner which was lying heavily on her stomach. There was little else to do out in this wilderness, while her father and fiancé were busy carving up their little clay empires. She frowned, cut adrift from these entanglements and intrigues which would shape her future. Banished from the weighty discussions and complex decisions which would decide her life. Why, she had no more say in her own affairs than poor Mary Keziah, her absent maid! Bella wished her dark-haired conscience was here. It was horribly lonely when the men were busy about their affairs, and there were no masked dances to attend or guests to entertain. In addition to that she had been forced to unpack her own trunk, and hang her creased gowns on the back of the door in the spittoon which passed as their boudoir. Lord Clavincale's much vaunted influence had only managed to secure the couple a second-rate room in a third-rate inn, four miles from the closely pressed town. Four miles from the King's colourful headquarters. Why, out here she was the last to know what was going on, relying on the serving wenches or their soldier sweethearts for news of the siege, or details of the fantastical Cavaliers' latest adventures. She had almost burst into tears when the surly footman showed them to their draughty garret, dropping the trunks and backing out of their hideous loft tugging his greasy forelock.

'Don't worry, my dear, it is but a base for a few nights. We'll be tucked up tight in a nice four-poster in the best house in Gloucester by the end of the week!' he had boasted, rifling through the bundle of correspondence which had been waiting for them at the miserable inn, the aptly named Black Dog on the Cirencester road.

Amongst the dispatches was a short note from her father proposing a rendezvous at their desperately off the beaten track lodgings. Sir Gilbert greeted the pair of them with his usual brand of smothering good humour, clapping Clavincale on the back and giving Bella's arm painful squeezes every few moments. The couple endured a bombardment of anecdotes from the merry merchant as he described his adventures on the road and subsequent historic meeting with His Majesty King Charles.

'Quiet sort of chap,' Sir Gilbert reflected. 'Lacks a certain, what would you call it, power of projection. Yes. But other than that, kind and considerate. Very wise. A regular sage!'

'His Majesty's consideration and intelligence is well known throughout the court,' Clavincale said, before Sir Gilbert launched into a fresh reserve of royal observations.

'Of course, he agreed with me when we got to the nub of it. "Gilbert," he said, "if it hadn't been for you those men would have mutinied, and been halfway to Scotland by now. Aye, and that ingrate Slaughter would have been six foot under Much Hindon churchyard feeding the grubs!"'

'A remarkable stroke of fortune,' Lord Clavincale inter-jected when the merchant paused to catch his breath. 'Quite remarkable.' He flicked his eyes towards the scowl-ing girl waiting impatiently beside him. Sir Gilbert took the hint at once.

'Here we go again boring you silly, my dear. You get off and rest yourself, I know I'm not the only one to have had an eventful and wearisome journey.' He threw his heavy arm over her shoulder and steered his daughter for the door.

'But what am I to do?'

'Why, you've travelled halfway around the country by yourself, my dear, I'm sure you'll be able to amuse yourself here as well as Oxford!' Sir Gilbert said rather testily. She paused at the door, but her father had already clamped himself on to Clavincale's arm like a lamprey, and was steering him towards the small card table in the corner of the room. She had closed the door on the plotting pair and left them to their own devices.

The night was cool and soft, a walk would clear her head a little after enduring the stuffy coach and dusty inn. She paused on the step, peered through the shadowed trees at the brightly twinkling campfires which surrounded their narrow island. A topsy-turvy atoll set in a rough sea of men and mud. The soft rise and fall of the soldiers' muted conversations reminded her of wavelets lapping gently over a sandy beach, the sudden blare of laughter comforting, reassuringly alive amongst all that death and destruction.

Bella wandered down the unkempt garden at the back of the brightly lit inn, followed the rough cinder path towards the row of poplars along the lane. She climbed the stile and found herself in a narrow close, a bower of overgrowing trees which led her off into the darkness. She heard the muted croak of a dozen frogs, and sensed the brittle shimmering of a mass of sedge to her right. A thousand stars were reflected in the frog-studded surface of the pond, a black mirror a few feet from her slippers.

'Bella?'

The girl leapt inside her cloak, jumped away from the water, and peered into the dark brushwood at the dim figure who had called to her. The shadowy figure lurched behind the drooping willows, coming towards her, his hat pulled down over his darkened features.

'Who's there?' she called, with considerably more confidence than she felt.

'It's me. Hugo. Hugo Telling!'

Lord Clavincale sat back against the waxy panelling of their poor lodgings, resting his weight on the narrow card table which separated him from his future father-in-law. By God, it wasn't enough! He would need ditch and wall and turf and woolsacks to protect him from the merchant's disembowelling business methods. They had talked for half an hour, the merchant describing in rather more detail their bizarre progress north.

'Do you think the boy will do something stupid?' Clavincale asked quietly, well aware the scruffy inn had just as many ears as an Oxford cloister. 'He wouldn't go as far as to challenge the Prince to a duel?'

'Hugo's cracked up enough, God knows,' Sir Gilbert frowned, taking another bite at his frugal supper of bread and cheese, washed down by a glass or three of strong sack. His features had settled back to their more usual florid pink, his eyes glistening in the candlelight.

'As long as we couldn't be accused of encouraging him. Lord knows I wouldn't like to face the brute if anything went wrong,' Clavincale observed. At least with Sir Gilbert he didn't have to pretend to be anything other than what he was: a gifted courtier and master of intrigue who accomplished his goals with pen and tongue rather than boot and sword. Sir Gilbert took another slurp at his sack, nodding reassuringly.

'I'll try and keep the silly hound busy over at Gaudy Green. He'll have plenty to think about in the trenches without picking quarrels with his commander.' Clavincale relaxed slightly, sipped his brandy before he played his trump card— 'I presume you've heard the rumours? Richmond parading his whore in front of him?'

Sir Gilbert was taken aback slightly, his merry blue eyes flickering from the rim of his tankard. 'What rumours?'

Clavincale waved his hand dismissively. 'The Teutonic Tetrarch has developed something of a fondness for Mary Villiers, Duchess of Richmond.'

'Ah, yes, of course. Richmond's wife?' Sir Gilbert's mobile eyes closed conspiratorially.

'Wife, indeed. The iron-jawed bastard wouldn't dare lay a finger on her, of course, he's far too superior for those sort of tricks, you know, but they say he can't tear his eyes off her!'

'Ah, Clavincale, good marriages they don't grow from seed. They take careful nurturing, and years of—'

'Yes, I'm sure they do, Sir Gilbert,' Clavincale interrupted. 'But it could be another way under Rupert's armour. I'm making some enquiries into it now, one of Nybb's men knows somebody up at Prinknash Park where the swine is staying. Pity young Telling wasn't married to her, I fear the duke might prove rather more difficult to usefully manipulate.'

'Telling? Why he's still blubbing over' – Clavincale's lazy grey eyes studied the blustering merchant – 'some serving girl,' Sir Gilbert corrected himself, smoothing his closely combed grey curls. By God, that had been a close one. It wouldn't do to list Bella's numerous beaux to her prospective husband, would it?

'Well, then, I think we can quietly congratulate ourselves on a good week's work,' Clavincale allowed. 'One of Rupert's creatures discredited, the camp lousy with rumours about his visiting mistress, and his damned siege stuck fast. Not to mention four hundred extra recruits for our regiment!' He raised his stained goblet. 'Here's to the brave lads!' They clinked their tankards and drank their dregs, each wondering how far he could trust the other. Sir Gilbert nodded, his lurid imagination running away with him again as he poured fresh drinks.

'If my ... our brigade ... can get in to the town first, we'll be the toast of the whole country. We'll get a paper put out, brave Cavaliers storm defences, smash Roundhead fanatics, save the King from wretched rebellion.' Sir Gilbert gloated over the tantalizing prospect. 'And when the fighting's all done ... you and my Bella can get hitched, aye, in Gloucester Cathedral!'

Clavincale sat back in his seat, stunned by the merchant's inexhaustible ambition. 'A fine idea!'

'We'll be the heroes of the hour, why, I wager we'd be able to pick our own titles,' he said significantly. He glanced at the portly lordling over the rim of his brimming cup. Clavincale smiled weakly. The much discussed unification of their families depended on Sir Gilbert being raised to the peerage. His daughter Bella would become a lady, a suitable enough partner for a nobleman like Clavincale. He could hardly marry her as she was, the low-born daughter of a grasping tradesman.

'As soon as I get a moment with His Majesty I'll bring the matter up. With all you have achieved recently, I am sure there will be no objection to your, er, deserved award.'

Sir Gilbert Morrison, merchant, colonel, and turncoat. To be raised to the peerage as Lord Marleward. It was enough to make one weep.

'If not a barony,' Clavincale ventured, 'you can rely on a baronetcy.'

Sir Gilbert's jovial features rearranged themselves in moments. He leaned forward, glared over the table at his prospective son-in-law.

'Lord Marleward, that was our agreement. Baronets went out with King James,' he growled. Clavincale smiled.

'Lord Marleward, of course. It's just that . . . with one thing and another, our stock might not be quite as high as it . . .'

'Lord Marleward,' Sir Gilbert repeated.

Clavincale pursed his lips. 'The thing is, Fath— there I go, calling you Father again,' he quipped, trying to deflect the merchant's suddenly cold gaze. 'The thing is, Sir Gilbert, our scheme to launch a new trading cartel in the west, on His Majesty's behalf of course, has not exactly come to fruition at this moment in time.'

'We decided to get the fighting done with first, Clavincale,' Sir Gilbert said warningly. Clavincale nodded.

'Absolutely. There will be plenty of time to retrench our merchandising opportunities, once the war is over and done.'

'Wait a moment, Clavincale. The offer was this: I set up

the Royal Westward Society of Oceanic Venturers, to compete with those overstuffed braggarts up in London, and in return I get the governorship of the society and my title.'

Clavincale smiled winningly.

'Of course, that was it in a nutshell. You secure the cooperation of the Bristol trading cartel and I obtain a peerage for you from the King.'

'Well?'

'Well. The trading cartel has yet to divert as much as a penny piece into His Majesty's war chest.'

'And?'

'And I have yet to receive the appropriate recompense for my little speculation in Dorset.'

'You mean the Spanish swineherds you sold those men to haven't paid up? What did old Nybb bring back from Penmethock, then, a basket of sprats?' Sir Gilbert snarled. Clavincale flushed, a little disconcerted to discover the extent of his future father-in-law's knowledge of his various affairs, official and otherwise.

'The sum Colonel Nybb brought back from Dorset was merely the downpayment, sir,' he said falteringly. 'There was some trouble on the voyage, and part of the cargo was lost. Count de Meola is withholding the arms and ammunition until I send some replacements.'

Sir Gilbert sat back with a sigh. 'And you were counting on the guns to grease your way into the King's favour?'

Clavincale hesitated to put it quite like that, but nodded anyway.

'So because your bilge-breathed captain can't do his job properly, you're in no position to ensure I get my peerage?'

'I wouldn't put it quite like that,' Clavincale reasoned.

'Well, look here. We'll get the men over the wall. We'll make the breach for the fancy Prince. And when it's all over, we'll put aside another hundred or so of the prisoners, and send them off to your dog of a Spaniard.'

Clavincale sat back, shook his head in admiration of the merchant's endless store of profitable invention.

'Admirable. We must ensure we keep the whole thing to ourselves, of course.'

'Of course.' Sir Gilbert puffed out his chest like the great Gustavus Adolphus himself. 'Military legends don't grow from seed, you know, they have to be nurtured. They need regular composting, you might say.'

'And with Slaughter's extra men, we have all the compost we need,' Clavincale laughed.

Sir Gilbert's eyes glittered. 'Gloucester Cathedral, eh?'

'The day after the city falls!'

'We'll invite the King and Queen, we'll even invite that braggart Rupert!'

'If he's not too busy dribbling down the Duchess of Richmond's cleavage!' Clavincale said, raising his eyebrows. 'You know, I believe I'd think more of him if he did something about it, staring into space and wishing on the stars. Platonic love is so tiresome, don't you think?'

Sir Gilbert nodded ruefully. 'Aye, but it saves the sheets.'

Clavincale looked up in surprise, but the merry merchant did not appear to be joking.

'Married? What?' Hugo Telling's eyes widened in surprise as he stalked along the water's edge beside his wayward heroine, a fustian moth hanging about a candle flame. 'Marry him? He looks as if he'd need one of Dr Chillingworth's siege engines to haul him over the bed!' Hugo

cried, rather crudely, Bella thought. She had allowed her
errant knight to accompany her as she made her way along
the deserted lane beside the pond. Bella had barely
recognized him at first, so thin and drawn in that awful
brown suit. The only thing he wore with any Cavalier
colour was his scarf, a present from her father and bearing
Sir Gilbert's fanciful crest of a rutting stag holding up a
treasure chest. If it hadn't been for his bright blue sash he
would have been indistinguishable from the unwashed
rabble the other side of the hedge.

'He manages very well, thank you,' she said primly,
reddening under her enormous hood.

'Oh, he does, does he?'

Bella's dark eyes flashed dangerously. 'Don't you dare
use that tone with me,' she snapped. 'You made your
choice when you lay with that red-haired whore of yours!'

'She wasn't my choice,' Hugo said bitterly. 'She was just
there . . . when I needed someone,' he said limply.

Bella snorted with derision at his feeble imaginings.

'Just don't presume to lecture me on morals, Hugo,'
she warned. 'I know full well what I'm doing.'

'I expect you do.'

'And what is that supposed to mean? I came looking for
you, you know? When you were made a prisoner? I drove
halfway around the country trying to get you out.'

'I heard,' he said sulkily. 'I meant to thank you.'

'Don't bother.'

'And as soon as you bumped into that fat frog of a
lordling you forgot all about me!' he cried. 'It's a good job
I managed to escape, if I had to wait for you I'd be chained
up in Bristol Keep by now!'

'If you insist on using that tone with me I'll see you're
taken straight back there!' she exclaimed, shoving the

scowling youth away and striding off down the path beside the pond. Hugo stumbled, straightened himself and his hat.

'I never know what to think,' he called to her rapidly disappearing back. 'I never know what you're thinking, that's the truth!' he declared. She halted. 'You pick me up and throw me down like an old shoe. I never know whether to worship the ground you walk on or box your ears!' Tears sprang into his pale eyes, as the mortifying, humiliating frustrations of the last weeks came bursting to the surface once more. Bella turned, glared into the gloom over the mirror-calm pond, her lip twitching in confusion. She glanced at him, his silly moustache and hangdog expression, his thin nose and quivering cheeks. She took a step towards him, touched his arm with a guilty little smile.

'Well, you took liberties,' she said, her hand dropping to her side. 'Parading that polecat in front of me with her bad hair and baggy bosoms.'

'She was only a girl,' he insisted. 'It's you, Bella, it's always been you.'

'Don't talk such nonsense,' she stammered. She was secretly thrilled to have acquired her very own errant knight, even if he was a thin, irritable, ill-made Cavalier in a patched coat.

'I've loved you from the moment I saw you. In the wagon with that, that Sparrow!' he growled. They completed a circuit of the quiet pond, listening distractedly to the croak and splash of the frogs.

'I thought ... you see ... I thought you were sending me away, because I was a mere boy,' he whispered. 'I thought you might like me more, if I came back to you a man.'

Bella halted, drained and scoured by his heartfelt confession, his innocent devotion. Clavincale and her father measured out affection as if they were buying tea, at so much per spoonful. Hugo threw his affections around like a dog shaking itself off after a dip in a ditch. She was cruelly, fatally undermined by his thoughtless confession.

'Hugo,' she said softly, overwhelmed by his simple-minded declaration. Bella was adrift, floating beside the pool like a phantasm, the ghostly shadow of a wood nymph trapped by his true-hearted spell. She had fortified herself against Clavincale's slippery insinuations and sudden tantrums, against her father's brusque affections. She had even learned to keep the crowding Oxford rakes at bay, the polished, perfect ladies' men who made bed their business about the bored court. She had been so long exposed to their calculated crocodile love that Hugo's breathless, boyish fumblings seemed like a breath of fresh air. Bella let his cold mouth close over hers like a dungeon door, sealing her spirit within her trembling frame. He tugged her closer, slipping into her cloak and soaking up her vital warmth, sensing her elemental presence flow through his moribund body.

'Bella!' They leapt apart like electric eels at the sudden shout from the other side of the tangled willow wands. She peered up towards the dimly glimmering lamplight, realized they had wandered further than she had intended, into the heart of a small, impenetrable wood.

Hugo slipped into the bushes like a slow-worm, and wriggled away into the darkness as Clavincale came striding down the cinder path, a lantern in one hand and his sword in the other. The lamp cast a sickly yellow light over the fluttering leaves.

'There you are! Was there someone with you?' he called, striding up to the bewildered girl and tugging her under his heavy grey travel cloak.

'A cutpurse ... or a tinker, I think,' she stammered, recovering her wits in an instant.

'Slinking away like a thief, all right. Be off with you!' he called into the surrounding vegetation. 'Come back at once, girl. Your father and I didn't intend you should wander the grounds until we had finished!' he chided her, escorting the girl back to the busy inn, their footfalls crunching the cinder path. Moths and flies and flutterbyes bobbed in the eerie light, attracted by the spluttering lantern. The inn was lit up like an enormous pumpkin.

'What do you think of that?' Clavincale asked at length.

'Pardon?'

'Your father is quite beside himself,' he went on.

'Oh, well, he would be,' Bella replied, wondering what she had missed. 'I'm not sure what to think of it,' she improvised.

'Think of it, girl! Your father's regiment takes the town, and we are married, the very next day, in Gloucester Cathedral itself! The whole country will be talking about it!' he blustered on, reminding the girl sharply of her father.

'Married?'

'My dear, I don't believe you have heard a single word I said,' he protested. 'We're to be married in Gloucester, as soon as they take the town. Now, what do you say to that?'

136

BY
FRIAR'S ORCHARD,

*GLOUCESTER,
17 AUGUST 1643*

The officers had completed their morning tour of the walls, inspecting the enemy trenches and seeing for themselves the damage their guns had inflicted on the reeling walls. They could see the crows and ravens plucking and jabbing at the half-naked bodies sprawled in the wilderness, or lying in the half-completed ditches beyond the walls. The Royalists were already moving cautiously about the slag heaps and puddles, dragging their dead away to the pits away on the far side of their entrenchments.

Sir Edward Massey studied the bloody defences and the gory puddles beneath the crumbling walls. There was as much wool as stone now, the huge bales bulging out of the breaches like horrific buboes on a dead man's chest. And yet the walls held.

Massey strode ahead, his lips moving furiously as he thanked God for his good fortune. For all their threats and taunts and ceaseless bombardments the Royalist forces were no nearer breaking the town than they had been a week ago. Seven precious days used up. But what of the next seven, and the seven after that? He did not dare hope the city could hold out that long. They survived from day to day, thanking the Lord for every sunset, dreading every dawn. 17 August. Surely the Parliament was aware of their desperate straits? Surely their relief was on the way by now? The governor had no way of knowing, apart from the rumours collected by the townsfolk as they slipped in and out of the water-meadows to collect turfs and possibly idle away the odd hour with a bored Royalist musketeer. According to the sketchy reports he had collected, Essex's army was eaten out with typhus and river fevers, and Waller was away in London raising a new force to replace the command he had lost on Roundway Down. It would be weeks before he could even think of moving. The enemy sappers had tried to trick the brave garrison, firing messages into the city by bow and arrow. *Your God Waller hath forsaken you, Essex is beaten like a dog. Yield to the King's mercy.* How long would it be before the townsfolk began to lose hope, their nerves gnawed by the hideous uncertainty of their situation?

Massey watched a file of musketeers picked from the southern walls make their way along the ditch towards the Northgate. Major Pudsey was to lead a large-scale assault on the enemy batteries which were being dug to the north-west of the city. It was a desperate gamble, taking men from the battered southern defences, but all he could do was juggle his meagre forces and try and make do.

Nicodemus Burke trudged along beside him, his blue coat massively baggy over his puny frame. A favourite around the walls and now a veteran of half a dozen sorties, he had become a token of their luck. Massey would miss him.

'Nicodemus,' he said, pausing by the heaped rubble and broken beams which marked the line of Brook Street – pulled down to reinforce the battered walls around the vulnerable gate. 'You won't be going with Major Pudsey tomorrow.' The red-haired boy looked up sharply, his features collapsing with disappointment.

'Not going, sir? Why I've been out—'

Massey held up his hand, smiled shortly. 'You've proved your worth. But I need you for something far more important.' He stepped aside as a caravan of rickety carts was pushed along the dead street by a gang of dusty women, barefoot children, and old men. The citizen's army had been put to work tearing down the old hovels and using the stone to reinforce the wall. The poor inhabitants had been transferred to their neighbours or friends, or put up in the big houses lately vacated by several city aldermen with pronounced Royalist leanings.

Still the siege went on.

'We won't hold the town for ever, as well you know,' Massey said shortly. 'We must have news of our relief.' Nicodemus was about to protest, but the governor went on, his thin features intent with concentration, his large eyes fixed on the boy's scowling face. 'I want you to go over the wall, and go through the enemy lines. If you are caught you may say you have been orphaned, I am sure you would not be put to any harm,' he said carefully. Nicodemus swallowed with difficulty. Over the wall? Alone? 'We must have news from London. I am not sure where to suggest you go for it, but Mr Layton's house on Wainlode Hill might be a start. You know it?'

Nicodemus nodded. Simon Layton had been on the town council before the siege, but had withdrawn to his comfortable mansion when the King's men had arrived. He was neither a rebel nor a royalist, preferring to occupy the rather dangerous and dilapidated fencing between the two parties. He might know the latest news from London, however. Nicodemus could be there and back in a day – or two. The boy nodded again, thrilled at the prospect of such a responsible assignment.

'You do not have to go, boy. I won't think any the less of you for wanting to remain here, with your friends.'

'Oh, no, sir. I'll go, sir! Right away, sir!'

Massey nodded, his thin features set.

He felt like a slaughterman. Slaughtering the innocents.

Ella Clamp had nodded and grinned at the young colonel, but he didn't seem to notice her that morning as she struggled by with her barrow, helping to clear the rubble from the flattened houses. A lot on his mind, probably, the poor splinter. Not an ounce of fat on the boy. She finished her shift and went on home to prepare the dinner, hardly relishing the prospect of sharing her front room with her mother-in-law. John's old mum was one of those turned out of their homes on Brook Street, and was presently grumbling in their back room, surrounded by her own personal parapet of trunks and baskets.

'Why di'n't they take their quarrels and sichlike some-where else?' the toothless old crone complained as Ella flustered about the house trying to put things straight. 'Come up 'ere botherin' ordinary folk? Sempty years I've lived there, and me mother afore I,' old Gwen went on, shaking her stick as if she was a cavalry captain at the head of a hundred men.

'Sir Edward said the roofs'd catch on foire, and stop his men from gettin' to the walls,' Ella explained patiently, cutting cheese for her menfolk's dinners.

'Yer father'd turn in his grave if 'e could see 'em making sport with his vigitible garden,' the old crone moaned. 'Pulled it all down around wi'out so much as a by your leave!'

Ella finished the dinners, wrapped the bread and cheese in a muslin cloth, and placed it in her basket. She lifted the old pail from the scullery and waved to the muttering old woman.

'I'm off to take John 'is dinner,' she said, relieved at being able to get out of the crowded house. She marched to the pump at the bottom of the street, and gossiped with her neighbours as she waited her turn.

'I see you've got old Gwendoline back then, El?'

'They should 'ave 'ad her set a spell on the King's men!'

'She'll be settin' spells on me if I 'ave to put up with much more of 'er,' Ella laughed. There was a sudden dull boom from the other side of the tumbledown wall. They were used to the barrage now, and mightily relieved the enemy shelling had not been as ferocious as they had anticipated. Damage was widespread but relatively minor: tiles and chimneys, the occasional window. Casualties were remarkably light. The honest folk of Gloucester reckoned it was another sign of God's favour.

'Goar, that's a big 'un!' The womenfolk straightened up over their brimming pails, shielded their eyes as they watched the smoking ball sail over the defences trailing a white comet.

'Christ Jesus, it's comin' for us!' They scattered like a flock of hens, throwing themselves down behind the walls and rolling under their groaning carts. There was a piercing whistle and a gust of hot air as the enormous iron ball hurtled down and buried itself up to its hissing neck in a heap of clay.

Ella peered through her fingers as the dust settled. The great ball had stuck fast in the heavy soil, the sparking fuse cut far too long. It hissed and popped, giving off a cloud of angry sparks and a foul sliver of grey smoke. Ella rolled over and leaped to her feet, snatched up the nearest pail, and threw the fresh water over the hellish bomb. The fuse was extinguished in an instant, the enormous ball no more than a lump of useless iron. The womenfolk emerged from their fanciful fortifications, eyed the missile warily.

'By God, Ella, you saved us!'

Ella shook her head, hardly able to comprehend their escape.

'Good job you 'ad yer pail!'

'Ah, we could 'ave fished old Gwen out, got 'er to piss on it!' a neighbour called, nudging Ella in her well-upholstered ribs.

'There's a bounty for used balls, as well as all that powder!' another excited neighbour pointed out. Ella nodded, quickly recovering her scattered wits.

'Get that cart over 'ere. I'm taking it in!' she cried. It took six of them half an hour to dig the enormous ball free from the cloying clay. In the end they had to run the barrow beneath the great iron pot, and roll the monster into the creaking cart by sheer force.

They trundled their prize off through the streets, laughing and waving to the soldiers as they shouted witticisms from the battered walls.

John Clamp's dinner remained where it had been left, beside the pump at the end of the road.

BY
FRIAR'S ORCHARD,

GLOUCESTER

Colonel Nybb shook his tousled iron-grey head in frustration as he watched the junior officers and elder sergeants herd his men up to the trenches the other side of Gaudy Green. He strode forward and hauled a couple of tall farm boys out of the sorry-looking ranks, snatched the pikes from their unprotesting fists.

'What d'ye mean to do, mineers, lugging pikes to a breach? Yer wants en feure pikes,' he told the bewildered brothers.

'Feure pikes?' the elder asked, shaking his bushy head.

Colonel Nybb couldn't trust himself to complete his explanation without beating the stupid great oaf senseless. Instead he rounded on Cully Oates, whistling along the miserable file with his halberd over his shoulder. '*Wo sind die feure* ... where's yer feure pikes, mineer?' he demanded, tugging the sergeant out of the ranks by his straps.

Cully Oates shook his head. 'Foire pikes? They'm stuck at the rear somewheres,' he replied, unperturbed by the bandit's fierce stare and even fiercer breath. 'Nobody 'as thought to bring 'em up!'

Fire pikes were particularly useful in siege warfare, consisting of a sturdy leather sleeve filled with a sulphurous concoction of pitch and nitrates fixed to the end of a long

143

pole. The bearer could thrust the burning firework straight at defending musketeers, setting sparks among the powder charges clinking about his chest. No musketeer in his right mind would remain at his post if he had to share it with a fire pike.

Nybb released the sergeant and waved the nervous farm boys back into line. No fire pikes? This siege was being run by house doves and green boys. They had less idea of getting into a town than into a whore's drawers! He strode along the shuffling file, his pistols rammed into his belt and a devilishly curved sword clamped in his fist. His men regarded him as if he was half man and half bear, a shape-changing demon stalking along their ranks glaring at the worthless mob. It was just dusk, and they could see the town walls lit up by the glare of the fires burning sullenly in the surrounding ditches. The men trooped past an abandoned hovel and followed the shouting sergeants towards the first of the outlying Royalist works, dropping into the puddle-filled ditch one by one, fustian lemmings in patched coats.

Nybb scowled at the officers who had gathered on the step of the looted ruin to study the town's defences through their perspective glasses. He couldn't be bothered with them: trinkets and toys had no place in Nybb's well-travelled armoury. They'd even brought missy along, the *Bella fatale* with the pert little bubbies.

'Ah, there you are, Nybb,' Sir Gilbert Morrison observed. 'I'm glad we caught you.' He pointed his glass towards the dimly lit walls, tracing the molehill saps which radiated like the spokes of a wagon from the battered south-eastern sector of the defences.

'There, look, you see? A little to the left of that leaning tower. Do you have it?'

Nybb snatched up the glass and took a cursory look at the rubble and turf wall. He'd seen more formidable pigpens. 'Ah, mineer. A bit of a breach, eh?'

'They've tried to fill it but we had Findlay and the sharpshooters out in the works picking them off,' Sir Gilbert commented, anxious to demonstrate his immediate grasp of the military situation. 'They haven't been able to do more than stuff a few woolsacks into the gap, see?'

They peered through their glasses at the glimmering walls, lapsing into silence as they studied the brooding, tumbledown towers.

Lord Clavincale wrapped himself in his grey cloak and joined the soldiers at the front for a change, equally anxious to be present at the historic storming. To his extreme annoyance, Bella had refused point-blank to stay at the inn and threw her cloak on as if she would join the soldiers in the saps.

'The trenches are no place for a woman, madam,' he scolded her with all the authority he could muster.

'No place for most of the women you are used to, perhaps,' she admitted, taking up her kid gloves and slipping them over her long, elegantly tapered fingers. 'But I'm not sitting in this fleapit while you go off without me. You were the one who insisted we come up to this godforsaken hole in the first place.'

'All the same, my dove, you could be injured by a stray shot, you could be . . .'

'I could have been ravished and sold into slavery on my own doorstep before now,' Bella reminded him, her hazel eyes sparking with determination. 'I can take care of myself,' she sniffed.

Clavincale shook his head. That was true enough at any rate. Why, the dragoon deserter who tried to hold her up back in Chipping Marleward earlier that eventful summer had ended up dead, shot the moment he turned his back on the whiplash girl. By God, if her father had been made of the same stuff the war would have been over by now! 'Have it your own way my dear,' he invited, 'but don't blame me if you end up covered in filth at the bottom of some ditch!'

Now Clavincale waved his perspective glass dismissively. 'The defence won't last the hour. A set of milkmaids and old tapsters? Why, one good push and they'll be on their knees,' he predicted.

Sir Gilbert nodded in agreement. 'Your men can use the trees as cover, look,' he invited.

Nybb shook his head sourly. How many more fat worms were going to come crawling out of the apple telling him his business? He had been fighting when they had been wetting their cosy beds!

Captains Telling, Allington, and Slaughter's man Shea stood by, fully armed and buckled into their buff coats. Shea had decided to stay with his command rather than join his apoplectic commander on his march south.

Michael Slaughter had collected what little gear he had brought out from Ireland and stowed it behind his horse, his pinched features black with fury. He had received instructions to join Prince Maurice's army in the far west as he marched with all dispatch towards Exeter. His mutinous regiment, however, was to go to that blundering oaf Morrison. It was too much to bear. Shea had stood by holding his former colonel's bridle, trying to catch his furious eye.

'You'll get another regiment,' Shea encouraged. Slaughter mounted, straightened his hat, and scowled down at his trusted captain.

'Oh, I'll get another regiment all right,' Slaughter growled. 'And mind you take care when I do, because they won't be bearing blue ribbons!' he had warned, tugging at his reins and cantering off down the Barton road as if all the fiends of hell were after him. He meant to go through with his threat, then, and seek service with the Parliament? He wouldn't be the first, nor the last.

Each of Morrison's five company commanders were to approach the walls from different angles, splitting the thinly spread defenders. Nybb would lead his company straight for the alleged breach, with the rest of them packing in behind. They would pour into the orchard and penetrate the heart of the defences, aiming for the spire of St Mary de Crypt, the church which had been pressed into service as the garrison magazine. If the attackers could secure the church the defenders would be without ammunition, according to Findlay, the gamekeeper who would lead the sharpshooters out of their holes to second the assault. Even Nybb had admitted it was a sound enough plan, if only these rabbits had the grit to carry it through, which he very much doubted. Give him a regiment of Wallenstein's conglomerate soldiery and he would take the town in half an hour. Ah, but Wallenstein was long dead now, and so were most of his old troops.

Nybb grunted something under his breath and handed the merchant his glass. He nodded to the junior officers, and stalked off into the night like a bad-tempered bear.

Sir Gilbert took Telling's arm, held him back for a moment.

'No heroics, Hugo,' he said quietly. 'You've nothing to prove to us, we don't doubt you,' he said reassuringly.

Telling tugged himself free and hurried off after his fellow officers. He couldn't resist taking one nervous look back at Bella, standing silently behind her fiancé, shrouded in her enormous hood, which shielded her features from the staring youngster.

Clavincale snorted in resentful agitation, all too aware these sullen heroes, these marvellous Cavaliers, had left him behind again, left him at the rear with the old men and the women.

'What dull fellows these soldiers are,' he breathed. 'They're all the same. No more sense than a rutting ram,' he commented.

'Even so,' Sir Gilbert allowed, 'he's worth more to us alive than lying in a bloody ditch.'

'Maybe,' Clavincale agreed, taking a quick glance at the quiet girl. Bella was biting her lip concernedly, but looked up and smiled brightly when she realized he was watching her.

'I do hope they'll be all right, the silly great things,' she said distractedly.

Clavincale blew a gust of air down his fleshy nose and turned to watch his silly great things storm Gloucester.

Nybb ducked his head down below the crumbling parapet and led his company along the muddy communication trench which linked the variously successful Royalist saps. The complex network of ditches and dugouts honeycombed the slag heaped wilderness beyond the south-eastern walls of the city, the same walls which had withstood the brunt of the Royalist bombardment. Captain Allington's men had already filed through the stagnant ditch to their assault positions to the north of the scraggly orchard. The main wall dissected the old friary, enclosing neat rows of gnarled and withered fruit trees. The few shot-blasted crabby survivors beyond the ditch would make a good marker for the storming parties as well as providing some cover for the attackers. Nybb paused to take a crafty look over the rim of his trench, searching for the breach he had heard so much about. Ah, there it was, just along from the crumbling tower. The scoured wall had been pitted and cracked by a storm of shot, the protective turfs torn away by successive blasts. The freshly mangled masonry glimmered in the gathering gloom, giving the old veteran another good mark.

He ducked down and peered along the trench at the wide white eyes of his company. The musketeers had lit their match and were blowing on the glowing ends to keep them from being blown out by the night air. Behind them a dozen and more had been pressed into service as sappers. Each had a tightly bound bundle of branches to throw into the ditch, others were crouching beside long siege ladders. Behind them swordsmen, clubmen, sergeants with handy halberds. The fighters who would beat the enemy from their precious stockade. Nybb tugged his helmet straps tight, dragged a pistol from his belt, and checked the complex mechanism.

'All ist klar,' he breathed. 'All right, mineers, are we ready? Voorwaaaarts!' He roared the command over the network of expectant ditches and diggings, levering himself over the duckboard palisade and lurching forward across the ploughed and puddled wasteland.

'Charge, ye slack-bladdered poltroons!'

He glanced right and left, saw the rest of his company leap out of their holes like so many sand eels. A baby-faced ensign struggled to unfurl the large blue colour, the broad silk flapped in his eyes as he stumbled forward.

Nybb took an enormous leap over a corpse-red puddle

and threw himself down behind a stony embankment ten yards short of the walls. He could see the black eyes of their muskets bobbing up and down to find a target. In another second a scattered volley dropped half a dozen of his men at once. The ensign dropped the colour and grabbed his chest, pirouetted into the puddle over the waxy corpses half submerged in the filth. Nybb spat out a mouthful of foul water, raised his pistol, and fired at the enemy musketeers. More and more men jumped into his ditch, the pioneers carrying their awkward faggots balanced on top of their hats. They hurled their bundles into the ditch and ducked down again as more and more musketeers opened fire at the attackers. Nybb squinted to his right, and watched Allington's company fan out towards the wall a hundred yards further to the north. Shea's company were attacking the tumbledown tower from his left.

'*Schnell! Grosse Gott im Himmell, schnell!*' Nybb lapsed from his camp vernacular as the sappers quailed before the defences. 'Get yer faggots in the ditch!' he roared, grabbing a frightened farm boy by his collar and hurling him out from behind their doubtful defence. The terrified boy hurled his hateful bundle at the wall, spun round and fell over as a bullet grazed his forehead. Nybb cursed in Armenian, hurled himself forward, and scooped the boy's twitching body into his arms. He staggered forward and deposited the limp youth over the badly aimed faggots. A trio of men in outsize morion helmets doubled up with a siege ladder, threw the wooden frame across the partly filled ditch, and jumped down into the puddled clay trench to hold it steady. Nybb turned and waved his company forward towards the gaping breach. Now he was closer he could see the powdery mortar between the soft blocks of stone. His musketeers doubled forward, raised their weapons, and fired a sudden volley at the frantic townsmen. Shrieks and screams and rolling smoke. Bright flames dancing in the dusk, illuminating the hate-racked features of attackers and attacked. He could see their hats bobbing on the walls, frightened white faces gaping beneath. They were reloading frantically now, their womenfolk hurrying up with spare muskets, powder horns, bags of newly cast bullets.

Nybb crossed the ladder in three steps and hurled himself into the heaped soil and refuse beneath the wall. He peered up at the black barrels protruding over the parapet above him, shoved himself to his knees, and chopped at the belching firesticks. A musket toppled over the wall and fell with a splash into the puddle-filled ditch. A fearful face peered out of the breach at him. Nybb wrenched his other pistol free and fired. The man fell back clutching his eyes. The bellowing bandit doubled forward like a two-legged rhinoceros, pushing the screaming Roundhead out of the way. His musketeers pressed in behind him, jabbing the flag towards the yawning breach, the clean stone gap in the wall. Nybb ducked as a musketeer swung his weapon at his head. The brass-bound butt clanged on his helmet but Nybb had already thrust with his sword, disembowelling his attacker. A woman screamed and dropped the pail she was carrying.

'Charge! This way!' Nybb roared encouragement to the screaming mob behind him, scrambling like monkeys up the crumbling earth wall or tottering over the creaking ladder. A grenade went off, toppling friend and foe from the breach. Men and women wrestled this way and that over the six-foot gap, smeared and splashed with sticky blood, ground to powder by worn boots. Nybb kicked and hacked and spat and roared, pressed back by a surging mob of Roundheads who sensed they must either close the breach or lose their city.

The ladder broke, depositing six screaming musketeers into the ditch. The rest hung back, watching for a moment the vanguard's bloody struggle on the far side of the obstacle.

Zachary and Eli Pitt scrambled down into the refuse-filled trench and staggered through the bloody puddles, clutching their pikes like candlesticks. No use in the furious cut and thrust on the walls, they dropped them to find more useful tools. A discarded axe, a broken stave. The two men led another surge up the slag heaped soil, barging their way through the packed mass of men at the breach. Zachary caught a Roundhead by the scruff of the neck, pulling him out of the mad scrummage and sitting on the man's chest. He peered down at the whiskery features, and then brought his club down on the man's skull.

'Watch out, Zach, for the love of Christ, that could 'ave been our Mordy!' his brother wailed, crouching above his brother as fists and swords and stones and empty pails crashed and thumped and flew around their heads.

'Wos fink Oi 'ad a gander at 'un first?' Zachary snapped, ducking his head as a goodwife swung a pail at his helmeted head.

'Gah, I can't hurt no woman!' Eli moaned.

'Ged on an' 'it 'er one afore she brains Oi!' Zachary shouted.

Eli brought the stave back and swung it at the goodwife's bonnet. She fell over the breach and toppled down the far side of the wall. A furious red-eyed scarecrow in a flapping green coat darted forward, grabbing the farm boy by the

152

rim of his helmet. Eli clubbed his hands away, dragged his brother back from the hateful carnage.

For all their pressure, Nybb's men were stuck fast, unable to force a passage from the mass of rebels coagulating about the dangerous breach. They simply could not pack enough bodies on the narrow soil slope to force the Roundheads back off their stony platform. Enemy musketeers clambered out onto the crumbling tower to their left, and opened an enfilading fire against the men stuck hopelessly in the filthy moat. Royalist musketeers dropped like flies. Pioneers dropped their faggots and ran. The swordsmen at the rear took cover where they could.

Nybb picked up the broken shaft of the regimental flag, the blue silk torn and stained, singed by an exploding powder horn. He elbowed himself to the wall, chopping and hacking at the rebels who had packed in around him. A blade pierced his thigh. A pail caught him another ringing blow on the side of his dented helmet. He staggered back, lost his footing over the slippery breach, and was shoved and kicked back over the wall. He rolled head over heels down the muddy slope and splashed into the blood-stained puddle, the wrecked standard clutched in his bloody fist. The Pitt brothers hauled him out of the mire and dragged him up the other side. The Roundhead musketeers would surely have shot them all dead, but Telling's men had reached the tower at last, and scrambled up the sandbagged defences distracting the sharpshooters. Nybb blinked and spat, face down in the dirt as the frightened farm boys hauled him off like a dead horse they meant to butcher.

'All right, all right, let me go!' he yelled over a mouthful of filth. He climbed to his feet, panting like a goat as he watched the remains of his company stagger and limp back to the trenches. Behind him, Telling's men had been thrown back from the leaning tower. Allington's had filled the ditch with faggots but had by some mischance attacked a particularly lofty section of the wall, and had been unable to make any headway. Shea's had gone to ground before they had reached the wall, and Findlay's men had hung back, sniping at the defenders.

Sir Gilbert's grand design to end the siege in a single night had ended in bloody failure.

Midnight, and at last the firing died away. The enemy had kept up a remorseless barrage against the walls all day, steadily increasing the pressure on the defenders until darkness, when their long-expected assault had flooded towards the sandcastle towers around Friar's Orchard. Blue-coated musketeers who had been sent to the northern suburbs for the dawn sortie against the guns at Kingsholm were hurried back to the threatened sector, but in the meantime the fanatical defence had fallen to the town militiamen and their wives. The citizen soldiers rushed out of their homes with spades, clubs, and assorted ironmongery to join the few soldiers at the bloody breach.

For a moment it seemed the wall must fall. A determined band of Royalist attackers fought their way onto the parapet, but were beaten to a standstill and pushed back over the slippery stone breach. John Clamp took a dry wound to the head, and was hauled off groaning. Ella thought the worst, staring down at his lifeless body as the fight raged to and fro. She dropped the dented pail she had been wielding and ducked down to haul her man off the wall by his heels, dragging his corpse away and laying him out beneath the black stump of an apple tree. He had been knocked senseless by a black-faced brute in a spiked helmet, and was equally fortunate to survive his bumpy rescue.

'Goar now, John Clamp, tell me you're aloive!' Ella cried, crouching over her husband as he blinked and worked his stubbled jaw. The fires on the wall cast bold red shadows over his thin features, making him look like some undead servant of Satan. He prised himself up on his elbows, wincing with pain as he examined his bruised skull.

'Thank the Lord for that. I thought you wuz a goner,' she said, hiccuping loudly. She squatted back on her heels, too tired to cry.

Morrison's regiment went into the attack by seniority of companies, one after the other. Lieutenant Colonel Nybb's company led the way, followed by Allington's under the senior captain, with Shea and Telling, the junior captains, following on behind. Findlay, the sergeant major, took his sharpshooters forward to second the assault and cover the subsequent retreat.

They came back in a wildly mixed-up mob, a filthy flock of ditchwater-dipped sheep, their colours torn and shredded by the splattering musketry. Three of the enthusiastic ensigns who had borne the banners were lying dead under the burning walls beside several dozen others. The breathless, shoaling survivors divided around the scattered works, scrambling in and out of the ditches and trenches to make their getaway, slipping off into the night like hungry wolves, footsore fugitives before some appalling pursuit.

Sir Gilbert didn't even try to halt the stampede. He stood behind the partly demolished wall of the hovel, scowling and shaking his head as the sudden flood of men flowed by his improvised headquarters. The wounded hobbled in as best they could, using muskets or broken pikes for crutches. Some crawled, others, blinded by flashes of powder or blistering blows across the head, staggered along mumbling incoherently, their trembling fingers groping for the shoulder of the man in front.

Stragglers came in by ones and twos, and made off after their more fleet-footed colleagues, regaining their breath and brawn beneath the eaves of the dripping plantation just across the road. The ashen-faced fugitives looked as if they expected the undaunted merchant to try and halt the rout, but he waved them on towards the sanctuary of the trees, nodding and calling after them familiarly.

'Bravely done, boys. They'll never stand another attack like that,' Sir Gilbert called, wondering where the wretched officers had got to. He and Clavincale couldn't be expected to hold them steady, could they? His prospective son-in-law drew his dress sword and threw his arm around Bella's shoulder, dragged the protesting girl into the ruined hovel as if he would fight off every Roundhead in the country.

Cah!

Sir Gilbert raised his eyebrows. Trying to impress his daughter with a bit of belated bravado, eh? The canny merchant had noticed the way Bella had stared after the moody young Cavalier. She had better watch her antics – making eyes at every daft blade in the army was hardly conducive to Bella's imminent metamorphosis into Lady Clavincale, was it now? His future son-in-law would do better to leave the fighting to others. Clavincale was no more a warrior than he was, after all. Sir Gilbert wasn't bothered by his want of military prestige. There were more ways to serve than at the head of a bunch of ragged-arsed recruits. But then, the merchant reflected smugly, Clavincale was still a young pup, he lacked Sir Gilbert's beatific blend of wisdom and maturity.

The merchant turned away from the pathetic spectacle Clavincale was making of himself, and squinted into the gloom as another set of scoundrels pulled themselves out of the pit, only to turn on each other like yapping dogs.

'Where were you, mineer?' Nybb crowed, bristling up before the rangy gamekeeper who had led the rearguard. Findlay scowled at the red-eyed giant, his legs planted apart, hands clamped around the barrel of his firelock.

'I was told to give covering fire, that's what I did,' he said quietly, with his usual bucolic menace. Telling and Shea stood panting to one side, shoulders hunched as they fought to get their breath.

'Covering fire, mineer, cowering fire I calls it,' Nybb growled.

Sir Gilbert, as sharp as ever despite the bloody over-throw of his forces, stepped between the formidable fighters, holding up his hands.

'Findlay did just as we said, Nybb,' he said smoothly, smiling up at the scowling bandit with the muddy mask. 'By God, you came within an ace of getting over,' he congratulated his murderous mercenary. 'They'll never stand another attack like that!'

'The lily-livered candle-wasters won't stand another attack, is what you mean, mineer,' Nybb sneered, spitting a mouthful of dirty spittle into the trampled earth.

Sir Gilbert frowned. 'Now now, Nybb, they did well enough, aye. Good troops don't grow from seed, man! There now, didn't they do well enough, Telling?'

The dazed youth blinked and nodded, opening and shutting his mouth in agreement. He took off his lobster-pot helmet and absent-mindedly put it straight back on again. Bella, watching him over her fiancé's cloaked shoulder, held her white hand to her mouth in momentary concern. Why, he hadn't gone all funny like her brother, had he? Lost his wits in the stormy murk of battle?

Clavincale jumped at the sudden movement behind him, turned round to scowl at the concerned girl. Bella smiled weakly.

Shea, apparently unaffected by the ferocious fighting, shrugged carelessly, interrupting the lordling's suspicious wonderings.

'They did better than I expected,' he said grudgingly. 'Although they went after me and Colonel Slaughter with a sight more venom than they did the enemy,' he said casually.

'Ah, let bygones be bygones, sir. They'll shape up well, aye, in time, in time.' He pursed his generous lips for a moment, as if reconsidering. 'Nybb, I suggest you get into that wood and keep an eye on the rogues.'

'Aye, mineer,' the mercenary crowed, with one last vindictive look at the unblinking gamekeeper.

Findlay watched him stalk off, muttering, into the dripping trees.

The garrison had thrown back a determined Royalist assault, but it was business as usual at daybreak as Massey unleashed a similar number of men from the northern suburbs of the smoke-clogged, shaken city. The furious counter-attack swept through the enemy trenches in a vicious right hook, surprising the King's engineers and catching the gunners napping once again. But this was no small sally party of a dozen or so blue-coats. Pudsey had four hundred heavily armed musketeers and pioneers, far more than the Royalist commanders had imagined Massey would risk in a single sortie over the walls.

The King's men took to their heels, scattered through the maze of trenches they had delved into the gloomy wilderness around the gates. Pudsey's men kept in a compact mob, firing as they went. They cleared galleries and threw grenades into pits, snatched up the enemy's discarded tools. The blue-coated mob surged down the communication trenches and reached the big Royalist battery at Kingsholm where they beat down the remaining gunners and spiked a number of their pieces before the enemy hurried reinforcements to the stricken line. By then the damage had been done: soft lead nails driven into the touch-holes on top of the gleaming guns would prevent them from being fired. Picking the nails out was a long and frustrating task, and it would be hours before the cannon would be ready to open fire once more.

Nicodemus Burke, hat on his head and a snapsack full of provisions at his side, slipped out with the main raiding party, but had thrown himself into a ditch on the far side of an abandoned trench and remained there like a piece of flotsam left by a retreating tide. He crouched in his hole listening to the furious Royalists reoccupy their bloody saps. The officers seemed to be as much in fear of Rupert as the Roundheads, nervously speculating on who would be blamed for the loss of the guns.

'You heard about Mortlake? Ball in the gut and he still had him cashiered. They say he died of shame!'

'The bastard will get his come-uppance one day,' another officer sneered. 'They say he fancies the crown for himself!'

'If he can keep his hands off Mary Villiers!'

'Ah, we can't blame him for lustin' after 'er!'

'He wasn't well chuffed with last night's work either, so I heard.'

'That fat moth Morrison? They say half his men had deserted by this morning!'

'That wouldn't surprise me, spineless rats the lot of 'em!'

'Spineless or no, they got a sight nearer the walls than Rupert's boys.'

Nicodemus lay still, listened as the officers passed by followed by their nervous men. Compared to the buoyant spirit of the men on the other side of the walls, the dirty diggers in the trenches seemed miserable and listless, only motivated by the fierce shouts of their belligerent officers. They took up their back-breaking work with gloomy forebodings, as if they sensed victory was slowly, tantalizingly, slipping away between their filthy fingers. He lay there shivering until the sun went down, and then doubled back along the deserted trench, his hat pulled down over his fiery red head. He reached a larger communication trench and picked up a broken shovel, as if he had been sent on some errand from the saps. He passed surly musketeers and grim-faced pioneers, chattering officers in their mud-splattered finery. Away to his left he could see the damaged guns being dragged out of the ruined battery, the wounded crew members trudging after their broken pieces. Nicodemus fell in behind the miserable crew, lending a hand pushing a groaning master gunner in a bloody barrow. The fleshy artilleryman cursed every bump and pothole, but waved away the few Royalist guards who seemed to take their duties seriously. They pushed him as far as a busy inn on the Kingsholm road, and Nicodemus slipped off into the night. For all his fears and fancies, getting out of Gloucester had been as easy as standing on his head.

Getting back in might prove a little trickier.

HOUNSLOW HEATH,

NEAR LONDON, 22 AUGUST 1643

William Sparrow had never seen so many people in one place. It seemed as if the whole population of London had turned out in their Sunday best to cheer and wave their sons and brothers, husbands and lovers off to war. They had surged out of the city and gathered in a vast multicoloured mob on Hounslow Heath, turning the sober march into a cavalcade, the God-fearing camp into a fairground. Pious psalms rang out over the common, bellowed with equally ecstatic fervour by Puritan and peasant alike as they mingled beneath billowing pavilions and beside the grubby market stalls. Traders and tinkers, hawkers and piemen, barbers and innkeepers had set up their stands to serve soldiers and civilians. The cheerful tumult was drowned out every now and then by the warlike clatter of the drums and merry whistles of flutes and pipes as another regiment arrived to swell the relief force being assembled in dark hedgehog-backed blocks on the heath.

William trudged along with his new halberd over his left shoulder. His wounded right arm was still heavily bandaged and quite sore, and he could only just lift the heavy cutlass he had carried throughout the doomed defence of his home town. He would make sure and practice his sword drill using his left hand before they went much further west and all.

William came to a halt beside a flock of Parliamentarian staff officers who were busy recording the arrival of each unit and trying to allocate the men to the correct brigade according to their complex, ink-smeared charts. They were wearing their Sunday best, sober broadcloth suits bedecked with orange sashes and ribbons despite the fearsome heat, and their tempers had frayed accordingly. The red-faced officers reminded William of farmers at market, anxiously attempting to ensure their livestock was penned up to take best advantage of the curious crowds. They were shouting and pointing, contradicting one another like a gang of fishwives.

'Mercer's? Straight past the big marquee, right over the far side,' a sweating major pointed out their position ready for the afternoon's big review. Sparrow turned to face his thirsty men, holding his halberd out longways as his company swung off the dusty road to take their place in the vast chequerboard of forces the capital city had collected. The Earl of Essex's army had been reduced to a pale skeleton of the force which had fought so hard on Edgehill the previous October, and would need massive reinforcement if it was to take the field once more. Luckily for the desperate Parliamentarian greybeards, the fickle London mob had confounded the Jeremiahs at Whitehall and responded with all its former vigour.

Only two weeks before, the city had watched Nathaniel Fiennes' poor garrison shamble into the capital like so many slaves. A thousand beaten curs who wouldn't have held the city an hour against His Majesty's rampaging Cavaliers.

Everybody was suffering, merchant and commoner alike. Trade had been ruined, markets closed up, and supply routes shut down by gloating Royalist garrisons.

The news from the west was disastrous: Waller smashed at Roundway, Dorchester, Portland, and Weymouth lost, and Exeter under pressure from Prince Maurice. Nathaniel Fiennes had returned to London only to be court-martialled and condemned to death for failing to hold on to the enormously important port of Bristol. Only the energetic influence of his father Lord Saye and Sele had saved him from being executed. The summer campaigns in the north had been almost as unsuccessful: the energetic Fairfaxes – principal Roundhead commanders in Yorkshire – unable to hold Bradford. Leeds was seized by escaping Royalist prisoners, who had taken over the magazine and held the town until relieved. Only a handful of quick-witted civilians had prevented the Governor of Hull from selling out to the King. Thank the Lord for this man Cromwell, the Huntingdon MP turned soldier, who had at least managed to win a victory at Gainsborough over the feared and despised Cavalier cavalry. But his short-lived triumph had not prevented the marauding Royalists from taking the town soon after, and marching into Lincoln a little while after that.

The despondent Londoners had pinned all their remaining hopes on Gloucester, as if their mystical belief in the town could save their own necks. Twelve days the defiant, God-fearing citizens had held out, twelve days in which the mood of the fickle London mob swung from total despair to feverish delight, blind faith in their very own general, the splendidly brave Earl of Essex.

The news-sheets had picked up the quickening pulse in the capital, and instead of sneering at the earl's notorious reluctance to come to grips with the enemy they praised him to the heavens. The adulation of press and public alike shifted away from Sir William Waller, erstwhile master of the West Country, and swung back behind the rejuvenated earl once more.

Old Robin would save Gloucester, and resurrect the tottering cause into the bargain!

Their superstitious enthusiasm filtered down to the wild-eyed street gangs, the idlers and loafers and barefooted, loose-tongued troublemakers. Regiments which hadn't managed to enlist as much as a crippled cat in the last few months had suddenly been besieged by bawling recruits. Every man, woman, and child who had flocked to the common to see them off believed in Essex and his brave boys. They dared not contemplate anything else.

William Sparrow spied his sweating friends in the unfamiliar files, and he fell in beside them, completing the dusty march past the enthusiastic crowd with all the swagger he could muster.

He came to a halt and took off his hot helmet. The bright light and open space had made him giddy, and he thought for one awful moment he might faint right in front of the cheering crowd, but Muffet was there as always, easing his calloused palm under Sparrow's elbow to keep him straight.

'If you can't march this far without collapsing you'd best get back,' the elder sergeant warned with a shake of his grey-flecked head. The captain blinked, mopped his red face with his neckerchief, and wiped his running eyes.

'I'll be all right,' he growled. 'I've been stuck in that damned inn too long.'

''Ow cudger be stuck in an inn too long?' Billy Butcher piped up from the next rank. 'They could leave me there long as they bleedin' liked!'

Muffet glanced over his shoulder at the grinning sharpshooter, proudly brandishing a brand-new firelock. The

164

musket had a longer barrel than the usual issue firearm, and a more complex trigger mechanism which used flints to spark the charge rather than a lighted match. The weapons had only been issued to the artillery guards and the very best shots in each regiment. Butcher was loudly reckoned to be the best shot in the army, let alone the regiment, not least by the Peckham dyer's apprentice himself.

'You can bugger off back there and all,' Muffet snapped. 'I'm not marching all the way back down west with you blatherin' on like a damned jackdaw! I 'ad more than enough of your opinions on the way up!'

Sparrow laughed, immensely cheered by the few familiar faces in his newly raised company.

As well as Long Col and young Butcher there was Hereward Gillingfeather, his coat buttoned up to the collar as if it was a chill January morning and not a furiously hot summer's afternoon, and Caleb Cruickshank, the simple-minded cabin boy who had shared their horrifying ordeal, thrown into the stampeding currents of the English Channel by his piratical father. With them were a hundred fresh-faced apprentices, crop-haired hooligans from the city stews, who seemed to regard a fortnight's soldiering as a fantastic summer's adventure rather than a military campaign. They had rushed to the colours in sweaty droves, buoyed up by the sudden wave of enthusiasm which had unexpectedly swept London. The only question was how long this terrific willingness would last.

'You just wait. Five miles down the Reading road this lot'll be bellyachin' to go home to mum,' was Long Col's phlegmy assessment.

*

165

'Henry Mercer's regiment, have a care!' the furious bellow rolled out over the shuffling ranks. 'Advance, advance your pikes and muskets!'

William watched his newly recruited company fumble and trip over their weapons, the long pikes tricky to handle in the stiffening breeze, the clumsy muskets clinking awkwardly against chestfuls of powder charges. Some of the musketeers had brought old-fashioned musket rests and didn't exactly know where to put them. Others had swords strapped to their belts which were proving as much a threat to the man behind as any enemy might be, and a few enthusiasts had even cut themselves some Swedish feathers – sharpened staves which they would hammer into the ground in front of them as a deterrent to cavalry. In addition to their assorted arms and accoutrements every man had a snapsack of hard-baked bread and a good round cheese, as well as any bottles of ale, hunks of fatty bacon, and ham bones they had been lucky enough to acquire back in the capital. Although most of his new company had volunteered and turned up in their working clothes, a good number of Sparrow's men were substitutes – shifty-eyed sharpers who had been paid to do another man's service. Some of the more well-to-do citizens, every inch as inspired as their lowlier neighbours, had decided against taking this easy way out, and had turned up to do their soldiering for themselves. These worthy individuals had equipped themselves with the best weapons available, lobster-pot helmets, and back and breastplates. Their brand-new buff coats, though, were rather too fresh from the tannery, and the badly treated hides reeked in the hot afternoon air, stifling and gagging their eminently respectable owners. They were slightly older than the mob of gap-toothed apprentices: artisans and professionals who had joined up to help make ends meet over the slack summer months.

Their spokesman and unofficial corporal was a round-faced banker's clerk with close-set powder-blue eyes, and a rather formidable beer belly lashed up behind his bulging buff.

'Gah, what a damned stink. The fellow swore it was beeswax and that it would clear up in a few days,' he said, bending his head to sniff the greasy shoulders of his coat.

'Seems to be attracting the flies.' His colleague, an undernourished, sallow-faced publican wearing an ancient morion helmet, beat at the gnats which had formed a buzzing guard of honour about their stand-offish section.

'Oy! Shut your mouths at the back there! Get in line with the rest of 'em!' Colston Muffet barged through the tired files, and waved the well-dressed musketeers back into their rank with their rather more excitable colleagues.

'Excuse me, Sergeant Moffat, is it?'

'Muffet. Colston Muffet. What d'you want now?' the exasperated veteran glared at the spotlessly turned-out young blades, who hadn't stopped asking stupid questions since they had left Holborn.

'Which one's in charge, do you know?'

'Captain Sparrow's in charge of the company. Him with the black hair, look.'

The wealthy layabouts peered over the front rank towards the steaming officer. 'Ah, yes. The fellow from Bristol. I wonder if you wouldn't mind asking him if he needs any assistants?'

'Assistance?'

'Assistants. Lieutenants, ensigns, you know. We've all served in the Trained Band, you know.'

Muffet nodded slowly, shaking his tangled head. Sunday

afternoon soldiers who spent three hours in the alehouse for every twenty minutes drilling. Muffet, a Londoner himself, knew the type.

'And what was your name again?'

'Talbot. Stephen Talbot of Wietzmann and Goldstein, you know them?' the portly clerk enquired. 'But what with this damned war and one thing and another, we're rather slack at the moment, and they had to let me go.'

Muffet shook his head, a gesture which the banker's clerk mistook as shocked sympathy. 'And what about you two?' Muffet asked his companions.

The diminutive publican in the ancient helmet gave his name as Rodney Sark, formerly of the Green Bottle in Cheapside, and his colleague was John Jewell, coal merchant. 'Only seein' there ain't much coal about these days, there ain't much point in bein' a coal merchant!' the third man reported, his soot-encrusted fingers clamped around his newly turned pike.

Muffet raised his tired eyes, squinted up at the iron blade, sparkling in the bright afternoon sunshine. 'You've cut a few feet off, then?' he asked casually.

The coal merchant grinned, his teeth startling white against his dark features. The coal dust seemed to have worked itself into every crease and seam in his face, turning the smiling soldier into a Moorish warrior. 'Easier to lug about, innit, with a bit lopped off.'

Muffet pulled at his nose, as if deciding whether to shoot the rogues on the spot or save them for later. 'And what happens when—'

His fascinating discussion was interrupted by a roll of drums and a warble of flutes. Muffet looked up to see the regimental commanders arrive to a loud cheer from the front-rankers. He hurried to his place alongside Captain Sparrow as the regiment came to a ragged attention.

Colonel Tobias Fulke walked his bay mare along the front rank, nodding at the few familiar faces he recognized. The gallant old gentleman had left off his burnished black armour, and rode along in the leather jerkin he had brought back from his service with the Swedes. He had taken off his hat to wave to his men, and to introduce his delighted patron, Henry Mercer. Sir Henry had financed the recruitment and equipment of the regiment, but made sure he had a sound field commander in the eminently reliable Fulke.

William straightened his helmet and presented his halberd. He caught a quick glimpse of a tall, rather stooping stranger in a black coat with whiskers to match. His enormous ivory-coloured collar had ruckled up over his jacket, giving him a rather dishevelled, threadbare appearance.

'Huzzah for Sir Henry! Huzzah for Colonel Fulke!' William called. The men responded cheerfully enough, equally eager for a glimpse of their new chief.

'Is that him? That the colonel?' John Jewell asked eagerly.

'What about the old duffer with the white hair? Don't say they've put a damned dotard over us!' Stephen Talbot shook his head, the rather daring plumes he had inserted into his hat band bobbing gaily.

Cheesemonger Mercer looked as if he had grown too quickly, his towering height had certainly outstripped his flesh and muscles, and he slumped on his horse as if his long spine couldn't hold him up straight. He had oiled his long black hair to his skull, but had not managed to control his rather bushier whiskers, which stood in tufts between his large red ears and small, mean mouth. Mercer allowed himself a small smile at the greeting, raising his hand to acknowledge this great mob of men who would bear his name and honour. He saw a dense thicket of pikemen, their variously pruned weapons forming a formidable phalanx against the blue sky. Their brother musketeers were grouped about either flank as they would be in battle, ready to crowd in behind the rapidly dilating ranks of pikemen if the enemy cavalry approached too close. To one side were his captains, drummers, fifers, and ensigns bearing the regimental and company flags. Mercer had designed them himself and chosen the colour. His personal banner was plain dark green. Fulke's, as his lieutenant colonel, would be green with a small red cross of St George on a white square in the top left-hand corner. Each of the other officers' banners was similar to Fulke's, only identified by one or more yellow circles in the middle. The sarcastic soldiers had already made their mind up what the yellow circles represented.

'Huzzah for the Cheesemongers!' one wag shouted from the anonymity of the back.

''Ere, is that your feet kickin' up that stink?!'

'Well, if they never recognize the flags it won't matter, they'll smell us a mile off!'

William glowered at the giggling ranks, so many boys who were lucky enough to have no idea what was coming.

It was different for the few veterans amongst them, the old hands like Muffet and Gillingfeather, stony-faced child soldiers like Butcher and Caleb. They knew what lay at the other end of the Great West Road. They knew that they would never get all the way to Gloucester and all the way back without a fight. A vicious, bloodbath battle against the King's principal field army.

Prince Rupert's unbeaten Cavaliers.

And so the enormous relief force stood in great chequerboard squares beneath their blowing banners, surrounded by hordes of ecstatic civilians convinced they were witnessing the birth of a new crusade. The small crosses of St George they had worked into the top corners of their flags were identical to those their ancestors bore on their shields and lances. The Crusaders faced hundreds of miles of trackless desert, snow-capped mountains, and brown hills crawling with heathens before they reached the Promised Land, Jerusalem.

Now the Earl of Essex faced a hundred and fifty mile march across England's green and pleasant land, over hills and down dales where the King's dreaded cavalry lurked like Turks. Where Rupert, the new Saladin himself, waited impatiently with his demon hordes. The earl rode past his cheering legions, lifting his enormous hat and bowing at the knots of officers crowded beneath the cracking colours, the shuffling packs of musketeers eager for a look at the legendary commander, the pikemen shielding their eyes to catch a glimpse of the Lord General himself.

'Hey for Robin! Huzzah for Essex!'

Colston Muffet raised his greasy felt hat with the rest of them. It was going on a year since he had first stood in a rank behind the red-faced nobleman, back in the heady days before Edgehill, when they imagined their crushing superiority in numbers and resources would allow them to chase the Cavaliers from the field in an afternoon. Twelve months on, and the King had damned near chased his subjects all the way back to their starting point.

They weren't marching out to bring their monarch to his knees, they were marching out so that they might stay off theirs.

THE BLACK DOG INN,

NEAR BROCKWORTH,
GLOUCESTERSHIRE,
23 AUGUST 1643

Clavincale's throat ached and his eyes watered. He was having to practically bawl his business to make himself heard over the raucous tumult of the ale-house, the overcrowded common room thick with pungent tobacco smoke interlaced with the inevitable reek of unwashed bodies. There must have been sixty men crowded about the busy bar, elbows tucked in like so many salt fish as they swigged their ale and sucked on their pipes. The ruffian squatting across the upturned barrel was in familiar company, nodding and winking and rolling his busy brown eyes. Clavincale, despite disguising his fortune behind a rugged travelling cloak and a pair of mud-splattered boots, stood out like a prick in a nunnery. The distracted nobleman dabbed his eyes on the hem of his cloak and leaned forward once again.

'Could you not have written any of this down for me?' he bellowed, as a wide-hipped wench sailed by like a galleon in a gale, her fleshy red arm braced beneath a tray of foaming tankards.

'Goar, don't mind me, love!'

''Ands off, you cunny-bloats.'

'And another couple over 'ere, Annie me beaut!'

Clavincale's grey eyes flickered back to the stable hand, scratching the side of his nose with a filthy fingernail.

'What's that, sir? Writen down? Ah, sir, many's the secret slipped 'cus a bein' writen down,' the scrofulous horseboy theorized. 'An 'sides that, sir, I in't niver bin one fer fancy quill work 'n' sichlike.'

Clavincale wondered whether this simpleton could possibly perform the tricky assignments he had in mind for him. The lousy oaf in the ancient coat had, however, come well recommended. Clavincale had asked Nybb, Nybb had asked Cully Oates. Cully Oates had become acquainted with a cross-eyed serving wench over at Prinknash Park whose brother Gideon worked in the stables. He was a familiar figure around the hall, and often carried messages between the scattered Royalist outposts. Nobody would question his comings and goings. Nobody would notice him, an ignorant farm boy, riding half a furlong back from the tireless Prince on his furious gallops through the night. And where were they taking him, these furious gallops through the night? Why, to snatch a private moment or two with the woman he loved. Mary Villiers, Duchess of Richmond.

If this scraggy dog had his facts right.

It was the worst kept secret of the war, of course, endlessly embroidered by a bored and distracted court. The Chinese whispers had been carried from hall to cloister, kitchen to bedchamber by the highest and the lowest in the divided land. The few scant details of the famous liaison had been taken apart and tinkered with, reassembled to fit the latest lie.

That the duke knew all about his restless friend's infatuation with his bold-eyed wife – called the Butterfly by her jealous admirers – and dared not gainsay either of them. That he had been instructed by the King himself to overlook Rupert's butter-fingered passes. Or even, most malicious of all, that the austere duke preferred Rupert's morose younger brother to his voluptuous lady.

What rot.

Clavincale snorted to himself. The great Rupert turned on his head, the iron-willed warlord brought to his knees by the sly glance of a woman? He thought for a moment of his Bella. The poor girl was terribly bored and distracted by the whole tiresome business of war and wild life, and wanted nothing more than to go home to Dorset as Lady Clavincale. To lord it over the servants and ride around the county on a dapple-grey palfrey. Where did she get these strange notions? The inn, of course, did not agree with her. The place was crowded out every night, the ribald singing grating her delicate nerves. Clavincale's frequent business meetings in their rooms or down in the snug were far too tedious to hold her wandering attention, and she had taken to having a stroll around the lanes with one of the old maids round about with whom she had apparently struck up a friendship. Not like Bella to spend time with servants, but the brisk walk certainly seemed to clear her head. She always seemed refreshed when she returned. A delightful girl, and a regular minx between the sheets, and yet had she turned him on his head? Of course not. He was surprised at Rupert, if he had fallen for her as the gossips maintained. Letting himself slip over a mere woman. One of the most beautiful women in the land, perhaps, but a woman nevertheless. Perhaps she was in the employ of Parliament, perhaps the dried-up crows at Whitehall, removing their pious beaks from their Bibles for a moment, had remembered the legend of Samson and Delilah and planned to lead the mighty Prince astray, entangling the demonic Teuton in her coiling hair.

Delilah, Medusa, Jezebel. A succubus to ensnare his alabaster soul.

Hah! Clavincale smiled, pictured the bewitching beauty prancing on some Puritan's glove like a nervous hawk, her silver bells and leather jesses clutched between his gripped fist. He hated Rupert with all his being, and would have happily sown black-hearted, maggot-riddled roses on the Prince's grave, but Clavincale didn't believe the fanciful stories for a second. But then again . . .

He might be infatuated, his brain might be reeling and his pitted heart crushed to vinegar, but Rupert would never have betrayed his friend Richmond. Would he?

So what to do, if he could not hope to catch him red-handed in her bedchamber? Why, then, to spark a scene, to bank up a blaze from the few fuming ashes. To bring the raging demons in Rupert's tempestuous character to the fore in front of reliable witnesses. These breathlessly alleged midnight liaisons in dripping woods, brief sentences exchanged beneath the swinging sign of a lonely inn. Clavincale would stalk and snare his arrogant quarry, expose his boyish back-door intrigues, and then take cover from his wrath, take cover behind the swirling skirts of Her Royal Highness Henrietta Maria herself.

She despised the Prince as well as he did, jealous of his sway over her fickle husband, and nervous of his role as the most admired Protestant Prince in all of Europe.

Why, it was all very well for Rupert to rid the country of his uncle's enemies, but would he ever be content to be a mere nephew? What if this Cavalier crusader was to lead an army of veteran English warriors over to the Continent? The Catholic empires of Austria and Spain had already been crippled by going on thirty years of desperate carnage. One last Protestant challenger could tip the delicate balance of power all over again, tip the scales for good. Clavincale knew he had an ally in the Queen. Knew he could, as a last resort, take sanctuary behind her holy cause.

'Tell me again what you heard,' he prompted.

Gideon Pike sucked in his windrushed cheeks, took a shifty glance over his sagging shoulders. 'Well, I heard a sight, sir, a regular sight, if you'll believe me.'

Clavincale closed his eyes, blinked to clear his fogged vision

'"By the stars," he says, "Zwounds," he says, and a whole lot of sichlike stuff.' Pike waved his leathery hand, declaiming the small talk he had overheard. '"I'm for Oxford with His Majesty," he says.'

'He's going back? When?'

'Late tommorer, if I did 'ear aright.' Pike screwed up his thin bird's bill of a nose. 'So she says, "When am I to see yer agin?" and 'e says, when he can, he'll get away, only he can't tonight, as he's got to see the doctor. As is why I'm 'ere along with you and not back there keepin' me eye on 'im as yer bid me.'

Clavincale nodded thoughtfully. 'The doctor?'

'Chillingworth. 'Elps out with the mathematikals and whatnot for the mines and sichlike.'

'He could be seeing her later,' he exclaimed.

Gideon Pike shook his head. 'Horses are all in an' bedded down. He's 'avin' a night off, I'd wager me life on it. I wager he needs it too, eh?' Gideon winked.

Clavincale sat back on his bow-legged stool, ran his thick tongue over his teeth. He could hardly believe, hardly dare credit what this dribbling cretin was reporting.

'That isn't much. Twenty score rogues are saying the same to other men's wives within a pistol shot of where we

177

sit now,' Clavincale growled, undermined by another surge
of doubt. 'Didn't he say anything else?'

Gideon Pike frowned. 'Not as I could rightly recall, sir.
They'd gone off the lane b'then, see, sir, and followed the
cinder path t'wards the fishponds. Them'd 'eard I a mile
off, cracklin' along, like.'

'So you didn't see him kiss her? Interfere with the lady's
clothing?'

Pike's amber eyes sparkled as he considered this tantalizing possibility. 'They were's close as you or I, sir,' he
leered. Clavincale leaned away an inch. 'So close their
very breath intertwined in the lewdest way you'd 'ave
thought . . .'

'Did he kiss her?'

''S 'ard to say rightly, sir. They looked certain to, if
you'll take m' meanin', then leaned apart all cutesey like,
's if they wuz 'fraid to!'

'And then they parted?'

'Tother side o' the 'edge.'

Clavincale paused for a moment. What twist of fate had
deposited him here, in a secluded inn on the Cirencester
road, miles from the furious activity centred on Gloucester? There was no room anywhere nearer the King's
cramped quarters, no room for a gentleman of his standing at any rate. And Bella would have turned up her pretty
nose at the thought of sharing a tent with Nybb. He smiled,
tweaked his velvet-clad elbows in smug delight. They had
imagined themselves stranded in a social wilderness, left
high and dry in this lousy backwater, a couple of lepers
isolated from the delightful round of suppers and parties
at the King's temporary headquarters. Four miles from the
nods and whispers, the gossip and the glamour of the
travelling court.

They hadn't chosen the Black Dog, why, no man of manners ever would, but Rupert had chosen it for his midnight tryst right enough. What better rendezvous, away from the flickering lanterns of the camp and the flickering tongues of the serpent court? A well-known landmark which ought to have been safely out of earshot of any spy, a coaching inn on a remote crossroads surrounded by thick woods with leafy lanes and shadowed clearings, a short gallop from the King's headquarters, a lazy trot from the various military encampments scattered about the county, and a thoughtful walk from the whistling trenches and waterlogged mines.

Fate had delivered this precious peacock of a prince into his lap. All he need do was watch and wait. Rupert had set snares enough of his own.

'And he rode straight back to the Park?'

'By the main road, aye, and then ways I've never found in all my twenny-odd years,' Gideon Pike allowed, grudgingly.

Clavincale slapped his dry palm on the upturned barrel. 'You've done well.' He lifted his fingers, Gideon Pike's eyes focusing on the silver shilling beneath.

'I 'eard you'd done well too, sir, you and your boys. Came within an ace of gettin' in ter town, if I'd 'eard aright? They say the Prince was reg'lar pickled, when he 'eard 'ow you'd done.'

Clavincale's smile slipped. 'Our attack on Friar's Orchard, you mean?'

Gideon Pike screwed up his eyes, raised his chin as he scanned his ale-fumed memory. Had there been any other attacks? Clavincale couldn't tell whether the man was serious or enjoying a sly dig at his non-existent military abilities.

'The calf slaughter, he called it. All them Wil'sher boys butchered, he says, and for what?'

Clavincale scowled, wondering whether the whole camp was discussing their disastrous assault. Thirty-eight dead and twenty-two missing, the same number again wounded, and the same number again made off into the night. God's wounds, nobody had suggested Gloucester was going to roll over and play dead for the King's Cavaliers. At least Nybb's men had reached the walls, which was more than could be said for this damned Prince's performance so far. He pursed his thick lips, rose to his feet, leaving the coin where it was.

'You'll have an eye on him? If he's for Oxford with the King as you say, he'll have to meet her tomorrow night. You'll bring word to me if he comes this way again?'

Gideon Pike nodded up at him. 'He's shown me short cuts I'd never have thought of, set my mind thinkin'. 'F 'e takes one again, I'll be after 'un like a lurcher on a coney.'

'And you'll be sure to call me out?'

Pike rubbed his sparse rusty moustache. 'I'll be sure, sir, rely on it.'

Sixty yards from the crowded inn and the dim lanterns were little more than flickers behind the trees, blinking like the bright eyes of night beasts.

The woman bowed her head, her hood falling over her forehead, masking her smoky features as the man tugged and pulled at her outer clothing. He grunted with delight as his hands confirmed what his fevered imaginings had promised. She was naked beneath the cloak, her slim body warm, as sweetly scented as a cinnamon pastry. She lifted the folds of her cloak and threw them about his hunched shoulders like a night heron's wings. His feverish devotions were smothered as she lifted her hands and eased her coral-tipped breast between his moist lips. She threw back her head, cracking it against the crouching willow.

'Are you all right?'

'Yes yes,' she snapped, impatiently twining her fingers in his lank curls.

MARKER HOUSE,

NEAR NORTON, GLOUCESTER

Goodwife Duckett, the gaunt-featured and beady-eyed cook, had taken an instant dislike to the boy, what with his outlandish city ways, flamboyant mannerisms, and dishevelled mop of dusty red hair. Why, he was no more than the whelp of some clever-tongued imp, sired on some doxy in the Gloucester stews, lousy as a hedgepig with manners to match. She gave him a black-eyed frown, watched the unwanted intruder as he slurped his mashed oats from the laden spoon. Goodwife Duckett didn't hold with Gloucester folk arriving unannounced on her doorstep, winding up her menfolk with stories of siege and strife. She wouldn't stand for it. If the master had been there she would have gone straight up to him and warned him off, although God knows Simon Layton wasn't exactly the most formidable man on the hill. It was good riddance her husband was dead, or he would have been filling up his head with rebel talk and traitor notions himself.

She scowled across the broad deal table, the knife-scarred altar where she prepared meals for the whole household.

'If 'e's got to stay till Mazur Lay'n gits back, 'e don' need ter go on about the war and sichlike while 'e's yere,' she complained, pushing the broad-bladed knife through a turnip in a particularly vindictive manner. Nicodemus Burke looked up from his gruel, swallowed nervously. The stable boy and the smith's young son were used to the old cook's vinegary observations, and waved the boy on.

'Don't pay no mind t'er,' Randall Planter encouraged him. 'Mazur Lay'n's as strong for the Parl'ment as Gar and Oi.'

''E's no sich thing,' Goodwife Duckett snapped back. ''E's strong fer his pocket and little else besides!'

'Yer wrong, Mary.' Elgar Maynard, the well-built, sulky-lipped stable boy, piped up. 'Many's the time we've sat by the foire talkin' on the war and all.'

Goodwife Duckett tossed a turnip top at the dirty fingered teenager.

'Well, 'f 'e's so strong for Mr Pym and all, why's he sittin' up yere while them daft folk in Glo'zer get 'emselves sieged up by their ritful King?'

''E's bidin' 'is time,' Randall Planter theorized. The cook threw the diced turnips into an enormous black iron pot and turned the wet blade at the three numskulls by the fire.

''F it weren't for Mazur Jackson tellin' I otherwise, I'd niver have had him in th' 'ouse, spreadin' all his traitor talk!'

'It's not traitor talk, Mary,' Gar told her soberly. 'The King's goin' ter take men from over Oirelan way and ship 'em back ter fight us. What'll you say when 'undred Papist heathens come lookin' for supper, eh?'

'He'll do no such thing,' the cook argued. 'Not to his own true subjects, anyway.'

Nicodemus kept his red head lowered over his plate. He'd had more difficulty getting in to Alderman Layton's house than he had getting out of Gloucester.

The roads had been alive with troops, Cavaliers on steaming horses cantering this way and that, messengers galloping off to all points of the compass. He was forced to go through the woods, or take long detours across hideously open fields to avoid the carelessly manned checkpoints along the busy main roads. Nicodemus headed off towards the east, skirting the bustling camps about Kingsholm before heading north towards Cheltenham. He had spent the night rolled in his coat under a dripping hedge, risen the following dawn with his clothes weighed down by the dew. He flapped his arms about his chilled trunk to spark his sullen circulation and hurried on, taking a circuitous route roughly parallel to the busy main road. At midday he turned north-west, bypassed the tiny hamlet of Norton, and headed towards the river, keeping his eyes on the steep wooded ridges of Wainlode Hill. The humped shoulder reminded him of a resting giant, a great green travelling man taking his ease beside the broad, brown and silver Severn. The hill ran north roughly parallel to the Severn, rising suddenly from the windswept water-meadows and willow-crowned lanes round about. The southern spur which overlooked the beleaguered city was thickly wooded, but the local farmers had cleared the central plateau and northern slopes for the plough, enclosing the clay furrows in a series of converging drystone walls.

Nicodemus made out more details of the prominent landmark as he got nearer, skirting thorn bushes, jumping ditches, and tramping wearily across abandoned water-meadows. He had eaten the last of his bread and cheese and had been forced to supplement his diet with blackberries picked from the brambles along the way. It was late afternoon before he reached the old road which dissected the northern corner of the hill, and saw the tall red chimneys of the great house rising from a girdle of protective elms. Alderman Layton's comfortable if somewhat sober residence of dry red brick and undressed stone.

Trouble was, Alderman Layton wasn't at home, and his overseer Master Jackson wasn't in the habit of admitting strange ragamuffins off the roads. Nicodemus, reduced to tears of helpless rage, had been sent away with a flea in his ear.

He had wandered off in misery, completely at a loss as to how he was supposed to continue his sacred mission, only to bump into a pair of sweaty youngsters struggling to get a wilful colt into the rambling stables. House martins peeped and whistled as they darted in beneath the beams to their muddy nest on the far wall. Their constant comings and goings had unnerved the young horse, which kicked and bucked as the boys pulled and pushed it towards its stall. Nicodemus watched them complete their task, dismally wondering what he should do next.

'Oy! You boy! Clear off!' Master Jackson, the sandy-haired foreman, waved his fist from the kitchen door, immediately identifying the red-headed intruder as an enemy and impostor to the long-suffering household. The over-excited youngsters tied up the kicking colt and ran out to vent their sweaty frustrations on the weedy-looking stranger. They marched him off by the scruff of the neck, hauled the hapless boy behind the sheds to beat his all too apparent impudence out of him. Come up the hill after their jobs, would he? Nicodemus fumbled in his sack as they clamped him against the wall, and finally managed to prise his tobacco pouch out as a belated peace offering. He dangled it in front of their slow, wide eyes.

'Old Rustic, best Winchcombe leaf,' Nicodemus yelped

185

as they prepared to beat his face into the mossy bricks. The youths stood back, snatching the pouch, and sniffing the contents.

'Baccy, eh? I'm partial to a bit of baccy meself,' Randall Planter announced, putting his bad-tempered suspicions aside for a moment. 'Where did yer get it?'

Twenty minutes later the three of them had become firm friends for life, squatting down behind the pigpen wall with their dirty boots stretched out, blowing blue rings over the delightful hill sloping away before them.

'From a dead muskiteer, you say? Was he very bloody, then?' Gar Maynard enquired.

'Most of his head shot away,' Nicodemus said breezily, not caring to bring the unfortunate soldier to mind. The older boys had never seen a man crouch at the bottom of a trench with his blue gizzards slopping over his hands all steamy like. But the more he went on, the friendlier they became.

'Why dincher say you was out from the city? Old Jackson's a reg'lar Roundhead, ain't he, Randall?'

'I can't go spoutin' off to everyone I meet,' Nicodemus told the ignorant farm boys. 'They might be Royalist spies or sichlike.'

'Ah, I hadn't thought of that.'

His new-found friends helped Nicodemus finish the last of his precious tobacco hoard, and wandered rather uncertainly back across the yard after Master Jackson. The gruff overseer stalked back out from the cool shade of the kitchen, and took another squint at the messenger.

'Is it right, boy, you're out of Gloucester?'

Nicodemus nodded dumbly, thinking he could always claim to be a wandering village idiot if the grey-eyed foreman proved to be of the opposite political persuasion.

'I've been sent to ask news of Master Layton, and to take messages for London,' the boy volunteered stoutly. The foreman scowled at the miserable youth for what seemed like an age, his tired black suit rusty with wear, the buttoned collar of his shirt waxy with grime. At last the overseer nodded, and laid his calloused palm on the boy's trembling shoulder.

'Well, he's not due back till tomorrow, so you'd best come indoors.'

Master Simon Layton, city alderman and cloth merchant, turned out to be a stout little man with long grey hair and a neat goatee beard. His eyes were bright and mobile, his fingers constantly drumming against his chin, his table, or the side of his red nose. The long ride across country had flushed his spare features, and spotted the grey travelling cloak which he unclasped and passed to his scowling cook. He marched into the kitchen, one brown eye fixed on the ragamuffin boy shuffling from one foot to the other beneath Jackson's iron grip.

'You say you've brought some message out of the city? For me?' he enquired, casting a nervous glance at the door. Randall Planter, Gar Maynard, and his father Handy Michael had stationed themselves beside it, as if they were the guardians of some impregnable castle. Handy Michael was still wearing his greasy leather apron, his drooping canvas nail sack hanging from his belly like some terminal growth. His son had armed himself with a scythe, while Randall had tucked a crowbar into his belt and sawn the end from an old crook he had found in one of the outhouses. Layton was an indulgent enough master, but he didn't relish his entire household eavesdropping on his business. On the other hand there was little point in throwing them out now, as they all seemed to be equally entangled in this particular piece of mischief.

'Sir Edward bid me get news from you, sir. He thought you might be able to get a message sent on, sir.'

'And why would he think that, eh?' Layton turned round sharply, peered at the boy as if he had been dropped by a passing stork. 'I don't know him from Adam, or you, for that matter. You might have been sent out by His Majesty to sound me out,' he accused. Nicodemus swallowed, found his tongue at last in his dry mouth.

'Beg pardon, sir, but I know you. I've seen you at Braintree's sir, the solicitors in St Mary Street?'

Layton frowned, tapped his nose, nodded. He stalked over to the dusty bubble-eyed window, and took a quick peek into the yard.

'I was runner to Mr Rice, sir? Before he took off home, sir.'

'Took off home, boy? He made a choice, same as we all did,' Layton snapped. 'We have families to consider, as well as businesses.'

Goodwife Duckett raised her sharp chin a notch, and gave Nicodemus a superior grin as if she had just won a valuable point.

The boy bit his lip in anguish, took a deep breath. 'Yes, sir. It's just that Sir Edward felt you might, bein' a man of considerable clout hereabouts, have the wherewithal to git a message out to the Parliament. Sir. Before the city falls, that is.'

Alderman Layton sucked in his red cheeks and sighed heavily. 'Doesn't he know there's a war on? I could be clapped in irons for talking to you, let alone harbouring a rebel fugitive!'

Alderman Layton had been among the hard core of Puritan-minded gentry who helped run the city corporation, but he had stopped short at outright rebellion against the King. Rather than choose one side or the other, he closed up his business interests in the St Mary's district of the city and retired to his home to the north of the troubled town to 'let things die down a little'.

The confounded course of events that diabolical summer had borne out his eminently pragmatic approach, proved the wisdom of his deliberate caution. Waller was campaigning around the county with some success until he was called away to meet the growing Royalist threat from the far west. The loss of his army on Roundway Down, and the subsequent capture of Bristol by the Royalists, completely undermined Parliamentary influence from the Avon to the Severn. And now he might be called to task for any number of unguarded utterances which had been dutifully minuted by John Dorney, the town clerk. The loudest rascals were still shut up behind Gloucester's defences, but it wouldn't be long before the roving Royalists would be paying the cautious merchant a visit.

If that wasn't enough, here was that damned Massey sending him messengers, bold as you like across the lines, with Prince Rupert the black-haired demon himself sleeping a few miles down the road at Prinknash Park! The house might be watched already, some of the staff might even be secret Royalists!

'And I suppose you've some kind of note? Some written confirmation of what you're telling me?' he asked at last.

Nicodemus shook his fiery red head. 'Sir Edward said it would be better to learn his words rather than be caught with a message, red-handed like.'

Alderman Layton winced. Red-handed? They'd have

189

a sight more than red hands if the King's men caught them!

He glanced up at Jackson, his steely eyed foreman. A good, sound, godly man with a clever head for figures, right enough. His foreman was a frequent visitor to the local church, an impassioned preacher whose endless tirades against the heathen influences on the royal court and the hellish excesses of the Papist hordes in Ireland had turned a good number of his law-abiding tenants thereabouts into committed Parliamentarians. Layton was mortified at the ever increasing bitterness of his overseer's diatribes, but he couldn't afford to lose him. Away from the church he was as quiet and as God-fearing a chap as one could wish to meet, and the merchant needed someone he could trust to watch over his various business interests when his affairs took him off over the county.

He looked around at his small workforce, Jackson's Praetorian Guard. Planter and Handy Michael, and young Elgar carrying that . . .

'Git that bliddy stick out of here, boy,' Alderman Layton rasped. 'D'you want to fight all Rupert's horsemen by y'self?' he shouted, his country accent becoming more marked as he lost his temper. The downcast boys lifted the latch and made themselves scarce in the yard. Layton paced the kitchen and worried his beard.

'I'll be on my way, sir, if you can't help,' the boy piped up. 'It's a long ways up to London, but the city can't hold for ever, not without some hope, sir,' he said shrewdly. Layton winced as if Nicodemus had driven burning tapers into his vitals. 'How far would you say it was, sir, hundred miles? I can hitch a ride, sir, I can cadge a pony or something along the way.'

Layton waved his hand dismissively. 'All right, all right,

boy, there's no need to start strumming your harp around here.' He raised his chin, nodded at Jackson. 'I've been over to see Belcher – you know, the clothier at Stow. He's had word from his people in Buckingham that the Earl of Essex is going to march any day now.' Jackson absorbed this intelligence with a sober nod of his sandy head. Alderman Layton pulled his lips together nervously. 'Of course, you know what it'll mean if he does? There'll be a battle. A big, bloody battle.'

Nicodemus was vibrating like a freshly struck tuning fork, electrified by the wonderful news. The Earl of Essex, marching at last? He had to get back, right away, tonight!

'Belcher says they'll be lighting bonfires along the way, to warn them all they're coming.'

'They'll warn the King too,' Jackson pointed out.

Layton shrugged. 'As long as the city knows relief is on the way, they'll grant 'em surprise.'

Jackson seemed to swell up in the narrow kitchen, pushing out his chest beneath his tired black coat. He gazed expectantly at his master. Layton paced the room, came to a restless halt beside the fire. He closed his eyes in silent prayer as he came to his decision at last. He would help, aye, where he might.

'I don't want no fire lit on my land,' he growled.

'No, sir.'

'Better do it over by Saddle covert. Take the horses round the long way and then double back down the road.' Layton's red features had paled visibly despite the fierce heat from the range. 'You'd best get them rubbed down double quick and all, we don't want Rupert's nosy swines finding a set of lathered horses in the stable if we're to claim we were all here in bed,' he said, miserably inventive.

Jackson nodded, looked up to Handy Michael. The

alderman regarded his employees as they exchanged a quick, secretive glance.

'And for the sake of God, be careful,' Layton warned.

Nicodemus swore he hadn't slept a wink that night. He had imagined Layton would order his enthusiastic amateur spies out into the night, to set every rick on the broad hill ablaze and tell the city Essex was on his way. But instead the crafty alderman sent the farm boys patrolling the lower roads for Royalists while Handy Michael and Master Jackson busied themselves bringing down the dry withies from the hayloft and lashing the broomstick bundles down on the running-board of Layton's broken-down wagon. Nicodemus, unable to sleep, stayed up past midnight, trussing up the loose straw into handier sized faggots and rolling dozens of torches from the brittle stems by the light of their rush lamp. He sat up into the night, watching the men bending over their incendiary bundles, humming psalms and whispering as if Rupert himself was patrolling the yard. Their quiet conversations soothed the boy to sleep, and they carried him into the house and laid him in the corner by the dreaming dogs.

Next morning, Nicodemus was woken by Goodwife Duckett's bad-tempered mutterings as she banged and clattered about her invaded kitchen.

The excited boys rushed in and gobbled their meal while Jackson cut his bacon precisely, refusing to be rushed by the impatient youngsters.

Layton took one quaking look at the firebomb wain waiting in his yard and instantly cursed his hasty decision to support the hare-brained venture.

'By God, sir, do you want all the world to see it? Get the

tarps pulled over the wretched thing and get it under cover!' he instructed, heart in his mouth. Jackson and Handy Michael followed his instructions, taking a shaft between them and manoeuvring the heavily loaded wagon into the great barn. Randall and Elgar hurried over and draped the laden wain with grubby canvas rick covers, and dashed across the yard to prepare the horses. Layton couldn't bear the tension any longer. He called for his saddle horse and rode off to Uckinton to see a man about some geese. Please God the damned fools would be gone by the time he returned.

Nicodemus felt faint with frustrated excitement, closing his eyes and wishing for the night. Goodwife Duckett had prepared cakes and ale for their dinner, and the three youngsters took the loaded basket off across the hill to eat it. They straddled the drystone wall and shielded their eyes as they studied the magnificent panorama stretching away before them. The red-headed messenger gulped the breeze as if he was intoxicated on fresh air. He could see half the world from the windy mount, the winding roads and furrowed enclosures laid out neatly beside the broad meanders of the brown Severn. Away to his left, beyond the covert and over another looping circuit of the long drystone wall, a defiant farmer was still at work, his clay-shanked plough glinting dully in the afternoon sunshine. Why, a good bonfire here would be visible for miles around. The crowing King's men would see their light from Bristol, let alone the rat-trap trenches beneath Gloucester's walls. Nicodemus could make out the tiny white puffs of the cannons, and a few moments later the dirty brown cloud of smoke as an invisible ball thudded into the tumbledown towers. The city was still holding out, precious days after he had managed to slip out from under their noses. As soon as the damned fires were set he would be off, back to Gloucester and a delighted governor. Nicodemus Burke, hero of the city!

The dull rumble of the guns seemed louder by the hour. He realized the furious cannonade had picked up sharply since he left, as Prince Rupert brought up more guns and lavish supplies of powder and shot. The garrison had set up their own powder mills, of course, just as they had dug wells, diverted supplies, and boiled the brown Severn water. Nicodemus knew, however, that his master Sir Edward had been particularly concerned that they would run out, that they would be unable to meet the next Royalist attack with the usual volleys of musketry. He dropped his head into his hands, and watched the one-sided bombardment as the slow afternoon crawled past.

At last, long ages later, Master Jackson waved them in from their vantage point on the summer hillside. Randall and Elgar hurried to bring out the horses to draw the hastily patched cart. Handy Michael thrust an elderly blunderbuss under the sandpaper-dry bales, and shoved a bandolier and powder horn beneath the seat.

Goodwife Duckett scowled from the step as the boys brought out their own impromptu armoury, the farmyard tools with which they would rout the crowing Cavaliers.

Master Jackson squeezed past the muttering woman, an elderly buff coat thrown over his sober black suit, a broad leather belt tied around his middle. He had selected an ancient pistol and a dented, rusted morion which his father had worn in the days of the Armada.

'Ye're fools, the lot of ye,' Goodwife Duckett said

waspishly. 'Ridin' off like dirty hedge runners settin' fires and sichlike.'

Master Jackson pulled on his gloves, gave her a short stare. 'We can't stand by, not with folk fighting and dying in Gloucester,' he said soberly. 'Besides, there'll be no trouble, if we're careful,' he predicted.

The cook watched her remaining menfolk complete their preparations as the long-awaited dusk settled over the yard and the whistling bats replaced the house martins about the eaves. Handy Michael sat beside the grim-faced overseer, waiting while the eager boys tied the half-broken colt behind the wagon and clambered up delightedly on the swaying load. Handy Michael clicked the reins and the heavy shires between the shafts took the strain, easing the great splintered wheels over the cobblestones. The wain rolled and creaked alarmingly, surely alerting every Royalist between there and Bristol.

'God help you,' the cook muttered, closing the kitchen door with a final, fatal clunk.

The last seven hours had dragged like slowly melting lead, but the night seemed to accelerate away with them, carrying them off into the darkness on their great adventure. Nicodemus rode the rustling load, spreading his legs to balance himself against the sudden shifts and shimmers beneath him. Master Jackson had taken out his lantern, the dim light filtering eerily though the holed sleeve. Nicodemus could see the broad rumps of the horses, and hear the soft jingle of their harness as they took the long way around the great hill, the overgrown tracks over the deserted slopes.

Night beasts scuttled in the hedgerows and bats flapped and danced in some grotesque parody above their nodding heads. Nobody spoke. It was as if they were afraid of breaking the spell which surrounded them, helped haul the vital load towards the wind-blown summit. They left the track, and bumped over the rutted field towards the brooding plantation, a closely packed bonfire of thirsty trees and broken boughs on the southern brow of the hill.

'Bring the wagon around the front, and set it in the trees. We'll fire the whole covert if necessary,' Jackson whispered. Handy Michael manoeuvred the awkward vehicle down the slope, and dragged on the brake. The boys slid down the rustling tarpaulins and began to feverishly pick at the knotted ropes with which they had secured the covers.

'You, boy, off to the wall there, and keep an eye out towards the road.'

Nicodemus dropped the ropes and doubled across the furrowed field towards the drystone wall which marked the enclosure. He peered down the gloomy lane, but his eyes were immediately drawn to the bright fires which ringed his home city further across the dark valley. Great plumes of smoke were rent and torn by arcs of orange flame, by the sparkling comets of red-hot roundshot. The walls and towers seemed to be made of cake, poor seed cake all dry and pitted, gnawed by a hundred ravenous rats. The moonlight glimmered on the river, a black and silver snake recoiling from the man-made commotions. As he watched, a bank of fleecy cloud drifted across the moon, followed by the streaming outriders of a rather more formidable weather front. There was a bite in the air, a breath of moisture. Don't say it was going to rain!

God wouldn't soak their tinder before they had set match to it! Nicodemus's fragile spirits sank. All their efforts for nothing? He glared at the sky as if he could turn back the storm which was hurrying up from the far west, its black belly pregnant with rain and garishly illuminated by Rupert's puny fireworks.

He peered back across the field towards the silent copse, picked out the peculiar hedgehog silhouette of the wain as the rest of the party unhitched the horses and rolled the wagon into the crackling, tinder-dry undergrowth. He turned again, and watched the clouds encircle the silver moon, pull down its glittering defences in an instant. Nicodemus wondered about shouting a warning. Hurry up with the match or we're all undone! He cricked his neck, peering from left to right and back again. At last he spied a sudden orange glow beneath the black fingers of the trees. Jackson's face, lit up like an avenging angel as he thrust the tinder to his torch. Handy Michael, grim and silent, took a light from Jackson, and shared the spluttering flames with the farm boys. Nicodemus watched in frustrated fascination as they lit the wagon, corner by corner. Wheel by wheel.

Suddenly, a great tongue of fire leapt out from the massed bundles, the compressed faggots of withies and twigs. The flames twined into the living trees, sent sparks dancing into the packed undergrowth. The firestarters edged back from the conflagration, as if in awe of their creation. Jackson came to his senses first, waving the boys off with the snorting horses. Handy Michael shadowed the overseer with his blunderbuss as he strode over the field towards his lookout post. Nicodemus ran forward to meet the sooty foreman, lit up like a demon by the roaring blaze behind him. It seemed as if half the hill had caught fire, engulfing the sheltered copse in an instant. Jackson turned to the farmhand, nodded.

'I'll get the boy back, you get yourself off to the farm,' he ordered.

Handy Michael grinned, his teeth glowing white. 'It's a fair blaze though, eh?'

'Aye, and it'll bring every King's man as can ride up here within a quarter-hour. Get off with your boys while you can.' The overseer gave the farmhand a simple salute, and watched him hurry off over the lumpy furrows after the horses. Jackson patted the boy's shoulder.

'Right. Down the hill, fast as we can,' he instructed. Nicodemus had to run to keep up with him as he doubled down the steep bramble-studded slopes, tacking this way and that against the grain of the old hill. The light faded behind them, but the bright bonfire twinkled on the summit, clear for all to see. They picked up the rock-strewn bed of a dry stream, and half ran, half slid along its stony course as it dug deeper and deeper into the lower slopes of the hill. They hurried through another copse, then ran across a broad, furrowed field and took cover behind a drystone wall. Jackson threw himself down, crushing the boy into the nettles and brambles. His face was cut and stung and he would have cried out if it hadn't been for Jackson's calloused hand wrapped about his mouth.

Nicodemus heard the hoofs a moment later, a staccato clatter on the stony track on the other side of the wall. Muffled voices, an angry shout as the Cavalier riders spurred their tired horses up the steep slope. Jackson lay like a buff and black stone amongst the brambles and nettles, the boy's heart thumping like a culverin beneath him. In a moment the riders were gone, heading for the enormous beacon they had lit on the hill.

GREYFRIARS,

GLOUCESTER, 24 AUGUST 1643

T he guns crashed and thundered to a deafening crescendo before suddenly giving way to an unfamiliar and rather sinister silence. A moment later the brassy clang of the alarm bells rang out along the battered walls, from battered tower to woolsack-packed breach, as the dazed defenders waited for the final, inevitable assault.

But no assault came.

Instead of a squall of musketry and the hoarse yells of ten thousand blood-crazed attackers, the bewildered citizens heard the feeble tap-ta-rap-tap of a drum, and peered over their bruised works to see a pair of nervous envoys pick their way through the churned wasteland towards the gate.

Sir Edward Massey breathed a heartfelt sigh of relief and loudly praised the Lord when he heard the bombardment had been halted to allow the rather fearful emissaries from the King to approach the gates under a drum.

Talk wasted time, time he didn't have.

The weary governor made his way up to the threatened south-eastern sector of the city, pausing to inspect the inner defences he had ordered dug at right angles across Friar's Orchard. The new earthwork ran from the Southgate to the Eastgate, reinforcing the hastily patched wall which had borne the brunt of the enemy fire. Now if the enemy succeeded in getting over the wall they would face a new obstacle – a six-foot earth and turf bank protected by a water-filled ditch.

Their last attack had not even gotten that far. The Royalist musketeers rushed the vulnerable breaches along the south-eastern wall, but determined resistance and disciplined musketry once again blunted the furious Royalist thrusts.

Massey hadn't waited for the enemy to recover their strength. He responded by launching more sorties from the town, attacking the enemy saps up and down the line in a determined pincer movement as well as unleashing a river-borne assault towards Severn Street. His constant jabs and feints kept the King's men guessing, inflicting many casualties and seriously sapping the enemy's morale. Their men went about their work fearfully, wondering whether they were going to be attacked from flank, front, or rear. The officers shouted and bawled and pointed and threatened, but five more days had slipped by without a dreaded storm.

Massey was reasonably confident in the battered defences and the dog-tired fighters crouching behind them, but by then he had more pressing worries.

The enemy, thrown back from the walls, frustrated in their muddy saps and harried in their smoke-banked batteries, had burrowed deeper and deeper into the pummelled and ploughed ground beneath the towers.

The restless governor, an expert engineer, laid himself out in the dirt, his ear pressed to the ground to listen for the tell-tale tap and click of Royalist miners. He set up cunning devices inside the threatened sectors, balancing small glasses of water on top of carefully positioned drums.

He stood back with his red-eyed officers, and watched the water tremble, the nervous ripples exaggerating the faint tremors under their feet. They regarded the governor as if he was a buff-coated Merlin, a wondrously resourceful soldier/scientist who could match Rupert blow for blow – whether he was using his fists like a schoolyard bully or using his head like some student at his astrolabe. Here was Achilles and Archimedes in one skin.

Massey smiled modestly at his officers' admiring observations, leaned over and lifted the glass from the drum, and drained it in one businesslike gulp.

The enemy were undermining the walls. Picking apart the very sinews of the city.

He had been drawing up plans to begin an immediate counter-mine to thwart their efforts when the enemy heralds approached through the drifting gun smoke, the dubious drummer beating a frantic and unmistakable tattoo while the King's messengers waved a large white sheet.

'Does he mean to treat or draw our attention?' Massey wondered aloud as the nervous heralds were shown into the inner city under the suspicious stare of their former neighbours. They were blindfolded and escorted through the rubble-strewn streets to the governor's battered headquarters at Greyfriars, where Sir Edward met them with his usual dignified restraint, and listened patiently while the shifty-eyed lawyers rubbed their hands apologetically and repeated the King's gracious invitation for them to surrender.

'His Majesty is making a personal appeal to you, sir,' Mr Bell chimed. 'You must know Prince Rupert is satisfied as to his dispositions, and is even now preparing to unleash the final assault. I need not remind you, sir, of the consequences for the population should their Majesties feel themselves obliged to take that fearful decision.'

Massey nodded gravely, his large brown eyes immensely sad. The crafty lawyers wondered for a moment if the exhausted young man would see reason and agree to negotiate. Instead he wiped his finger beneath his eye and gave the negotiators a wry smile.

'Why, His Majesty made much the same request two weeks ago, when he first came before the walls,' Massey said reasonably. 'I do not find our case much altered since last we talked. My casualties are trifling, although I hear a pig was killed out by the orchard.' Massey's officers and staff stifled their smiles behind their gloves. Mr Hill frowned, taking a quick glance at the battered walls of the command post.

'A storm, sir, once unleashed, is notoriously difficult to contain. Your women and children would suffer grievously...'

'The women and children have decided to throw in their lot with their husbands and brothers on the walls,' Massey explained with a small shrug, as if he could not be held personally accountable for such lunacy. 'I am sure they are well aware of the consequences of their decision. Besides, it cannot be long before we have news of our relief.' He thought quickly of Nicodemus, wondered where the red-haired imp had got to. Was it too much to hope he had penetrated the enemy lines, that he had reached friends with news of Essex and his relief force? Massey glanced up at the envoys, but his fanciful thrust was far too clumsy to disconcert the hugely experienced lawyers. Neither of them moved so much as an eyelid in response. The unsatisfactory interview was terminated, the King's men blindfolded and escorted back to the walls. They seemed stung by the almost supernatural assurance of the defenders, blandly trusting in God to deliver them despite their impending doom. 'The King's men have taken over my house, you know,' Bell said apologetically. 'I had no choice but to bear their messages!' The messengers hurried back across the broken wilderness to the ominously quiet trenches.

A few precious moments later a saker gave a rust-bellied cough and destroyed the fragile silence. The bombardment continued, redoubled in intensity. Back in the mines below the smoky saps, a battalion of clay-smeared miners from the Forest of Dean resumed their work, picking, prodding, and propping the reluctant earth. If the King's men couldn't get over the walls, they would tunnel under them. Gloucester would, Gloucester must fall.

Sir Edward Massey walked the walls, quietly acknowledging the greetings of the sooty townsfolk, wondering what would happen to the same simple-hearted inhabitants once the battered parapets finally succumbed to enemy attentions and collapsed beneath their feet. The emissaries had been right. A storm, once unleashed, would be impossible to bring under control until the fighters had sated their bloodlust, thrown off their bestial battle frenzy and become men once more. He had seen storms for himself. A taken town was never a pretty sight in the morning.

'God bless you, sir!' Massey looked up from his gloomy promenade, and smiled weakly at the toiling goodwife pushing another barrowload of turfs along to the battered rampart. 'Ella Clamp, sir, from down b' the Southgate, sir, you remember?'

Massey nodded, wondering where he had met the

grinning matron with the formidable arms. 'How are you, madam? Bearing up despite the inconveniences?'

'Oh, I'm well, sir, and the old biddy's taken to the back room with all 'er b'longin's in a barrow!' Massey raised his eyebrows at this startling intelligence. 'And our John's well on the mend, you'll be glad to hear. Took funny when the buggers tried to get over the breach, sir, seein' double ever since. "No," I sez to 'im, "I'm over 'ere, you silly bugger." Not that it'll make much difference to 'is work, mind you, sir. Don't need to be able to see like a 'awk when yer laying turfs, eh, sir?'

'Indeed not.' He stared over the woman's rumpled shoulder as the grubby, gap-toothed Amazon continued her breathless commentary on the siege thus far.

'And there's my boys— Whatever is it, sir?'

Massey opened his mouth, nodded vaguely at the horizon. He had memorized every dip and hollow, every wind-blown peak, and could identify the familiar features despite the surrounding darkness. A darkness which was rudely illuminated by a sudden glow, bright as a wolf's eye in the night.

As he watched, the glow became a beacon, a great yellow glare on the humped shoulder he knew to be Wainlode Hill.

All along the line the agitated defenders raised their heads and squinted at the burning landmark. A great boiling brazier clear for all to see.

'What is it?'

'It's Essex,' Massey breathed. He turned, clutched the bewildered goodwife by her formidable forearms. 'It's Essex! He's on his way at last!'

*

The young colt took a snoutful of smoke from the wind-blown bonfire and reared in alarm, tipping Randall Planter onto the rocky path. Handy Michael cursed, turning around the heavy shire he was straddling and hanging on to the heavy harness as he slipped down awkwardly to help him. Elgar peered over his shoulder to see what the sudden commotion was about. He saw the smith haul his friend to his feet, the bay colt stamping and rearing as it tried to wrench the reins from the youngster's sprained hand. The figures were etched like black-lead statues against the orange glow mushrooming up from the wooded southern spur of the hill, the crisp summer night alive with wind-blown sparks tumbling over and over themselves in the fire's raging slipstream.

And on the ridge behind them, a lone horseman, his hellish mount clawing the sky with its front hoofs, whinnying to raise the dead.

O sweet Jesus, save us!

Gar Maynard's terrified shout stuck fast in his constricting throat. Even as he struggled to scream four more riders joined the intruder on the skyline, took one look across the open plateau, and urged their horses towards them. Gar gave a strangled yelp, loud enough to warn Handy Michael of the danger. Randall hopped beside the bucking pony while the smith tugged at the reluctant animal, beating it across the snout with the back of his hand.

The fire-spawned Cavaliers seemed to Gar to fly across the illuminated arena, closing in on their quarry in a moment. Behind him, the hill fell away steeply towards the broad barrier of the river. The Severn had chewed the north-eastern slopes of the hill away completely, leaving a steep shingle cliff rearing like a red wall above the wind-blown water-meadows. Gar's only escape route lay towards the open eastern slopes, the heavy clay fields which fell away towards Master Layton's house.

'Stand in the name of the King!' an angry rider bellowed, holding his pistol in his fist. Handy Michael boosted the boy into the saddle and slapped the pony's rump. It needed no further urging, hurtling away at right angles across the furrowed field. A shot rang out, clipping the smith's tall felt hat from his head. The terrified man raised the ancient blunderbuss, squinted down the trumpet barrel as the howling riders swooped out of the darkness and wheeled around him. Before he could squeeze the trigger the leading rider had ducked along his horse's neck, leaned forward, and tipped the farmhand into the cold furrows with the point of his sword. The killing blow looked almost elegant, a delicately precise lancing which hardly looked likely to break the smith's cheese rind of a skin. Elgar Maynard shook himself, kicked the heavy shire, but it did not seem to understand his desperate haste, and walked in a great ponderous circle towards the killing-ground western slope. Gar looked back over his shoulder, saw Handy Michael sit down heavily in the clay as if he'd been at the cider again, his stubbled head lolling on his twitching shoulders. Gar watched as the smith tipped his head back, stretching his dirty neck and releasing a sudden, shocking spout of black blood.

All of a sudden a red-clad arm reached across his breathless chest and grabbed the shire's heavy harness. Gar looked around in surprise at a young Cavalier in an enormous plumed hat. The rider had spurred to a halt alongside and caught the apprentice Roundhead napping.

'Sit still, lad, or I'll stick you like a pig,' the rider – no older than he was himself – growled with all the authority he could muster.

The other four Cavaliers spurred after the faster colt as it stampeded for the cover of a small copse on the eastern flank of Wainlode Hill. Randall would have been sure to get away if it wasn't for the drystone wall on which they had taken their leisure that afternoon. The colt refused the sudden obstacle, digging its hoofs into the soft furrows and hurling Randall out of his saddle and over the wall. The whooping riders spurred along the cart track, turned through the gate, and leapt off their horses. Randall Planter sat up with a wince, spat out a mouthful of dry clay, and looked up into the merciless black eye of a pistol.

Just then, the skies opened.

The storm Nicodemus had watched looming across the sky like a night beast crawling up a castle wall had arrived at last, unleashing its pent-up fury on the burning hill and cowering town.

The rain pelted the blazing copse, drilled into the surrounding furrows, and hammered men and beast as they made a dispirited return to the glutinous Royalist camp. Hoofs sucked at the suddenly churned mud as the two surviving Roundhead spies were dragged up to the watch commander's tent.

'Here's your firestarters. Crop-headed bastards,' the triumphant Cavalier cornet called, handing the reins to the captain of the guard. Randall turned in his saddle and looked at Gar. His hair was soaked through, and hung in long black snakes down his long white face. The watch commander picked his sticking boots from the muck and glared up at the stupid farm boys.

'You didn't think to put it out, then?'

'Too big for us, Richard, but this rain'll damp it out, aye, quick enough.'

King Charles stared out at the unexpected rain from under the dripping flap of the command post. An agitated runner had already brought news of the beacon – surely a sign that the enemy were on the move at last – and now they were told two of the three mines they had prepared to topple the walls had already filled with water. A number of miners from the Forest of Dean were either trapped or drowned. Two weeks' back-breaking work lost in a blink of the eye!

Rupert was furious, pacing the command post in sullen rage while the rain thundered and drummed on the taut canvas roof.

'Now all we've succeeded in doing is running them a nice bath,' his nephew growled, mortified with fury. 'No doubt that insolent wretch Massey will delight in taking the waters, cocking a snook at us while he's at it!'

The King turned, smiled weakly at his scowling commander. His desperately mournful expression shocked the young soldier to his core.

'Well, no matter,' Rupert snapped. 'We'll continue the bombardment in the morning,' he announced with a careless flick of his wrist. 'The walls can't hold much longer, and Essex couldn't keep pace with a three-legged tortoise.'

The King overlooked his nephew's hollow boast. His Majesty was completely at a loss. What had he done to antagonize God, that he should look so cruelly on their efforts to finish this wretched war, to stamp out this hellish rebellion once and for all? The bewildered monarch sucked in his cheeks and examined his surely immaculate conscience. What in God's name had he done to deserve this? The country tearing itself to pieces before him, a city prepared to be hammered into the ground before it obeyed its sovereign lord once more? Was he Charles Stewart or some evil, moustachioed sultan, a stammering Genghis Khan come to hang the heads of all the inhabitants from his saddle bow? All he wanted the fanatical fools to do was to remember their first allegiance to the crown. He would not punish them, he would make no examples of his own, misguided citizens.

Now even the weather conspired against him. He knew it, Rupert knew it, every soldier in the trenches knew it. The siege had been a disaster from the beginning. And yet what had he been supposed to do? Hide himself and all his friends away in Oxford? Allow the rebels to run his kingdom?

Rupert coughed.

'There is little more to be done tonight, Your Majesty. With your permission, I will retire. An early start for Oxford.' He bowed low.

King Charles waved his hand, and watched his glowering nephew tug back the flap and stalk off into the night. The King sighed wretchedly, desperately alone in this fetid wilderness of tents and steaming men. He would be glad to get back to his new capital, away from the filth and mud of this hateful outpost. A few hours with his queen and his excitable children, away from the war and the warriors. A few moments of peace was all he asked.

Rupert leapt on his horse and galloped to the guard post. He strode in and cast his furious black eye over the ignorant Roundhead farm boys his patrols had caught on the burning hill. The sooty boys looked up fearfully at the towering stranger, wondering who or what on God's earth he was.

'Who are they?' Rupert snapped.

'Boys, yer Highness. From Layton's place, sir.'

'They set this blaze?'

'Look at their hands, sir, covered in soot and sichlike. Besides, they stinks of smoke,' the gleeful cornet reported.

Rupert glared at the crying boys. Crop-haired apprentices, rebel ranters with all their shouting knocked out of them now.

'Well? Are you out from Essex or what?' Rupert wanted to know. The boys shook their stubbled heads miserably. 'Where are your friends?'

'We caught one, sir.' The cornet ran a grubby finger across his neck.

'Any more of them? Any more of you? Speak up!'

Randall Planter opened and closed his mouth like a dying tench. Elgar Maynard swallowed.

'N–no, sir. No more, sir.'

'Where are your flints, where is your tinder? Well? Did you find their flints?' Rupert enquired, shrewd as ever despite the drenching, brain-belting rain. The cornet frowned, shook his head.

'No flints, sir. Not on the dead man neither.'

'Then you're lying. Where are your friends?' Rupert snapped.

'Gone, sir,' Randall Planter blurted out.

'Where? Here? Into the camp?'

Elgar shrugged. 'Gone, sir, don't know where.'

Rupert sneered, glanced at the guard commander, who was looking as stern as possible despite the trails of

210

rainwater running over the brim of his hat. 'Let them draw lots,' Rupert decided.

'Lots it is, sir,' the guard commander agreed with a businesslike nod.

'Lots?' Elgar Maynard wondered aloud.

Rupert strode out of the tent and remounted his horse. He took one scowling look at the rushing clouds and spurred off into the night. Damn it all to hell. Now he would be late.

PRINKNASH PARK
AND THE CROSSROADS,

Gideon Pike was slumped in the warm hayloft, overcome by the lateness of the day, the stifling, mote-heavy heat, and by the rhythmic munching of the horses as they contentedly digested their supper. The rain drummed and rattled on the tiles, its varied cadences somehow satisfying – if you were lying up snug and out of it. He had positioned himself beside the loft door, where he had an excellent view of the yard and the busy lodge across the way. The squat, functional building was situated at the bottom of the steep slope just below the old grange where the mighty Prince had set up his headquarters. The various outbuildings had been taken over by a company of Rupert's blue-coats. His long-serving lifeguard had assumed responsibility for the security of the massive horseshoe-shaped park, and posted sentries at the gatehouse up the lane, and at the studded doors of the big house. Some of Rupert's more fortunate sentinels had obtained drier quarters inside the old abbey, and watched the surrounding road from the warmth of the attic window, where they occupied their time by carving workmanlike reliefs of the King in the waxy panelling.

Gideon Pike had fully intended to keep his watch through the night, but the warmth, the soothing lullabies of the shifting horses, and sieving rain, had undermined his good intentions, and he had fallen into a dreamless sleep.

The clatter of hoofs in the yard below tugged him abruptly from his slumbers. He peered out of the loft trap as three riders, cloaked and hatted, threw themselves from their rain-black horses and dragged the steaming beasts towards the stables. Gideon threw off his mouldy blanket and dropped through the loft hatch as the sodden Cavaliers shook the rain from their drenched clothing.

'Evening, sirs. A rotten night for it.' He nodded his sleep-fugged head, rubbing his knuckles into his eyes as Prince Rupert pulled off his plastered hat and ran a wet hand through his black hair.

'Rub them down and be sure they're fed and watered,' the German snapped, hardly noticing the servant's miserable existence. 'Have the grey saddled and ready to go in one quarter of an hour.'

Gideon bowed, fully alert now. 'Yer niver goin' out agin', sir, you'll catch yer death!' Gideon protested. Rupert had already turned on his heels and stalked out of the barn, his bone-tired officers barely able to follow him up the steep lane towards the welcoming lights of the big house.

'Well, we're done for if he isn't,' one muttered, wringing his sodden hat out over a straw bale. Gideon hurried to unsaddle the horses, hanging their gleaming tack on a nail. The two officers wandered out after their master, shaking the heads as they peered out at the rain.

'Tonight? He's welcome to it.'

'I wouldn't have the strength, the man's got melted iron for blood, if you want to know.'

'Melted? Ah, it'll be stiff enough,' the other replied with

213

a bark of laughter, ducking out into the deluge after his energetic master.

Gideon grinned to himself as he gave the three steaming beasts a brisk rub down with a handful of straw. He fed and watered them as instructed – woe betide the creature who didn't take proper care of one of Rupert's teeming menagerie – and hurried to the next stall along. He patted the great grey mare across the rump.

'Come on, girl, yer on,' he crooned to the wide-eyed horse.

'By Heavens, Clavincale, you might just as well have taken a bed at Tullymallock,' Ross 'Roy' Dunblane told the portly lord as they clattered rather uncertainly up the steep stair to the young lord's gloomy apartments at the Black Dog. The Scottish nobleman's outlandish costume of trews, plaid, and blue bonnet had silenced the rowdy clientele in an instant, and even Annie, the red-cheeked serving wench, was struck for words for once.

'Well, don't stare so, you damned hussy,' Clavincale scolded. 'Have another jug of mulled wine sent up, the best, mind you, not that rot-gut vinegar you tried to palm us off with last night.'

'Las' night, sir? Sir Gi'bert drank it all down, sir, sure enough,' Annie responded sharply to this outrageous slur.

'Sir Gilbert wouldn't know a good wine from wolf piss. Mind you, now, your best bottles, we've a long night ahead of us!' They clanked and tapped up to the draughty garret on the third floor, already three parts inebriated, flung open the door to find the merchant in question propped up at the table before a tray of pullet, cheese, and new bread. The jolly gentleman was as flushed as ever, his mouth smeared with grease and speckled with crumbs.

'Ah, Clavincale,' he said, waving the pair of them into the room, his merry bluster managing to raise the temperature a few degrees above the usual pest-house chill of the draughty garret.

'Where's Bella?' Clavincale enquired with a belch, flinging his hat onto the rumpled bed and easing his fleshy buttocks over the slovenly kept mattress.

'Oh, her! She's buggered— she's gone off for a walk. She says we are becoming too tiresome for her, with all our little meetings.'

'But it's pouring with rain,' Clavincale complained.

'Is the wee honey blob taken leave of her senses, wandering about on a night like this?'

Clavincale glanced at their shifty, moist-lipped guest. The Scot was clearly disappointed Clavincale's ravishing mistress was not about to drool over. Perhaps it was not a bad thing Bella had decided to take herself out of his way. She said she couldn't stand men with ale and brandy on their breath. By God, he'd breathe over her when she got back!

'Ah, well, she's wilful, there's no denying it,' he told her father, who didn't need to be told at all.

'Good wives don't grow from seed, you know,' the red-faced parent ruminated. 'They have to be guided, persuaded to your way of thinking, that's my way of thinking, anyway.'

Dunblane, a dapper, dark-eyed little Scot with a rather old-fashioned forked beard, leaned against the doorpost to regard this wonder of a merchant his friend Clavincale had told him about.

'You know Ross, of course, Laird of Tullymallock.'

Clavincale waved his wrist at the sardonic and clearly tipsy newcomer. Sir Gilbert exchanged a furtive glance with Clavincale, sucked in his rosy cheeks, and nodded enthusiastically.

'By reputation only, and a worthy reputation it is too, sir. An honour, sir, do make yourself comfortable, I'll send for more vittles.' He had already demolished the supper for three Clavincale ordered sent up to the room before he left for his rendezvous with the lively laird.

'You're too kind, sir, but I have already eaten.' The laird nodded, rolled one fork of his wet beard as his rather more formidable associates made themselves comfortable – tucking in to what remained of the feast with their usual gusto. Dunblane drained his goblet and allowed Sir Gilbert to fill him up from the half-empty bottle on the table. He gave them a minute or two, and then enquired what manner of evidently pressing business they had summoned him to discuss.

'I told you, Ross,' Clavincale said around a mouthful of succulent chicken. 'It is an exceedingly delicate matter, requiring the attentions of a, how shall I say, exceedingly experienced courtier.' Dunblane had heard it all during his long and wasteful sojourn at the royal court, whether in London before the war, in some whisper-filled Oxford cloister, or a damp henhouse outside Gloucester. The apparently aimless preliminaries introducing some dubious piece of mischief in which he would be prime mover. Aye, the scrapes he'd gotten himself in to, his old father would have thrown fits if he'd heard the half of them, Ross thought with a rare twinge of remorse.

Dunblane was the youngest son of Rory George Dunblane of Candlewood, one of the principal Covenanter Lords who were presently running Scotland in league with the all powerful Marquess of Argyll. Young Ross, a sprightly fencer and notorious rake, hadn't seen eye to eye with his stuffy Presbyterian parents, and had left home with name, reputation, and very little else four years before, hoping to find a place at the colourful and glamorous Stewart household in England. Auld Rory had cut the boy out completely, left him with one draughty old tower at Tullymallock, but Ross had more than enough cunning to live off his wits (and his various mistresses) and had managed to hold on to a slender toehold at court ever since.

If he had kept up better relations with his powerful father the lad might have been a useful ally to the King in his clumsy and blundering attempts to pacify his unruly Scots subjects. Dunblane could have been sent north with the King's sweetest greetings and protestations of undying loyalty to the land of his forefathers, and to their most deeply and truly respected religion. A useful feeler to the stony-faced cabal which ran the north and highlands. Auld Rory had the ear of the great clan Campbell chieftain Argyll himself, and if he could have been convinced of Charles Stewart's honourable intentions then between them they might even have managed to form some kind of alliance against the tumultuous power of Parliament.

But the Scots, united in one religion and boasting a large, well-trained, and disciplined army, seemed to be drifting instead towards an understanding with the rebels rather than their rightful King. That was according to the rumour-mongers at court, anyway. Dunblane doubted the Covenanters would ever risk such a dangerous liaison. If his father was anything to go by, the Covenanting grey-beards wouldn't share the steam off their piss let alone do the English Parliament's dirty work for them.

As it was, Charles Stewart had more undernourished and penniless young noblemen than he could point a stick at. Young Dunblane continued to hang on to his precious place at the bottom of the table, but until something turned up he was just another nobody with a shite-pit of a castle and a funny title.

The arrival in the camp of the powerful and influential James Graham, Earl of Montrose, had rekindled his interest in matters Scottish. What was a Graham doing in Gloucester? Straying so far from his wind-blown glens? Clearly matters were stirring back home, but in which direction? What was Montrose up to, trying desperately to obtain an interview with the troubled King? He would have liked to have asked the great Graham himself, but ancient family feuds prevented such a meeting. When he and Montrose had met in a rutted lane between the crowded camps they had stridden past each other with their noses averted. By Heavens, he would have liked to have been a fly in Montrose's tent. The court gossips had it that he was friendly with the great Rupert, and all.

Dunblane drained his goblet with a vengeance, looked up sharply at the overstuffed intriguers. 'Somebody who can hold his tongue, ye mean,' he asked sourly. 'What is it ye have in mind now?'

Sir Gilbert munched his cheese, allowing Clavincale to do all the talking. He poured the last of the strong sack into the Scot's slightly trembling glass.

'The thing is, Ross, we've received certain intelligences, about some of our esteemed commanders.'

Dunblane nodded, wondering if they meant his unspoken enemy Montrose. He wasn't surprised or offended by their sinister approach: intrigue and accusation were meat and drink to anybody who had spent more than an hour at Oxford. 'Our commanders? Which one?'

Clavincale smiled. 'Is it right that Montrose is down from Scotland? Trying his damnedest for an audience with His Majesty?' Dunblane nodded carefully. 'We hear Rupert has taken a shine to him, kindred spirits if you like.'

Ross Dunblane's smile slipped a notch beneath his foxy moustache. 'Aye, well?'

'Well, then. We hear Montrose has been offered a command with the Covenanter army.'

Dunblane tried to keep the surprise from his thin features. He mastered his mouth, smiled sourly. 'James Graham is a distinguished soldier. It is an understandable choice,' he mouthed, wondering if it could be true. Would the arrogant earl serve Argyll? Obey the powerful Covenanter lords, take instructions from the likes of his father? Dunblane doubted it. 'Well, if this be true,' he said slowly, 'what would he want coming to the King?'

If the recent rumours were correct, the Covenanting forces were more likely to side with Parliament than with their monarch. So what *was* Montrose up to?

'It seems to us,' Clavincale said guardedly, 'young Montrose is having second thoughts about this alleged command. Perhaps he would prefer to remain loyal to the King, should the Covenanting forces side with the enemy.'

Dunblane frowned, thinking through the puzzling possibilities. Keeping an eye on Scottish politics was like trying to track a red herring through a shoal. His head ached, the room swam like a barrel of apples. Big red apples with rosy cheeks and maggoty mouths.

'Whatever he's up to,' Clavincale continued breezily, 'it

seems he is having difficulty persuading His Majesty of his case. So he has turned instead to Rupert.'

That was true enough, the Scot thought through his alcoholic haze. Montrose would try to get to the King via his nephew.

'So Rupert holds the key to Montrose's immediate and apparently undecided future.' Dunblane nodded, listening now rather than trying to puzzle the angles. 'Now it has come to us that you and Montrose don't exactly see eye to eye. Something about an old family quarrel? I am told there was even talk of a duel?' Dunblane raised his red eyebrows. Where did this overstuffed Englishman get his information? 'Many more meetings like the one in camp the other morning and the Provost Marshal will be clapping you both in irons. I hear various insults were repeated at the Gay Lion Inn at Barton? Along the lines of "If that penniless shit-finger steps in my way again I'll run the wee cunt through,"' the pudgy nobleman recalled mockingly.

Dunblane's thin face paled behind his bristling, ale-tamped moustaches. 'He said no such thing. Did he say so? The rogue,' he muttered under his breath, staring at Clavincale through a beady, ale-addled eye. 'Duelling is expressly forbidden, by the King himself,' he whispered, belching into his balled fist.

'Ah, it's forbidden,' Clavincale nodded serenely, 'but that doesn't mean a man should allow such slights to go unchallenged. I'll get straight to the point, Ross. Sir Gilbert and I have as much cause to despise Rupert as you despise Montrose. Their promotion is our downfall, their success sours our spirits. Damn the braggarts, they need to be taught a lesson!'

Dunblane prised himself from the doorpost at the sixth attempt, nodded vigorously. 'Aye, yer right!'

'Why, I've a good mind to ride straight over to Prink-nash Park and confront the swines right now!'

Sir Gilbert grinned at his remarkable son-in-law to be. He was good at this, he would have to admit it.

'Why, sirs, I heard they meet at a crossroads not a mile from this table, and scheme and plot long into the night, safely out of earshot of all decent folk!'

Dunblane staggered, clasping the hilt of his formidable sword. 'Ye don't say?'

'I do!'

The wiry laird with his outlandish trousers blinked in furious delirium. Clavincale, who had been surreptitiously watering down his own wine all night long, leapt to his feet. Sir Gilbert glanced at him, nodded quickly.

'By God, if we're quick we'll catch the buggers red-handed!' he announced.

Dunblane was cursing in Gaelic and struggling to open the door.

'Let me at the scoundrel!' he said brokenly, staggering out into the gloomy landing with the blustering Englishmen hurrying after him.

Sir Gilbert ducked back out of the driving rain and gnawed his fleshy thumb in agitation. It was a risky business, cutting cards with devils like these, but he couldn't back out now – such craven behaviour would result in an immediate loss of faith. He shivered, blew a drop from the end of his red nose, and tried to get a hold of his jittering nerves. The three of them were standing beneath the dripping porch of the Black Dog, watching the puddles spread across the yard. Sir Gilbert had grabbed a bottle on his way down, and was trying to stoke Dunblane's alcoholic ardour. The sudden damp seemed to be sobering the hot-headed idiot as quickly as they had intoxicated him in the first place!

Clavincale took his place, peering out into the miserable downpour to watch the road. Sir Gilbert pulled him back, gave the nobleman an encouraging wink. Their plan was too ingenious to comprehend failure, he told himself for the fortieth time.

'They'll be along, don't you fret yourself,' he said with a deal more conviction than he felt.

To give credit where it was due, the broad outline of the cunning scheme had been formulated by Clavincale. A fine brain for mischief that one, he was sure to go far. What a stroke of fortune it had been to get hitched up with him!

Clavincale's sources had to some degree confirmed the breathless gossip about Prince Rupert's pie-eyed obsession with his friend the Duke of Richmond's bewitching wife. Clavincale's stable boy spy had apparently followed the Prince from his quarters at the old abbey to a secret liaison with a woman, and all indications suggested the lovestruck pair would meet again tonight, not half a mile down the road! It was too good an opportunity to miss, a marvellous chance to take the precious Prince down a step or three and improve their standing with his sworn enemy, Her Royal Highness Henrietta Maria.

To this promising end they planned to set a devilish trap for the headstrong warrior.

First, Gideon Pike would shadow the Prince from his headquarters at Prinknash Park as he rode north around the great horseshoe-shaped valley and along the main road towards Cheltenham. The old road ran straight as an arrow towards the crossroads near Brockworth. Shortly before the main crossroads, however, there was a small lane branching off to the left. The short-cut track ran through the woods and joined the main Gloucester road a mile or so beyond the crossroads, a short distance from the Black Dog. It was along this lonely stretch of track that Rupert had allegedly met with his lady love. If young Pike had his facts right, that was.

Cully Oates and Eli Pitt had been told to watch the lane and wait for Gideon. If and when the Prince rode past, Cully Oates and the stable boy would shadow the Prince at a safe distance while Eli Pitt galloped back to the inn to alert the rest of the party of the Prince's imminent arrival. Ah, it was trickier than a greased porker, clever enough to warm the cockles of your heart, Sir Gilbert thought, giving his waterlogged outer garments a vigorous shake.

'Why are we waiting?' Dunblane complained, his fiery spirits somewhat dampened by the dreadful downpour. 'To horse, man, to horse!' he urged, leaning precariously far away from the porch post where they had propped him. Clavincale patted the Scot's thrusting arm, although he was equally frustrated at the delay. He tugged the merchant closer, whispered in his ear.

'The fool was wrong. Rupert's tucked up in bed, not even that Teutonic halfwit would come courting in weather like this!' Sir Gilbert was about to reply when he heard the distant drum of a horse approaching through the sheets of slanting rain. The rider steered his foaming nag into the yard and pulled up in front of them. Nybb strode out, a great grey bear in his soaked coat, and grabbed the pony's reins.

The rider raised the shapeless, waterlogged rim of his felt hat and peered at the three gentlemen on the porch. Sir Gilbert squinted, recognizing his old employee Eli Pitt. The former farm boy and militiaman had, since their abortive attack on Gloucester's walls, become one of Cully Oates' trusted corporals, and had been enlisted as a messenger and clubman for the desperate night's work.

Sir Gilbert ran over their intricate and devilishly cunning plan once more, marvelling at their endlessly inventive scheming. Why, the great Machiavelli himself would have shaken his head in wonder.

Neither Clavincale nor Sir Gilbert relished the prospect of confronting the lovelorn Prince by themselves, and had wisely decided to take half a dozen hard men along with them. Nybb, of course, had agreed to come along – as much for the prospect of a good scrap as anything else. Telling was supposed to be there, but the idiot sniveller was away pining somewhere. Still, as well as Nybb they had Cully Oates, a reliable rogue, Zachary and Eli Pitt, who never asked too many questions, and the crafty stable boy Pike. Together, they should be more than enough to bring the errant Prince to heel.

Clavincale had also decided to bring Dunblane along. According to his would-be son-in-law the strutting game-cock was capable of just about anything, and would be a respected witness if it came to an inquiry into the Prince's nocturnal doings, helping to insulate the pair of them from the Prince's wrath.

Nobody could know how the night would turn out, but everything was falling into place so far, the merchant thought with satisfaction.

'He's on his way, sir, down the blind lane!' Eli Pitt reported, his excited features jewelled with rain. Nybb peered over his formidable shoulder.

'He's on his way, mineers. Time we were on ours,' he repeated.

Dunblane frowned at the burly bandit, wondering for a

moment what he had been drawn in to. Clavincale clapped him on the back.

'Come along, Ross, we'll teach the arrogant bastards a lesson!'

The young Scot blinked at him, his fume-laden mind sliding and slipping about as he tried hard to concentrate. Who were they hunting? It was that scoundrel Montrose, wasn't it? Wasn't it?

'Sir, wait a moment, if you please,' he mumbled. 'Ma heed's on fire, man, can we not go back to yer rooms?'

'Nonsense, Ross. We'll confront the saucy devils, we'll not stand by and let them drag your name through the mud!'

Nybb grinned at the drunken lord, winked at his crafty master. He had stuffed his pistols into his belt and drawn his sword. The notched blade glinted in the dim lantern light filtering from the inn.

'Come on, mineers, or we'll miss our quarry!'

The rain had turned the fishpond into a cracked and pitted mirror, forcing the frogs to take cover under the rustling sedge. The cinder path between the pressing, sway-backed trees had turned to mush, trampled and splashed by a dozen heavy boots.

The cloaked company strode towards the dark rendezvous, swords drawn, clubs handy.

Nobody spoke.

Nybb raised his hairy fist, bringing the plotters to a sudden halt. In the distance they heard the single frightened whinny of a horse. The German mercenary waved them on again, lengthening his stride. Sir Gilbert let the younger men press ahead. No point in being in the front rank if things got unpleasant. Dunblane was staggering along with them, barely able to put one foot in front of the other. Clavincale silenced his ale-addled enquiries by holding a wet finger to his generous lips.

Nybb held his lantern up, peered into the gloom. Rain slanted in over the trees and dripped from the hanging branches. Sir Gilbert squinted against the squall, and made out two riders crouched unawares against the storm, their horses stamping and tossing their bedraggled heads as their owners leaned towards one another, clutching white hands.

'Stand, sir!' Nybb bellowed, striding towards the hunchbacked pair.

Sir Gilbert jumped in his soaking-wet coat as a small dark figure leapt from the bushes to their right. Nybb whirled round, astounded by the unexpected apparition.

'Hold hard, you wretch,' Nybb growled, shaken.

The frightened figure clutched at his breeches, which seemed to be in danger of falling down. Nybb looked up at the unexpected intruder.

'Tellink!' he crowed, mightily amused.

BY
THE BLACK DOG INN,

NEAR BROCKWORTH,
GLOUCESTERSHIRE

'Telling?' Clavincale stared at the slack-jawed youth, caught with his breeches down like a boy in an orchard. He peered into the twitching bushes, and saw a white arm tugging at the corner of a grey cloak as its owner desperately tried to mask her nakedness. He knew without thinking it was Bella. His bones whispered it, his internal organs glistened and slithered with her lies and hideous deceptions. His hair crawled over his scalp like a handful of centipedes as he realized how she had enslaved and betrayed him. The arrogant flick of the wrist, even in extremity, was her all over. His mind boiled over in jealous rage.

'Telling!' Clavincale yelled, stumbling forward towards the wide-eyed youth.

A dozen yards away, the cloaked rider had registered and evaluated the sudden threat in an instant. He brought his left palm down on the wet rump of his partner's horse, and drew his sword with his right in one practised, fluid movement. He saw two riders reining in behind them, blocking the narrow path with their sweating nags.

'The pond, through the pond,' he yelled, as the

frightened brown mare reared, the startled rider clinging to its neck.

Nybb looked from his right to his left, saw the alerted Prince urging his lady friend away.

'Fly, fly!' Rupert yelled, tugging his own startled grey about. The moment's warning afforded by Telling's unexpected appearance had given the Prince the vital seconds he needed. His partner, swathed and hooded in a voluminous and rain-saturated cloak, sat up in the saddle, tugged her horse across the path, and spurred through a rank of spindly sedge into the shallow pond. The brown mare reared and bucked, crossing the obstacle in a series of spectacular leaps which drenched Cully Oates to the bone and spoiled his sight of their bellowing quarry.

'Stand, gentlemen!' Sir Gilbert, mortified at this sickening twist, shouted from the rear. Eli and Zachary Pitt stood by, drenched statues with nailed clubs, waiting for orders in the sudden chaotic swirl of the night.

Clavincale launched himself at the unarmed youth, lunging with his sword as Telling leapt out of his furious path and hurled himself over a log. Bella emerged from the bushes, clasping her cloak to her neck and staring wide-eyed at the gang of intruders.

Nybb ignored the boy, strode towards the Prince, at bay on his snorting grey mare.

'You'll stand, sir!'

'I won't!' Rupert roared. In the same moment he drew his saddle pistol and fired. The bullet screamed off Nybb's worn breastplate and careered into the night like an angry wasp. The impact stopped the big man in his astonished tracks, dumping him on his backside in the slush. He dropped the lantern, which rolled over twice, its frail yellow glimmer extinguished.

'No firing!' Sir Gilbert yelled into the sudden darkness. Dunblane staggered forward, his rain-tamped head rotating like a child's top as he tried to make sense of this midnight madness.

Cully Oates wiped the spray from his face, spurring his skewbald nag across the path to block Rupert's escape. He drew his carbine and held it upright, the butt resting on his thigh as he squinted into the confusion of shouts and blurred movement. Gideon Pike, terrified and chilled to his bones, didn't see the elder sergeant turn his horse across his path. He rode straight into the back of the bucking cob, spilling Oates forward in his saddle. The carbine spluttered in his fist as he accidentally pulled the trigger, the powder damp.

'Ballocks!' Oates spat, trying desperately to stay on his unfamiliar mount, and flinging the useless carbine away into the bushes.

Rupert wrenched his mare about and crouched low over its neck. He dug in his spurs and charged for the snorting horse, his sword gleaming wickedly six inches from the grey's flattened ears.

'The lantern!'

'Where's he gone? You bastard, Telling, come out and fight!' Clavincale yelled at the drenched undergrowth.

'Hugo, stay where you are!' Bella yelled back, shrill in the darkness.

Rupert flicked the grey mare's reins to the left, brought his horse in front of the rearing skewbald. In the fraction of a second he made out the bewildered rider, he struck. The sword clipped Cully Oates' left forearm, cutting through coat, skin, and muscle. Oates cursed, flung himself away from the dancing blade. The unbalanced pony tripped over its own hoofs, tipping the wounded man over its steaming neck. Oates landed in the bushes with a back-breaking groan, prised himself to his knees, and crawled away from the disastrous ambuscade. Rupert tugged the grey to the right and spurred alongside Gideon Pike, who in one terrible second saw a frenzied face and a silver scythe arc towards him. He raised his right arm to parry the blow, and hung on to his saddle bow as the frantic nag splashed and reared in the slush. He blinked, his face splattered with sticky warm blood. He tugged at his suddenly loose reins as the pony skittered away side-ways. Shocked by the whirlwind of steel and beast, he glared down at the trampled track, focusing through a pink mist on the bloody stump of his right arm, the trembling fingers still clutching the greasy ends of the neatly severed reins.

The ghost rider clung on with his thighs as the pony shook its head and cantered on up the path towards the inn, the rest of the patrol scattering out of his way.

Rupert took one look over his right shoulder and watched his partner disappear into the trees on the far side of the pond. He crouched over the saddle and galloped around the sodden cinder path after her.

'Telling! You scum-raking low-born candle-wasting whore-son, where are you?' Clavincale bawled hoarsely at the close-packed trees. He leapt over the log and thrust his sword into the tangled undergrowth, a brittle mass of creepers and vines, brambles and rustling ferns.

A white hand shot out of the dense vegetation and closed with supernatural force about his wrist.

'Hugo! Run!' Bella screamed, hysterical with fright.

'Clavincale,' Sir Gilbert warned, catching hold of his daughter's cloak and spinning her around. The wet hem flapped, revealing her cream thighs. Nybb, lolling on the ground, focused on her kicking legs, her neat auburn triangle which elongated and stretched as she scissored away from her fearful father. Dunblane staggered, his head splitting as he tried to comprehend what had happened. Where was Montrose? Wasn't Montrose here?

Telling blasted out of the bushes like a roundshot, came face to rain-streaked face with the panting nobleman. Telling butted him on the nose, depositing the lord on his back-side in the tearing, scratching brambles. Clavincale raised his sword but found his blow jammed by the undergrowth. He screamed in defiance, blinded by rain and blood.

'Hugo! NOOOOOO!' Bella screamed.

'Come away, girl!' Sir Gilbert implored. Nybb prised himself to his feet, lurched after the lantern.

'Where's Montrose?' Dunblane called. 'Montrose, you damned crofter, come out and fight!' he yelled in his drunken delirium.

Telling threw himself over the spluttering lord, squashing the furious man into the cramped boughs and lashing branches. Clavincale rolled over, his greater weight easily pressing the youth aside. Telling's breeches had come down, twined his kicking boots like chains and restricting his struggles.

'Anthony!' Bella implored.

Clavincale snarled like a cornered wolf, locked his hands about the boy's throat. He twisted savagely, pulling Telling's head back. Bella threw her father back and raced into the undergrowth, leaping over the log and landing like a cat behind her fiancé. She locked her fingers in his thick blond hair and tugged him back with all her might.

'Agghh! Bitch!' Clavincale released his hold and gripped her by the wrists, pulling her off balance. She stumbled over his hunched shoulder, landing in a heap of drenched cloth and bare legs. Telling prised himself up and landed an awkward punch on the side of his rival's head.

Nybb retrieved the lantern and peered into its darkened chest. Sir Gilbert had grabbed Dunblane by the coat and was pulling him off towards the hidden inn.

'For God's sake,' the merchant hissed, 'come away before he brings help!' Nybb, who had been in too many scrapes to lose his head over a bit of screaming, nodded dumbly, shoving his broad paw under Dunblane's armpit and boosting him back along the trampled path. Eli and Zachary had already taken to their heels.

Bella rolled onto her knees and saw Telling scramble off on his bare backside through the tangled undergrowth. Clavincale wiped his mouth, examined the blood-smeared back of his hand, and got to his feet, lifting the sword from the cinder path.

He turned, infinitely slowly, towards Bella.

'Bitch,' he breathed, vapour jetting down his bloody nose like a slaughtered bull. He took a step closer to the girl as she straightened up slowly, backing in to the mossy trunk of an ancient oak. 'Marry me for my money and make sport with your wastrel friend, eh?' Bella stood still, whimpering with fright. Clavincale raised the sword, the dirtied hilt glimmering in his smeared fist. He glared at her face, the beautiful features framed by the saturated hood of her cloak, her eyes filled with terror as she focused on the wicked point. He was close enough to make out the tiny flutter of a pulse in her throat, mesmerized by her superb neck.

He couldn't do it.

He couldn't pierce that satin skin, grate his worn blade against her delicately fluted breastbone and free the warm blood which pulsed so strong through her treacherous heart.

Clavincale blew out a huge plume of breath into the damp air and lowered the sword, just as Telling leapt back out into the attack, swinging a broken bough in a two-handed grip. The wormy wood broke in pieces as it impacted with a sickening crunch against the base of the nobleman's skull. Clavincale staggered forward, his knees folding up under his corpulent body. He dropped the sword, clutching at the terrified girl as he tried to save himself. Bella screamed, holding on to her cloak as his fat fingers clawed the soaked material, bunched in desperation around her midriff. Bella pushed his face away, propelling the pole-axed lordling to her left. Clavincale flopped over the moss-backed log, his trembling hands trapped beneath his stranded bulk.

His final gasps of agony were drowned out by the

sudden waterlogged clatter of hoofs as an unknown rider galloped back down the cinder track towards them. Telling bent down to lift Clavincale's sword, threw a protective arm across Bella as she trembled and pointed beside the tree.

Prince Rupert reined in his foam-flanked grey mare, stared down at the panting, bare-legged youth. The moment he had ensured his companion was safely hidden beneath a dripping elm on the far side of the pond he had reloaded his pistol and turned back, despite the woman's wretched appeals for him to come off.

He spurred back the way they had come, following the murky tracks of the bandits who had tried to cut off his escape. The scoundrels had fled, leaving a bloody stump of an arm and a spray of rosewater-red droplets over the path and surrounding vegetation. Rupert saw the commotion beneath the trees and closed in on the fiends, who seemed to have fallen out amongst themselves now. One look at the cowering girl and the lean-shanked youth told him all he needed to know. He glanced over his shoulder, peered on up the cinder path towards the inn. His grey mare jumped at the sudden shot which rebounded through the woodlands. The swine were coming back!

'Who are you?' Rupert snapped, holding his pistol steady as his horse stamped and thrashed the puddles. Telling wiped his mouth, his thin features as pale as a barn owl's belly.

'Hugo Telling, formerly captain to your brother's regiment of horse,' the careless youth snarled back, dangerously antagonistic given the Prince was reputed to be the best pistol shot in England. Rupert gave the near-naked Bella a cursory examination, as if her tantalizingly revealed shoulder and thorn-scratched thighs were completely beneath his interest.

The woman he loved with all his iron-bound heart had just ridden off into the wood – there was no other female on the entire planet who would have held his attention for more than a moment.

'Tell me you had no business with this ambuscade before I drill you a third eyeball,' Rupert threatened. Telling thrust out his chin, a posturing scarecrow in his ragged coat and splattered shirt-tails. Rupert had shot the weathercock from a steeple fifty yards high before this night. Now he was just a couple of feet away.

'I had nothing to do with it,' Telling announced, peering back up the path towards the inn hidden in the trees. They could hear shouts in the distance. Lights danced like glow-worms behind the shimmering vines and branches. He looked down at Clavincale, sprawled motionless over the log, the back of his fleshy neck seeping blood.

'This is her fiancé,' Telling said simply. 'I wasn't expecting him or her father.'

Rupert allowed himself a snort of derisive amusement.

'Your alfresco liaison seems to have saved me from certain embarrassments,' he breathed, ducking down to pat the nervous grey's neck. 'I shall not forget it. I wasn't here,' he leered, turning the grey's head and spurring off into the darkness.

His flight seemed to bring Bella to her frantic senses. She clutched and wailed at Hugo, who held her firmly with one hand and tugged on his ripped breeches with the other.

'We've got to get back,' he cried, trying to shake some sense into the half-naked girl. 'We can't be caught here,' he concluded. Bella was staring at the carcass of her fiancé, opening and closing her mouth in silent accusation.

'He would have killed you,' Telling reminded her, dragging her off into the trees. He used Clavincale's sword to beat a way through, dragging the blubbering girl behind him. Further into the tangled copse, deep into the woods. Away from the suddenly triumphant pursuit.

'Here's one! In the trees, look!' A wide-eyed musketeer stood splay-legged over the body, pointing it out to his company commander. The alarm had brought dozens of variously inebriated soldiers out of the inn and outbuildings, terrified they were being attacked, that the energetic garrison of Gloucester had launched another ambitious sortie. They milled about the yard in blind panic, dragging on coats and buckling on swords while a terrified gentleman pointed and swooned, peered about him as if he had fallen into a den of thieves.

'What is it? What knavery is this?' Captain Andrew Malvern, an undernourished and rather dour professional, threw the squawking troopers aside and peered down at the breathless colonel, who reached out and grabbed his knee as if it was a splinter of the true cross.

'Robbers! Bandits in the trees!'

Malvern looked up, his calico shirt spotted by the squalling rain. He tugged out his sword and waved his men towards the stile where their unfortunate victim was pointing.

'They've got my daughter! Fiends!' the portly gentleman cried as he tried to stand. Half a dozen men hauled him to his feet. The man peered about the yard as if he was getting his bearings. He took a deep breath.

'We were out walking, my daughter and my friends, when we were set upon by the path there.' An advanced guard of musketeers had already doubled over the gate and were hurrying down the cinder track, holding their lanterns up to illuminate the ghostly trees and bushes.

'Who fired that shot?' Malvern wanted to know

The white-haired red-cheeked gentlemen's busy eyes flickered from him to the woods. 'Why . . . the robbers. My daughter! My lord Clavincale!'

'Clavincale? He's with her?' Malvern demanded.

The mortified gentleman nodded, mopping his sopping brow with the corner of his cloak.

'No shooting till I say so!' Malvern bawled, and doubled after his men.

They found the first of them a hundred yards beyond the gate, a small, boyish body partially concealed by the overhanging vegetation. Malvern hurried over to the shouting musketeer and squinted down at the man. He was wearing trews, long riding trousers popular in Scotland, and a short leather coat beneath his ruckled-up cloak. The musketeer bent down and tipped the man over on his back. He had been shot in the side of the head, his pale features and foxy red moustaches sooty with the discharge and clogged with blood despite the rain which sluiced down over them. The musketeer bent down and rifled through the man's saturated clothing, holding up a small leather purse.

'The robbers are close, they've not had time to strip 'em,' he observed.

'Or they're not robbers at all,' the captain muttered, glaring at the closely packed trees. There seemed to be any number of fresh trails stamped into the undergrowth, as if the bandits had just taken to the heels.

'You lot get in there after them,' he barked. 'The rest, with me!'

Malvern wiped his eyes and hurried on along the trampled path after his noisy men. He saw a gang of them tugging and tearing at a prancing pony, the rider swaying drunkenly as they restrained his terrified mount.

Malvern sprinted down the path and barged his way through the shouting mob, grabbed the bridle as the frantic pony tried to buck and kick its rain-splashed captors. Malvern glanced up at the rider, a thin, sickly looking farmhand in a blood-splattered short coat. He was gazing disbelievingly at his right arm, severed below the elbow and gushing his lifeblood in a scarlet stream over the horse, the sodden saddle, and trampled cinder path. His white face was pinched, his lips blue.

'Here's one of 'em, at any rate,' a corporal yelled.

'Aye, but not for long. The bastard's bleeding to death. Take him back to the house and get what little he's got left bandaged!' Malvern ordered. He reached the trampled path beside the fishpond, and shook his head in wonder as he saw his men crowding about another body. A gentleman this time, in a filthy light-blue suit, smeared in mud and soaked through. He too had kept his full purse and five fingerfuls of gold rings. Malvern's feverishly excited troopers were walking up and down the path, following the confusing trails of hoof prints and boot steps, pointing out the variously converging tracks.

'More than one horse. At least three,' one shouted.

'And they came through 'ere, look, see how they chopped the brambles down!'

Malvern straightened up and examined the breach in the surrounding undergrowth. He frowned.

'You fools. The coils have been pushed in, not out.

238

They went that way!' He ducked his head and hacked his way through the tunnel, his men pressing in close behind him.

Three hundred yards back up the path, Telling and Bella slipped out of the tangled brush and hurried towards the inn. The yard was still in an uproar, and the terrified youth pulled the girl back before she walked right out in front of the milling soldiers. He thrust her towards the kitchens, ducking under the bright windows. They could hear the cooks chattering excitedly as they crawled on their hands and knees to the side wall of the massive inn, and threw themselves down in the shadows for a moment.

'We can't go in like this,' Telling moaned, his face smeared with blood as if he had washed himself in a flannel made from fish hooks and thorns. His bare shins were worse, slashed and bleeding and trembling with cold as the chills crept through his bones. Bella swallowed, collected her reeling thoughts.

'I must go. I'll bring you a cloak or something.'

Telling, paralysed with fear and mortified with cold, could only nod dumbly as Bella straightened up and stepped out towards the front door of the busy inn. Luckily for her the attention had focused on the yard, and nobody noticed her slip in the hall and hurry up the stairs, leaving a cold grey trail of water on the worn panelling behind her. She reached her room and peered inside. In another moment she had snatched up the damp cloak which was airing by the wardrobe, and turned on her heel.

Sir Gilbert Morrison stood in the doorway, his grey curls plastered to his livid red head. His fleshy mouth was opening and closing like a dying roach.

'Father,' Bella said warningly but without any determination. The merchant crossed the room in one bound and slapped her across the face, knocking the astonished girl over the bed to the floor.

'Idiot harlot! Where's Clavincale?' he hissed, closing the door behind him and bending down beside his sobbing daughter. Bella backed away from her furious father, peering up at him through a squall of bitter tears.

'Where is he, fighting with that putrid sack Telling? Well? You've gone too far this time my girl, way too far!' Sir Gilbert lifted the crying girl by her ear. She yelped, prising herself up on her muddy arm.

'You're hurting!'

'I'll do more than hurt you if any harm has come to him! He's your future, girl, not some ragged-arsed horse-boy! Whatever got into you?' he snorted, as much upset by her woeful lack of reasoning as her wayward morals.

'He's in the woods,' Bella snapped, pushing her father away and shoving herself to her feet. Sir Gilbert eyed his daughter, a fearful grin splitting his flushed features.

'Tell me he's unharmed,' he encouraged. Bella dabbed her eyes.

'They were fighting. He fell.'

'He fell.'

'Hugo hit him with a stick. He's still there.'

Sir Gilbert covered his eyes with his pudgy paw, pinched his nose in agitation.

'Where's Hugo?'

'By the front door. He's scratched to pieces.'

Sir Gilbert felt another tidal wave of fury rush up over his grasping senses.

'I told them we were attacked by robbers,' he wailed. 'If this gets out, we're done for, all of us!'

Bella strode past him. 'I must get him in, you'd best take him back to the camp with you.' Her father rolled his watery blue eyes in exasperation. 'Tell them you found me wandering outside and put me to bed, all right?'

Sir Gilbert's mouth moved mechanically, as if he was chewing a sleeping wasp. He nodded slowly.

'Telling got knocked on the head trying to protect us,' he reasoned, as if he was testing his elaborate explanations on himself. 'I'll get word to Nybb to keep his mouth shut. Where's Dunblane? Who fired that shot?' Horrifying new panoramas opened up before the mortified merchant. Bella ducked past her fretting father and hurried down the stair past a gaggle of shouting soldiers. She let herself out into the night, and located Hugo hiding in the bushes.

'Here. Come in with me,' she encouraged the shivering youngster, crouching miserably in the mud. Bella hauled him to his feet, flung the cloak about him, and helped him towards the inn.

Straight into the path of the grim-faced captain of the guard.

BY
GAUDY GREEN,

GLOUCESTER, 26 AUGUST 1643

Decent quarters were rarer than hen's teeth outside those dismally standing walls. Every hovel, shed, and shithouse had long since been commandeered by some exasperated Cavalier anxious to make as good an impression as he could in front of his sovereign. Colonels shared rickety bedsteads while their disgruntled owners curled up on the straw. Lords and ladies made do with cramped garrets, and junior officers were glad to find elbow space in a broken-down barn.

Captain Andrew Malvern's pestilential living room a mile or so from the sodden saps of Gaudy Green doubled as a guard house and interrogation room, while the cellar and shed had been pressed into service as lock-ups, horribly crowded with filthy prisoners, drunkards, thieves, and would-be deserters.

A set of ruffian dragoons squatted on the holed porch, dismally regarding the rainwater gushing from the broken-down guttering and streaming past the haphazardly laid tiling. A scarred sergeant was running a length of hemp through his tobacco hands, checking for any wear and tear. A couple more prisoners had been lined up for that morning's work, and his squad had gotten the duty.

The storm had abated somewhat since the previous night's unexpected downpour, but the camp had been transformed from an admittedly muddy wilderness to a waterlogged morass. Men paddled through the unfamiliar paddies, or woke to find the brown slush had run into their tents or shelters, slowly soaked into the patched socks they had left out to air the night before. The broad virgin moats around the defiant city were filled to the brim by the obliging Roundhead rain, while the mines which had come so close to toppling those woolsack-packed walls were no more than vast mole traps for the unfortunate pioneers. Sodden bodies had been carted off to the depressingly busy pits behind the main battery, and still the city held out.

At this rate, it would be the King's cause lost at Gloucester, not Parliament's.

Captain Malvern stared out of the fish-eyed window at the miserable panorama of browns and greys, his weary bones gnawed with doubt about the conduct of the increasingly hateful war.

He turned on his heel and nodded his head as the garrulous merchant warbled on. And on.

'Yes, yes, Sir Gilbert, I know all that.' Malvern interrupted his choleric flow at last. 'But neither Lord Clavincale nor the Laird of Tullymallock are with us to verify your version of events.'

'So you're saying I'm a liar?' Sir Gilbert snapped, bated beyond endurance by this unblinking monster in the tired red suit. Too clever for his own good, poking his nose into his business!

'I am not saying any such thing, sir. But you must understand my difficulty, as captain of the watch. Two gentlemen murdered under my very nose, and this intelligence from Prince Rupert.' He clicked his fingers at the overworked clerk who was trying to work his way through a dog's breakfast of reports and dispatches ready for the morning muster. The dragoon corporal fished in his bundled correspondence, handed up a scrap of rain-damp paper which had been torn from Rupert's pocketbook earlier that morning. Malvern held the scrap up to his bloodshot eye.

'Having heard of the incident at blah blah blah, I proceeded to blah blah blah and can identify the body as that of Gideon Pike, a horseboy at my headquarters.'

'I don't see what His Majesty Prince Rupert has to do with this,' Sir Gilbert sniffed, mortified by the idiot German's continual and unhelpful involvement in his affairs. Why, he could turn the lot of them over to his uncle! No wonder he hadn't managed a wink of sleep last night.

Telling, beside him on the uncomfortable settle which had been pushed against the whitewashed wall of the decrepit hut, seemed to stiffen beside him. Aye, and he'd best make the most of it because he'd never stiffen ever again if Gilbert Morrison had anything to do with it! All these loose mouths ready to go off like a spark in a cellar full of powder! He'd be lucky to get out of this scrape with his skin intact, and that was the truth of it!

'I was rather surprised myself,' Malvern admitted. 'But he was here looking over our spies and happened to notice the blackguard's body lying outside.'

Sir Gilbert gave Malvern a beatific smile while rubbing a soothing hand over his raging belly. Didn't that Teutonic tyrant ever sleep? It was only just dawn, and yet Rupert must have safely secreted his lady friend – whatever her mysterious identity – returned to the park to change, and been back on his horse in a matter of hours. He'd pay for it one day, carrying on like Satan's favoured son.

Rupert had already dropped in to see the guard commander to hear the 'full and exact relation' of the night's activities, no doubt making sure his own precious name hadn't been mentioned. Well, if he kept his mouth shut, the few poor buggers left from Sir Gilbert's party would certainly be intending to do the same. If he started pointing the finger the whole sorry mess would come out in front of His Majesty. Sir Gilbert prayed to God the Prince would take the easy way out, put his pride aside and let sleeping dogs lie. Sleeping dogs? Why, Clavincale and Dunblane were doing a sight more than sleeping!

'Amazing powers of recognition,' the merchant allowed with a tight smile.

'They're sending the man's sister over to identify the body. But if it does turn out to be this chap Perch, well, obviously he was in league with these cut-throats who attacked you.'

'Obviously.'

'Even though there were . . . how many of you?'

Sir Gilbert studied the impudent captain through his merry blue eyes. How many? He'd never find out, not from him at any rate. As long as Nybb had managed to shut Cully Oates and the other two fools up. By God, he'd done a good enough job on Dunblane.

Hugo Telling had admitted fighting with the merchant's prospective son-in-law, but had strenuously denied having had anything to do with the Scot's death. The brainless young clot had been caught in Bella's room by Captain Malvern as he continued his investigations into the bloody affair, and Sir Gilbert had been forced to swallow his bile and admit that the snot-nosed sprat had 'developed something of an affection for my Bella here'.

Well, it was either that or expose the scoundrel and risk having the whole affair thrown out into the open. Luckily for the anxious survivors of the abortive confrontation with the Prince, Sir Gilbert had a damned good head on his shoulders.

Malvern had been eyeing the errant Cavalier with suspicion until Sir Gilbert threw a fatherly arm around the boy.

'He's been knocked about something cruel,' he improvised in a flash. 'He was dragged off into the bushes by the bandits, and has only just managed to stagger back to us. We were just on our way to find you, as a matter of fact.'

Malvern eyed the trembling youth, his blue body wrapped in a borrowed robe, his lank hair plastered to his numb skull.

'He was with your party as well?'

'That's right. We generally take a tour of the lines about that time.'

'The lines are four miles away.'

'The outer ring,' Sir Gilbert modified smoothly. 'My men are spread over a surprisingly large area,' he explained.

Malvern could believe that. From what he had heard about the old goat's regiment most of them would be over the county line by now.

'So you had been touring your outposts with Lord Clavincale, the Scotchman Dunblane, and Captain Telling when you were set upon by how many?'

'A dozen or so,' Sir Gilbert mused, nibbling the pad of his well-worn thumb.

'Mounted men.'

'Aye,' Sir Gilbert agreed.

'And you managed to run back to the inn to raise the alarm?'

'I fought the devils off as long as I could,' Sir Gilbert vowed, reddening.

Malvern nodded. 'And lopped a few arms off while you were at it, eh?'

'I dare say,' the merchant allowed modestly.

'And the sword you are wearing now, you were wearing the same last eve?' Sir Gilbert nodded. 'Do you mind?'

Malvern reached over and pulled the merchant's expensive Pappenheimer out of the long whistling scabbard. He examined the finely wrought weapon, nodding with appreciation.

'A good blade, Sir Gilbert. And one which would need careful attention. Have you washed the blade since the incident?'

The wily merchant scented a trap. 'Yes, I had to get all the blood off,' he explained craftily.

'Only there is a minute residue of rust . . .' Malvern ran his thumb along the flat of the sword, and examined the tell-tale red dust. 'Which would have in all probability been removed if you had washed the blade as you suggested.'

'I must have given it a quick wipe, then. It was damned wet last night, you know,' Sir Gilbert said indignantly.

'Only we managed to recover Lord Clavincale's weapon, which was also strangely devoid of any bloodstains.' Sir Gilbert was one jump ahead of him. 'And the Scotchman's blade was also clean. Captain Telling had not apparently strapped his sword on at all, not surprising really in the circumstances . . .' Sir Gilbert glanced at the miserable wretch squatting alongside. 'So you see, gentlemen, I am slightly puzzled how it is one of you managed to lop that wretch's arm off without getting so much as a drop of blood on your blades.' Malvern smiled devilishly at the red-faced merchant. Sir Gilbert pursed his lips for a moment.

'You disappoint me, Captain,' he said at last. Telling glanced around at him, as surprised as the gloating captain of the guard. 'You assume that we were forced to use our swords against these rogues? No, no, no. There wasn't time for fancy fencing, you know, it was the middle of the night, black as a witch's tit if you want the truth. All we could do was grab our bilboes and slash about as we might. I can distinctly remember giving one chap a most horrible blow to the arm, but a second later one of the rogues knocked me over and I can remember dropping my dagger. Gilbert, I thought, you're done for. But the rascal seemed pleased enough to pick up the knife and make a run for it *before* I could draw my sword.'

Even the distracted dragoon clerk looked up from his heap of dispatches at the merchant's increasingly outrageous fabrications.

'Clavincale will tell you how . . . Oh, my word, but my Lord Clavincale is no longer with us.' He dropped his head onto his chest, filling up with uncontrollable emotion. Malvern scowled at his curly grey head.

'Is this right, Captain, you defended yourselves with dirks which were subsequently lost in the struggle?'

Telling nodded miserably. 'I hit him with a lump of wood,' he said, wiping his running nose over his sleeve.

'Who?'

'One of the robbers,' Telling explained.

Malvern sighed. 'I see. And then they dragged you off into the woods before releasing you?'

'I escaped.'

'And ran straight to Sir Gilbert's daughter's room?'

'It's no secret he's giddy over the girl,' Sir Gilbert interjected quickly.

Malvern concentrated on Telling. 'The room she was apparently sharing with the late Lord Clavincale?'

'It's no—'

Malvern held his hand up, determined to pursue his point. 'Well?'

'I have been seeing Miss Bella,' Telling admitted, colouring slightly despite his deathly pallor.

'Behind Lord Clavincale's back?'

Telling nodded miserably.

'And your rival discovered your sordid little deception and challenged you with it, is that right?'

Telling's horrified features turned to stone. He was about to reply when there was a sudden commotion on the porch outside. The door was flung back and Prince Rupert ducked under the leaning frame and glowered at the miserable defendants. Malvern bowed his head as the Prince studied his mortified victims.

'Captain Malvern. You have completed your investigation into this nasty little affair?' Rupert asked, scowling at the red-faced youth sitting beside the worried merchant.

'I was just about to . . .'

'What are your preliminary conclusions?'

Malvern hesitated, knowing the Prince's reputation for dispensing summary (and effective) justice. 'I feel there is more here than meets the eye,' Malvern began.

'The colonel's party was attacked by a gang of cutthroats including the armless fellow outside, isn't that correct?'

'Well, yes . . .'

'But the intruders were driven off by the prompt alarm, yes?'

'Well, apparently . . .'

'Well, then, Captain Malvern, I don't feel we need detain these gentlemen any longer.' He gave the guard commander a fierce grimace of a smile. 'It's been a long night for all of us, and Captain Telling has his kit to collect.' Telling looked from the Prince to the startled captain. 'He's been transferred with immediate effect to my lifeguard,' Rupert snapped. 'I'm sure we'll manage to keep him out of mischief, don't you?'

Malvern blinked, his lawyer's brain pondering the puzzling permutations.

'His Majesty is well aware of the damaging effects these internecine quarrels can have on his officer corps,' he explained, as Malvern continued to look determinedly at his astonished prisoner. 'He simply will not countenance these domestic outbursts, and has charged me with stamping it out.'

'Well, yes, your Highness, that is . . .'

'So I will expect to see a full report, outlining the incident we have discussed, when I return from Oxford.'

Malvern opened his mouth, but thought better of arguing with the mighty Prince. Rupert turned to Sir Gilbert, sitting up hopefully beside the young blade in question.

'And you, Sir Gilbert,' he said with a small sneer. 'I feel it would be best for all concerned if you took yourself off to your bed for a few weeks, please, to ensure you have fully recovered from this . . . unfortunate incident,' he said, 'before you take to the field again.'

'Your Highness is too kind, remembering an old man's aches and agues,' he said coldly. 'Time was I too could have gone gallivanting about the country at all hours of the night without raising a sweat. It is a different matter now, of course.'

Rupert gazed through the merchant and the wall behind him. 'Then we understand each other perfectly,' he said shortly. 'Captain Telling, you will fetch your essentials and see me here in one quarter of an hour.'

Hugo got to his feet, the dingy room revolving around him like the uneven deck of a storm-tossed trawler. 'Yes, sir,' he spluttered, as the Prince stalked out into the weak morning sunshine.

Malvern compressed his lips, gave Telling a sour stare. 'A commission in Prince Rupert's lifeguard,' he said evilly. 'Not a bad night's work, as it turned out,' he observed waspishly.

Sir Gilbert prised himself to his feet, hauling the dazed youth up by his sleeve. 'As the Prince so rightly pointed out, the King wouldn't want all his officers' dirty laundry waved about in public.'

Malvern sighed. 'Another time, perhaps, Sir Gilbert.'

The merchant waved his pudgy fist dismissively, and shoved the bewildered boy out into the sunlight.

'By God, Telling, you were this close to hanging.' Sir Gilbert held his finger and thumb together, shaking his grey head in disbelief. 'You could have taken the lot of us with you,' he complained, standing back under the leaking porch as the dragoon guards opened the outhouse door and dragged out a couple of bawling prisoners by the scruffs of their shirts. The crying boys were covered in soot, the tracks of their tears shining clearly on their grubby cheeks. Hugo noticed the youngsters' knuckles were black where they had been rubbing their sooty eyes.

'Gawd save you, sir, it weren't us, like,' one complained. 'We was only along 'em to push the wain, sir!' The protesting pair were frogmarched into Malvern's hastily evacuated guard house past the wide-eyed couple.

'You could have hanged us sir,' Telling hissed. 'Whatever were you thinking of, creeping up on the Prince?'

'He shouldn't have been there, you ungrateful little fool. Don't you see that? He was in as much trouble as we would have been. Don't you realize who that was he was meeting?'

'I didn't see her face,' Telling accused. 'And neither did you. It could have been anybody.'

Sir Gilbert snarled with laughter. 'It was her, everybody knows it was her.'

'You dared draw a weapon on . . .'

'Never mind that, Telling,' Sir Gilbert answered, reddening again. 'We were only doing our duty, bringing the arrogant bastard down a peg or two. If it hadn't been for you making sport with my Bella under that tree it would have been Rupert in the dock, not you and me.' The merchant stamped off across the slurry, Telling hurrying to keep up with him.

'I never asked you to come creeping up on me,' Telling rasped, thin features flushing with unhealthy colour. 'And it was Clavincale as attacked me, not the other way around.'

'Because he caught you . . . embracing his fiancée.' Sir Gilbert boiled and hissed like an old kettle, unwilling to acknowledge his daughter's infidelity. 'Well, you can rest assured of this, Telling, you'll not come creeping around her quarters again. I'm taking her straight back home! Aye, I thought that would take the wind out of your sails.'

Sir Gilbert Morrison could hardly hear himself think over the wretched Roundhead's frantic screeching. He peered over the muddy road at the improvised gallows, an elderly and arthritic elm, and watched the dragoon squad wrestle the screaming boy towards the limp noose. The hemp rope had been flung over the lowest bough and tied off under a broken stump. He noticed Captain Malvern had come out to witness the execution, no doubt imagining how sweet it would be to see the merchant hanging there with his tongue sticking out. Malvern watched the mechanical preparations with grim-faced intensity. The men knew their work. The crying boy didn't.

'They tole us to do it, Maz'ur Jackson said so,' Randall Planter wailed, pulling and tugging at his stony-faced captors. 'For God's sake, sir, it were niver none of my doin'!'

Malvern waved the struggling men under the waiting elm, taking off his hat to wipe his flattened hair. The Roundhead spy who had escaped the decreed death penalty stood beside the officer as pale as a corpse, clutching his lucky long straw in his bunched fist. He looked to Sir Gilbert as if he had been hanged already, tearfully craning his neck about the bustling and completely unsympathetic camp.

'No use averting your eyes, laddie,' Malvern told him curtly. 'You knew what you were about. Spies get hung and that's it and all about it!'

'I'm no spy, sir, and nor's 'e! They made us do it, sir, they took us along 'ginst our will!' Gar Maynard maintained, rubbing his running nose, his thin features soured with shame and fear. His luckless friend flung his terrified weight about, trying to free his pinioned arms. A crowd of Royalist soldiers, sappers, and camp followers coagulated out of the murky swamp like a legion of the lost, attracted by the condemned prisoner's bullock bellowings. They seemed to sense that the siege was lost, that their chance to finish the rebellion once and for all was slipping away from them. These Roundhead bullies, these crop-haired apprentices were tough enough in a thousand-strong mob, but rope 'em out alone and they cried like lambkins, called for their mothers like milksop babes. They had been quick enough to join the traitors, and here they were swearing they had done no such thing. The boy's plight hardly moved the softer-hearted amongst them, let alone the crowds who had lost house and home and loved ones through their vile warmongering. Instead, stung by their miseries, they heaped scorn on the doomed youth's head.

'No Bishops for ye now, boy! That'll serve you for treacherizin' against yer rightful King!'

'Hang the bastard and all his kinfolk with him!' a gap-toothed old crone shrieked, her soiled skirts black with the moisture seeping up from the puddles. The river fever would take her inside a week, and she'd not go alone.

There was a dry cough behind Sir Gilbert's shoulder, and the merchant wheeled around to find himself nose to nose with his errant field commander. Nybb gave him a sideways grin, his yellow incisors gleaming like a particularly menacing wolf.

'How do, mineer?'

'Where have you been?' Sir Gilbert hissed.

Nybb raised his buzzard's nest eyebrows. 'Looking for you, mineer, all ist klar, ja?'

'All ist nicht klar,' Sir Gilbert rasped, lapsing into Nybb's peculiar camp vernacular. 'What happened to Dunblane? Telling swears he was all right when he last saw him!'

'Must have been hit in the mêlée,' Nybb volunteered, watching the shouting youth being held up beneath the gallows tree. The guard commander stepped forward and slipped the noose over the boy's terrified head.

'Mêlée, my arse,' Sir Gilbert snapped. 'You were the only one there with a loaded pistol. That could be us swinging there, not some damned misguided idiot of an apprentice.'

'Hold yer vasser, mineer,' Nybb objected, *sotto voce*, 'the blibber-klecker would have undone us all, shooting on.'

Sir Gilbert balefully regarded the buff-coated bear alongside him as the crowd suddenly surged forward to get a better view of the hanging. A dragoon beat a slow, mournful tattoo on a drum. The desperate boy was silent for a moment, staring about him as if somebody somewhere would come to his rescue.

'Randall Planter of Norton, you have been found guilty by military tribunal of spying for the enemy,' Captain Malvern bawled for the gloating soldiery. 'And as such you will hang by the neck until you be dead. May God have mercy on your soul!'

''Tweren't Oi, Oi tell yer, 'twas Mazur Jackson made Oi do it!' Planter yelled, his wrists bound behind his sweating back.

'Hang the rebel hound!'

'Burn the firestartin' bastard!'

Malvern raised his stubbled chin and the dragoons took up the slack, walking backwards away from the blasted elm. Planter stood on tiptoe, his filthy boots stuck to the earth by the clogging mud. The dragoons hauled back on the rope, raising the bundled boy off his feet. Planter's face flushed with hideously ripe colours. Blood red, beetroot purple, royal blue.

'What about Cully Oates and the other two morons? I

don't see them about this fine morning,' Sir Gilbert snarled.

'I've had words with my mucker Cully, and he with the lads. They'll keep their mouths closed, aye, and their bowels open,' he promised, watching the youth twitch like a hooked carp on the end of his hemp rope. The dragoons took the strain, holding the swinging boy aloft in front of the baying crowd.

'Rupert's been here already. He's suggested I take a holiday,' the merchant reported as the youth's right leg kicked comically, a dark stain spreading about his worn-out breeches.

'Ah, he's pissed 'isself an all. I fancied those for mysen,' a leering musketeer told his grinning cronies.

'Well, then, mineer, I reckon you'd best do as die Schwarzer says. The regiment's safe with me,' Nybb crowed.

'You?'

'Aye. Mebbe it will be helping me forget all I saw, in the woods, you know.' Nybb gave him a sickly grin. Sir Gilbert scowled back at him.

'Hand over my regiment to you?'

'I could always get to see Princey mysen,' Nybb suggested.

The merchant's shoulders slumped. He nodded his fleshy chin. 'Aye, well, then. Until I get back, at least,' Sir Gilbert allowed.

'Until you get back, mineer.'

Randall Planter finished kicking, and the dragoons lowered the soiled bundle into the trampled puddle beneath the old elm.

And still the siege went on.

PART THREE

REMEMBER, REMEMBER, THE FIFTH OF SEPTEMBER . . .

Humpety Dumpety fell in a beck
with all his sinews around his neck
and all the King's surgeons and all the King's knights
couldn't put Humpety Dumpety to rights.

Roundhead rhyme written about the
Siege of Gloucester

BY

THE SOUTHGATE,

GLOUCESTER,
3 SEPTEMBER 1643

The hushed congregation filed out of the church like so many shameful sinners, hats pulled down low over their creased brows. There was no time to stop and exchange pleasantries with the cabal of black-coated clergymen who hurried through the prayers that Sunday morning. No time to peer up at the lopsided weathercock on the steeple or the tiles clipped from the mossy tower. Sermons could last anything up to two hours or more, with the bristling preachers working themselves and their congregations up into a frenzy of righteous wrath.

But there had been no sermon this morning, only curt instructions to proceed straight to the Eastgate and help with the defences.

The citizens had assured themselves their city was safe, that the enemy floundering about in the trenches outside were dying like flies from the plagues and agues. They had almost begun to relax, joking and whistling at the Royalist works, flinging refuse and trading insults with the toiling sappers. They had all heard of the great fire on Wainlode Hill, sign surely that the Earl of Essex was on his way to relieve the town. They had rejoiced at the sudden deluge which had swamped the enemy camp and flooded their mines.

But the siege continued, inch by bloody inch, foot by

muddy foot, the snail-like progress of the saps and mines heralded by vicious bombardments which wiped the smug smiles from the citizens' faces. Red-hot roundshot blazed and crashed against the punch-drunk walls, paralysing the deafened defenders who quaked and trembled behind makeshift barricades, their features coated with a fine layer of grey dust so that a goodwife could barely recognize her man returning from his exhausting duties. Ghostly blue-coats shambled along behind the crumbling parapets, stopped to shoulder blocks of masonry back into the flaking defences.

Sir Edward Massey patrolled the length of wall between the South and East gates, the most vulnerable stretch of the pitifully battered defences. He had ordered a second rampart constructed across Friar's Orchard, and then reinforced the sector with a sconce – a broad star-shaped earthwork mounting four guns. Now, if the defences did fail, the attackers would find themselves channelled about a formidable inner bastion.

Massey had ordered a counter-mine dug near the Eastgate, to intercept and possibly collapse the enemy tunnel below. But the downpour which hampered the Royalist miners prevented the townsfolk from making any headway. As fast as the toiling drones emptied one pailful the filthy hole filled itself up again, draining the water from the surrounding swamps. Human chains handed buckets back and forth, but still the pit refused to dry. In the end, they gave up. The crippling work was sapping their strength and pulling fresh men in from the walls. Massey could not afford their sweating sacrifice.

Now, it seemed, the townsfolk could not be spared for their Sunday morning sermons. Hundreds of the bewildered citizens went back to their homes to change their clothes, gloomily convinced their end was at hand.

Ella and John Clamp had packed the children home, watching their tireless offspring leap the puddles and throw stones at wrecked hovels along the way. They hardly had the strength to walk home, let alone reprimand the gleeful boys.

'Ah, I tell 'ee what. I don't like it and tha's a fact,' John Clamp theorized, patting his pocket for the last of his preciously hoarded tobacco. Ella nodded grimly, her arms hanging like lead along her sides. She hardly knew what to do with them, without a bucket to haul or a barrow to heave.

'When was the last time John Hale missed a sermon, tell me that!'

'They can't be long away now,' Ella complained. 'You saw the signal fires same as I.'

'Another of their tricks, my dove. We don't know woss goin' on out thar,' her husband replied gloomily. 'Could be play-actin' to draw us out.'

The enemy forces to the north-east had already staged a bizarre mock battle in an attempt to convince the town the expected relief force had been beaten off in disorder. Shrewd citizens noticed the heaps of dead they left behind them later clambered to their feet in disgust and tramped back to their positions.

The weary pair shuffled back to their battered house, now minus a chimney breast and a half-dozen roof slates, and clambered stiffly into their dusty work clothes.

The enemy forces pressing in from the north, no doubt stung by the failure of their previous pantomimes, finally realized it might be a good idea to stop the citizens collecting turfs from the Little Mead. They opened a murderous fire on the collection parties, sending the startled women and children scuttling for cover. Now Ella had to walk even further to find what little green grass had been left in the safer quarters of the city. They picked up their tools and followed the crowds towards the battered walls, and were herded into a work party by a red-faced captain.

'Where we diggin' today, then, Cap'n?' John enquired, settling the long-shanked shovel over his creaking shoulder. The flustered officer pointed back down the wall towards the smoke-clogged rubble which was the South-gate. He was already wearing a thick bandage about his forehead, but the city was in such desperate straits that not even the wounded could be spared from working on the walls. The grubby youngster hobbled along using his halberd as a crutch, a wandering pilgrim leading the weary citizens into the boiling cauldron of smoke and shell around the beleaguered bastion. They tied neckerchiefs about their mouths to keep out the soots and smokes, and weaved their way under the groaning towers towards the woolsack-packed breaches. Soldiers and citizens were staggering this way and that in the drifting smog, hauling logs and heaving great slabs of stone. Their womenfolk followed behind, bent double under baskets of loose rubble and sandbags.

Ella and John ducked down below a great chewed corner of the walls, the stone blasted to choking dust by a constant flurry of roundshot and musketry. The continual soft thuds as the balls impacted into the punished rock reminded Ella of an army of woodpeckers, taptaptapping in some petrified forest. Larger balls hammered whole blocks of masonry free, sparked avalanches of powdered mortar and crushed stone. Some shots fell short, landing with obscene raspberries in the splattered slag heaps and puddle-filled ditch, sending up great spouts of liquid mud to add to the defenders' misery.

The siege had been going on for three weeks and more, and Ella hadn't seen anything like it. Musket balls whined through the perilously gaping breaches as the enemy snipers crowded into the dirt and ditches outside, trying to keep the townsfolk from repairing the vulnerable wall. Their long-range musketry was dangerous rather than effective, the lead pebbles they fired slowing as they lost what velocity they had. Men leapt up, startled and screaming, as the balls impacted against stretched arms or bent backs with enough force to cause vicious bruising without breaking the skin. Several shocked citizens were helped back towards the casualty clearing station which had been set up in the almshouses near the church, convinced they had received mortal wounds. They shook their heads and gaped when the red-eyed surgeon's mate pointed out the ball had not even punctured their thick hides.

'Keep down, girl,' John Clamp called, following his wife under the yawning breach and flattening himself against the soil bank alongside. Ella straightened her bonnet, her eyes running with the acrid fumes coughed out by the busy guns.

'Keep moving there!'

'More woolsacks here!'

The morning dragged by, a punishing cacophony of shrieks and thumps and yelling men, lost in a swirling sea of black and grey smokes which writhed like snakes up and down the shifting walls. Just when Ella thought her ears must burst with the hellishly grating noise, the bombardment ceased.

The defenders rose from their holes, took fearful peeps over the rearranged slag heaps and demolished rubble. It seemed as if an army of giants had made sport in the weary wilderness, tramped new pits and puddles in the shot-blasted mud.

And that was when they saw the fearsome enemy engines rolling over the petrified wastes like enormous crabs, their broad wooden tongues bobbing and rising as they waddled towards the reeling walls.

'To arms! Alert! Alert!'

The King's engineers had played their final cards.

A small army of carpenters, sawyers, hauliers, and rope makers had been labouring for weeks in the quiet grounds of Llanthony Priory, transforming newly hewn logs and badly cut planks into machines of war. The bemused engineers were directed by Dr William Chillingworth, a quiet, cultured theologian and mathematician who had been sickened by the foul rebellion which contorted the vitals of the island, turned father against son and brother against brother. He had stridden through the bustling grounds, tramped over heaps of sawdust and springy coils of newly turned timber as his woodworkers hammered and planed and nailed and roped long into the night.

He carried a roll of complex drawings under his arm at all times, and had become a familiar sight to the troops as he commandeered tables and chairs or broad tree trunks to spread out his confounded plans. He lectured the doubtful officers standing by with their arms crossed and faces set. He shoved careless carpenters aside and demonstrated exactly how his painstaking creations were to be assembled.

The Royalist command seemed as amused by his contraptions as the bored soldiers, but allowed him to form working parties to keep the rascals busy as the storm dragged on, day after sultry day. Only Rupert had taken the trouble to examine his plans, fascinated as always by the application of science to his business of warfare.

One by one, tower by tower, platform by platform, his medieval machines had taken shape. The siege engines had been fashioned from the heaviest ox carts, the reinforced axles supporting a broad bridge of stripped logs. The good doctor had explained the design a dozen times to his doubting artisans. The wooden pontoon would be rolled towards the town and driven into the broad ditch beneath the southern walls. The wheels would drop into the trench, bringing the broad wooden platform down to bridge the yawning gap. The troops hiding behind the three-tiered armoured tower on top of the unlikely contraptions would then lower the raised drawbridge over the battered walls and scramble over the completed pontoon, hurrying through the breaches while their companions gave covering fire through the loopholed shields. The rear of the platforms had been constructed like vast wheelbarrows, to allow the men sheltering behind the mobile wall to manoeuvre the complex trolleys. The wooden arcs were the size of a small house, bristling with gunports and held together with miles of hemp rope, hundreds of iron nails, and buckets of horse glue. The broad drawbridges which would take the brunt of the punishment had been coated in pitch and looted hides to stop the defenders attacking them with fire arrows.

The leviathans looked like monstrous engines from another age, some abandoned design of Archimedes shipped over the seas and centuries from ancient Syracuse.

A wheeled testudo from the armoury of Julius Caesar himself.

The doubtful Royalist soldiers weren't so sure.

'Wooden horses went out with the siege of Troy,' Sergeant Major Findlay, former gamekeeper and sharp-shooter, observed waspishly as his musketeers assembled like reluctant hoplites behind the oak-ribbed hulks. They had laden themselves down with extra bandoliers of powder and sacks of bullets, ready to keep up a storm of fire against what they hoped would be terrified and completely surprised defenders. Colonel Nybb eyed his scowling lieutenant, his pirate's beard parting to reveal a mouthful of conger-sharp teeth. For once, he agreed with his officer, though he wouldn't have admitted it for a moment.

'A learned fellow, eh, mineer?' Nybb asked sarcastically.

Findlay, the stone-eyed sniper, was the only man in the regiment who would dare gainsay the brutish commander. He held his feral stare, raised his chin a notch.

'I'm just saying. They'd be right enough if they were running over a bowling green. Those ditches aren't even, they're up and down and all over the place, I know because I've been in 'em.'

Nybb rolled his great turnip husk of a head, his eyes glinting with delighted malice. He enjoyed a good scrap, and Findlay was the only bugger in this damned outfit who was worth fighting. The rest of them were striplings and sprats, cannon fodder of the lowest sort.

'Been in 'em, mineer, but not up the other side, eh? Worried what you'll find other side of the wall, I'm thinking.'

Findlay remained impassive, leaning on his long gun

and regarding the commander with his usual carefree impudence.

'You just worry about pushing the effort over there,' he suggested. Nobody in the army would have dared challenge Nybb's tyrannical hold on what was left of Morrison's regiment, but Findlay seemed to relish their continual murderous exchanges.

'Right you are, mineer. Yours and Allington's men can push the barrows, I'll bring in a stand of pikes behind you.'

Findlay nodded, lifted his musket, and ran his eye over the carefully cleaned mechanism. Nybb watched him stride off towards his troops, anxiously waiting about the huge wheels of the war towers. He grunted something into his chest and drew his sword. The curved blade was notched from a hundred battles, but had been sharpened to a razor edge by a bewhiskered armourer back at the camp.

The bewildered dregs of half a dozen regiments climbed from their holes and shelters and formed up in front of their howling captains. A hundred yards behind them, a troop of horse went through an elaborate display, closing up by the right, wheeling to the left, trotting and then cantering into imaginary attacks. The weary footsloggers got the message. Nybb waved to his officers. Shea had buckled himself into his helmet like a hermit crab, his fearful eyes protruding as if on stalks. Allington, a lean and lanky veteran, had taken up a position on the right-hand corner of the shuffling pikeblock. If Findlay's marauders could hold the breach, the pikemen might just form an impregnable hedgehog within the walls, keeping the garrison from mounting an effective counterstrike. The great tottering towers creaked and groaned as the men bent their backs and took the strain.

'Have a care, mineers,' Nybb bawled. 'Vorwaaaaarts, march!'

Thomas Minter wondered if he was seeing things. Great jungle creatures crawling over the pitted wilderness towards the beleaguered city, the broad platforms wobbling like a shithouse door in a gale. The unlikely contraptions bucked and reared over the torn trenches and sullen ditches, their rope sinews stretching as the heavy drawbridges craned forward.

'By Heaven,' the bewildered musketeer snorted, crouching in a hole near the battered breach. 'Take a look over 'ere, Robin.' His colleague was taking a break, back pressed to a damp woolsack while he took great fragrant puffs at his long-stemmed clay pipe. As usual, the strong tobacco had taken the edge from his nerves, reduced the popping and banging bombardment to a soothing lullaby. He pushed his greasy felt hat back from his brow and peered up at his astonished colleague.

'W'is it now?' he slurred.

Thomas snatched his musket up and rested the worn barrel on the earth rampart. 'Houses are movin'.'

Robin Fry snorted with laughter. 'Go on?'

'No, they'm really movin',' the musketeer insisted. 'All swingin' and rollin', like. Pulled up from their foundations and rollin' along on wheels!'

Robin Fry blew out a gust of acrid blue smoke and prised himself to his feet.

'What are you loike?' he smirked, leaning on the splattered sod and trying to focus on the great brown woodlice which seemed to be crawling towards them, ladders and towers sprouting from their black backs like an ant's waving antennae. Robin Fry frowned, rubbed his eyes and looked again.

'I swear, Tom, we'd best give this stuff a wide berth from now on,' he said, shaking his head and taking a suspicious look at his innocently fuming pipe. He tamped the glowing tobacco out on the wall and ground the embers into the soil with his broken-toed shoe. 'It's fair 'avin' Oi on,' he said.

Findlay cursed and snorted, back bent to the groaning timbers as he helped push the ridiculous contraption towards the burning walls. The roughly hewn logs were grating his hands and tearing his nails to pieces, but he leaned over and dug deeper, his muddy boots raking the mud as he tried to find a foothold.

'Push harder, you candle-wasters!' he shouted, lungs bursting with the effort. His toiling troopers took him at his word, the engineers stripped to their shirts as they tried to keep the enormous engines moving. The solid oak wheels turned reluctantly, the squealing axles sounding like slaughtered pigs as the engines ground through the slurry. Half a dozen musketeers were being carried along behind the loopholed barricade, taking potshots at the defenders as their colleagues toiled in the hold below them. They were pulling back their pieces and reloading, gazing down as the red-faced galley slaves attempted to launch their towering triremes into Gloucester's moat.

'Push, push, damn you!' Findlay roared.

The pockmarked landscape between the priory and the southernmost stretch of the town defences had always been fairly flat. The defenders had not had the time to widen the medieval trench beyond the earth rampart, concentrating instead on the vulnerable south-eastern sector and gate. The good Dr Chillingworth had examined the defences through a perspective glass, estimating the height of the earth rampart and the breadth of the ditch which ran along beneath it. He had sensibly concluded this long, straight wall would be most vulnerable to his engines. In addition to the relative weakness of the defence, the broad heath beyond the priory walls seemed fairly level, and although the dotted tussocks and crops of sedge suggested low-lying water, the ground seemed firm enough to support the heavy machines. The priory where he had set up his workshops had been built on the eastern bank of the Severn, and Dr Chillingworth had reasoned that the broad river would prevent the enemy garrison from launching a counter-attack on his vulnerable contraptions.

But for all his brilliant designs and his unquestioned mathematical genius, the determined doctor omitted two crucial calculations. Firstly, the effect of the weather on his chosen ground, and secondly, the extent to which the besieging forces had unintentionally altered the meticulously balanced topography of the town's vulnerable underbelly.

The weather stayed fine for weeks, drying the ground, so that when the observant doctor ventured out on his nocturnal reconnaissances he was satisfied it would hold his engines. The sudden downpour a few days earlier had hampered his final preparations, but he did not judge it sufficient to soak the exposed heath.

In fact, the lonely wilderness absorbed the water like a sponge, turning firm ground to slimy morass in a moment.

270

In addition to Mother Nature's trying connivances, the Royalist engineers had diverted hundreds of gallons of rain- and ditchwater from their works about the Southgate. Bucketful after bucketful had been laboriously drawn from the moats and ditches and emptied into the narrow gutters they had dug towards the river, the muddy engineers hoping the swirling waters would drain along the newly dug canals into the Severn.

Swollen with rain and unwanted ditchwater, the new channel cut across the heath quickly flooded, spilling hundreds and hundreds of gallons into the quaking, shot-splattered ground.

Now, instead of a firm flat field of tussocks and tough grasses, the hopeful Royalist engineers had to contend with a waterlogged morass criss-crossed with natural springs and becks, and a narrow but deep and swift-flowing drain filled with filthy water.

The fearful soldiers were pushing Dr Chillingworth's precious devices straight into a marsh.

Sergeant Major Findlay knew something was wrong. The broad wheels were sinking further and further into the boggy ground. The former gamekeeper watched the muddy watermark creep up the solid oak structures as if they had strayed into a sedge-studded estuary against a swiftly rising tide. He grabbed the roughly hewn log walls as the tower tipped alarmingly to the left. The toiling soldiers looked up, so many muddy moles up to their knees in churned filth. The tower came to rest. Findlay ducked under the rear of the stalled engine and peered up at the men crouched behind the raised drawbridge. They were hanging on for dear life.

'Move to your right, you're overbalancing it,' Findlay shouted above the slow squall of musketry their advance had attracted. The men did as they were told, crowding in to the right-hand wall of the rickety tower. The engine creaked and settled.

'Right, push on!' Findlay ordered. He glanced behind him, saw Nybb and his pikemen creeping forward like a human pincushion, a forest of spikes above a patchwork press of red and green, blue and grey coats. The men advanced slowly, anxiously waiting for the engines to breach the walls.

The ungainly devices were peppered with musket balls as the defenders opened a frantic fire. Splinters and chips scored cheeks and blinded eyes. Still the machines rolled on, driven by the desperately sweating Royalists.

But for every foot they went forward, the huge wheels sank six inches. Findlay, peering over a clipped spar, saw they were still fifty yards and more from the medieval trench.

'Push, push!' he bellowed over the bedlam, the mad crackle of wheels and spars and twanging bullets. A lucky shot snapped the hemp rope holding the right-hand side of the drawbridge upright. The top-heavy platform immediately lurched forward, the drawbridge hanging by its left-hand hinge like a badly fitted cupboard door. One of the musketeers fell out, entangled by the ropes and sandwiched between the chopped logs. His shrieks of fright cut through his colleagues like a knife. The engine halted once more, up to its axles in black water. Findlay cursed. What idiot had ordered them to push the wretched things through a swamp?

'Pull him out, you jobberknols,' he yelled at his white-faced storming party. The idiot weasels hardly moved,

272

clutching the creaking structure as if they were balanced beside a bottomless chasm. They tried to take the strain once more, but the engine refused to budge, settling rapidly on its foundations.

To their left, a second engine at first found the going easier, the crew taking advantage of a slight ridge running left to right towards the walls. The firmer ground aided their progress across the whistling heath. But just as Nybb imagined the engine would make it to the walls it tipped up on its haunches, hovered for one gut-wrenching moment, and then toppled over altogether, its oak wheels trapped by the narrow, practically invisible drainage ditch. The hemp sinews snapped and cracked about the broken towers, the timber shell bursting like an addled egg. The terrified crew took to their heels to the jeers and catcalls of the relieved defenders. Nybb watched them run, a furious snarl contorting his warthog features. Before he could shout an order, the pikemen had begun to edge back from the ruined enterprise, opening wide gaps in the closely packed formation. Nybb stood and stared as Find-lay's men emerged from their ridiculous engine, popping out of the woodwork like rats from a burning barn. The last engine stopped as if afraid to go on alone. Nybb watched it tip to one side and come to rest at an alarming angle as its crew too decided enough was enough. The exhausted, mud-splattered men splashed and waded back towards the decapitated priory under the terrible glare of their terrible commander. Dr Chillingworth hurried up, his papers and charts shoved under his arm. He opened his mouth and pointed, and then looked down at his shoes. The water was already seeping over the buckles, staining his grey boot hose black in an instant.

Nybb shook his head and shouldered his halberd, and

followed his relieved regiment off the stricken field. He noticed the cavalry regiment which had been performing elaborate caracoles in the field beside the main latrine had gone. Taken itself off on some other errand or marched away from the damned town? Nybb's disgruntled speculations were interrupted by Dr Chillingworth, stamping his feet as if he couldn't quite believe the weather could have played him so foul.

'The ground was dry, I went out there and walked it myself!' the doctor told anybody who would listen. 'It was as hard as rock, as hard as rock, I tell you!'

Now it seemed even the elements were lining up behind the righteous garrison.

There was nothing more to be done than dig. Dig and dig and dig and dig until Essex arrived and caught them with their breeches down.

STOW ON THE WOLD,

GLOUCESTERSHIRE,
4 SEPTEMBER 1643

Long Col's pessimistic prediction that the new men would be whining to go home before they had reached Reading had proved a little too hard. But the combination of a cold snap, swiftly dwindling food supplies, and strict orders against looting along the way had certainly dampened their spirits. They marched past the cheering crowds on Hounslow Heath as if they belonged to Caesar's finest legions and were off to finish with that upstart Pompey. The first night under the stars was cold but cheerful, the new men too excited to complain about the creeping chill. They squatted about the watchfires while the old hands described their experiences at Edgehill, Lansdown, and Roundway.

'They should niver have kept still, see, the cavalry sitting there like brick shithouses while the King's men charged,' the grey-haired sergeant remembered with a shake of his head. 'We should have 'ad 'em, by rights.' The new recruits tugged their coat collars around their suddenly cold necks, while some of the more confident newcomers imagined their presence on that fateful day might have made all the difference.

Their long march west had already trimmed Stephen Talbot's baggage. He had lost several pounds from his snapsack and another couple from his waistline, despite the fact he had already consumed the rations which had been intended to get him all the way to Gloucester and back.

'Blackberries?' he squawked when he finally summoned up the courage to ask the glowering sergeant where his next meal was coming from. 'Very nice with a few apples and a pinch of cinnamon under a nice bit of pastry,' the banker's clerk and part-time soldier complained, 'but who's going to cook 'em?'

Long Col studied the overweight youth for a moment, running his tongue along his streaked teeth. 'You can pick as much as you like from the hedgerows, as long as you keep up,' he replied serenely.

'Hedgerows? Pies don't grow from hedgerows, man!'

'That's Elder Sergeant Muffet to you,' Long Col snorted, his thin veneer of patience cracking up before Talbot's thoughtless onslaught. He jabbed the musketeer in his chest. 'Now bugger off and bother someone else,' Long Col suggested, making his muttering way over to the drystone wall where his comrades had rigged up a temporary shelter beneath an old horse blanket. They had picked up discarded musket rests and pressed them into service as tent poles, and were relatively comfortable beneath the dew-soaked sheet.

'Moanin' again, is 'e, the bleeder?' Billy Butcher enquired, opening an eye as Long Col thrust himself into the reeking billet.

'A few Sundays with the Trained Bands and 'e thinks 'e's Hannibal,' Long Col said wearily. 'He'll change his tune when he sees the King's army lined up in front of him.'

But the King's army had not lined up in front of them. Not yet anyway.

They marched on, the formidable force dividing like a delta to follow several tracks and pathways.

Then the food ran out.

Then the order went around that there were to be no more fires at night for fear of advertising the relief force's position to the enemy.

Then the weather turned even colder.

Mercer's muttering men tramped along the narrowing lanes, suddenly aware they were being funnelled towards the full force of the King's army. At nightfall they herded together like cattle, hunched in their coats and whispered amongst themselves. The carefree legions which marched out of London bellowing psalms to the heavens had metamorphosed within days into an anxious mob of suspicious individuals, all too aware of their own frail mortality.

Dawn cheered them for a while, until the few berries they could pick along the way for their breakfasts set to work on their digestive systems. Within an hour or two of the sunrise the shuffling soldiers were passing whole files of cursing men squatting over ditches, their buttocks displayed to the mightily amused horsemen in the fields beyond.

The Roundhead cavalry hooted and whistled at the suffering foot soldiers, who tugged up their breeches and shook their fists at their aristocratic comrades. Somehow the cavalry always seemed to get better billets and better vittles.

'Course, they can bugger off over the country, can't they?' Billy Butcher observed indignantly. 'The country folk can 'ide all their gear out of the way of the likes of us. But them strawheads can track 'em further, do a bit of moonlightin' off their own backs. Why, I ran in to one of

277

Essex's lifeguard the other day who had more gold and goblets in his saddlebags than the entire bleedin' commissariat column!'

The furious foot soldiers peered over the hedgerows as long lines of immensely wealthy cavalry trotted over the open fields, their orange and tawny sashes and cornets snapping in the crisp breeze. They certainly looked a well-fed lot to the emaciated infantry toiling along behind them.

'Share your loot with us, you buggers!' Billy Butcher yelled. 'You can't take it with you!'

Long Col smirked on his pipe, content to let the men let off a little energy – as long as it took their minds off the coming battle. The presence of the horsemen seemed to buoy their spirits for a while, encouraging and reassuring them as they hurried on.

'There must be thousands of 'em,' Billy said, shielding his eyes to squint at the solid russet-coloured squadrons.

'There were thousands on Roundway, di'n't make no difference,' Long Col said gloomily.

'God was not with us on Roundway,' Gillingfeather piped up, working his heavily bearded jaw as if he were chewing a wasp. 'We should have pressed our attack on the town while we had the chance. Sitting on the outskirts waiting for them to give up, pah!'

'Sir William would have lost half his army, and us an' all, if he'd gone in mad-'eaded like that,' Butcher claimed.

'The Lord of Hosts despised us,' Gillingfeather wailed. 'He tore away our swords and shields as we were unworthy of the work ahead. He . . .'

'Well, it's a bleedin' good job you're not the general, that's all I can say,' Butcher interrupted before the ranter

worked himself up into another righteous tirade. 'You'd
'ave 'ad us all dead and buried long since!'

The Earl of Essex's army rendezvoused at Brackley, picking
up more reinforcements and some desperately needed
supplies before turning sharply south-west. They followed
the old Roman routes across the Cotswolds, long stretches
of well-made roads jammed with men and equipment, a
vast and multicoloured anemone, popping and swelling
with prickly spines and colourful antennae. Mercer's men,
marching in the middle of the immense column, could see
as many men shuffling behind them as shuffling along in
front. The columns pulsed and shrank as they wound their
way down into the sudden dips, climbed back up the
hidden hillsides. Many of the London recruits had never
been so far from their home city and were completely
overawed by the magnificent views, striding along in such
a vast (and surely unstoppable) force across the top of the
whole world. They could see for miles, from dim green
horizon to dim green horizon, roads laid out like spilled
ribbons from a goodwife's basket, rivers like sparking
necklaces at the bottom of the sudden, steep-sided valleys.

A wintry sun lanced through the low clouds, turning
the stubbled enclosures to fields of gold, the chalky slopes
to jewel-studded robes.

And below the tree line away over yonder, the sunlight
suddenly glittered and winked on a thousand breastplates
and drawn swords. A magnificent force of knights with
silver helms and fluttering pennants appeared as if by
magic, rising from the earth like gaudy scarecrows to set
their spirits scuttling.

'Cavalry!' John Jewell the coalman saw them first. Or imagined he had. He gripped his pike in his soot-encrusted fist, wishing to God he hadn't lopped so many feet from the pole. Long Col pushed the wide-eyed blackamoor back into line.

'They've been shadowing us all morning, you candle-wasting prick,' Billy Butcher called over his shoulder, contemptuous as ever of his over-anxious new comrades.

'Keep moving, they're not interfering with you,' Long Col shouted, waving the gang back on again.

The column resumed its march, repeatedly bumping into one another and tripping over their pikes as they kept their eyes glued to the treacherous horizon. A large force of Parliamentary cavalry trotted across their line of vision, keeping themselves between the slow-moving infantry, baggage, and artillery and the mysterious Cavaliers along the next ridge.

'They'll attack at night!' Stephen Talbot whispered to his anxious companions. 'They'll charge through us with flaming torches!'

'I'll stick my flaming torch up your arse if you don't stow that clatter,' Long Col bawled from the flank. 'They're as scared of you as you are of them. Just keep together, that's all. Don't stray from the main column!'

They came out of the ground like demons.

Red and blue and green silks and velvets and taffetas swirling and sparkling like fireworks. A swiftly moving blur, a flock of kingfishers tumbling along a lonely brook. The Roundhead advance guard was stunned, staring in drop-jawed horror as the enemy horsemen erupted from the invisible valley, spurring their horses up the steep slope and on to the higher ground. They flowed like lava along either side of the jammed road, enveloping the flank regiment in jaws of steel.

William Sparrow had seen the King's horsemen at close quarters before, but he was as horrified as his quaking men when he saw the enemy force rise out of the road like a fiery rainbow. He could have sworn the road ran straight across the field. He hadn't noticed the treacherous dip in the hills but the experienced enemy scouts had. Their ever watchful commander had ordered his men along a stony gully, right across the relief force's line of march, and laid out an ingenious ambush for the bumbling Roundheads.

Mercer's men were following a farm track parallel to the main road, and their easier progress across the empty fields enabled them to overtake several of Essex's veteran regiments which had become entangled with their carts, guns, and baggage on the busy highway. Suddenly Mercer's green regiment found itself in a narrow enclosure with the road running behind an impenetrable hedgerow to their right and a steep, freshly ploughed slope to their left. Before William even registered the unexpected threat the front rankers had halted, turned in panic, and barged their way into the mass of men away from the Cavalier squadrons coming up the hill at them.

'Charge for horse!' Colonel Fulke bellowed as his terrified horse was compressed by a frightened mob of musketeers and pikemen. Their colours swayed above them as the ensigns were bundled back with the rest.

'Stand!' Fulke bawled, drawing his sword and waving it above his white head. 'Stand, you swine! Pikes to the front, muskets to the flanks!' The men were in no mood to obey their field commander. All they knew was they had walked into a trap and that they were surrounded by hordes of screaming imps on panting horses. Two brightly clad squadrons raced across the ridge and scattered a flank guard of Roundhead horse while the main force fell on the crowded road. A splutter of ill-aimed musketry from over the hedge heralded another desperate surge which carried Fulke and his horse back a good ten yards.

'Stand, you rogues!' William recognized his mentor's furious bellow, and was finally galvanized into action. He grabbed hold of John Jewell's coat sleeve as the errant coal merchant was about to run for his life.

'Stand! Stand by me!' he roared, using his halberd to prise the milling mob into some kind of line. 'Charge for horse!' John Jewell held his shortened pike up in the air. William grabbed the pole and dragged the point down to the proper angle, level with a charging horse's chest.

'Stand with me!' William repeated. The enclosure was blocked by a milling crowd of men. The front-rankers couldn't run, and had no choice but to face about and take a grip on their weapons. Some had already dropped their pikes and were standing about like useless clots trying to squeeze their way through the packed crowd.

'Get your pikes down,' William shouted, looking along the wavering rank. The terrified men had followed Jewell's example, ramming the butt of their weapons into the turf and placing their right boot over it. They crouched down just in time, packed together like mackerel and bristling with steel-tipped spines.

The earth drummed and rocked under their feet as the Royalist horsemen careered past, emptying their pistols into the shoal of screaming men.

Long Col had kept a burning match with him at all times, and had spent precious seconds sharing his glowing point with his wide-eyed musketeers. Gillingfeather and

Butcher had fired already, dropping a cheering Royalist trooper as he galloped by with his mouth wide open. The astonished rider landed with a spine-shattering crash on the trampled furrows and lay staring up at the sky for a moment before the rest of the marauding band veered away from the panic-stricken Roundhead mob and galloped straight over him. The thundering hoofs transformed the bewildered rider into a shattered turnip sack, his broken bones sticking up through the bloody rags of his flattened carcass. The screaming cavalrymen spurred off down the hill towards the bitter cavalry mêlée at the foot of the steep slope.

'Reload!' Long Col shouted, streamers of white smoke sidling through the mob like vapours of fear. William blinked against the foul smoke, using his halberd to herd the terrified pikemen into a straight line, their suddenly fortified fellows packing in behind them with their pikes held at varying angles. In another minute the mob had mutated into a compact phalanx, squads of musketeers forming on either flank, six men wide by six deep.

'Loaded?' Long Col bawled at the first rank, trembling recruits with twitching fingers staring fearfully at the churned field.

The second Royalist squadron had formed up in two lines and were trotting forward as if they couldn't quite decide whether to charge the alerted regiment. A fierce young Cavalier on a huge black horse seemed to make up their minds for them, spurring ahead with his hat held high in his fist. The rest spurted after him in ones and twos, a cornet ducking down low over his horse's mane, a bareheaded trooper tucking a carbine under his arm.

'Steady! Aim for the horses! Fire!' A dozen muskets coughed and spat like old gin blossoms outside an alehouse. Before their owners could study the damage they had inflicted they were unceremoniously barged aside by the second rank, who raised their muskets and fired into the smoky mass of twisted legs and rearing horses. The third rank and the fourth rank took their turns, keeping up a withering fire against the confused horsemen. The enemy squadron disintegrated in a hail of red-hot lead. Horses screamed with terror and plunged into the soft earth. Riders threw up their arms or fell from their saddles. Most of the others pulled up suddenly and veered away after their colleagues. The disciplined volleys had missed the shouting Cavalier who led his men into the murderous fire. He charged straight at the Roundheads, who would have undoubtedly turned and run if they had had the room. But there was a great mass of men behind them and a thick hedge to their right. They had no choice but to draw their heads into their coats like turtles and take a firmer grip on their pikes. The enemy rider's fiery mount dug in its hoofs before it reached the jabbing spearpoints, bucking the youngster into its mane. The youth held on, holding his pistol to the beast's sweating neck. He stared down at the massed Roundheads, his feeble moustache twitching above his small round mouth, his thin face streaked with powder and sweat.

William pushed his helmet back, recognizing his old rival Telling instantly. The Royal Wool-Gatherer himself, with a brand-new coat, brand-new arms, and a superb charger, come to try to stamp the upstart rebels into the earth! He had gotten the better of the bastard half a dozen times, and still he came back for more! William gave a strangled cry, outraged that he should have to risk his life fighting the rat-faced candle-waster all over again. Here, in this undernourished wastrel of a Cavalier, were all William's miseries, woes, and terrifying uncertainties brought to horrifying life. Here was his past, present, and future, the war which had swallowed him up and would no doubt spit him out. The hound had pursued him across half a dozen counties, chasing him from the familiar comforts of his home and exiling him to serve with strangers. Taking his livelihood and ripping him from family and friends. If that wasn't enough, he'd already had the house dove at his mercy and let him go, unable to lop the head from the hateful human hydra.

He growled with rage and strode forward, jabbing the halberd at the snorting horse and making it rear back in confusion. He was filled with furious excitement, deliriously intent on performing some feat of arms in front of his terrified men. Before he could think straight he had lowered the halberd and grabbed for the loose reins. He took a grip on the greasy leathers and tugged the horse back. Telling regained his balance in an instant and swung his sword straight at him. William saw the gleaming blade arc towards his head and then clatter with shattering force against John Jewell's pikeshaft. Before William could register anything else Telling had booted him square in the face, the big black horse leaping away over the dazed and wounded of both sides. William collapsed onto his backside, clutching his gauntlet to his smashed face. It came away sticky with blood.

He was still staring at his gory glove when he started to choke. Long Col had seen his foolhardy charge and darted out to pull him back, dragging the heavy man by his coat collar. William tore at his throat, blinded by bloody fury. Long Col deposited him in the grass and shoved another jibbering pikeman into the rank he had vacated.

'You'd got 'em all to stand and then led 'em all back

out again!' Long Col reprimanded his senior officer, his grey eyes glinting with anger. 'Pikes have got to stay together!' he yelled into the captain's bloody face. William shook his head, compressed by strange legs and smelly boots and wavering pike butts. Long Col hauled the idiot to his unsteady feet.

'You know who that was? That lousy prick Telling!' William spluttered, wiping his glove repeatedly across his split lip and bloody nose.

'By God, William, you can't take your quarrels into battle! You could have broken the line playing your schoolyard pranks! Kill yourself by all means, but not these men!'

William's spirits dropped like lead through water. He blinked rapidly, stunned by his narrow escape. The bastard wouldn't have hesitated to cleave *his* skull! Long Col strode through the press of men, muttering under his breath.

Gillingfeather watched the Cavalier captain spur off down the slope shouting challenges. He raised his musket and took careful aim, closing one eye and squinting along the barrel. He squeezed the heavy trigger with patient precision, a draughtsman of death.

Telling's big borrowed bay threw up its back legs as the heavy ball smashed into its sweat-caked rear, cracking its pelvis. The stallion squealed like a stuck pig, its front legs twisting as its heavy body slewed to the right. The rider was catapulted out of the saddle and sprawled in the churned clay furrows. The cornet who was spurring his horse on down the slope pulled up sharply, peering over his shoulder at his captain's sudden fall. The blue and black pennant he carried in his clenched gauntlet curled around the chipped lance enticingly.

'You got 'im, Gilly! Let's get 'is 'orse rag!' Billy Butcher yelled excitedly, about to race out after the dazed horseman and the vulnerable colour.

'Stand where you are! Reload, you scoundrels,' Long Col roared to the suddenly delighted musketeers. They had driven off an attack and were ready for anything now.

Mercer's men watched as a bare-headed trooper drew up his horse behind the prostrate youth, took careful aim, and fired his carbine. A sandy-haired musketeer in a grey coat twisted around as if he had been stung, clutching his face and screaming. Butcher cursed, raised his musket, and fired in one frantic movement. His shot whined over the man's head as he stooped over his saddle and shoved his hand out towards the crawling Cavalier.

'He shot him!' A furious musketeer pointed towards the bare-headed horsemen, as if he had broken some unwritten law of combat. He staggered back holding on to his companion's limp body as the stranger slipped to the ground, clenched up suddenly, and then writhed in the dirt. The wounded man's fingers twitched and scored the earth as his elbow and wrist joints locked up in agony. The carbine ball had clipped an artery beneath his jaw, and his lifeblood jetted over his shocked comrades, spraying their horrified faces with ruby bright droplets as they backed away in tangle-footed horror.

The determined rider ignored the flurry of ill-aimed shots from the shouting mob, leaning over to haul his dazed companion to his feet and boosting him up behind him. The cornet urged them on as he covered their cumbersome retreat. He had tugged his unwilling horse's head about and was walking it in agitated caracoles before them, screaming challenges to the Roundhead rogues and brandishing the silk-fringed flag as if it would deflect their bullets. The musketeers surged forward after the precious prize once more, but this time William was there to stop them, hauling them back by their coats and turning to face the surging mob. He bent over and walked backwards, lowering his halberd across their straining bellies and leaning in to them. They ground him back like a door jamb another few feet before William could dig in his heels sufficiently to halt their surly progress.

'Let's at them!'

'Back in line,' William growled, short of breath and gagging on his own streaming blood.

'Stand and fire,' Long Col bellowed, tipping the contents of one of his wooden powder pots over the trampled grass as the idiot musketeers crowded forward, almost knocking him down in their new-found enthusiasm.

Before the angry musketeers could sort themselves into ranks and reload, the three Cavaliers had spurred off down the hill after the rest of their squadron.

'Stand straight in your ranks and files!' The familiar refrain was bellowed out by the frantic sergeants as Colonel Fulke beat his way towards the open ridge to see what had become of the ambush.

The Roundhead tide subsided as suddenly as it had flowed. Mercer's bloodied regiment shuffled and panted, leaning on their weapons as if they had run a race over a boggy field.

Long Col shoved and kicked his way through the sweating scrummage and bent down beside the sandy-haired soldier. Sudden spurts of blood were jetting over his comrades' legs as he panted with terror, the whites of his eyes bloodstained tallow. The veteran sergeant jabbed his dirty fingers at the whistling hole, jamming the spasmodic spurts. The youngster was trying to speak, his blue lips trembling over his bared teeth.

'Give me some room!' Long Col yelled.

William stared down at the wounded musketeer, startled by the sergeant's desperate glare.

'Give us your neckerchief,' Long Col yelled again.

William picked the sweat-soaked rag from beneath his buff coat and tore at the knot. The sandy-haired soldier was trembling like a freshly caught codling, his boots kicking a tattoo in the trampled furrows.

The relieved regiment opened ranks as the Cavalier threat receded, Long Col shoving intruders away from the downed man. His bright blood flowed from the gash in his throat, pouring around Long Col's searching fingers. William wrenched his neckerchief loose and thrust it towards the crouching sergeant. Long Col slid the sodden bandage under his bloody fingers and clamped the dressing to the youngster's mortal wound. By the time the rag had staunched the flow the sandy-haired musketeer had stopped kicking. His face, scrunched into the clay, was waxy and his wide eyes bittersweet bright.

Nobody could even remember his name.

Prince Rupert's attempt to interfere with the earl's lumbering relief army had failed. He fell back to the town of Stow on the Wold, gathering in his scattered squadrons, and retired down the steeply wooded hill towards the crossroads beyond the ridge. The agitated commander was still pondering where to strike next when his scouts reported that the Earl of Essex had resumed his advance on a broad front, in full battle order. Colours were unfurled and carried to the front by ecstatic ensigns. Ten thousand voices could be heard from a mile and more off, singing psalms and cheering their own brave general as he rode to direct the historic advance.

The terrified but triumphant relief army had formed up on the ridge in a vast rectangle, a thousand men wide and six lines deep. Hundreds of pikemen stood practically shoulder to shoulder as they began the steep descent, long files of musketeers fanning out between the compact cores of each regiment. Fresh regiments of Parliamentary cavalry were drawn up in solid russet blocks on the flanks, while other horsemen divided and flowed about the lower slopes, seeking easier ways off the plateau.

Prince Rupert, black with fury and spent powder, could have chewed his sword in frustration. He sat on his stamping charger near the crossroads and watched the enemy mass roll down the wooded slopes like a slow brown tide, all shifting shapes and kaleidoscoping colours. He ordered the rearguard to harass the enemy outriders for as long as possible, turned his horse, and spurred away to find his uncle.

THE CITY OF GLOUCESTER

The crypt was dark and gloomy and reeked of urine as if it had been pressed into service as a latrine by every tomcat in Gloucester. Sir Edward Massey had to duck to avoid braining himself on the vaulted ceiling as he followed the powder master along the narrow aisle between the stacked barrels, their greasy pot bellies and looping iron belts illuminated by the minuscule glow from his well-shuttered lantern. The weary governor paused, gagging at the sulphurous saltpetre stink. He wiped the corner of his eye on his gauntlet – he had developed some kind of infection due no doubt to his near-terminal lack of sleep – and raised his chin expectantly as the powder master settled the lantern on a beam and stood back.

'I brought you down here, sir,' the powder master whispered, 'so as not to alarm the rest of 'em, like.'

Massey nodded. 'What is it you find so worrying that you dare not repeat in front of my officers, Mr David?' he enquired, his undernourished body screaming for some urgently needed rest. The crypt at St Mary's was narcotically quiet, a haven of peace buried beneath the shot-blasted town. All he wanted to do was curl up beside the stinking barrels and close his eyes.

'Well, sir,' Thomas David observed, trim and business-like in his smeared leather apron. 'I've kept the barrels

down here so as the boys wouldn't go carrying no tales.'
Massey, blinking with exhaustion, smiled serenely. The
powder master peered over his shoulder and leaned
forward conspiratorially. 'But they're all empty, see? Apart
from these three here, we're out.'

The desperate news lanced through the governor's
reeling mind like a freshly honed dirk.

'Out?' he croaked. 'All out?'

Thomas David nodded grimly.

'We had that bit of trouble with the mill down the quay,
and there just ain't the raw materials to keep tother one
going for long,' he explained. 'Start of the siege we had
forty barrels, and we've milled about ten more in the
meantime. But you've bin usin' up about two a day, so now
we're down to three!' Thomas David glanced at the
bemused commander as if he had used up most of their
precious supplies putting on firework displays for the
children.

''Twun't goin' to last for ever, sir, after all!' he
reminded him.

Massey nodded, took a deep breath in the stinking pit.

Three barrels would last them another day or two at
most. After that the musketeers would be reduced to using
up what was left in their powder horns, or what they could
steal from raids on the enemy saps.

But the Royalist works were too close for surprise
assaults now. The garrison had hung on by the skin of its
teeth for twenty-five days and was too exhausted for any
more desperate sorties. He could barely spare a man from
his post on the thinly held line as it was. He had tried to
cover the most vulnerable sectors, the city gates, its castle
and quay. In addition he had stationed men at other key
locations inside the city walls and had set up a flying

reserve at the Wheat Market. But a good half of them were already carrying an assortment of light wounds and all of them were on short rations. He could have the murky waters of the Severn boiled for them to drink, but they couldn't use mud to fire muskets.

'I thought I'd better say, sir,' Thomas David apologized awkwardly.

The governor sighed, shook his thin, careworn head.

'You have done all that was asked of you and more, I am sure,' Massey reassured him. 'No garrison could have done more. I was . . .'

'Sir!' The excited bellow from the stairs caught the murmuring men unawares. They peered down the barrel-lined aisle as one of the town runners leaned over the iron handrail, waving his hat for their attention. Sir Edward made his way past the stacks of empty barrels and peered up at the youngster.

'Sir . . . beg pardon, sir, but Sergeant Gray is looking for you urgent, like. Something you ought to see, sir!'

The broad river ran swiftly between the featureless banks, small eddies and whirlpools scouring the broad earth bays as the tide turned. The powerful brown flow lifted the small boats which had been tied up near the priory, their masts clinking merrily above the busy decks. The tiny armada of skiffs and rowing boats formed bobbing jetties beside the larger lighters and fishing smacks which had been dispatched upriver from Bristol to rendezvous with the King's troubled forces. The priory grounds nearby remained a hive of activity despite Dr Chillingworth's ignominious absence, with carts and wagons and long files of men winding through the abandoned orchards and forming disorderly queues along the water's edge. But they weren't disembarking badly needed supplies, or collecting more powder to finish the siege once and for all.

They were loading their sick and wounded aboard and evacuating them away from the accursed town.

Sir Edward raised his perspective glass slowly, as if any undue movement might bring the enemy forces running back to the quietly fuming trenches and abandoned saps to resume their deadly labours. He focused on their great siege machines, rickety towers stuck up to their axles in mud, wound about with hemp ropes like massive maypoles. It would need an enormous effort to move the things now, surely?

Sergeant Major Gray was standing alongside the governor on the southern ramparts, nodding his head impatiently and pointing a blunt finger towards the enemy headquarters beyond the marsh.

'Yes, sir, there, look. A little to the left of those old Humpety Dumpeties, look, see? They're putting their wounded aboard, sir!'

Massey squinted down his narrow glass, studied the unhurried evacuation in silence. Improvised stretchers were being carried aboard while others, more lightly wounded perhaps, were hopping past the watchful officers and being helped on board by the blue-jacketed seamen. Massey swung the glass around the bustling harbour and focused on the main camp, partially obliterated behind columns of slow grey smoke.

They were setting fire to their huts. Taking down their tents and rolling the filthy tarpaulins on the back of creaking carts. The long horse lines which had been laid out beside the latrines had been pulled up or left deserted, string sacks of hay abandoned like Saracens' heads at some

Crusader fortress. The huge pavilions belonging to their lords and ladies had gone, swallowed back up by the trampled earth. Massey swung the glass around to his left, focused on more deserted emplacements and empty batteries. Great wickerwork squares which looked as if they had abandoned by some giant's grandchild. Heavy wheel ruts criss-crossed the filthy fields, horses whinnying as they dragged the last guns away from the undefeated walls.

'You see, sir, they're going! They've only gone and given up!' Gray called, his young face flushed with excitement. Massey blinked rapidly, unable to comprehend their sudden salvation. All this simple hero of Gloucester could manage was a stupid, lopsided grin at his cheering officers.

'Going, going?' he repeated, shaking his head as the word was passed along the lines, from tower to woolsack to breach to battered rubble-filled gate. 'Then God has spared us,' he concluded simply.

'Praise the Lord!' Gray yelled. Their excited exclamations and triumphant cries of relief were drowned out by a sudden, swelling uproar of joyous shouts as the soldiers and civilians in the beleaguered town registered their deliverance and roared their gratitude to the smiling heavens.

It was dark now, and streaming rain clouds had rushed up from the west to complete the King's downfall. Sector by sector, sap by sap, the sodden Royalists clambered from their filthy, rat-infested holes, crawled out of their leaking huts, and formed up before their bedraggled officers. As fast as the dispirited troops could be withdrawn and re-assembled they were marched off to the north-east, heading for Sudeley Castle. Within an hour of the movement orders

being issued by the hollow-eyed staff officers the roads
were churned to slush. In another two they were choked
with every cart and coach in creation. Wheels splintered
and snapped, whips cracked and tempers frayed. The
entire army seemed to be in a particularly foul mood, from
the filthiest corporal to the fattest lord, from mud-shanked
carter to shivering earl. The fact they had come so close to
crushing the town made it seem doubly galling to comprehend the bitter truth that they had not. A few short weeks
before the Royalists imagined they had all the time in the
world to finish this business, to crush the rebellion like a
one-legged bug.

They remained boastfully unbeaten but frustratingly
unable to proclaim the victory they had set their hearts
and minds on. The end of the wretched, filthy war was as
far away as ever. Gloucester had held out like a valiant
vessel in a landlocked Sargasso of enemies, defying everything which science, invention, and a soldier's ingenuity
could throw at it.

Now the mud-soaked survivors of the saps and sorties
cursed and muttered, vindictively splashing through the
blood-red puddles and shoving anybody who stumbled in
their way.

Nybb strode along in the middle of the reeking column,
watching Eli and Zachary Pitt shove and steer his baggage,
piled high onto a rickety dog cart. The few hundred or so
survivors of Morrison's fanciful brigade sloped along
behind, miserable and stuffed with sin, more than ready
for a good fight whether their enemies were careless
carters, sullen cavalry, or those mad gabbler Welsh from
the grand works up by the Vineyard. Cully Oates tramped
along beside his chief, sucking the damp air from his
empty clay pipe.

'Someone's dropped a right ballock,' Oates commented, striding over a series of waterlogged rills in the running road. 'Who was in charge anyway, is what I want to know.'

Nybb marched on, his boar's head hunched up in his weather-washed coat of greens and greys. It had been blue and red when he took it from the body of a Hungarian mercenary after the Battle of Wittstock six long years before.

'That cunny-hunter Rupert was in charge, mineer. Never ye mind that alte Skatch-man Ruthven,' he snarled under his evil breath. 'Too busy mitt die fräuleins to do his proper duties,' he spat.

Cully Oates pushed his hat back to scratch his lousy hair.

'Ah, we'd best keep mum about that business now,' Oates recommended, glancing at the toiling pikemen as they manoeuvred their barrowload of assorted loot and cast-offs along the hellish track.

'Keep mum?' Nybb cursed in Turkish, rolled his beastly eyeballs. 'I'll tell you mineer, what we saw,' he tapped his Neanderthal brow, 'will come useful to us, aye, one day.'

Cully Oates wasn't so sure. 'He's got powerful friends, see? We were lucky to escape without' avin' us necks stretched.'

'Pah! He was lucky, mineer, lucky that house dove Telling was there to save his hide. If he hadn't warned die Schwarzer I'd 'ave bagged the bugger mysen!'

'What about old Hugo, eh?' Cully Oates asked, anxious to change the subject. He thought Rupert would have had a pretty good look at his attackers, and would be only too pleased to come across them again. Best keep your nose clean and your eyes down, when that braggart was about.

Nybb snorted, ran his hairy paw across his tusk-studded mouth. 'I bet he kacked hisself when he had the call, and all,' he sniggered. 'The weasel-arsed candle-waster was always running to and from the scheissehaus!' The saturated soldiery roared in appreciation at their commander's assessment of their absent colleague's unreliable bowels.

'Two shits together, is what I say,' Nybb went on vindictively. 'I'm glad to be shut of the pair of them.'

'And old Morrison and all,' Cully Oates put in, jabbing his clay pipe as a reminder. 'We've seen the last of that shyster!'

Nybb frowned. 'Ah, mineer. If I thought that was true, I'd dance a jig in a polecat's petticoat!'

Cully Oates grinned weakly, horrified by the appalling prospect.

The men marched on through the dismal, drenching rain towards their suddenly uncertain destiny.

The principal object of Colonel Nybb's multilingual scorn forced his way through to the King's lifeguard about midnight that same dreary night. The rain had stopped but the surrounding trees seethed and dripped, the filthy road practically washed away. A convoy of coaches, carts, and heavily laden wains had stalled at the bottom of a short, steep slope, and a saturated chain gang of grumbling lords, fully armoured cuirassiers, standard-bearers, and gentlemen of the royal bedchamber had been pressed into service to get them moving again. The despondent monarch was squatting on a milestone a little way from the activity, his hands clasped in front of him. He stared at the muddy patterns over his boots while his delighted sons charged about the verges shouting and screaming like savages. They had been cooped up in Matson House so long they were glad of the change of scenery, no matter how wet and windy.

A muttering cabal of cloaked officers stood by, nodding and whispering to each other as their grim-faced troops shuffled on up the rutted track, gawping at their down-hearted sovereign as if he had grown a couple of extra heads.

Prince Rupert spurred his mud-splattered mount down the embankment and leapt out of the saddle. A soaking-wet marquess hurried to hold his bridle as if he was a common stable boy and not a powerful magnate in his own right. Rupert strode through the bowing officers and swept off his sodden hat.

'Your Majesty. That rogue Essex is at Naunton. We tried to stop him on the downs before Stow and three miles beyond, but he came on in battle order. He has upwards of ten thousand men,' the towering Prince reported in short, agitated bursts, clearly impatient that he should have to spend time making such reports to anybody. His uncle glanced up at the raging Prince, the tireless Cerberus on whom he had bestowed so much hope. The King raised his hands in mute appeal.

'We could not afford to be caught between the relief a–a–army and the garrison,' he explained with a bitter stammer. 'You knew our counsels, my lord,' he added shortly. The volatile Prince held his tongue with difficulty. Of course he knew their counsels. He had expressed himself with his usual blistering forcefulness at their acri-monious councils of war, and had not complained (to anybody apart from a few trusted friends like Will Legge and the Duke of Richmond) when His Majesty had chosen to disregard his advice. He had warned from the beginning they could become bogged down in a long siege. Now it appeared the Royalist army had lost as many men through sickness and sorties as they would have done if they had been unleashed in one bloody assault. But his uncle the King had refused to contemplate such butchery, and Rupert's imperative arguments had been overlooked.

Nevertheless, if the crotchety old halfwits who had inherited direction of the campaign had known their business they would have been inside the town within a week. How was it such a massive force had been repulsed by so few?

'I am aware of the provisions made in case a relief force arrived,' he replied with a flash of his dark, unwearied eyes. ''Tis a pity we allowed the old cuckold time to perform such a miracle.' The eavesdropping officers gathered nearby growled with anger at this apparent slur on their military abilities.

'Are ye saying we should hae ta'en the toon sooner?' the elderly Earl of Brentford snorted, his florid face flushed with anger. Rupert raised his eyebrows. 'Is there something you wish tae say to ma face, your Highness?' the worn-out warrior asked.

The King raised his thin white hand, unusually irritated by their petty-minded squabbles. 'Nobody can be blamed, my lords, as nobody could have imagined the Earl of Essex would ever have been capable of such a march.'

The staff officers nodded their sodden beards in full agreement with His Majesty's startling insights.

'My Lord Wilmot sends word he attempted to intercept the rebels at Bicester, but was prevented from falling on their flanks when an *enclosure* was held against him,' the scowling Prince observed archly, anxious to deflect as much of the blame as possible. He wasn't about to allow his impeccable military record to be tarnished by another man's mistakes. 'Essex was in full strength by the time I had assembled the cavalry,' he added petulantly, glaring at the muttering staff officers as if he dared them to gainsay him.

'I will return this minute and lead them on again, if you wish it, sire,' he offered, knowing the King would not permit such an operation at that crucial juncture. The army would be needed elsewhere now, to block the Roundheads' route to London. 'I suggest an immediate march on Burford. We can command all the approaches to London and force Essex to fight us on our ground,' he said loudly.

'Burford? The men need to rest and refit, sire. Surely your original intention to march on Sudeley is the wise solution,' the gouty old earl suggested smoothly. 'If the army can be brought up to strength we will have an excellent chance of beating Essex just as we have beaten Waller.'

'We will have to catch him first, my lord,' Rupert sneered. 'It appears the earl has found his legs at last.'

The gruff council of war broke up as quickly as it began. Rupert stalked back to his horse, which lifted its sodden head in weary wonder. The staff officers, earls, and lords hurried back to their coaches to rage and fume at his ill-mannered outbursts. The King climbed wearily to his feet, and waved his overtired but still active sons to his side. The muddy princes hurried over, looked up eagerly at their feebly smiling sire.

'Are we going home now, Father?' James asked, stifling a huge yawn with his small fist. King Charles of England smiled wanly, his brown eyes watering in the night gloom.

'We have no home,' he said in an undertone, but loud

enough for the puzzled princes to exchange a concerned glance. They followed their father back to the freed coach and clambered up behind him in silence.

They had been in hiding for days, hurrying away from the bright and horribly incriminating star they had left on Wainlode Hill and taking refuge in a lonely sheepfold out on the waterlogged flats along the river. Jackson knew the water-meadows like his own master's yard, and led them on a wide circuit around the hill along paths that Nicodemus wouldn't have been able to pick from the tangled tussocks and coiling willow wands. They hid in ditches and watched the road, leaping out like mud-striped tigers on likely looking travellers. Ragged and weary country folk, tinkers and wanderers set adrift by the fluctuating fortunes of the King's war. From the garbled reports they had managed to collect from these fearful messengers, it appeared the 'London men were acomin', eatin' every poor body out of 'ouse and 'ome on the way'. One old crone had the Roundhead crusaders at Stow, another said the treacherous whelps were at Cheltenham.

Wherever they were, the crucial intelligence had to be passed to the long-suffering garrison of Gloucester. The hard-pressed governor might even be contemplating surrendering the town that very night, with relief so near at hand.

They decided to risk returning straight to Layton's house, travelling through the night, spied on by ghostly owls and beady-eyed foxes, and working their way back towards the alderman's grand house by cautious fits and starts.

The master – safely back from his own extended travels

about the county – was astonished to find them shivering in his kitchen the following dawn, sipping bowls of gruel under Goodwife Duckett's cauldron-watching stare.

The overseer listened to the agitated alderman rave and rant, sipping his gruel from the bowl of his spoon without raising an eyelash. It seemed to Nicodemus as if the Midlands preacherman could not comprehend any harm ever coming to him. The boy munched his bread and listened as the softly spoken overseer described their adventures.

'Well, never mind your adventures,' the white-faced alderman snapped, 'we've had the King's men here turning over everything in the yard.'

'And stickin' forks in all the 'ay out in the barn,' Goodwife Duckett added with a gloating relish. Alderman Layton flicked his wrist as if he couldn't give a cuss for his hay.

'They brought Handy Michael here on the gelding's back,' he announced with a furious shake of his small head. Jackson barely blinked, his pale eyebrows kinked in concentration. 'Aye, shot dead,' Layton confirmed. 'And the boys taken off to the King's camp for all your fun.'

The overseer held his hat in his hand, shrugging imperceptibly.

Further debate was interrupted by the clatter of hoofs upon the cobbled yard. Before they could even think of hiding the muddy fugitives they saw shadowy figures moving towards the house through the misty fish-eyed window. They held their breath as a straw-headed cornet rapped on the door and ducked into the room, looking about him like a hungry wolf in a henhouse.

Nicodemus Burke felt a chill finger of doubt run up the back of his neck, prickling his stiff red hair beneath his shapeless felt hat. He glanced at the dour overseer, thinking he must have morning dew in his veins and frost on his brain to remain so full of fire and zeal and yet so punishingly remote from the deadly dangers of their thankless mission behind the Royalist lines.

Layton only just managed to keep his head, resisting the temptation to invite the suspicious soldiers into his hearth.

'What, you again? Garrison a bit lively for you, is that it?'

The straw-haired cornet's lip peeled back from his bad teeth. He took off his helmet, shook out his matted yellow locks, and stepped aside as his captain followed him into the delinquent's kitchen.

Captain Andrew Malvern took off his gauntlets and studied the assembled household, noting the mud-splattered newcomers by the fire. The dapper little councillor looked momentarily pained at the unexpected intrusion, but quickly rearranged his features into a jovial grin.

'Your pardon, sir, I was under the impression these men were merely making a nuisance of themselves after eggs and whatnot,' Layton said briskly, 'as they did the last time they were here.'

Malvern wasn't about to be deflected by complaints about a few fowls. He lowered his chin and fixed his grey eyes on the mobile alderman.

'Alderman Layton, back from your travels at last,' he said. 'And your weary footmen with you,' he added, glancing at the serenely staring overseer and the paralysed boy by the fire.

'Footmen? I wouldn't have the rogues within an inch of me, sir. They're just back from the water-meadows, where they've been hedging and ditching,' Layton explained.

Malvern nodded, unconvinced. Before he could question the men any further the city councillor launched into a lengthy complaint about his ungrateful workforce, loudly asserting that Handy Michael and 'them young hotheads' who set the fire had been planning their daft stunt for a while.

'I hadn't taken much notice of 'em, of course,' he added hastily. 'They were always carping on about one thing or other.'

The Royalist captain had left the rest of the army as it prepared to march off towards Sudeley, deciding to make a detour to the north-west in order to personally investigate the mysterious beacon they had observed the week before. He was determined to get to the bottom of the crucial signal, find out who was behind the warning blaze and what its unmistakable glare was intended to represent. According to this Roundhead snake in the grass Layton, the warning fire which was lit not two miles from his own home by three of his own employees was a complete and utter conundrum.

'Former employees,' Alderman Layton corrected him, testily. 'I'll not have hotheads on my farm,' he insisted.

Captain Malvern pulled at his silky beard, eyed the double-dealing councillor with distaste. Why, he was almost as slippery as that rogue Morrison back at Brockworth! Give him an honest, God-fearing, psalm-singing Roundhead and he would fight the man fair and square. Getting to grips with these damned moneymen was like trying to catch eels in a tub of honey.

Malvern took another sideways glance at the alderman's household, assembled in a shuffling line beside the kitchen range. The ragamuffin boy with the bristling red hair looked familiar, although he couldn't for the life of him remember where from. The dried-out overseer seemed to look about the gloomy kitchen without focusing on anything at all, while the goodwife sobbed into her apron and burst into tears the moment she was addressed. Malvern glanced over his shoulder at the burly cornet who had captured the fire-starting spies.

'Do you recognize either of these two hedgers and ditchers, Wilkes?'

The cornet shook his head. 'In that dark, one Roundhead's much the same as another,' he replied.

Layton smiled sweetly. Well used to the cut and thrust of local politics, he knew a bluff when he saw one. 'How could your brave cornet recognize anybody here? We were all at home at the time,' he said stoutly.

'I thought you said you were away on business?' Malvern enquired.

'I was away, yes, but everybody else was indoors.'

'How do you know?'

'Because they had no business being out of 'em!' Layton replied shortly.

'These two weren't here the last time we called,' Cornet Wilkes observed slyly, still annoyed at the unwarranted reference to their unauthorized foraging.

'I've just told you they've been hedging and ditching out by the river!'

Malvern sighed. 'Is this right?'

Samuel Jackson nodded absent-mindedly. 'Hedging and ditching, sir. Yes, sir.'

The captain was rapidly losing patience with these idiot farmhands. He clicked his fingers at the sneering cornet. 'Have the boy sent in.'

The fearful household stared towards the kitchen door as the broadly built cornet stepped outside and returned in a moment with Gar Maynard. Layton compressed his lips, choked back his colour at the sight of the badly beaten boy.

'I said,' he said thickly, 'that I'd not have hotheads on my farm!'

Goodwife Duckett gave a little broken cry and hurried towards the boy, cradling the bewildered youth in her cloying embrace.

'By Heavens, Gar, tell us it ain't true!' she cried. 'And your poor father dead and all!'

Her heartfelt query took the Royalist captain aback. Could it be the rest of the household had been unaware of their friends' little escapade?

'Were any of these men here with you the night you lit the beacon? Be honest now, Gar,' Malvern encouraged.

Gar Maynard held the crying woman away from him, and gave the officer a wall-eyed stare. Nicodemus felt Gar's stony eyes run over his terrified features. He shook his tousled head.

'You ought to know,' Malvern said sternly, 'that as well as your man Maynard getting himself shot while setting the fire, your lad Planter has been hanged for his part in the business. You, sir, should know the law when it comes to spies.'

'Lawks, they weren't no spies,' Goodwife Duckett wailed, the tears splashing from her contorted features onto the plain stone flags. 'They was just plain boys same as these.' Malvern nodded.

'Well, they're in your care so you'll be held responsible if they try anything else,' Malvern warned the alderman, straightening his hat on his head.

*

Simon Layton remembered the captain's dire warning as if it had been branded on his forehead with hot coals. He closed his eyes and prayed for strength, then opened them and glared at his unapologetic overseer.

'You heard the man, Jackson. You're all in my household, I'm to be held up for your behaviour.'

Jackson nodded his sandy head, serenely calm despite the uproar in the kitchen. Goodwife Duckett bawling and hanging on to poor orphaned Gar, who kept pulling himself free in obvious, sullen embarrassment.

'The poor orphan boy! Look what trouble yer games 'ave caused 'im!'

Layton glared at Nicodemus with his snapsack packed and his hat squashed down over his red hair, and then leered at Jackson, strapped back into the buff coat he had recently recovered from its hiding place out in the pigpen.

'We're not in your household no more, sir. No blame to you, sir. We're off for Gloucester to join up with the earl,' the overseer replied calmly. 'Me and the boys have talked it through.'

'Oh, you have, have you? What about letting me in on your deliberations? Don't I count? I've paid yer wages these last twelve years, Christ knows!'

Jackson nodded. 'And very grateful I am, sir. But they've wronged God and wronged the people and now they've wronged us, sir,' he said, his preacherman's voice ringing in the enclosed kitchen. 'Shooting down poor Michael and hanging up the splinter of a boy there. There was never any need for 'em to draw lots, sir.'

'Draw lots? I think Gar got off light, I do straight! Lighting fires to warn the town under the King's men's noses? What were you thinking of? Of course they were—'

'What, right to hang him? Sixteen years old, sir? The

boy didn't hardly know what he was doing, sir, and they went and hanged him for it!' Jackson exclaimed, a trace of colour on his drawn cheeks.

Layton held up his small, pudgy hands. 'Don't you start preachin' on at me, Samuel Jackson,' he warned. 'It was your rebel foolishness that led them on the first going off!'

The overseer sucked in his cheeks at this vicious attack.

'Sir,' he responded quietly, 'I make no apology for what thee and I have done. If I led them on, it's a matter for me and my God,' he announced.

'By God,' Layton cursed with a shake of his head, 'you're a self-righteous bastard, you know, Jackson.' He took a short, red-cheeked breath. 'You mean to go back, and then join up with Essex?' the alderman exclaimed. 'After all that's happened?'

'Don't be a fool, man,' Goodwife Duckett scolded, mortified their nocturnal activities might once again attract inquisitive Royalist officers into her kitchen.

'The earl's on his way, we've seen the signs. The city must be warned of it,' Jackson said darkly.

Layton gazed at the foreman as if he had begun foaming at the mouth, unable to believe his own ears. Go back and light more fires, is that what he was about?

'I forbid you to step out that door, do you hear me? I'll ride after that captain myself and warn him, so help me!' the merchant screeched, dumbfounded by their suicidal foolishness. Jackson gave him a ghostlike smile.

'We're driven by other wills than yours, sir, begging your pardon,' he replied, begging no such thing.

Alderman Layton watched them go, three hunchbacked pilgrims following the stony road out of his yard. He slammed the door and shook his head at the crying goodwife.

'By the thorns of Christ, sir, they'll all kill 'emselves afore they're done,' she wailed. Layton nodded grimly. And kill him and all, if they weren't damned careful.

'Not far now,' Master Samuel Jackson said, peering down the broad shoulder of the dark hill. Nicodemus Burke didn't need a torch or stars or anything else to guide him. The place was as familiar as his own narrow garret back in Gloucester. The wind carried sullen sheets of rain in from the river, and unleashed spiteful squalls at the exposed ridge.

Wainlode Hill. Scene of their fatal encounter with the enemy cavalry those few brief days before. Handy Michael shot down as he ran and poor Randall hung up for their crimes. Nicodemus pictured his friend sitting beneath the drystone wall a few days before, smoking his pipe and coughing on the eye-watering smoke without a care in the whole wide world. He imagined him now, blue and cold and naked in a ditch full of dead men. He shivered. His eyes were watering now, right enough.

Going back? Layton was right. They were mad to risk it, the three of them against the King's entire army. But the enemy cavalry were away towards Cheltenham now, and the roads would be empty enough, Jackson told them earnestly, desperate to reassure the boys their fool's errand would be as uneventful as collecting the eggs back at Layton's farm. Gar Maynard, lanky and sullen, lifted his boots and ground them down as if he couldn't feel the rough path beneath their feet. He walked straight into the whipping branches of the trees as if he was immune to their skin-splitting stings. Jackson ducked down like an old poacher, sniffing the stiff breeze. He waved the boys down

310

but Gar marched on, shoving his way through the thicket to the enormous scorched ring they had left on the brow of the hill. The soot-blasted limbs of the incendiary wagon lay like the remains of some fox's midnight feast beside the singed trunks of the trees. Nicodemus glanced at Jackson as he watched the orphaned Roundhead begin to gather boughs and branches from the copse.

'Run to the wall like you did last time, and keep a watch,' the overseer told him, eyes glimmering in the watery moonlight. Nicodemus nodded, prising his cold body away from the womb-like bower of scorched under-growth and scuttled off across the familiar furrows towards the wall.

All of a sudden the black valley below was lit up by garish flames. Thick black smoke tumbled up into the gathering storm, the glowing clouds splashed and scarred, illuminated by zigzagging comets showering sparks.

Gloucester lay prostrate, surrounded by tormenting fires. To Nicodemus, watching dumbly from the rain-lashed ridge, it seemed as if the town must be swallowed up at any moment – swallowed up by a coiling, pulsing dragon decked out in the King's colours.

He shivered with chills and terrors, but kept his watch through the night.

KILMERSDEN HALL,

NEAR CHIPPING MARLEWARD,
SOMERSET, 5 SEPTEMBER 1643

Bella Morrison had wished herself dead, or at least deaf, a thousand times over. She would have gladly endured a week on a rack rather than be subjected to her father's sanctimonious tirades about her behaviour. Sir Gilbert was in such a filthy mood he hadn't even trusted himself to be alone with her for two whole days. He had locked her in the gloomy garret at the Black Dog while he settled his affairs under the suspicious eye of that interfering swineherd Malvern, only returning when the stubborn captain had given up his fruitless hunt for clues and witnesses and taken himself off to annoy somebody else.

Those endless days wrapped in her cloak against the damp chill seeping through the old panelling had been the worst hours of her whole life. She could see the soldiers moving about in the yard, long files of musketeers and pikemen making their way back along the Brockworth road. Surely Gloucester lay in the opposite direction? Their bewildering marches were nothing to do with the fight in the wood, were they?

Bella dropped the mouldy curtain over the webbed glass, listened for the urgent footfalls on the narrow landing. The deliberate tread of a man in spurred boots, his scabbard scraping against the woodwork. What was it about a pair of leather boots that made men strut so? Perhaps she would borrow a pair of Clavincale's and try them out, see if the change in footwear would alter her personality.

Bella held her long white hand to her clammy forehead. She wondered if the wet weather had permeated her brain, shut up so long on her own in this third-storey dungeon. Perhaps the enforced isolation had milked her mind just as that terrible night had drained her spirits, quenched her restless thirst for excitement. Locked up in the inn she was just another poor drudge, no better than the poor red-armed cooks busy in the kitchen below. A grinning goodwife waiting for her men to come and release her, to set her to her chores all over again.

Well, she wasn't having it.

Bella paced the room and gathered her thoughts, concentrated her arguments the way a general would assemble his troops.

Clavincale had been a boor and a bully, rich but tight-fisted and all too ready to use them on her if she didn't bow and scrape before him like some Egyptian whore. Her father had been after a lucrative marriage, not her happiness. If he thought so much of his money he ought to sell her off to some travelling bordello, to entertain the drunken Cavaliers for a few shillings. Is that what he wanted? Bella coloured, gripping the bedknob as if it was her parent's fleshy throat.

She had always loved Hugo. Hugo could be the only man for her. There. She had decided, made up her mind at last. As soon as her father sorted out their present difficulties she would go straight to the boy and swear her undying allegiance to his troubled cause. She might even compose a tearful testimony for Her Majesty Henrietta

Maria, and enlist the Queen's support in her troubled causes! That would make her father sit up and take notice.

But Sir Gilbert's livid features and bulging white eyes forestalled Bella's outraged assaults and scattered her precisely reasoned case. When it came to the inevitable clash of wills, her father's white-hot temper routed her watered-down spirits, brushed her aside like steam off the kettle.

He had stood in the doorway like a newly cast cannon, glowing with rage as if he had spent the previous two days squatting in a furnace. He scowled at the miserable girl for a moment before closing the heavy oak door with a bang which shook the whole house.

'No,' he said quickly, waving his stubby forefinger at her, 'don't say a word. You'll listen for a change, listen to me for the first time since you were born,' he promised her, striding into the room and gripping her chin. He held her like a newly caught perch, ignoring her defiant stare.

'Your little liaison could have hanged us all, do you realize that? Do you?' Sir Gilbert nodded her head up and down for her as if she had lost control of her muscles. 'I spent hours, no, days,' he corrected himself, colouring furiously, 'arranging this marriage. Talking Clavincale into lowering his sights a little, lowering them to a common tradesman's daughter like you. Like you, Bella, do you hear me?'

Her tears ran down her cheeks and ran in tiny crystal deltas over his bunched fingers and twisted wrist. She choked with rage and shame but dared not interrupt his vitriolic flow.

'You'll never again have the chance to marry as high, you see that, don't you? Clavincale was a dream come true, he had money and prestige and power, and he could have made you into a lady, a *lady*, Bella,' he croaked.

The miserable girl went limp, limp as a boned fish in his furious grip. He unlocked his trembling fingers and let her slide back over the unmade bed. She lay staring at the ceiling, trails of tears running over her face and onto the soiled bedding.

'And what do you do? Keep your damned mouth shut for a change and go along with it? Put up with him for the sake of your name and my name and your blasted brats' names? No. You go behind his back as if he's a senile old pot-walloper, playing the polecat with that candle-wasting clot Telling. Telling,' he repeated, shaking his head. 'Do you know he could have killed us all? I had to stand there while you dragged my good name and your own through the mud, admitting you'd *developed a certain affection* for the dog? By God, Bella, you've pulled some strokes in your time, but I tell you straight, you've gone too far this time. Let me tell you, young lady, things are going to change around here, right now.' He had turned on his heel, paced across the worn floorboards as Bella glared at the hateful ceiling.

'I was too soft on you after your mother died, I know it now. I should have brought in a governess or packed you off to a nunnery. Ah, I thought that would make you blink! You bloody polecat, you don't deserve any better, do you? Eh?'

'No, Father,' Bella admitted, realizing at last he was coming to the end of his tempestuous tirade. Sir Gilbert puffed and blew. 'I'm sorry, Father. Truly,' she said, turning her head to look up at her furious parent. Sir Gilbert seemed to soften for a moment, then boiled up all over again, shaking his finger at her.

'Oh, no, you don't, my girl! You'll not get around me making cow eyes and sobbing your heart out! Three men are dead, Bella. Dead!' He lowered his voice to a fierce whisper. 'Clavincale and young Dunblane done in. You can't go around murdering members of the aristocracy as if they were a pair of cross-eyed pullets! I came this close to hanging just because I was there!'

Sir Gilbert continued outlining the convincing case for the prosecution as he threw her belongings into her trunk. Clavincale's clothes were hanging where he had left them. He shook his head. Malvern had already collected his personal effects to send back to his family away down west. Both he and Dunblane had been given a full military burial in the nearby churchyard, while the one-armed bandit who attacked them had been stripped and rolled into a pit with that morning's crop of casualties. As far as the noblemen's families would understand both had been killed while on active service with His Majesty's forces. Malvern knew they had met no such end, but he could hardly gainsay Prince Rupert himself, could he? He might as well try ploughing with dogs as bring that Teutonic tyrant to book.

Sir Gilbert ran his thumb along Clavincale's best suit, a richly embroidered black- and red-slashed doublet with matching breeches. He held it up to his neck and scowled, then rolled the suit up into a compact bundle.

'What are you doing?' Bella asked, sitting up and wiping her eyes.

'I'm withdrawing my investment,' he snarled. 'Same as you withdrew yours. Now finish packing your trunk, and put all his stuff in the other, I'll leave instructions on sending it back to his people,' he growled, striding towards the door.

His people, Bella thought dumbly, overwhelmed with miserable frustration. I was almost his people.

Bella retreated into a ghostly world of narrow rooms and stuffy coaches, losing herself in gloomy imaginings as they hurried away from Gloucester like thieves in the night. She feigned fevers in order to forestall her father's continually renewed offensives, swooned and fainted and coughed and sighed in the face of a stream of punishing invective. They shared the Bristol coach with a frail solicitor and his family who had been eaten out of house and home by the troops billeted upon them, ruined by the third royal invasion in less than a year. They had had enough, and were moving to the newly captured city in the hope of avoiding the rampaging armies. Mr Rice and his family had packed themselves and their belongings into the coach, leaving precious little space for the Morrisons' much reduced household. Sir Gilbert was forced to whisper in his daughter's ear, a habit which Mrs Rice, already much distressed by her recent ordeals, found uncommonly rude.

'And let me assure you here and now, young lady, if you imagine for a moment I am going to stand by and let that upstart Telling come calling, you've got another thing coming, my girl.'

Tetbury.

'Yes, well, he won't last long with Prince Rupert's lifeguard, I can tell you that for nothing, why d'you think the arrogant swine wanted him in the first place? To shut his mouth, of course.'

Chipping Sodbury.

'And old Nybb won't have heard the last of it and all. I

317

hope those straw-brained buggers Eli and Zach know how to keep their mouths shut.'

And on and on and on and on until they were home. Well, Kilmersden Hall at any rate.

By which time Bella's imagined illness had become a fully fledged and very real fever. She was so weak with the shivering chills they had to carry her into the house under the black-browed stare of Lady Ramsay, widow of the late lamented squire, Cavalier, and hopeless debtor, Sir Marmaduke Ramsay.

The formidable woman stood on the top step while they helped the girl into the house. Sir Gilbert was in no mood for any of the widow's abrasive observations. He swept off his hat, bowed stiffly, and watched the servants assist his swooning daughter indoors.

'A touch of the chills, ma'am,' Sir Gilbert reported. 'Life in camp can be somewhat disagreeable at times.' The scowling widow's furious response was interrupted by the excited arrival of a tall youth with a shock of brown hair and an equally dishevelled girl holding her bunched gown about her knees. Sir Gilbert stared at the newcomers through one wet eye.

'Hello, Father-ing! Back from the war-ing already-ing?' the lanky youth called cheerily and somewhat obscurely. Sir Gilbert frowned.

He'd forgotten all about his daft son.

'She's cured him of everything else,' Lady Ramsay reported, when the family assembled for a late (and rather frugal) supper. Jamie Morrison sat straight beside his beaming nurse, staring ahead of him and nodding at everything anyone said. The dolt watched a fat cat purr along the panelling as if it was some striped tiger from the jungles of the east, fascinated by its fluid movements and disdainful glances at the noisy intruder. His father studied every inch of his face, noting his elegant and well-fitted clothing. The last time he had seen him the mad boy was dressed in a sweat-stained shift, all that the drooling idiot could be allowed given his virtual incontinence. Anneliese Ramsay, who had apparently found new purpose in her life nursing the poor splinter, looked from her patient to his red-faced father sitting beside the fire. It was as if she could follow Sir Gilbert's wandering thought processes just as well as his son's.

'They belonged to Thomas. I had to take a little off the arms and legs, but it seemed a shame to let them go to waste,' she announced, glancing guiltily at her black-gowned mother, who scowled from her throne opposite her unwanted guest.

Lady Ramsay would have delighted in taking the intruder by the scruff of his neck and hurling him out of doors herself, but the fact was her poor husband had been duped by this conniving rogue, tricked into borrowing hundreds of pounds which neither he nor his widow had been able to repay. In other words, they were in the merchant's debt. Morrison had been using Kilmersden Hall as his unofficial residence ever since poor Ramsay and young Thomas had gotten themselves killed on Lans-down. He had even brought his idiot son back from the equally destructive battle of Roundway, and left the batty boy in their care while he went off gallivanting with that honey blob of a daughter of his to Gloucester. Now it appeared their crooked schemes had run amiss, because they had come back with their tails well and truly between their legs.

'Well, I must say,' Sir Gilbert said with heartfelt sincerity, 'I can't believe the change. He's practically a new man,' the merchant said, smiling at the radiant Anneliese.

By God, the last time he had seen her she had resembled one of the kitchen drudges, not the eligible daughter of a great (if somewhat straitened) house. The girl seemed to have flourished up all over again since her terrible loss. She had never been reckoned a great beauty – Anneliese had been too often in the company of the bewitching Bella for that – and the tragic deaths of her father and brother had robbed her of what little presence she ever possessed. Now, though, she had blossomed, grown up into a tall, darkly pretty woman with a quick eye and smiling mouth. She seemed to be saving most of her smiles for his dim-witted son, and all!

Poor Jamie had never wanted to be a soldier, but with everybody dashing off to find their buff coats Sir Gilbert had wangled him a commission in his militia. He had served with some distinction and all, but finally lost his nerve (and his wits) at the appalling disaster on Roundway Down. One of the late Lord Clavincale's first acts of cooperation with the Morrison clan had been to arrange for Jamie's immediate release. The poor prisoner of war had eventually been fetched home by Bella's former maid Mary Keziah, in such a pitiful state that his father had barely been able to look at him. Sir Gilbert shook his head and looked again at his newborn son.

'What about all this Father-ing and hello-ing, what's all that about?' he asked.

Lady Ramsay folded her white hands in her black lap.

'I would have imagined the improvement thus far would have been enough for you, sir, rejoice that you have three parts of a son, I can assure you three parts are better than none.'

Sir Gilbert nodded his head at this familiarly barbed tune.

'Indeed, ma'am, I am in your debt,' he said smoothly, reminding the old trout just who it was owed nine hundred pounds to who. 'Your daughter has performed miracles.'

Anneliese blushed fetchingly, reached over to pat her patient's twitching knee. Sir Gilbert noted the movement, Lady Ramsay also.

'When Jamie returned, he would only make animal noises,' she reminded Sir Gilbert. 'Once he had rested I thought I would take him for walks in the grounds, down to the farm, around the park. I suppose he got tired of mooing and baaing at the cattle, and so at last came back to his senses,' she said with a winning smile.

Sir Gilbert shook his head in admiration. 'I don't know how we can thank you,' he said simply. For once, he found his emotions were not under full control. The blasted girl had brought his son back, after all.

'On the contrary, Sir Gilbert, we remain in your debt,' Lady Ramsay observed waspishly. 'How will we ever free ourselves of our duty to you?'

Sir Gilbert blinked rapidly. He didn't want to have to talk and tangle about money at a time like this. Anneliese lowered her head. Jamie beamed. The formidable widow scowled once more, indeed it appeared to the merchant her iron-mould features were incapable of representing any other expression.

'However, my daughter has naturally developed something of an affection for your son,' she growled, 'having been in his company, and none other, for so long.'

Sir Gilbert nervously licked his lips. The widow couldn't bring herself to elaborate on the distressing development.

'I . . . well, we really,' Anneliese began, 'have become fond friends. And, well, when he's fully better . . .'

'*If* he's fully better,' Lady Ramsay corrected.

'If he's fully better, we would like to marry.'

Sir Gilbert held on to his seat as if he was in danger of toppling into the grate. He opened and closed his mouth, looking from the girl to his daft-headed son.

'Well, Jamie,' he asked at last, 'and what have you got to say about it?'

Jamie smiled. 'Me-ing and Anneliese, Father-ing,' he said, 'are in love-ing.' He nodded his head, brows folded in deep concentration. 'And so-ing we want to get married-ing.'

'There!' Anneliese cried, 'What do you think of that-ing?' she asked with a laugh.

Sir Gilbert could have cried at this unexpected and marvellous twist. Just when he thought he had been bundled back to oblivion, fate had taken a hand (or two) and set him back up again! He leapt up as if he had been sitting on a pan of hot coals.

'A toast,' he called. 'To the happy couple!'

BY

PRINCE MAURICE'S HEADQUARTERS,

OUTSIDE EXETER

'Gentlemen,' Prince Maurice called to his assembled officers, his hoarse voice rather more heavily accented than his legendary brother's, 'a toast. To the early victory of His Majesty King Charles!'

'The early victory of His Majesty King Charles!' a dozen inebriated voices bawled back.

The sooty-faced, dusty-coated, and sweaty-shirted officers had crammed themselves into the command post, forcing the weary staff officers to gather up their maps and dispatches and orders and requisition forms and take refuge outside.

The night air was crisp, and a stiff breeze was blowing in from the sea, gathering up the smokes and fumes over the battered town and washing them away up towards the bustling Royalist camp. A mob of grinning Cornish musketeers made their way up the slope through the choking fogs escorting a squad of miserable Roundhead officers. They shivered in the cold wind, exchanging wondering glances as the drunken shouts rang out from the brightly illuminated pavilion.

'Gah, not so bliddy cocky now, eh, boys,' Jethro Polruan suggested, tapping a wounded ensign on his bandaged arm with the sooty barrel of his musket. 'Wiped the smile off your faces, you traitorizin' scum,' the giant leered. The bloody defenders avoided his fiercely glinting eyes, staring at the floor like sinners.

Exeter had fallen after a short, fierce siege.

The town had been hemmed in from any possible relief by land, and with all available reserves hurrying over the Cotswolds towards the desperately held city of Gloucester Parliament sent the Earl of Warwick to strengthen its beleaguered western capital from the sea. But although the favourable winds rushed the Roundhead ships across Lyme Bay, the fleet had not been able to negotiate the bottleneck estuary of the Exe without coming under enfilading fire from the enemy batteries set up along both banks.

One of the brave men-of-war which had tried to run the gauntlet had been struck by a lucky cannon shot which had carried away most of its rudder. The great battleship had run aground in the notoriously tricky channels, its guns blazing defiance as the gleeful Royalist gunners feverishly sponged and loaded their glowing culverins. The mighty ship lost its masts and was reduced to a blazing hulk in under an hour. The Cornishmen crowded along the banks, cheering and whistling as they watched the one-sided duel and the inevitable destruction of the oaken intruder. They had ducked down as a sudden enormous explosion tore the wretched hulk to matchwood and sent a pillar of orange flame soaring into the night sky.

Twenty minutes later a dozen or more waterlogged survivors had been fished out of the shallows and frog-marched up the slope to the Prince's headquarters, where they stood in a sullen, shivering circle beside their land-locked brethren. Jethro Polruan left off baiting the sorry officers and shoved his way into the gang of wretched castaways.

'And 'ere's some seamen, boys,' he called over his formidable shoulder, his grinning cronies packing in behind their straw-headed champion.

Polruan and the rest of the hard-fighting Cornish infantry had fought their way through Devon and Somerset and half of Wiltshire, driven Sir William Waller's Roundheads off Lansdown, rushed out of Devizes to finish his army on Roundway, and then helped storm Bristol in the space of a few short weeks. They had then returned home to tackle the Roundhead garrisons they had left behind them. First off, Exeter. A pious little scorpion's nest just the same as Gloucester. The town had rudely rejected the King's summons to remain loyal to the crown, and now, all these months later, it had paid the price for its disobedience.

The unruly mob of cursing heathens had poured through the burning corpse-choked breaches like giant rats, driving the defenders away from their walls and securing the town for their scowling commander.

'Yer webbed feet couldn't save you, lads,' Polruan chuckled, eyeing the dripping, shivering seamen in their sodden blue jackets and striped canvas trousers. 'Ah, 'tis a pity we sank her, I wager she's stuffed full of vittles and strong liquors and all.' There was a furious blast of shouting and bawling as the hungry Cornish contemplated the prospects of salvaging the vessel. Polruan jabbed a scowling sailor in the shoulder, disliking his impudent grin. 'Nah, they would 'ave drunk it all down themselves, trying to steer that bliddy tub up under us guns!'

'Might as well try buggerin' an 'alf-starved tiger!'

'You prickless plover, Judd, keep yer dirty 'abits to yerself!'

'Bastard cowards, the lot of 'em!' Simon Shevick shouted from the back.

'Throw 'em all back for the fishes, is what I say,' Gideon Woolly roared.

The dangerously milling mob were illuminated all at once by bright yellow light. The Cornish officer corps had completed their council of war and threw back the tent flap to go about their duties. Colonel Scipio Porthcurn recognized the surly mob at the centre of the disturbance, and ground his teeth in fury.

By God, as soon as they had finished with the enemy they were at each other or up to mischief! His regiment was like a gang of starving cut-throats, forever on the lookout for more trouble. The black-bearded officer drew his sword and used the bloody hilt to batter his way through the milling musketeers towards the eye of the storm. His men called warnings, shoved and tripped him, but dared not disobey their commander within spitting distance of the Prince's quarters. He had a bliddy temper on him, mind, that Maurice fellow.

'You again, Polruan?' Porthcurn called wearily, frowning at the familiar silhouette of his giant sergeant. The enormous red-suited rogue rolled his eyes.

'Why d'you always pick me out?' he complained. 'It's never Downderry or Shevick or bliddy Woolly there.'

A small waterlogged officer stepped out of the ring of wide-eyed prisoners, took off his battered leather hat, and pointed it at the bandit in chief in question. 'This man has been threatening my men and these prisoners,' the pale-faced castaway reported angrily. Porthcurn regarded the bright-eyed sailor, the brown hair plastered to his scalp still wound about with bits of stringy weed from the muddy estuary. 'I demand to see the officer in charge.' Porthcurn left Polruan snorting and stamping to one side and bent down to peer at the plucky Roundhead.

'And who might you be, shouting the odds at my men?' the Cornishman demanded, his black eyes blazing. Didn't these dogs ever give up? Washed up on a beach in front of five thousand Royalists and the fanatical bastard still wanted to pick fights!

The undernourished seaman settled his hat back on his head, as if he had a commission from the King himself to order the Cornish about as he felt fit.

'I am Captain Gallen Fey, of Parliament's ship *Conqueror*.' He nodded over his trembling shoulder at the fiercely blazing wreck they could see out on the black tide.

'Is that right? Well, you're a prisoner of Prince Maurice now, my old matey,' Porthcurn sneered. 'And if I were you, I'd watch what I was saying, from here on in.'

'Ah, you tell 'im, zor!'

'Thrash the bliddy knave!'

Fey ignored the ribald advice. 'I've taken dozens of you lot prisoners, and always treated you fair and square,' he retorted. 'Now will you please get my men under cover before they take a chill?'

'Take a bliddy chill? I'll give 'ee a chill, you jiggumbobbing bastard . . .'

'All right, Polruan.' Porthcurn held his hairy hand up for silence, and regarded the game captain. He couldn't help but admire the man's guts, standing there in his piss-wet drawers arguing the toss with his regiment of murderous cut-throats. He hadn't come bleating for quarter like others he'd come across, leaving his men to rot on the surf like a netsman's cast-offs.

'See these men into the barn there,' he ordered his muttering desperadoes. 'They can change clothes with the dead up there or go buck naked, it's up to you.'

Fey could hardly ask for more, given that most of the

Cornish troops looked like badly dressed scarecrows themselves.

'Well, don't stand there gawping, get to it,' he bellowed as the reluctant mob shuffled and mumbled. He took Fey's elbow, guiding him through the surly throng. 'And you, Captain, maybe you'd like to come along to my quarters. I've acquired a bottle or two from your town there.' Porthcurn eyed the shivering stranger.

Fey shook his head slowly. He was trembling so much it was difficult to make out the gesture from his sea-racked shivers.

'You can keep the liquor, sir, but I'll not say no to a glass of water. I must have swallowed half the Exe.'

Porthcurn ignored his muttering men, and escorted the frozen fanatic towards his mean billet.

'Fuckin' kelders! Mebbe we ought to cook 'em all a nice plate of parsnips while we're at it!'

'Polruan! I heard that!'

THE BRICKWORTH ROAD,

NEAR GLOUCESTER,
8 SEPTEMBER, 1643

Hugo Telling stretched his aching arms, yawned like a culverin, and blinked to clear his foggy vision. He felt as if he had been galloped over by all the King's horse at least a dozen times, every sore muscle, brittle bone, and taut tendon stretched slack with nervous exhaustion. Hugo peered down at the crowded road, still clogged with the Earl of Essex's equally exhausted relief army. They had succeeded in forcing their way through to the beleaguered town, but the sight of a dozen Royalist sentinels posted along the nearest ridge still made them jittery. Some of the nervier musketeers had even fallen out of the dense column to open fire at the shadows on the hill, and their wasteful shots were falling dismally short.

'What a damned shower,' his subordinate and saviour Benjamin Hazell called from his post along the end of the breezy plateau. The cornet lifted his helmet to run his well-manicured hands through his golden ringlets, which curled and sprang obligingly in the sudden blow. The young swell raised his immaculately shaven chin a notch, casting a disdainful eye along the shuffling files of anxious enemy troops. He stood up in his stirrups as if to expose himself even further, lifting the bright blue banner he carried in a silent challenge to the scowling old tapsters and crop-headed apprentices cowering at the foot of the

slope. Telling studied the cornet through the corner of his
eye, not quite knowing what to make of his new companion. He looked like a dandy but fought like a cornered
wolf, took as much care over his dress as a duchess yet
wouldn't think twice about sleeping under a hedge with
the men. He often spoke with a ridiculously affected lisp
but could swear like a trooper, and although he had risked
his life on his behalf he wouldn't hear a word of Hugo's
blushing thanks.

'Don't mention it, sir,' he told the bloody nosed captain,
his golden eyelashes fluttering as if he was in excruciating
pain. Hugo, mortally embarrassed by his supposed subordinate's clenched expression, imagined he had broken
some private code, violated some rule of etiquette by
thanking his rescuers. Alexander Gull, Hazell's heavily
built manservant and orderly, shrugged his shoulders and
pinched his raw cheese of a nose between his grubby
thumb and forefinger. The bow-legged horseman who had
proved so deadly with the carbine carried the new captain
all the way back to their temporary quarters at Compton,
holding out his arm as a buff-coated banister rail as Hugo
climbed down to the trampled grass with a wince.

'Ah, don't mind 'im, sir. 'Tweren't as if he was doin'
any of it for you, like.'

Hugo frowned, pushing back his hat to study the bare-
knuckle brute.

'Come now,' Hugo responded rather waspishly. 'If it
wasn't for you and Mr Hazell, I would be lying back there
now,' Hugo insisted, bewildered by the bodyguard's knock-
about banter. He had imagined that rancid bandit Nybb
was bad enough. Gull seemed to be operating on a level of
servitude somewhere beyond Hugo's reckoning. If Hazell

asked him to lie in the mud to stop his horse getting dirty, Gull would do it, and smile while he was at it.

'Ah, yes, sir, but his Highness was along the ridge, see, sir,' Gull leaned over his exhausted charger's neck, nodding his broad, freckled head. 'He was only showing off to the Prince, see, sir.'

Hugo frowned. 'I didn't see the Prince, not after we left the gully.'

Gull tapped his large, rather squashed nose. 'But he saw you, sir, and a pretty job you made of it, if I may say so, sir.' Telling shook his head, unable to fathom the oaf's bizarre sense of duty. 'Mr Hazell, sir, he's sworn, sir, see? He'll end the war dead or a general, sir, that's what he said.'

Hugo pulled at his sparse russet moustache.

'By performing heroics in front of the Prince?'

'Wouldn't be the first, sir, nor the last neither.'

That was true enough, Hugo supposed. He wondered if Gull suspected him of similar motives. Charging about with reckless abandon – so long as Rupert was there to witness it. Hugo shivered with disgust. *He'd* never stoop to such second-rate theatricals, he thought piously.

Hugo pictured his own true love, Bella, his very own angel, who had found a place in her heart for him at last. He grinned to himself, lewdly imagining the ravishing damsel stark naked on a dapple grey, watching him lead a charge from these superb heights.

'Course, he'll do tricks for serving wenches and tavern gals an' all,' Gull went on, tightening his helmet strap and bloating his red chins. Hugo snorted under his breath, returned his wandering attention to the road.

The raw red track threaded between the trees at the

foot of the slope like an open sore alive with brown- and red- and green-jacketed men, the deep and waterlogged ruts trapping the wheels of their heavily laden baggage carts and diverting them this way and that through the trampled mire. Hundreds of toiling soldiers had been detailed to lend a shoulder, pushing and hauling and kicking the creaking wagons free. The Earl of Essex's cumbersome artillery train was faring even worse, long lines of oxen straining and stumbling and shitting as the drivers whipped them along through the treacherous, malodorous morass. Every gun dragged by dug deeper scores into the track, tearing up ancient foundations laid by equally wet and weary Roman legions.

Gull followed Hugo's gaze, shaking his head at their sweaty antics.

'Well, it proves one thing, sir,' he said cheerily, 'it proves them Roundheads wrong, see, sir? God with us, they'll tell you. Well, if God was with 'em 'e wouldn't 'ave gone and plashed up the old road there, would 'e now? Why, it's no better for them than it were for us goin' on Chelnem.'

Cornet Hazell turned towards his burly bodyguard. 'I sometimes wonder whether you're on the right side, Gull, you seem to spend so much time wrestling with theological imponderables,' he quipped, twirling the waxed points of his golden moustaches. Gull grunted in bewilderment, watched the cornet spur his stamping horse on along the ridge, parading the colour to the distant marching men.

'He do trouble me so, when he comes out with his outlandish talk,' the loyal bodyguard complained with a frown. Hugo yawned once more, watched the young dandy's annoying progress along the hilltop.

'He won't last long waving that flag like that,' Hugo snapped.

'Ah, none of 'em do, sir,' Gull replied. 'A commission with the Prince's lifeguard? I forget how many we've had this summer alone.' He glanced at his stubby fingers as if the number was beyond convenient calculation. 'They never lasts more than a week or two.'

Telling eyed the simple-minded brute, wondering if the crafty cornet had left him behind on purpose to disconcert his new captain. 'Bring your own winding-sheet, is all I can say. Rupert'll 'ave you in it in a week or three.' He nodded wisely, as if he would say a whole lot more if requested. Hugo licked his pale lips.

He had barely clapped eyes on his notorious commander since his brusque appointment back at the camp. Telling hadn't imagined the Prince would be dropping by his quarters every night to share a bottle and a pipe and report the day's doings, but he had been looking forward to some closer contact with the single-minded warlord.

'Well, there's never any shortage of volunteers for the lifeguard,' he responded briskly.

Gull shook his head sadly. 'No, sir, there's not. Come queuing, they do. You were lucky Captain Neville got shot, sir, otherwise there would have been no place for you.'

Hugo snorted with anxious amusement. The Prince would have shot the fool himself to make room for Telling, he thought smugly. Why, he had saved his life, after all, when Sir Gilbert and his cronies came looking for trouble. Telling remembered the mad clash of steel, the shouts in the dark and the sudden splashing. By God, he'd damn near messed himself, leaping away from his beloved Bella as if she had been struck by lightning. If he hadn't been

where he wasn't supposed to be Morrison's fanciful depu-
tation might have trapped the Prince and his mysterious
lady friend by that pond, and forced him into some hateful
confrontation back at the court. The plotters had hoped
to enlist Telling as well, making him party to the unworthy
enterprise. He would rather have been shot through the
heart than be thought a willing hand in such dishonour-
able doings. He was a soldier, not a common cutpurse.

Telling remembered Clavincale, swaying in front of
Bella with his sword poised at her sweet neck. The blow he
gave him would have floored an ox. But just as he had
been unable to stand by while the Prince was appre-
hended, he could not have allowed that fat, greasy-fingered
bully to lay a hand on his lover.

He missed her like he would miss his lungs, his heart,
and all his innards. Without her he was an empty pot
rolling about the deck of a stricken ship, carried this way
and that by the—

The sudden shot twanged overhead, startling Telling
out of his lugubrious imaginings. He yanked his new horse
about and peered down towards the other end of the hill
in time to see a gang of enemy musketeers jump out of the
furze bushes and empty their muskets at the crowing
cornet. The sudden volley made Hazell's horse rear with
fright, but the stinging fusillade was aimed high. A ball
tore straight through his silk-fringed flag, almost yanking
the heavy lance out of his grip.

'Hazell!' Telling yelled. Gull ducked down over his
horse and turned to go to the assistance of his errant
master. Telling paused, collecting his prancing mount and
trying to register the perils. At least a dozen enemy snipers
had worked their way up the slope under cover of the trees
and bushes, and more might be lurking just over the rise.

He watched Gull thunder towards the disturbance and cursed under his breath. God's holy wounds, he already owed the braggart cornet a life!

'Patrol, charge!' Telling yelled, drawing his sword and pulling his snorting horse around towards the flurry of firing. Lazy lead bullets described ponderous arcs over the grassy knoll, like fat bees at the limit of their endurance. Telling imagined he might reach out and grab the burning balls, pick their bullets from the sky for them. He leaned over the big mare as she picked up speed, eyes bulging like brown apples as the inexperienced horse whinnied and threw her head in fright. The sudden charge took the wind out of the snipers' sails. They turned tail and fled back to the rocky cover further down the slope. Telling could see them reloading feverishly, ramming their charges down the smoky barrels with frantic haste. Cornet Hazell mastered his horse and trotted off as if he was at a parade, his pinched nose in the air as if he could not be bothered to punish such ungentlemanly scoundrels. Telling sighed with relief, tugging the reins to the right to take the big mare away from the hill. The Royalist patrol swirled away over the green hill in a sudden riot of flashing steel and confusing colour, and disappeared over the ridge. The watching Roundheads gave themselves a hoarse cheer, and traipsed back down to join their friends for the last few miles of their long march to Gloucester.

'Christ Jesus, they couldn't hit a tent from the inside!' Billy Butcher moaned, shielding his eyes as he watched the brief firefight unfold at the top of the hill. Most of Mercer's men had fallen out from their duties in the mud-clogged hollow to watch the Royalist popinjays driven off by a sudden sortie by a detachment of the Red Regiment of the London Trained Band. The city militia forces were loudly reckoned to be the rock of the cause, the most reliable unit in the entire army (not least by themselves) and had been unable to resist interfering with the forlorn Cavalier rearguard silhouetted on the top of the ridge. The grumbling soldiers replaced their hats and helmets and resumed their duties, lending a hand with the cumbersome baggage train.

'What a performance. All that smoke for so little fire,' Stephen Talbot complained, closing one eye to squint at the rapidly retreating enemy horsemen. He had a clay pipe clamped between his teeth but still managed to spit on the road like one of Wallenstein's twenty-year veterans. Colston Muffet hurried back along the column, counting heads to make sure none of his section had decided to join the Red Regiment's little escapade.

'Get those carts moving, we're supposed to be in Gloucester tonight,' he growled, annoyed all over again at the noisy new men who had fought one brief battle and thought themselves experts.

'What about a little detour? There's plump houses away up the lane there,' John Jewell asked, transferring his pike from one chafed shoulder to the other.

'Yeah, what about a bit of plunder, eh? We've walked far enough for it, that's for sure.'

'My cousin marched to Etch-Hill, and he says they looted every house on the way!' Rodney Sark piped up, his beady brown eyes glittering with mischief.

Hereward Gillingfeather coughed menacingly, his livid berry of a face flushed red. 'We're soldiers of Christ, not fornicating horse thieves!' he snarled. Stephen Talbot raised his left leg and gave him a moist fart.

336

'Anybody who turns his back on the Lord's work should fall out now, I'll not march with thieves and whoremongers,' Gillingfeather ranted, his thin, hairy features pinched and paling with righteous anger.

Long Col caught his arm, held the wiry little fighter back. 'Don't tell 'em that, Gilly or they'll all be off,' the elder sergeant advised with a wink.

The distracted soldiers looked up as Captain Sparrow strode back through the mire, his knee-boots sucking and plopping in the liquid filth. The towering champion had earned grudging respect from some of his men since the fight at Stow. They were impressed as much by their own feats of arms as by his leadership, but he had stood his ground so they had stood theirs. The fact he had a running quarrel with some upstart Cavalier made him appear almost glamorous to the crop-headed apprentice boys who were but lately come to the colours. Their very own hero of a captain earned even more respect when the youngsters heard that the row had started over some flirt-gill of a merchant's daughter. Why, it was like something out of that Shakespeare fellow.

'Hello, Captain, almost there, are we?' a tousled musketeer called cheerily, nudging his idle mates into line. William snorted something non-committal and wiped a dirty hand over the heavy stubble on his jaw. Once again, the long march had flayed the spare flesh from his frame and features, turning the portly youth into a sunken-cheeked, black-bearded pirate. Long Col looked deeper, noting the red rings beneath the captain's bleary eyes and his short breath. He straightened up beside his friend, nodded familiarly.

'You all right there, Will?'

Sparrow nodded bleakly, rubbed the worn leather of

his tender right forearm. 'It's the damp, it's got into the muscle or something,' he complained. The skin was still puckered pink from the sword wound he had received back in Bristol trying to fence with a Royalist officer who clearly knew his business. If the King's man hadn't been cut down in the vicious, swirling street fight near the Frome Gate, William would have been run through.

He had tried to practice his swordplay on the long march from London, testing the weight of his heavy naval cutlass and even going through the strokes with his left arm, but he was normally too exhausted to do anything more than collapse in whatever miserable billet they had managed to secure. If it came to another fight, William would rely on the halberd. It was shorter and handier than a pike, the broadleaved blade capable of slashing and smashing as well as prodding and jabbing. If it came to the crunch, he would have to defend himself as best he could until his aching arm had healed completely. If it healed completely, he thought gloomily.

'You were lucky to keep it at all, if you want to know,' Long Col scolded, falling in beside the captain as the company resumed its weary march, or rather, shove. 'Another couple of weeks' rest would have done it a sight more good than this.'

'It was all right for you, Col, London's your town! What was I supposed to do with a few shillings and a poxy arm? Dig graves? Sell chestnuts?'

'You could have had a nice billet writing them pamphlets,' Long Col reminded him. 'Talk about the easy life!'

William sighed. It was true he had already turned down the chance to earn his crust writing inflammatory propaganda for the Parliament. The Roundhead grandees had quickly realized the King's party held the upper hand when it came to spreading the word, to propagating their just causes. Parliament needed pamphleteers as well as pikemen, and yet here he was stuck with the pikes. He hadn't even held a pen since the spring!

All the details of his old life, family and friends, all the minuscule methods he had learned as an apprentice back at Greesham's in Bristol, were no more than idle memories, fast becoming as dim as his long-lost childhood.

'My mother always warned me about falling in with bad company,' he joked. The two of them made room for a team of sweating, lowing oxen, lashed to a culverin which seemed to be enjoying a life of its own, sticking and sliding in the slick swamp.

'Not far now, though, eh?' Long Col asked, his grey eyes caked with fatigue and lack of rest.

'Another mile or two. We'll be sleeping on feather beds tonight, Col, that I can promise you.'

Long Col snorted, fell in behind his captain. Feather beds my arse, he thought ruefully.

Mercer's Cheesemongers might not have been given feather beds, but the welcome they received from the citizens of Gloucester almost made up for the oversight.

They saw their colours first, blowing proud on the horizon, hanging slack between the pressing trees as the vast conglomeration snaked through the recaptured valleys. Red flags mainly, carrying the small cross of St George in the top left corner. Behind them masses of smaller banners sporting family crests. Clusters of yellow stars or sunburst streaks, white spots and wavy piles. Some of the cavalry cornets carried religious or political slogans, others bore Latin inscriptions which had been carried over English fields since the days of the Normans.

And beneath the spectacular shadowplays of flags and banners came the relief army.

Great shuffling hedges of pikemen, mobile thickets marching to the distant thunder of the drums and the wind-blown whistle of flute and pipe. Endless files of musketeers tramped alongside carrying their weapons butt up against the weather. Behind the troops came huge convoys of leaning wagons which reminded the garrison of ships under sail, their canvas awnings blown up like pigs' bladders in the fresh breeze. Behind them more guns than they could count, hauled by steaming oxen hitched in tandem. Drivers and carters and tinkers and hawkers threaded their way through the colourful procession, adding to the general tumult.

The garrison and townsfolk hardly believed their eyes when the red and grey columns finally appeared on the main road. Regiment after regiment of russet horsemen ushered the psalm-singing relief force the last few thousand yards, over the desperate wasteland the King's men had left behind. The weary, bloody, and bandaged defenders crammed themselves on the battered ramparts, endangering the walls which had withstood so much. They opened lanes through the dust and rubble and poured out into the scorched wilderness which had until the summer been pleasant pastures and market gardens. Hundreds flocked around the tottering towers to watch the glorious cavalcade approaching from the hitherto empty eastern hills.

And in the van the Earl of Essex himself, resplendent in gilt armour and attended by a sober congregation of senior officers in buff coat and sash. The rebelled nobility of

England, lords and knights, a smattering of MPs and a flock of veteran officers recently returned from service on the Continent. Behind their eye-watering assortment of personal banners came Essex's lifeguard of horse, followed by two thousand more cavalry.

Each troop, company, and regiment was greeted with a roar of welcome by the ecstatic citizens so loud that some of the men at the back of the immense column were convinced they must have marched straight into the most elaborate ambush of all. Hats were flung into the air with no hope of recovery. Armfuls of blooms were flung like fragrant grenades into the soldiers' astonished faces, forming a colourful slurry under their boots and hoofs. Even scowling Puritan matrons dashed forward to give the wide-eyed Roundheads a chaste kiss on their stubbled cheeks.

'By the bowels of Holy Moses, boys, did you see her?' Billy Butcher exclaimed, clutching his warm cheek as a particularly daring maiden darted back towards her black-suited parents. He tried to mark time to talk to her but he was carried along by the press of men crowding into the gate behind. He cricked his neck looking about for her, lifting his hat and giving the beaming girl a filthy wink. Gillingfeather nudged his young companion in the arm, nodded on towards the centre of the transported city, the tall spire of the cathedral standing proud of the hunched hovels and battered town houses.

'Remember, Billy, soldiers of Christ,' Gillingfeather reminded him.

Butcher jammed his hat back on, frowning at his elder and mentor. 'What street's this? By the gate, look, mark the spot, someone!'

Long Col seemed to have stretched himself for the

occasion, striding beside William Sparrow into the godly city, his ears ringing with their violent cheers. They had been given a rousing send-off back at Hounslow, but the capital's fond farewells would have been drowned out by these deafening shrieks of welcome. Sparrow had never seen such enthusiasm for the cause he had taken up. Maybe he had made the right choice after all.

'However did the King imagine he would take this place?' William shouted into the veteran's dirty ear. 'There must be more Roundheads here than in the whole country put together!'

Long Col nodded sourly. 'Aye, you're right enough. But those wagons we've been pushin' aren't carrying powder alone, you know.'

William raised his red-rimmed eyes. 'They aren't all after money,' Sparrow scolded him, shocked at his sergeant's lack of belief.

'No, mebbe not. But there'll never be enough there to pay 'em what they've earned. Remember back in Holborn, the money we drew? They'll be a sight quieter when we march out and leave 'em to it!'

The grey-haired veteran's gloomy prediction brought the captain back to earth with a bump. He'd forgotten for a moment the fact that they had only accomplished the first half of their dangerous mission. They had arrived, and now they would have to get back, across one hundred and fifty miles of woods and hills and under the noses of as many enemy garrisons as there were fleas on a dog. And worse than that, they would have to get around the King's entire army, which had never been beaten in a straight fight.

William tramped along, the throb in his arm flaring up all over again as he contemplated the punishing pre-dicament.

But Long Col's forebodings could hardly stem the celebrations. William spent a good minute or two pondering the strategic situation before he was carried away once more with the joyous clamour of their welcome.

'Praise the Lord! The day of judgement is at hand!' a merchant roared from the crowd.

'Amen, brother!' Gillingfeather retorted, beginning to enjoy himself amongst so many godly folk.

John and Ella Clamp, hungry and tired and cross-eyed with excitement, had screamed themselves hoarse, desperately hanging on to their errant offspring in the fearful crush by the gate. Even old Gwen had left off her muttering to join the family on the walls, loudly enquiring why them 'bliddy rebels had taken s' long t' get yere'.

'N' mind how long they took t' get yere, Mother,' Ella scolded her, 'they'm yere now, and tha's all that matters!' The old crone gave her a sour look.

'And who's goin' to pay for my house, eh? Turned out of me home at my age? It's a disgrace, if you want to know.'

Ella shook her head, beads of sweat running down from her grubby bonnet as she elbowed her place on the turf wall she had helped maintain.

'Never you mind yer house,' she cried. 'We'll have time to build you another one, now the King's finished his business with us!'

The King might have finished his business with the town, but he certainly hadn't finished with its worn-out rescuers.

BY

WAINLODE HILL,

*NEAR GLOUCESTER,
10 SEPTEMBER 1643*

'Two days. I ask yer. All that bleedin' way and we get two days' rest 'fore we're off again,' Billy Butcher complained, lifting his hat to wipe his forehead along his shiny coat-sleeve. 'It's bleedin' pack ponies they want to recruit, not men.'

'Get on, boy,' Stephen Talbot called from the next rank, 'they took one look down Rodney's breeches and couldn't tell a difference!'

'I bet he could whip the King's men out of Gloucester without crossing the county line!'

'He certainly floored that wench with the holed drawers!' John Jewell shouted from the back. 'She fell in a swoon as soon as he whipped 'un out!'

'She made 'un pay twice over, mind!' The vastly amused musketeers fell about as they shuffled along the steeply rising lane towards the bare shoulder of the hill. Now they had reached the safety of Gloucester the campaign seemed as good as won. Their nervous imaginings had proved groundless, and Prince Rupert's much vaunted cavalry had turned out to be a set of slinking shadows, forever darkening some woody horizon but reluctant to come to grips. They had raided Dalbier's quarters one night, Behre and Godwin's the next, but hadn't been seen since. So much for the King's mighty horsemen, the recently graduated veterans thought smugly. Now all that was left was to gather up as much loot as possible and get back to London before they had it taken off them.

The Earl of Essex's requirements were broadly similar to his more troublesome troops'. He had stayed in Gloucester just long enough to accept the heartfelt thanks of its brave citizens and garrison, and to replenish the excellent Colonel Massey's dangerously dwindling supplies of gunpowder. He had also left several jealously guarded treasure chests with coin enough to settle the city's principal outstanding debts: hard-earned wages for its toiling troops and labouring citizens. Food was collected from the outlying villages recently liberated from the swarming Royalist quartermasters, and carried in to the city under the watchful eye of the earl's cavalry. The worst breaches in the battered walls were quickly made good, and the abandoned Royalist works relieved of anything of value. Dr Chillingworth's laboriously constructed siege engines – the people had nicknamed the silly machines sows – had been dragged off for firewood.

With the city safely reprovisioned and his tired troops rested, the earl returned to his maps and charts, and pondered the best route home. The obvious way was to simply turn about towards the east and follow the Stow road, then cut across country to Chipping Norton and Buckingham. The trouble was, this was precisely the district into which the King's unfought army of up to twenty thousand men had apparently vanished. Rupert was reputed to have around six thousand horse alone, against his sober, God-fearing, but highly strung four thousand. He might well have the benefit of a few thousand more foot, but foot and baggage could only hope to cover eight miles in a day. Two weeks on the road with the King's army lurking on his flanks? It was enough to make the great Swedish warlord Gustavus Adolphus blanch.

Robert Devereux, Earl of Essex was a slow, serious-minded soldier, whose father had been executed after his disastrous dalliances with Queen Elizabeth. Ponderous but popular, dedicated but indecisive, Essex had been given the senior command of all forces loyal to the Parliament, and had managed to keep the King's resurgent forces from the capital for over a year. He knew in his bones the present campaign would either save his troubled cause or – if his army was defeated – leave the capital unprotected. His main priority needs must be the immediate return to London. The men might have enjoyed a few weeks' rest and relaxation in the west, but the King might have already set off for the unprotected heart of the cause. The earl had made up his mind to march north to throw the King's scouts off the trail, before swinging sharply around and making a headlong dash for safety. To this widely approved end, the entire army had marched out of Gloucester and taken the north road for Tewkesbury.

Mercer's regiment had been detached from the main body and sent off on a parallel course to forage the outlying farms and meadows between the north road and the Severn. The noisy, overconfident Londoners were delighted to be away from the confines of the camp, the vociferous preachermen and stern-faced Puritans who went scurrying to the senior officers the moment a fellow swore or went off for a drink. Some of the more thoughtful soldiers had saved a bottle or two of ale or strong liquor for the journey home rather than drink it all up during Gloucester's revels, prepared to risk a dressing-down from some half-drunken superior for the sake of a little Dutch courage when push came to shove. There had also been a fair number of illicit liaisons during their two-night stay in Gloucester, although the ungodly soldiers who had succumbed to the perils of the flesh derided the scandalous shortage of decent women.

'No wonder them Cavaliers didn't bother gettin' in after 'em. What a set of sour-gobbed witches,' Billy Butcher told his leering mates when he finally found his way back to their temporary quarters at the Boothall. Talbot, Jewell, and their well-endowed companion Rodney Sark had joined him on his nocturnal reconnaissances, eager to sample the bacchanalian lifestyle of the modern soldier which they had heard so much about.

But Gloucester was a strictly Puritan city with a rigid moral code. The staggering soldiers had expected brightly lit cat-houses stuffed to the rafters with ravishable fifteen-year-olds: instead they were forced to go further and further into the maze of alleys and leaning hovels of the city stews, seeking out rather more mature companions, drop-dugged widows who dragged them in off the filthy streets before some scowling goodwife could call the constables.

'I arsked after her, course,' Billy reported, rubbing his uncomfortably itching groin.

'Who?'

'The one with the green eyes that gave me that smacker by the gate. Fing is, by the time we found a decent bleedin' tavern we was 'alfway to Wales. I mean, I could 'ardly knock at every door along the way, could I?'

'Rodney could!'

'And he bleedin' did. Black and blue his bell-end was, time we got the stallion stabled!' Stephen Talbot, former bank clerk and now careless veteran of battle and bawdy house, roared with laughter at his own jokes.

'Bring out yer dead!'

'Aye, he was that pissed he would 'ave and all!'

William Sparrow couldn't help chuckling at their outrageous good spirits. They would sober up soon enough when they came on the King's army. He looked up, over the scrawny hedge and up the slope towards the long hog's back of Wainlode Hill. Beyond the steep ridge the wide, swirling Severn, broad enough to stop any but the most complex ambush as they marched north. North? What in God's name did they want to march north for? London was to the east!

Long Col smirked as the carefree company wept with laughter, holding themselves upright on their muddy weapons as they were transported with the hilarity of Butcher's amorous adventures.

'I swear she's given me the pox and all,' the straw-haired young sniper complained, hand busy in his breeches. 'Itches like fuck and the end's about the same colour as old Gilly's ugly mug.'

Hereward Gillingfeather closed his eyes and whispered heartfelt apologies to God as he strode along the verge beside the delighted mob, enduring the hateful boasting as if it was some Papist torture chamber designed to undermine his will. Puce with anger, the wiry little musketeer tried to block up his ears against their profane language. It seemed to him at last three-quarters of the regiment was made up of guttersnipe scum and whore-mongering bloats. The worst sweepings of every alehouse in London. He had fallen out by himself, his musket over his shoulder, and followed his own pious route along the top of the bramble-choked verge, a good head and shoulders above his verminous companions. He too had been transported with ecstasy by the townsfolk he met –

but not for their base reasons. No, these were godly people, sober men and dutiful goodwives who had laboured and fought beside their menfolk, keeping the hordes of Satan at bay. How was it those good citizens had allowed these fornicating Roundhead imps to come amongst them? Ah, the great Prince of Darkness, the stealer of men's souls, knew well his many-fingered servants. He had given them beastlike appendages so that they might go forth and multiply themselves on silly wenches and serving girls. He had given them vile serpent tongues so that they might talk their way into a goodwife's hearth, and seduce her from her duty to Lord and husband.

Ah, yes. He had heard of soldiers whispering secrets to blushing virgins, and because Satan their sire had loaned them lying tongues, they had triumphed, persuading those sweet girls that in times of war like these they could in true heart put aside their precious maidenheads. It would be their way of keeping faith with the cause.

Was he the only true Christian among them, was he the only pilgrim in this boorish battalion?

No. There was Caleb. Caleb the simple-minded captain's boy who had been cast into the great teeming oceans of Satan by his basilisk-eyed imp of a scum-spewing warlock father. The great strapping lad seemed to have grown like a weed on a diet of double-baked bread and fatty bacon, heavy-handed and slow-brained like an enormous two-legged oxen. It was as if he was afraid to grow too much on board that Satanic vessel for fear of attracting more blows from his vicious puke-eater of a father. Now he was with true friends he had blossomed, tearing his shirt and splitting his breeches so they had been forced to fetch new ones from the town.

Gillingfeather glanced down at the wall-eyed giant with

pious approval, watching him shuffling along unawares, swinging his left arm as he went. Caleb marched with head down and hunched back like some great troll of the underworld, his newly turned pike swinging on his right shoulder. He never moved it, despite the weals it left on his pale, hairless skin. He only removed his rusted morion helmet to sleep or to duck his broad, pale head in a stream or trough. Caleb hardly ever looked up, content to follow the rest where ever they led him. To eat and to sleep and to fight as they dictated. A perfect tool, a perfect Christian soldier.

'Captain Sparrow to the front!'

Gillingfeather looked up the lane, peering through the thicket of pikes and musket butts towards the head of their Satanic column.

Colonel Tobias Fulke, game as ever despite his advancing years, had climbed down from his brown mare to argue with the scouts. The old soldier's white head bobbed and ducked as he pointed up the lane and across the heavy clay furrows towards the ridge.

William pushed his way through his highly amused company and presented himself to his angry commander. He had hardly clapped eyes on the colonel during the last stages of the hectic march, the old man having accepted a place of honour riding into Gloucester with the Earl of Essex's senior staff. Now, though, the gallant old gentleman had returned to his beloved men, as bad-tempered and down to earth as ever.

Fulke looked as if he ought to be squatting outside his house weaving wicker baskets rather than leading four and a half hundred fighting men. His fine white hair was as usual blown in a dozen directions by the mischievous breeze, and his face was so flushed it reflected on his burnished breastplate like some snow-capped robin. The scouts were clearly discomfited by the unfamiliar (and ungodly) speech and belligerent manners of the strangers from up-country, stepping from one foot to the other as if they had fallen in with a company of barbarous Turks.

A broad, sallow-faced farmer had strapped himself into an old buff coat and armed himself with an ancient pistol with an elaborately carved stock which looked more dangerous to himself than any daft Cavalier. His two young companions were strange opposites: the one tall and silent, the other a red-haired little weasel with a faceful of sun-ripened freckles who seemed to be doing all the talking.

'Not 'ere, sir. You've gan wrong, sir, somewheres,' the boy exclaimed.

Fulke rifled his orders, squinting at his smudged instructions. 'No mistake, you young hound! Layton's, plain as day. Sheep and pigs and poultry! It's here in black and white!'

'Master Jackson 'ere was overseer to Master Layton, sir,' the red-haired tyke insisted. 'Master Layton's strong for the Parl'ment, sir!'

Fulke frowned. 'Well, he can't be that strong or he wouldn't be on my list! They didn't send you three to me to argue the toss, boy!'

'Beggin' your pardon, Colonel,' Jackson said quietly, nodding thoughtfully, 'but the boy's right, sir. Alderman Layton's as pure for the Parliament as any man here.'

Fulke snorted, rattled his papers in the man's expressionless face. 'Orders from the city. Forage the entire area. Layton's down here as having seven hundred head of sheep alone!'

'Not 'ny more, sir. The King's men went off with most of 'em,' Jackson reported. 'It was me and the boys here as set the fires on the hill to let 'em know you were acomin'.'

Fulke had no time for their incendiary adventures. 'I have my orders. Now either you lead us to the farm or you can bugger off back to Gloucester and we'll find it ourselves!'

Jackson absorbed his fiery outburst with a serene nod. 'We'll lead you up there, sir, but there ain't much left.'

'Right! Sparrow, you take your company and follow these men. We'll take a rest on the top of the cliff there, watch out for trouble.'

Sparrow nodded curtly and stepped over to the verge as the weary regiment resumed its march.

'He's got it wrong, sir, Layton's on our side, sir!' The red-haired boy tugged at Sparrow's coat, his lively blue eyes starting in alarm.

Sparrow glanced down at the pesky wretch, shook his arm free. 'This lot's our side, lad,' he said, nodding his head at the shuffling soldiery. 'So everybody else is their side, see?'

Nicodemus Burke let go of the big captain's arm, and waited impatiently while he collected his men. Sparrow turned to the talkative boy, his stubbled head tilted to one side like an inquisitive eagle. 'Well?' Nicodemus shrugged.

Jackson pointed over the hedge towards the cinder track which cut across the clay field like a rusty knife. 'Master Layton's house is over the way. But you'll find nothing.'

They found an old wagon without wheels and a damp cellar stacked with broken barrels. Apple cores littered the floor, crunching under their shoes as they searched the spider's stronghold for hidden vittles. A stack of ruby wine bottles had been pulled over and looted, the empty bottles broken against the mouldy wall. The stables had been stripped clean of straw and tack and spare shoes. Bags of nails and split saddles had been removed from the webbed rafters. In one stall they found a dead colt, too wild to take the saddle a Royalist cornet had tried to throw over its back. The kitchen was no more than a bare cave, the cold hearth littered with broken plates and dented pans.

Alderman Simon Layton sat in the shambles in his stained shirt, head in hands as the Roundhead troops completed their fruitless search of his scoured house. Sparrow stood in the doorway, one eye on the owner and another on his cursing men. Master Jackson stood and stared about the yard, Gar Maynard bewildered by the unfamiliar wilderness which had been his home.

'No, I don't expect you'd know the old place. They came back after you lit yer fire the other night,' the ransacked alderman called, recognizing their familiar faces through the fish-eyed kitchen window.

Sparrow leaned against the door jamb. 'They said you were for Parliament,' he said with a careless shrug. 'Only we had orders to forage the farms along the Severn, see?'

Layton looked away from the towering captain who lurked like a black shadow on his own threshold. 'Oh, I see, all right. I told 'em, I warned 'em, but they wouldn't listen.' Layton looked up once more, crying freely as he shook his white fist at the door, the treacherous rogues lurking in the sunlit yard. 'But it wasn't *your* house as they were going to loot, was it? 'Twasn't *your* property they made off with without a by your leave!'

Jackson regarded the bared house and stripped outbuildings, nodded piously. 'No, sir, it weren't. But it wouldn't have made any difference if it was,' he said soberly. 'And be thankful they spared you, sir, they weren't as considerate with Handy Michael or poor Randall.'

Layton jumped to his feet and strode to the door, wiping the back of his hand across his misted eyes. 'Good riddance, aye, that's what I say! I warned 'em, I warned 'em there'd be trouble if they went lighting signal fires for all the county to see!' he told the uninterested captain.

'We've all of us lost, sir. Keeps us trim and true to the cause,' a hairy-faced musketeer muttered from the stairs. Gillingfeather had been detailed to search the upper rooms, but had found nothing of any interest save for some vitriolic Cavalier propaganda carved onto a wall with a blunt knife.

Layton stared at the newcomer, hands on his hips. 'Come away bare-handed, have we? What a shame,' he snorted. 'Maybe you'd like me shirt, look, it's all I've left to give to your fucking cause!'

Sparrow waved the argumentative musketeer out of the room, and hauled his gauntlets on his dirty hands. 'We're sorry for your loss. But the place for you, sir, was down in the town, not hiding on the hill hoping the armies would pass you by. There's not a farm between here and London that hasn't been gone over just as bad as yours.'

Layton's eyes sparkled with malice. 'Is that so? Well you don't look as if you've starved yourself! Where did your last meal come from, eh?'

Sparrow straightened his greasy hat, gave a small, ironic snort. 'I wouldn't like to say. But then again, sir, I don't know where the next one's coming from, so it all balances out in the end, *eh?*'

*

In actual fact, William Sparrow's next meal did turn out to come from Layton's place. Billy Butcher, sniper and forager *extraordinaire*, had roved all over the deserted hill, noting fresh piles of sheep dung. The piled pellets were still steaming, as if a flock had grazed the broad green shoulder that morning. Billy notified Long Col, and half a dozen of them scoured the hedges for the mysteriously missing sheep. They discovered a gate hidden behind some browning brambles, which had been cleverly constructed to conceal a narrow rabbit track cut into the steep red-stone cliff on the western slope of the hill. They scrambled down the crumbling path, slipping on freshly deposited piles of dung, and found themselves in a small river-locked coomb. The natural enclosure was bounded on three sides by the cliff, and to the west by the water-logged meadows along the Severn. Closer inspection revealed that the coomb was enclosed by a narrow duck-weed ditch – a perfect and almost invisible wall preventing the two hundred or so sheep from wandering.

Billy Butcher found the shepherd sleeping under a willow, his holed hat pulled down over his ancient face. His skin looked more like bark than flesh, as if the lousy scarecrow had been caught up in some clever-woman's spell and doomed to be absorbed into the tangled roots of his own resting place. Billy kicked him in the thigh, stepped back as the frightened shepherd leaped to his bare feet.

'Lor' love you, sar, what're you loike creepin' up on a body loike that?'

Billy grinned, raised his dirty thumb towards his unguarded flock. 'Whose are they?'

'Them sheep? Mazur Layton's, sar, G'bless you, sar,' the shepherd replied, taking a look over the sniper's shoulder as the Roundhead troopers dropped their weapons and began shooing the bleating flock towards the steep red cliff. The old man's gap-toothed jaw dropped.

'Lord, sar, what you'm doin'?' he exclaimed, deeply alarmed at the soldiers' ham-fisted antics. The flock broke and scattered like the Roundhead cavalry on Roundway, retreating to all corners of the narrow meadow. They backed up against the ditch, bleating and snorting, staring at the emerald slab of water with their stupid wall-eyes. The shouting musketeers chased after them, driving the flock into the stand of willows in the corner of the field. Billy Butcher sighed.

'You'd best help round them up,' he advised. The shepherd had already pushed past the grinning sniper and was staring at the looters as if they had dropped from the stars. 'You can't have Mazur Layton's flock,' the shepherd wailed, 'he tole I to bring 'em down 'ere when the soldiers comes!'

Billy Butcher raised his musket and fired off one quick, deafening shot. A wall-eyed ewe trotted on for a moment before dropping on her side, twitching violently. The shepherd held his dirty hands over his ears, shocked and stunned by the loud retort and hellish blast of sparks. Billy lowered his musket, grinned at him.

'We can take 'em one way or the other,' he told the devastated custodian. 'Now get your ragged arse over there and round the bleeders up!' he snarled, making the hapless scarecrow jump with fright.

They finally managed to round up two hundred and six sheep and drove them up the steep track towards the road, while Caleb lurched along at the rear carrying the dead ewe slung over his shoulder. William shook his head as the flock came tumbling down the deserted slope, the rest of the company cheering so loudly they almost caused a sheep stampede. Billy grinned at the astonished captain.

'Where did you find them?'

'Over the cliff. He had 'em penned up in a little cove,' Butcher reported, grinning broadly.

William eyed Caleb, the dead ewe bleeding down his broad back. 'And what's that?' he asked, narrowing his eyes.

'Supper, sir,' Butcher reported.

BY
ORCHARD STOKE,

*NEAR CHELTENHAM,
14 SEPTEMBER 1643*

Nicodemus Burke sighed heavily, switching Captain Sparrow's snapsack from one chafed shoulder to another. This was some reward for all his service, carting his kit about like some damned slave boy! He prickled with anger as he thought of all the hideous hardships he had endured under Gloucester's bombarded walls. Despite the miserable, teeth-rattling risks he had run on behalf of the stricken garrison, nobody had thought to do more than give him a quick pat on the back for his troubles. On the few occasions he had managed to corner an acquaintance his lively description of his adventures on Wainlode Hill had been rudely interrupted by some other pressing business. He wasn't the only youngster who had a tale to tell about the siege. Half a dozen of his former cronies boasted they had been standing next to a little brother and sister when they were decapitated by a red-hot cannon ball. At least a dozen claimed to have personally extinguished sizzling enemy mortar rounds. Some of his absent friends had been eaten out with jealousy at their own miserable lack of battlefield experience, and responded by starting a vicious rumour that the brave messenger had embroidered his entire tale from beginning to end!

The staff officers he had got to know so well during the dark days of August were busier than ever, and unable to spare him a moment of their time. Greyfriars was a hive of activity, the headquarters of the replenished garrison coming under siege from citizens demanding payment or compensation for damage inflicted by the King's guns. Every penny of expenditure had been dutifully recorded in the city chamberlain's spidery handwriting, where weeks of back-breaking labour and nerve-shattering risks were reduced to a few laconic sentences.

'Item, payd John and Ella Clamp one pound eighteen shillings and thruppence eech for helping about ye Southgate and bringing up turfs thereupon.'

Cattle had been killed or looted or had simply strayed during the prolonged firefighting about the suburbs. Property had been misplaced, borrowed, or used to jam some hole in the wall. One scrofulous, toothless old crone complained she had been subjected to lewd incitements by the Earl of Essex's men. A party of rather shrewder townsfolk had put themselves about cutting down Dr Chillingworth's abandoned siege engines into more manageable firewood. All in all, Gloucester was noisier than it had been before the siege. The atmosphere of good-spirited cooperation which had kept the citizens going throughout their three-week ordeal had vanished just as quickly as the King's soldiers from the refuse-filled trenches outside the walls.

The most pressing complaint, as usual, revolved around money. Some of the long-serving soldiers were claiming huge amounts of back pay. Others were busy claiming cash for dead or deserted colleagues.

It was little wonder Sir Edward Massey had not been able to spare the prodigal red-haired waif more than a few moments of his precious time.

'The beacon was your work, Nicodemus? I can't tell

what the fire meant to the garrison. You must make sure and tell me all about it.' As it turned out he wasn't able to tell him anything at all. The governor had been called away on pressing business, a council of war with the great Essex himself no less, and Nicodemus had been left to lounge about the frantic headquarters, as unwanted as he was unappreciated.

The miserable youngster had been on the verge of going back to his damp garret in St Mary's Street when he had the luck to bump into Master Jackson and the gloomy Gar Maynard, still mourning his dead friend Randall. The farmhands had just enlisted as scouts with the departing relief army and Nicodemus jumped at the opportunity to extend his apparently doomed military career. He rushed about the town collecting what few bits of kit he could find before reporting back to headquarters to collect his piti-fully insignificant wages.

'Item, payd Nicodemus Burke, a message boy at Greyfriars, for severall duties within and without the walls, five shillings and sixpence.'

It was enough to make a fellow weep.

A black-eyed clerk from the Earl of Essex's commissariat column took a long and rather disdainful look at the red-haired ragamuffin before reluctantly increasing the boy's precious store of coins.

'I'll vouch for the lad,' Master Jackson called over his shoulder. 'He's risked as much as any of us, these last few weeks.'

'Well, he's a little small for a soldier, don't you think?' the exasperated clerk enquired, turning the coins in question over in his sweaty fingers. Nicodemus eyed the milled edges of the coins, licking his pale lips as Jackson argued on his behalf. 'There's boys no older hefting a pike in the Trained Bands. And this un's seen more action than most of 'em put together.'

The clerk shrugged, scratched the boy's name onto the growing roster, and dropped the coins into his dirty palm.

'Go with this man and see you report to Mr Donne. He's liaising with the general's own scoutmaster for the march north.'

Before he had time to think, Nicodemus found himself striding out at the head of the departing army with a dozen other local men, recruited to help find the quickest highways and byways about the beleaguered county. He pressed his vast hat down on his head and threw a small pack on his back, stuffed with his meagre worldly goods. His precious fortune was wrapped in a scrap of cloth and tucked under his belt against a rainy day. Nicodemus lengthened his stride to keep up with Master Jackson and the long-legged Gar Maynard, leaving his home town behind without another thought.

They hadn't gone more than ten miles before Nicodemus began to regret his rather hasty departure. For one thing, the three of them had been attached to a regiment of London men who spoke so quickly he could barely understand a word they were saying. When he asked the jabbering magpies to repeat something, they hooted and laughed and said he was a dumpy-doodle. Then there was the confusion over Master Layton's farm, the hateful orders to forage the poor gentleman's stock they had tried to challenge with such a singular lack of success. The London men were even more suspicious of their new guides when they had returned from their unpromising expedition driving an enormous flock of bleating sheep. The bad-tempered captain rounded on the boy, poking his dirty forefinger into his threadbare chest.

'I thought you told me the farm had been stripped bare?' Sparrow demanded indignantly.

'So it was, sir. The farmyard, that is,' Nicodemus explained petulantly, on the verge of breaking down in bitter tears. Master Jackson, the untroubled overseer, placed a fatherly hand on his twitching shoulder.

''Tweren't the boy's fault, Captain,' he explained with his usual pale-eyed serenity. 'As far as we could tell the place had been plundered good and proper.'

'Two hundred and six sheep hidden down the bottom of a cliff? I thought you said you knew this place?'

'We did, sir. Though we've been away lighting signal fires and sichlike so what Master Layton done with the flock is—'

'All right, all right, I haven't got all day,' Sparrow snapped. 'What's the quickest way back to the main road?' the captain demanded, impatient to complete his first independent assignment.

The bearded beginner had clearly been discomfited to find himself so far from the rest of the regiment – which was itself stuck out on a limb from the main body of the earl's slow-moving host – and couldn't wait to rejoin his friends. Jackson pointed over the willow-ribbed meadows towards the east.

'There's a good track over the fields that'll shave an hour off the road,' the sandy-haired guide reported as the first bleating bundles were driven through a gap in the hedge and into the narrow lane.

'Right, then. You get up the front and point the way, while you two jobberknols lend a hand with the sheep,'

Sparrow snarled over the increasingly irritating bleating of the agitated flock.

Of course to add insult to injury his fellow scouts Gar Maynard and Master Jackson very quickly proved their worth. The well-travelled farmhands knew most of the country roundabout and made themselves useful finding short cuts, locating shallow fords, and pointing out decent billets. What was he able to do so far from home? He had no more idea what was around the next corner than the snapping musketeers. The youngest scout in the regiment was about as much use as a three-legged whippet, and spent most of his time helping to herd the looted sheep or lugging Captain Sparrow's personal baggage. He hadn't enlisted to carry a sackful of sweaty shirts!

The bitterly disappointed boy had never been as far from home, and the closely enclosed country in which he found himself was quite beyond his unhappy reckoning. Narrow belts of woodland seemed to be funnelling the vast conglomeration of troops (and sheep) towards some unguessed destination, the low hills on every horizon preventing the marching army from getting its bearings and so adding to the growing sense of apprehension. As far as the bewildered youngster could make out they had gone north to Tewkesbury and then turned on their heels to march straight back towards the south. Nicodemus hoped the general knew what they were about, because he certainly hadn't a clue as to the earl's intentions. Perhaps he intended to march and countermarch his army until the King lost his temper and launched an attack? According to the muttering Londoners the Royalist army had made towards Evesham, and then turned about to shadow the

Roundheads back towards Gloucester. As far as Nicodemus could see all they were succeeding in doing was wearing out shoe leather.

Where they were now was anybody's guess. Some scout he had proved to be, the boy thought ruefully. The hero of Gloucester – commended by Sir Edward Massey himself – reduced to running errands for jumped-up printer's apprentices like this hulking Sparrow fellow. So much for *his* glittering military career.

'Cheer up there, lad, it might never happen!' Master Jackson said, allowing himself a small smile of encouragement.

Nicodemus grinned feebly. 'I'm all right,' he said as brightly as he could. The overseer was not convinced.

The regiment was taking a break beside a chattering stream, the soldiers chucking pebbles into the fragrant green pools beneath a hump-backed bridge. A few of the more enterprising pikemen had waded out into the weedy rills and were attempting to spear themselves some lunch. Master Jackson watched them splash and shout in the shallows, shook his head at their antics.

'Don't they have rivers in Lunnun?' he asked the miserable youngster. He led the way along the bank, past a stand of willows to a quieter corner. Nicodemus squatted down to watch as the wily countryman took off his old buff coat, rolled up his sleeves, and stretched himself out along the grass.

'How much further is it then, London?' Nicodemus asked as the former overseer slipped his long arm into the water and laid his ear to the soil.

'About hundred and fifty mile, I reckon,' Jackson responded quietly.

'Towards the east, you said.'

The overseer nodded silently, feeling under the over-hanging bank for a dozing trout.

'Then why are we going back the way we came?'

'To throw the King off the scent, of course.'

'Well, he must know where we are b'now,' Nicodemus cried. 'This lot stink like a shitpit!'

Jackson blinked in agreement, concentrated on the job in hand. 'His lot smell just as bad, you can rely on that.'

The boy lapsed into silence for a minute or two, watching the patient poacher tease the invisible fish from the swift-flowing brook.

'Well, what happens when the King comes across our—'

Nicodemus jumped back in alarm as Jackson wrenched his arm out of the water, flicking a plump brown trout into the grass. The fish flapped and gasped as the overseer grabbed for it, his wet fingers slipping on its polished scales. Nicodemus recovered in a moment, crouching forward and grasping the furious fish in his dirty paws. He held the squirming trout steady while Master Jackson crawled over, held it straight, and dispatched it with one quick and efficient blow to its steely head.

'Please God, if I've got to go, let it be as quick,' the sober-minded scout murmured. Nicodemus hardly said a word the rest of the afternoon.

'Out of the way! Make way there!' The furious shouts came from the other end of the crawling column, causing a concertina effect which propelled the apprehensive soldiers into the bramble-choked verge. William Sparrow clambered up onto a roadside tussock and peered up and down the blocked lane as a young officer with staring blue eyes strode through the press prodding the stragglers out of his path with his halberd.

'Come on, hurry up! Let them through!' he called, elbowing the slower-moving and rather surly soldiers aside. Mercer's muttering musketeers climbed up out of the sunken lane, the tired pikemen shuffling into the refuse-filled ditch as a regiment of sweaty men in tawny coats hurried up the slope, running a gauntlet of icy stares and ribald comments. Much to the astonishment of Mercer's bewildered recruits, the strangers in such apparent haste belonged to the Lord General's regiment of foot, Essex's own. Many of the bearded veterans had been in arms since the beginning of the war, and had already participated in half a dozen bloody fights from Edgehill to Turnham Green.

'Look out, boys, the King's men are up there, mind!'

'Rearguard's twenty miles back, mate!'

'Aye, and London's that way!'

The belligerent officer ignored the banter, standing aside as his ragged veterans made their own peculiar way through the jeering crowd, striding along using their outmoded musket rests as bizarre walking sticks. The musketeers would lift their rests, describe a peculiar circular motion with their wrists, and tap the steel-tipped stick back down again. The unusually rhythmic and rather soothing clatter sounded strangely discordant in the narrow lane as the veteran companies hurried on up the slope and disappeared from view behind another clump of trees. The pikemen were carrying their weapons at the trail, their faces running with sweat beneath the curled rims of their rusted helmets.

Behind the foot came a gaggle of officers on foaming horses, a whole crop of colours lowered behind them to prevent the huge red flags tangling in the treetops. Mercer's troops might have been new to the colours but they didn't need to be told the identity of the serenely smiling gentleman in the burnished armour. It was the Earl of Essex himself, riding to the wars at the head of his men.

'Hey for Robin!'

'God keep you, sir!'

'We'll thrash 'em for you, my lord!'

Green recruits and cynical old sweats alike crowded back into the lane to surround the lord general's party, patting his sweaty horse and calling his name as if it would bring them luck in the dangerous days ahead. The general nodded, acknowledging their greetings by raising his painstakingly engraved baton.

Behind the officers came the earl's lifeguard, élite cuirassiers in full armour and wrapped in orange scarves. Many of them were gentlemen themselves, with an annual income reckoned in thousands of pounds. Mercer's footsore soldiers respectfully made way for them, although Long Col had seen their brothers in arms on Roundway Down and had not been overly impressed by the monstrously fortified knights.

'Remember how they stood there that afternoon, Will?' the sergeant asked his bleary-eyed captain.

Sparrow, glad of the break from the crippling march, took off his hat to staunch the flow of sweat into his eyes, and wiped his hand over his sunburnt brow. 'Aye. Like five hundred brick shithouses,' the captain remembered, pinching his nose between his finger and thumb and blinking to clear his fogged vision. 'But not quite as mobile,' he growled.

Sir Arthur Haselrig's regiment of 'lobsters' – identically equipped to the earl's show troop – had been ground backwards and finally cut to pieces by the swirling Cavaliers. Almost a hundred of them had perished when their panicked flight had taken them straight over the nearest cliff, smashing man and beast alike to bloody ruin.

'All right if you're in a fix like this, though,' Long Col said, nodding at the steeply banked hedgerow which seemed to be strangling the tortuous column. He glanced at Sparrow, who was swaying from side to side as he tried to stand straight. Long Col frowned. 'How many more times? You're no good to anybody swooning like that,' he complained. Will straightened his hat, scowled back at him.

'Will you give it a rest? You're worse than my mother!' William bristled, thought fleetingly of his dead parent. By God, he doubted she would even have recognized him now. The curly hair she had ruffled clipped short against lice, the chubby features she had pinched shrunken up and covered in three weeks' stubble. And then he remembered Mary. Mary Keziah Pitt, his sweetheart and fiancée. Good Christ, the last time he had seen her had been ... what, the day before that disastrous encounter on Roundway? He hadn't even heard from her since. William wondered where she was and if she was well. Still working as maid to Miss Bella, he supposed. He realized with a guilty twitch he had barely thought of her for a moment these past two months, what with one thing and another. William wondered if she was missing him. She couldn't well write him, as she had difficulty with her letters. Maybe she would ask Bella to draft one for her. Bella, spare time on somebody else? That would be the day. Perhaps *she* had met somebody else? Some sprat from the King's army which had taken control of the entire West Country, if you listened to the latest reports. With Exeter gone William doubted there were many Roundhead garrisons left where the desperate girl could take cover. Poor Mary would be at the mercy of every cocky bastard who could ride a horse. The big man sighed miserably. Maybe he ought to find time to write her a letter, care of her mother Gwen, Chipping Marleward's red-armed laundress. He ought to try and ensure her safety, at the very least. The trouble was, with the King's army rampaging up and down the country, there were all too few places of safety left.

Long Col poked him in his good arm, distracting him from his gloomy and rather belated domestic tribulations.

'It's you as wants to give it a rest! Why don't you get back to the wagon, put your feet up for a bit?'

Sparrow resumed his troubled march, his stubbled jaw set firm. 'I'll not be carried to the next battle. What's this lot going to think, eh? A captain who can't march ordering them to hurry it up?'

The sergeant frowned, nodded his grey veined head. 'All right, it's up to you. But don't blame me if you're too shagged to lift your sword when we bump into the bastards.'

They trudged on in silence for a while. They would be bumping into the bastards any day now.

THE GREAT KEEP
OF BRISTOL,

18 SEPTEMBER 1643

T he old place hadn't changed much, Sir Gilbert
Morrison reflected ruefully. The enormous stone
keep seemed to have escaped relatively unscathed
from the late siege, the only visible alteration the newly
raised banner cracking crisply atop the battlements. Parliament's enormous flag had been shredded by shot and
singed by flames, taken down and wrapped around the belly
of some shell-shocked ensign. In its place the triumphant
Royalists had raised the King's personal standard, the
Stewart arms blowing free once more above His Majesty's
recently recovered city and port of Bristol. The great keep
had been built by the Normans in a sedge-banked bend of
the Avon, the eastern flank secured by the narrower,
swifter River Frome. It had been from this direction that
Prince Rupert had launched his famous assault on the city,
his hard-fighting brigades climbing over walls of their own
maimed to rush through the breach. Once over the
stubbornly held wall, Rupert's men had flowed around the
inner defences like a spring tide, surrounding the few
remaining strongpoints and forcing the stragglers to take
cover in the mighty castle.

From here, Parliament had expected the survivors to
defy Rupert for another week or more. In actual fact the
governor, Nathaniel Fiennes, had been persuaded to yield

before any more unnecessary hurts were done, a mistake for which he was currently lingering under sentence of death.

Sir Gilbert handed his pass to the surly guards at the Temple Gate, noting the pockmarked ramparts above his head. The soft stone towers and ancient walls looked as if they had been attacked by a flock of immense sand martins, bored and tunnelled by mole-clawed masons. Two months after that terrible storm, and the ditch beneath the battered embankment was still foul with Cornish blood and forgotten body parts, although the dozens of bloated corpses had thankfully been dragged out and burnt.

The dishevelled guard followed the merchant's gaze, nodded with gruesome satisfaction. 'Fair ol' fight they put up,' he commented, his teeth stained with cheap tobacco.

Sir Gilbert shrugged as if he had seen a sight worse. 'It was a fair old fight at Gloucester, sadly lacking the happy conclusion His Majesty was banking on,' he said smoothly.

The guard handed him back his sheaf of papers, passes, and arrays, all signed and stamped at the King's head-quarters shortly before Sir Gilbert's ignominious departure from the Royal headquarters.

'They all seem in order, mind how you go, sir, there's all sorts of rubbles and sichlike strewn about.'

The merchant smiled at this friendly advice and urged his patient grey mare in under the bruised gatehouse.

Bristol had suffered, that was for sure.

As well as burnt-out hovels and gutted town houses, there were whole rows of buildings lacking windows or roof tiles. Heaps of rubble and smashed firewood marked the sad end of some formidably defended barricade. Goodwives had been busy with bucket and brush, removing the gorier reminders of the late siege. Urchins poked amongst the ashes and rubble after cannon balls, for which they had been promised a halfpenny by the hard-working salvage crews scouring the city from St Mary Redcliff to Prior's Hill. Sir Gilbert rode by squads of sawyers and labourers, whole battalions of masons and carpenters, all busy rebuilding shattered corners of the shaken city. Stone dust hung heavily in the windless canyons of homes and warehouses, catching in his craw and making him cough. He turned the horse down ever narrower thoroughfares towards the heart of Bristol, the bustling merchants' quarters which had seen vicious hand-to-hand street fighting as the King's men had clawed their way towards the vital harbour. A whole row of houses beside the fish market had been gutted by a raging tempest of flame which had eaten up the timber-frame hovels one after the other. Sir Gilbert was obliged to ride backwards and forwards past the miserable ruins a few times before he located the littered course of the old lane which led to his West Country headquarters. Although the refuse-strewn alley was blackened with smoke and soots, the immense gates which guarded his warehouse yard seemed sound and relatively unmarked. The merchant spent another minute or two banging on the formidable barricade and hallooing to wake the dead before he attracted the wandering attention of a coughing stranger in a shapeless woollen hat. Clearly his clerk and confidant Algernon Starling had been throwing his money about like water, recruiting any old tapster who had taken his fancy. Why, there wasn't a day's work left in this old crock!

Bristol might have been transformed by war, Algernon Starling had not.

The wizened crow in the threadbare black coat emerged from his gloomy quarters beside the yard, blinking at the hateful sunlight which lanced between the surrounding walls and slid from the battered rooftops. He was an ill-kempt, suspicious fellow with knobbly knuckled hands and a large-domed skull, around which he had plastered his few strings of wax-black hair. The clerk nodded and muttered to himself as he watched his master dismount from the tired grey and peer about as if he was reminding himself of his squalid surroundings. Morrison grunted something under his breath – as near a greeting Starling was going to get from his bad-tempered master.

Damn it all, Sir Gilbert thought angrily, the yard was bare! He had ridden into the lion's den to pick up the threads of his various ventures, only to find that hunch-backed jackdaw Starling had sold his business out from under him!

'And what are we trading today, Starling?' Sir Gilbert enquired when he had finally found his tongue. 'Thin air? Mossy cobbles? Spider-webs?'

The horrifically undernourished clerk sucked in his transparent cheeks at his errant master's all too familiar sallies.

'Did you not get my correspondence? I wrote you a full list of all my transactions,' he said wearily, falling in beside the bustling merchant as he poked his head into the maze of normally busy storerooms which looked over the deserted yard.

'I know that,' Sir Gilbert replied testily. 'That's why I'm here,' he said, lowering his voice. 'I need to lay my hands on some readies,' he went on, conspiratorially.

Starling scowled, nodded his misshapen skull into the brush cupboard he called an office. Sir Gilbert closed the door behind himself and watched his not-quite-trusted servant unlock a chest and remove his precious ledgers.

Sir Gilbert, as fluent with figures as he was with his tongue, wrenched the volumes out of the clerk's mean grasp and held them to his formidable chest as if they were God's holy books. He cleared a space on the careworn desk and ran his fingers over the greasy pages, flicking the ledger open to squint at the most recent entries. His full lips moved like greased slugs as he silently shaped sums and calculated profit margins.

'Wherever did you get three hundred swords?' he snorted at last.

'Beadle's. He was having a clear-out before the city fell, so I bought the lot. Hopton's in charge here now, and they say he's been equipping fifty men a day for the King's armies.'

Sir Gilbert nodded, somewhat reassured by his clerk's business acumen. Ah, he'd had a good teacher, see?

'Three bargeloads of undressed stone?'

'Stranded in the harbour. The masters let me have it all cheap before they, er, evacuated themselves.'

The merchant snorted with derision, returned his attention to Starling's immaculately kept ledger.

'A ketch? Whatever do I want a ketch for?' Sir Gilbert spluttered.

'The governor needed a packet boat to keep in touch with the Somerset coast,' the clerk replied patiently. 'Most of the city boats were taken or sunk, and what few were left got sent upriver to Gloucester to evacuate the wounded.'

'Splendid . . . let's see . . . ah, yes, a nice tidy sum. Good work, Starling.' The clerk bowed ironically as the merchant finished his calculations. 'What are the rest of them doing?'

Starling shrugged his thin shoulders. 'As we expected.

374

Fitzherbert's sub-contracting to repair the walls. Him and Gibbons had stockpiled cement and mortar before the siege, so they're raking it in. Of course they did themselves a favour by betraying the merchant fleet to the King.'

Morrison frowned, gnawing the tips of his fingers as he contemplated his colleagues' dastardly doings during the recent siege. He had heard all about it, of course. The crews of eight vessels lying downriver at the King's Road had been encouraged to mutiny by the plotting rogues back in Bristol. The turncoat crews had locked up or knocked out any officer or gentleman still determined to save the cargoes for the Parliament and then sailed their new fleet under the protection of the nearest Royalist fort. The ships had been packed with valuables belonging to the principal local burghers as well as high-value cargoes of sugar, spices, cloth, coal, and arms. The rich booty had no doubt proved highly lucrative to its new owners, who had wasted no time in selling the cargoes back to the city merchants who had lost it in the first place!

They had made a pretty penny while he had been doing his duty risking his fortune for the King, Sir Gilbert thought indignantly.

'Nobody else has got a boat in yet so the garrison is having to pay through the nose for everything. The boatmen downriver are claiming they should have been contracted for the ships which went in just before the siege and all, the harbour master's still trying to sort them out.'

'Mutinous dogs. They ought to set the cavalry on 'em,' the merchant muttered. He sighed glumly, assaulted by fresh waves of doubt. It was no good swanning about the country and expecting business to run along fine without you. Healthy profits didn't grow from seed, after all.

He'd been up to his ears leading his regiment at Gloucester while all the local merchants had muscled in on his operations, cutting him under, cutting him out.

He closed the ledger and pursed his generous lips for a moment.

'I left you with a fortune back before the siege,' Starling hissed. 'Don't say you've gone through the lot?' he exclaimed.

Sir Gilbert frowned at his inquisitive agent for a moment before itemizing his recent expenditure on his chubby fingers.

'I had to send His Majesty King Charles a thousand for a start,' he reported gruffly. 'A nice little contribution to his war chest to encourage him to overlook my previous errors of judgement.'

'When you sided with the Parliament, you mean?' Starling pointed out shrewdly.

'Exactly so,' Sir Gilbert agreed, overlooking the clerk's sarcasm. 'The regiment cost me another thousand all told, although Christ alone knows when I'll see a silver penny of it back. You heard about that fool Clavincale? Well, of course I had to splash out to set him up with my Bella. Now he's dead the wedding's off and I'm down another five hundred.'

'An outrageously expensive dowry, and all for nothing,' Starling wailed.

Sir Gilbert squinted at the scrawny brute. 'Well, of course I had to make an impression,' he blustered. 'Convince him I was a man of means. He was a lord of the land, and wasn't about to marry some milkmaid. I picked up the bill for his quarters and all his vittles and all, right through the siege, mind you. It cost me another twenty pounds to send his daft corpse back to his family. The least I could do, in the circumstances.'

The clerk had been wondering what had prompted the merchant's rather hasty return from Gloucester.

'Never you mind,' Sir Gilbert warned. 'Anyway, when I got back, I had to settle that harridan widow-woman's most urgent debts.'

'How is Lady Ramsay?' Starling asked coldly.

'Still living. It's as cold as a witch's chuff up at the hall, if you want to know.'

Starling shivered in sympathy. 'I don't understand why you don't go home. There can't be many Roundheads left in Chipping Marleward these days,' the clerk observed.

Sir Gilbert rolled his busy blue eyes. 'Home? The hall *is* my home, or as good as. The place is lousy with dragoons so I can't say I've hung about long enough to open the old place up. No point in letting the bastards get their hands on the few bits I've got left,' the merchant complained. 'As well as that I've paid off her grocery bills, all her damned staff, half a dozen soldiers, *and* laid in a supply of coal for the winter. That cost me a pretty penny, I can tell you.'

But not above fifty pounds out of a fortune Starling had reckoned himself. Three thousand two hundred and sixty-seven pounds, nine shillings, and sevenpence ha'penny, to be precise. Surely he hadn't blown the lot?

'Then I've had to shell out for doctors for those dratted brats of mine, they're both moping about with every ache and ague they can think of. Doctors? Don't talk to me about those thieving Venetian stinkfingers! Have you any idea how much they were asking to mend the pair of 'em? Bed, possets, and brown paper is what I said would do 'em. Oh, no.' Sir Gilbert took a quick breath. 'And then there's new wardrobes for both, and for young Anneliese into the bargain.'

Starling wondered why the merchant had inclined to such an uncharacteristic display of generosity.

'Well, they're to be wed after all, my Jamie and young Anneliese,' the merchant announced fondly. 'We can hardly have them getting married in rags and borrowed breeches, can we?' He lowered his voice as if the formidable widow was eavesdropping on their conversation. 'Of course, Mouldy Dragon Tits has insisted on doing everything right, if we're going to do it at all. I can hardly gainsay her in her own home, can I?'

Starling shrugged. Well it wouldn't be the first time. Perhaps the merchant was losing his edge? He was however pleasantly surprised that Sir Gilbert had managed to arrange the match in the first place. Lady Ramsay had always despised the merchant and his low-born brood, borne bitter grudges which dated back before the war. Now she had apparently decided to forgive – or at least overlook – their recent political and commercial rivalry. Needs must when the devil – in the shape of the jolly merchant – drives, Starling supposed.

'So in other words,' Sir Gilbert sighed, 'I'm on my uppers.'

Starling tore up a floorboard and extracted a rusted old tin from the mouldy foundations. He produced a large key from around his scrawny neck and proceeded to open the box.

Sir Gilbert shoved his meaty hand in and closed on the precious hoard of coins. He picked out two pounds and slid the coins over the table towards the suddenly myopic clerk.

'That's for your trouble,' Sir Gilbert told him gruffly.

'And here's another fifty to go on trading where you can. I'm going to need the rest to get things moving up at the hall.' Starling nodded, replacing the coins in the tin and securing it in its hiding place. Sir Gilbert placed the remaining profits in his purse and tucked it away out of sight. He frowned, drumming his fingers on the open ledger.

'I need more, Starling. Two thousand down in two months, and I'm still no better off than when I left Bristol.'

'What about the house? I don't see any reason for keeping it up if you've got your feet under the table up at the hall.'

Sir Gilbert snorted at his clerk's naivety. 'Sell a house in the middle of a county lousy with soldiers? I wouldn't get the price of a cup of cold piss,' he scolded. 'You know they've quartered a company of dragoons on the place? They're eating the whole village up. If it wasn't for the fact I'm a commissioned colonel they'd have stripped the old place to the boards.'

Starling shook his head at this heinous outrage. 'Don't appear as if any of us is safe from 'em,' the clerk moaned, looking about the empty yard. 'Good job I cleared up all this when I did,' he sniffed.

'Aye,' Gilbert Morrison allowed, 'they'll beggar the lot of us if they're not careful, fighting their damned wars.'

Jamie Morrison had taken advantage of his bad-tempered father's temporary absence to take a stroll down the hill to see how things were doing in the village. He had for some inexplicable reason been confined to the hall, where Lady Ramsay scowled and squinted at him from dawn till dusk, and frequently poisoned his shoes and stockings. For this reason he tended to go barefoot. But if one went barefoot one would attract attention to one's breeches, so he had left them off and all. And also his drawers and shirt and hat and coat. It was a fine afternoon, though, the sky arching overhead, a perfect eggshell blue studded with hurrying white clouds which stopped and made faces at him as he made his whistling way down the overgrown driveway. He knew the way, of course, and even if he did get lost he could always follow the singing birds and muttering insects, which always flew downhill by preference. Jamie stopped, lifted his right foot, and examined the bleeding soles. Why didn't the stones roll downhill out of his path? he wondered. Perhaps because they weren't birds. If the stones had souls, they would roll away as well. Delighted by his insight, he continued on his way, down towards the village.

'I thought he was with you,' Anneliese cried, holding her white hand to her mouth. Bella, still pale and drawn after her debilitating fevers, shook her head mournfully.

'And I thought he was in the bath house. I found his clothes on the landing,' Jamie's sister insisted. Anneliese twitched with nervous embarrassment. He'd not gone off again, had he? Run off to hop and jump about the meadows like some Greek hero returning to some long-lost island paradise? She shivered with frustration at his haphazard impulsiveness. Would it always be like this? Plagued by doubts, she stood by hopeless and helpless in the face of her sweetheart's puzzling behaviour.

'Which way would he go?' Bella asked, reaching for her cloak from the hall stand. 'Anneliese, which way would he go?' she repeated, throwing the well-travelled cloak about her shoulders.

'Anywhere,' the dark-haired girl replied, tears running down her face in a silent stream.

The slant-eyed misfits who rode with Speedwell's troop of dragoons were a typically mixed bunch; a band of filthy, scruffy scavengers who cared little for whom they fought, as long as they didn't have to fight. They had been posted along twenty godforsaken miles of the Fosseway, safely away from the lurid attractions to be found beneath Bristol's battered castle. The vagabond troop was made up of the worst sort of scum, sweepings from the alehouses and deserters from a dozen regiments. Their shaggy, hard-mouthed ponies got them into and out of trouble just quickly enough for their liking, giving the roving bandits a considerable range over the great switchbacked slopes and sudden plunging valleys which made up the Mendip Hills. The company had been out of action for months, and what few decent officers they had possessed had long since found other commands. Those that were left were no better than the men, lazy, greedy freebooters who put all their martial efforts into scaring civilians. They were supposed to collect the village assessment, as well as gather foodstuffs for the garrison of Bristol. In actual fact, they had eaten the hills clean, driven off livestock, and sent precious few wagons on the long descent down Bitterwell Hill. They had made the Blue Boar tavern their unofficial headquarters, driving the fearful villagers back to their dingy homes as they drank the nights away and accosted the few womenfolk who still dared to go out.

It was Mordecai Pitt who spotted Jamie first.

At first the former soldier imagined the pale pink blob coming down the steep lane was a wandering pig, fleeing the greedy clutches of their unwanted masters. In another moment he realized it was a man going on all fours. He recognized the merchant's boy – Daft Jamie – although God knew it could hardly have been anybody else.

The lame soldier gripped his thigh and hurried along the street towards the naked man, wondering what on earth the mad boy was doing so far from his home up at the hall. Perhaps he had taken some strange notion to see his old house. Well, he wouldn't want to see it now, that was for sure. Mordecai hurled the stack of firewood he was carrying into a doorway, and bent down to haul the stupid boy to his feet. Jamie was splashed with mud, his face smeared with grass and soil where he had been imitating the absent cattle in the fields. His bright eyes wouldn't focus as Mordecai hauled him straight and shook him.

'Jamie . . . Captain Jamie,' Mordecai hissed, shaking the fool by his twitching shoulders. 'Whatever is the matter, sir?'

'Baa! Baa-ing!' Jamie hooted and bleated, bringing anxious faces to the grimy windows along both sides of the mean street. Scowling matrons peered out, covered their eyes, and ducked back indoors. Children pointed and jeered. The idle dragoons came out to see what the fuss was about.

'Hello! Made a new friend, have we? Oi, Sarge, come and have a gander at this!'

Mordecai ignored the catcalls and quickly threw off his own coat to wrap around the mad boy's shoulders.

'Must be getting desperate, eh, cripple? But that one's got no tits to speak of!'

'Fed up with the sheep, eh, Roundhead?'

The leering dragoons staggered down the steps into the road, nudging one another and pointing the stems of their long clay pipes.

'Now then, Mordecai, just because you've taken lame, no need to lower your sights!'

Mordecai grinned at the drooling gang as the boy shivered in the street, his thin body racked with chills. 'He's taken too much ale,' he explained lamely. 'I'd best get him back.'

'Hoo, now. Taken too much ale? That'd be a first, if I've heard right. Look, Henry, Mordy's found hisself a playmate!'

'Ah, he don't look too excited by it, though, do 'ee?'

'His father's got a sight more go in 'im, is what I've 'eard!'

'N'mind the father!' one of the Somerset men drawled. 'Oi'd rather have a tumble with his daughter!'

'Ah, shc'd shoot you first, Michael, and you'd not be the first!' The toothless dragoon beamed in merriment.

'Ah, I loike a gal wi' a bit of spunk!'

Mordecai frogmarched the idiot boy past the mob, ignoring their jibes and stepping over their carelessly placed boots.

'He's too good for the loikes of us, see, Peter. Too chummy with his Roundhead mates, I reckon.'

They all knew Mordecai had served at the recent siege of Bristol, laming his leg and hobbling home when the defeated garrison had shambled out of the battered gates. The fact most of them had also served the Parliament made them doubly suspicious of the unemployed farm-hand. His refusal to re-enlist with the Royalist forces had been regarded as some direct insult to the shabby guidon they had left propped beside the fireplace in the tavern.

A bow-legged dragoon stepped down from his perch beside the laundry house, preventing the pair of them from seeking sanctuary indoors. Gwen Pitt peered out of her doorway, biting her lip with anxiety at her son's plight.

Sergeant Joshua Lawton may have been just five feet tall, but he made up in menace what he lacked in inches. A broad, puckered scar ran along his stubbled jaw, set defiantly as he regarded the crippled villager.

'What, been laying with the fool, have you? You know the punishment for unnatural affections like that,' he said quietly.

Mordecai grinned feebly. 'He's taken too much ale,' he insisted.

'Ner mind ale, boy, you've been sodomizing him, is what I reckon,' Lawton accused. 'What does your Round-head code say about that?'

ALDBOURNE CHASE,

NEAR HUNGERFORD

Burdened with unnecessary baggage and slowed by sinking guns, the earl's army oozed like a slowly turning tide over the misty grasslands, the springy turf and surrounding trees deadening the usual creaking cacophony of an army on the march and creating an unnatural, sinister silence.

They had marched seventy miles and more already, feinting from Gloucester towards Tewkesbury before setting off on the mad dash back to London.

The earl's scouts had for once earned their shillings, probing the dangerous road ahead and discovering to their delight a convoy of supplies bound for the King's army drawn up outside the alehouses in Cirencester. Encouraged by this uncharacteristic feat of initiative, the usually lugubrious earl had immediately rushed his own regiment of foot up to the front of the dawdling column, and sent them ahead to seize the town while the cavalry worked their way around the outskirts in an iron-shod pincer movement. The surprise had been total, the haul of loot impressive. The distracted guards and drivers had been throttled or clubbed as they staggered out to see what the commotion was about, and a couple of weak Royalist cavalry units had been disarmed with hardly a shot being fired. More importantly, the gleeful Roundhead attackers seized forty wagons of foodstuffs and supplies destined for the hungry Royalists who were still shadowing them somewhere to the north.

Or south.

Or east.

Well, not even the King's Cavaliers could simply vanish off the face of the earth, could they?

To the hurrying Parliamentarians the broad swath of springy turf which ran like an immense green pavement between the close-packed trees seemed a hatefully exposed desert, a biblical wilderness which left them at the mercy of the wolf-pack Cavaliers. Since they had marched out of Gloucester they had become accustomed to close, hilly country intersected with narrow sunken lanes. Steep verges ran like battlements along the muddy tracks, the formidable obstacles supporting sprawling elderberry bushes, wiry brambles, and stiff-fingered hawthorns. Horse-tangling willows crowded into every ford and fold in the undulating landscape, keeping the hated enemy cavalry away from the nervous Roundheads, who preferred to follow the restrictive lanes rather than risk making faster progress in the open fields.

Here though they had no choice but to press on across the greensward, the treacherous trees falling back from the road to create a four-mile funnel, a killing field fit for kings.

Aldbourne Chase had been teased and tended by loyal woodsmen since the days of King John, a vast green rectangle, an elongated arena where princes and lords rode out with their hounds and hawks, honed their hunting skills.

The skills they would use today to trap their russet-coated quarry.

The morning mist was still rising from the heavy overnight dew as the Earl of Essex's vanguard tightened their helmet straps and spurred on into the chase, peering into the distance where the vast, all-encompassing arms of the King's forest met once more, great wooden jaws to chew and gobble an entire army.

Six regiments trotted across the lush turf as if they were lining up for the start of some military steeplechase. Long files of dragoons on skewbald nags spread out along each flank, keeping a wary eye on the close-ranked trees. Behind the cavalry came the general staff with the lifeguards of horse and the Earl of Essex's own infantry, Phillip Skippon's Londoners, and Lord Robarts' men in their newly issued coats. Behind them Holmstead's and Barclay's, most of whom had missed the issue and were still wearing the tattered remnants of their civilian kit. The noisy London Trained Band regiments were still in good spirits, buoyed up alternately by fire-and-brimstone sermons and the hope of more plunder. Behind the vanguard came the slow-moving artillery and baggage columns, struggling through the atrocious tracks and ploughing up what little road was left. They created a slimy, rutted morass for the cursing rearguard, who had to wade through their liquid filth to keep up. Finally, bringing up the rear, five highly strung regiments of Roundhead cavalry, forever peering over their shoulders for the swirling tornadoes of Rupert's despised cavalry. They had to be out there somewhere – surely Rupert wasn't going to let the earl's overloaded army crawl all the way back to London unmolested?

*

Unluckily for the nervous rearguard, neither Prince Rupert nor the brightly coated furies he commanded had vanished. He had been up since before dawn ordering his squadrons, briefing his eager captains. His uncle might have fallen into some all too familiar fit of despondency, but the energetic Prince was not about to give up the chase.

As soon as the sun peaked above the surrounding trees he ordered the advance.

No trumpet, no drum, no warning shout of triumph. They walked their prancing chargers through the dew-soaked gallops, colours hanging limply against their wet lances. Bridles jangled and horses coughed on the damp dawn air. Captains and cornets fidgeted in agitation, ducked their heads as they trotted out from beneath the dripping eaves of the forest.

Suddenly, a trumpet sounded startlingly loud from the front. A great shout went up from five thousand throats and the silent meadows erupted with furious alarms. The cavalry still waiting under the dank boughs of the wood felt the familiar thunder and rumble of the hoofs even through the deep mulch of the forest floor. The excited horses stamped and backed into one another as their riders urged them through the press, out into the glorious panorama of Aldbourne Chase.

Hugo Telling had been in the saddle for days, and his thighs were chafed red from the constant rubbing motion of leather and breeches on bare skin. But his breeches could have been on fire for all he cared now. The enemy were there before them, at their mercy in the gloriously exposed chase, a gently sloping gallop designed for horse and man.

The mottle-coated, ragbag Roundheads were no better than beaters, turned on by their masters in the absence of other game. Telling exulted in the pure, undiluted excitement of it all, revelled in the surging power of riding down another man. He did not even imagine he could be hurt, believed himself invulnerable to their panicked volleys.

The rebel scoundrels had hidden behind hedges and lurked in the sunken lanes all the way from Gloucester, but they wouldn't get away now, surrounded by a sea of scarlet Cavaliers on a featureless racecourse.

He glanced to his right, and watched Cornet Hazell gallop past with the colour held out as if he intended to joust with the panic-stricken enemy. Alexander Gull, his broad face blank beneath the tightly buckled helmet, spurred along behind watching his master's arched back. Telling seethed with fury to think they would beat him to the wailing Roundhead lines, and ducked down lower over the horse's wind-blown mane. Its black ears were laid flat, its great brown eyes rolling as it tossed its head to join the frantic gallop, to catch up with its stampeding cousins.

Prince Rupert's squadrons catapulted out of the woods and closed in on the drop-jawed rearguard. The Roundheads turned their horses to face the threat, dragoons bolted towards the great swollen mob of infantry, the snarled columns of wagons and guns.

There was a flurry of shots as the rearguard opened fire with their carbines and frantically drew their pistols. Rupert's men were on them in a moment, slashing with their swords while the feverish enemy riders fiddled with their firearms.

'Use your swords, you fucking numskulls!' a ruffian yelled, attracting a crowd of screaming Cavaliers straight to him.

Hugo saw Hazell charge right through a stumbling rank of Roundheads, knocking a tall captain from his horse with the point of the colour. Alexander Gull spurred into the gap, laying about him with a pole-axe, denting helmets and crushing skulls. Hugo's horse shied away from the imminent collision, hurling Hugo out of the saddle to straddle the terrified beast's neck. A Roundhead lunged at him with his sword, skewering the empty saddlecloth. Hugo lashed out, deflecting the man's sword while he hung on grimly with his left hand. He bumped back into the slashed saddle as the frightened horse reared, thrashing a smaller enemy charger out of its path and spilling the inexperienced cavalryman to the floor where he was immediately knocked senseless.

The russet-coated mob disintegrated on every side, riders pounding away after their infantry.

'Close up!' Hugo yelled belatedly, knowing his troop had already scattered beyond hope of recall. 'After the colour!' he yelled, spurring after the headstrong Hazell, who had caught up with a broken-wheeled wagon. Hazell switched the heavy colour to his left hand and thrust with his sword. A civilian driver doubled up on the running-board and toppled to the trampled grass. Hugo pulled his horse around the other side of the stalled wagon as a bare-headed man in his shirtsleeves jumped down and sprinted away like a hare. Telling went after him, his eyes, whipped by the frantic blast of the chase, running with tears. He brought his sword down in one whistling stroke, cutting across the fugitive's shoulder. His dirty white shirt blossomed with blood and he fell full length and rolled over in the turf. Telling looked up from the slashing, heart-thumping orgy as a hundred sheep stampeded across his path, their wall-eyes starting from their thick heads. His horse bucked back in agitation at this unexpected invasion. A flurry of shots flew past his head, superheating the smoke-ribboned wind like burning wasps. Startled, he looked up to see a tightly clustered band of enemy infantry who had formed around an improvised laager of abandoned wagons. He made out their fearful faces, white dabs beneath their rusted helmets and drooping hats. But they weren't running around like panicked partridges, they were standing their ground and reloading with ominous precision.

Telling's boiling blood cooled in a moment. The deafening shouts and splutter of muskets fell silent on all sides. He could see every hairy, sweat-beaded detail on every frozen face, every unbuttoned article of kit, every raised weapon. Even the bullets seemed trapped in mid-flight, like bumble bees flying through honey. In that tiny moment of awareness, the fear he had forgotten – the fear he had managed to fight down flat like the straw pallet he had gratefully left that dawn – returned like a dragon sliding through his innards. He remembered his last encounter with that oaf Sparrow on the hill before Stow, how he had been rescued from almost certain death by his despised new rival Hazell and left in the swell's dangerous debt. He pulled up abruptly, all too aware of his own mortality now. He ducked over the prancing mare's mane and spurred it away from this red-coated rock, joined the swirling squadrons which were still entangled with the enemy rearguard. It was a confused, cut and thrust scrimmage of horse and rider, where desperate riders stabbed opponents in the back and slashed at grasping hands. He caught a backhander from a bearded Roundhead on a black horse, and almost fell from the saddle before he broke free. By the time he had righted himself, he was almost in the trees. Hugo caught his breath for a moment, examined the blood smear on his gauntlet, and turned the panting animal back towards the chase.

Another blare of trumpets announced the sudden, spirited charge of Stapleton's horse, hurried down from the vanguard to save the threatened rear. The fresh troops pounded across the grass, herding the screaming stragglers back towards the isolated rocks of Parliamentarian infantry, and crashed into the disorganized Royalists. In another moment, Rupert's mob of screaming Cavaliers was pushed back a hundred yards. The Roundhead wedge had cut a huge hole in the crush, but their charge was slowed and then halted by sheer weight of numbers.

The din rose once more as six thousand swordsmen hacked and slashed at each other, an anvil chorus worthy of hell's fiery furnaces.

'Stand straight in your ranks and files!' Sparrow yelled, stepping out of the crush for a moment to check their formation. Not so much formation as white-faced, many-legged mob, musketeers and pikemen all mixed up. But he was determined to hold them together this time, determined to overcome his own impulse to run and hide and stand straight beside them. His legs were trembling in his boots so hard he had to stamp them up and down to regain control.

'Stand straight, pikes to the centre,' he bawled, his hair standing on end beneath his tightly strapped helmet. His single-minded concentration seemed to steady the would-be fugitives. The disorganized ranks sorted themselves out, stragglers hurried in from the woods or emerged from beneath the abandoned wagons. A dozen horses lay dead or dying in the slashed traces. A driver had fallen back over the running-board and impaled himself on a splintered shafts. His arms were still moving although he looked quite dead. Others were crawling for cover, desperate to escape the pounding hoofs as the confused mêlée flowed this way and that along the stalled baggage train. Sparrow was still trembling with shock, his whole body shivering beneath its straps and buckles and tightly pulled belts. He felt as if he would fall apart the same as his company, but somehow managed to swallow his fear, compress his doubts back into his breeches, and stabilize the terrified mob.

'Stand straight,' he croaked, his throat constricting with the effort. By ones and twos they sorted themselves out, lifting their arms and holding one another's shoulders to dress their ranks. Colston Muffet waved a file of musketeers forward, and hurried the next rank in behind them. Colonel Fulke rode along from the rear, holding his helmet on with his gloved hand.

'Thank God! You stay put, I'll send the rest back to you,' he shouted. Sparrow nodded and worked his chin. His teeth were clenched so hard he thought he might have developed lockjaw.

'Don't let 'em wander now, William,' Fulke advised, turning his lively horse and spurring off to gather the rest of his men. Sparrow peered after him, noted the rest of Mercer's regiment seemed to have broken up like a pearl necklace, the stragglers bunching in iron-spiked lumps around the wagons and guns. At least they hadn't all run for it. He looked up as more Roundhead horse cantered up from the front, taking the places of their battered companions. They seconded Stapleton's charge, giving the broken troops time to recover and re-form their ranks.

'Mercer's regiment, have a care! Advance, advance your pikes and muskets!'

Sparrow heard the command from the other end of the line, repeated it to the enthusiastic, wide-eyed volunteers behind him. He recognized John Jewell and Caleb, the new man Jackson standing like a statue in the agitated ranks. He wondered for a moment where the red-headed boy had got to.

Mercer's regiment had formed up with pikes in the centre and musketeers on the flanks. Fulke waved them on as they strode over the littered turf, stepping over bodies and slaughtered horses.

'Christ Jesus, we're goin' ter charge ol' Rupert hisself!' Butcher yelled.

'Shut your mouth, you damned jobberknol,' Long Col scolded him. 'Stay in line and keep the rest of 'em straight!'

'Charge your pikes!'

The front two ranks brought their weapons up to their shoulders, holding the quivering points out at chest height. The scattered cavalry who were still milling aimlessly between the heaps of dead and smashed carts spurred out of the way, seen off by the bristling hedgehog and a volley of shots from the screaming Roundheads.

Yard by yard, acre by acre, the killing field was cleared.

Rupert's devils were cast back into the tree line where they could be heard blowing fresh fanfares to summon assaults which never materialized.

'Advance your pikes and muskets!'

Mercer's men stood to, peering over the trampled turf and following the smears of blood where some rider had been dragged off by a comrade. The littered field looked as if it had been scoured by a tornado, torn up by the roots and flung back down again. Sparrow was amazed by the refuse the retreating men had left behind. Boots, helmets, bloody scarves. Purses, boxes, saddles, sacks. A neatly severed hand still clutched an elegant sword. Stephen Talbot had found it first, clenching his teeth as he pulled the frozen fingers from the dead steel. He drop-kicked the offending item away to a roar of delight from his fellow soldiers.

Two months before he had been calculating lines of figures in a London bank. Now he was a carefree killer, thoughtless, greedy, profane – and very much alive.

Sparrow shook his head, his body chilling with the heart-stopping anticlimax of it all. Rupert driven off in confusion, the way to London clear, and it was still only eight o'clock or so.

'Mercer's regiment, prepare to march!' He shouldered his halberd, loosened his straps, wondering what they were up to back home. Still abed, he supposed. Moaning about getting up for work. Enjoying a nice bite of breakfast. His stomach rumbled loudly.

'Oy! Who was watching the sheep?' Billy Butcher called, peering around the shambling pikemen, his face black with soots.

'That little red-headed bugger, last time I looked!'

'Oh, fucking marvellous, they've only gone and rustled our mutton!'

The girls found their missing patient in the lane, hurrying along with limp arms and staring eyes, a splash of blood across his chin, neck, and chest. He was stark naked, and covered in dirt and bloody weals.

Anneliese covered her mouth, stifling her cry of alarm. Bella, her eyes red raw so she could barely recognize her idiot brother, threw out her hands to catch him.

'Jamie!' she yelled, holding on to the terrified youngster as he squirmed and kicked like a landed cod. She pinched his wasted muscles, drew back her hand, and slapped him around the face. He staggered, gave a single, choked cry, and slumped to the ground covering his face. Anneliese was mortified by his pitiful condition, her hopes and dreams shattered in a moment by his obvious and completely unhinged distress. Bella brought her hand back, examining the bloodstains as the boy whimpered like a beaten cur.

'It's not his,' she exclaimed, wrenching his chin up and peering at his drowned face.

'He's soaking wet!' Anneliese backed away, struck dumb with horror at his bewildering predicament. He was gasping now, panting like a dog as he tried to speak.

'They're hurting him-ing, they're hurting hiiiim,' he screeched.

'Who? Who are they hurting?' Bella pulled at him, none too gently as she tried to make sense of his gibberish.

'The soldierings are hurting him-ing!' Jamie blubbered, squirming like a snake at their fear-frozen feet. Bella looked up, and heard the hatefully familiar tumult from the village.

The furious villagers tumbled out of their homes with every weapon that came to hand, surprising the gang of half-drunken dragoons who were menacing poor old Mordecai.

The naked boy had dashed away on all fours between

the compressed legs of soldier and civilian, leaving the cruel dragoons to concentrate their scorn on the lame Samaritan, who they shoved and punched into the hard-baked ruts. Infuriated, his mother had snatched up the nearest weapon and thrown her door open.

'Mother!' Mary Keziah, horror-stricken, cried. Her mother didn't hear her.

Gwen Pitt emerged from the laundry house with her enormous soap-smoothed ladle held in her red fists, screaming at the surly soldiers to leave her son alone.

Sergeant Lawton wheeled around in alarm, but broke into a fit of laughter as he spied the fat woman with the flabby red arms flounce down the steps. Mordecai, on his knees before the bow-legged runt, opened his bloody eye. They had beaten him to the ground and hauled him back up again, and were about to repeat the procedure when Gwen had sallied out to his rescue, precipitating the riot.

'You leave the boy alone,' she screeched. Lawton stepped back before her furious onslaught, glancing about for his cronies. They were laughing and pointing at the entertainment, their weapons loose in their fists. The mob of villagers swarmed in close – too close – behind them. Consumed by an immediate surge of furious panic, Lawton raised his pistol and fired. There was a splutter of sparks and Gwen staggered back, her stained bodice splashed with blood. Her fat pink hands clutched and fluttered at her ample bosom as she collapsed onto the steps.

Mordecai snarled with helpless rage, elbowed the bandy dragoon between the legs. Lawton doubled up, bringing the smoking pistol butt down on his skull as he fell. The startled dragoons gaped, giving the furious villagers the precious moment they needed.

Jeremiah Pitt dashed out of the alley, leapt into the air,

and landed on a dragoon's back, wrapping his arms around the man's throat.

Other villagers, exasperated and terrified by turns, hurried up the main street before the soldiers could wield their weapons. Crushed in the narrow gap between the hovels they were set upon by a dozen men and women while others screamed behind their doors. Lawton rolled clear and prised himself to his feet, wrenching the dagger from his roll-top boot. Mordecai groped for the weapon and missed, slashing his arm. The wiry little fighter jumped back towards the steps, knife held ready as the crowd closed in on him.

He didn't see the dazed woman sit up behind him. The careless dragoon had left his pistol beside his commandeered bed all night, and the damp had penetrated the powder. The spluttering pistol had propelled the bullet with just enough force to break Gwen Pitt's skin but without smashing her formidable breastbone. She sat up in sudden fury, astonished she was alive at all, let alone that her despised attacker was standing unaware not two yards in front of her.

'Get away out of it, strawheads,' Lawton snarled as the vicious brawl broke out in front of him. He lifted his unloaded pistol, confident half of them would immediately freeze.

'I'll shoot the first bastard I—'

Gwen Pitt had run the village laundry house for twenty years, lifting bales of waterlogged washing from the great smooth-ribbed tubs. Since her husband disappeared at the beginning of the summer she had been left to her own devices at home and all, trying to hold on to the disintegrating threads of her family. Two boys off fighting with the King, another back from Bristol crippled for life, another threatening to run off and join the Roundheads any moment, and her eldest daughter Mary up the spout from that jumped-up paperboy Will Sparrow.

Merciful Christ above, Gwen Pitt had already endured all the bloody war she ever wanted.

The big, fleshy woman lifted the washing paddle as if it was the mother of all her miseries and swung it with all her might at the bandy-legged sergeant. The horrifying blow caught him around the back of his head, splitting his skull like an egg and popping his left eye straight out of its numbed socket. The pole-axed sergeant hit the road with force enough to knock out several teeth, his umbilical eyeball smeared between his cheek and the unforgiving road.

The fight stopped immediately, both soldier and civilian alike struck dumb by the crushed corpse, his jagged skull leaking a lagoon of blood and dribbling grey brains.

The dragoons recovered first, dashing towards the astonished laundress – straight into the path of the pretty lass with the pistols.

Bella Morrison had already shot one man in similar circumstances, and right now she was ready to shoot another. Carried along like flotsam by the God-damned brutality of it all, she was sick to the stomach of fighting and misery and blood and hurt. Her friends sent away, her brother sent mad, her fiancé mouldering in his winding-cloth because of her disgraceful deceits. Bella was sick of it all, and would have happily fired off a cannon a hundred miles wide at her whole, hateful world, punctured her entire blood-drenched universe.

Now, though, she would make do with these looted

pistols, smuggled back into the village by her former maid Mary Keziah.

Good old dependable Mary.

The dark-haired girl had hurried out of the back of the house the moment she heard the fracas in the street outside. While her mother ranted in the doorway brandishing her ladle like a great iron mace she dashed out of the back door and recovered her own weapons from the secret armoury beneath the chicken shed, a brace of pistols she had brought back from her own days following the army. Neither the camps nor the roads these days were fit places for unarmed young women to go wandering. These vicious dragoons had dragged the village from its smug isolation into the same mean world, imposing the rigid doctrine of kill or be killed on civilian as well as enemy.

Mary had spent more than enough time around the soldiers to know how to load a firearm, and she hurried to the alley to see what the hideous argument was about. The sudden shot stopped her in her tracks, left her bent double with agonized uncertainty. She peered out into the confused street fight, bewildered by the murderous brawl. Her courage evaporated like the dead dragoon's grey brains as she surveyed the horrific tableau, and she was standing forlorn when Bella made her way down the passage behind her. Mary was startled by her former mistress's sudden appearance, and was about to shoot her down dead in blind panic. Bella reached out and grabbed the raised barrels, lifted the pistols from the maid's tearful grasp.

'What's going on now?' she cried.

How long had she got, Bella thought crossly. She hadn't seen her errant maid since she had gotten back from her adventures in Gloucester. They hadn't exactly avoided one another, but for half a hundred unspoken reasons they had grown apart. There wasn't time to catch up now.

Mary Keziah, poor pregnant Mary, stood forlorn while Bella brandished her pistols like a Turk, held a cocked finger to her lips.

'They've beaten Jamie and Mordecai, they're running riot,' she whispered. 'You run back to the house to fetch Lady Ramsay's people,' she instructed, mistress all over again. Before the girl could reply Bella had slipped around the corner of the alley like a thief in the night.

Run? She couldn't run anywhere in her condition . . . but of course Bella didn't know of her pregnancy.

And neither did Will. She would have written to tell him of her delicate condition, but she had never been skilful with letters. Mary Keziah held her hand over her mouth, paralysed with panic, and watched Bella step out into the furious street.

The dragoons froze for a moment, regarding the blonde-haired Amazon who seemed to have risen from the very mud in front of them.

She was paler than ever, her hair tufted and caught up by the breeze and the hedgerows. Her gown was rent along the leg, revealing her creamy petticoats beneath. Their eyes wandered over her figure. They licked their dry lips.

'Stand,' she croaked, determined to master her voice. 'Stand there!' she cried, louder. The dragoons leered at her and winked at one another.

'One man's dead already, I'll make it three, I swear,' Bella vowed, a tiny dab of furious colour appearing below her furiously blinking eyes. The dragoons chuckled, but none of them moved. The villagers crowded in behind them, with knives and clubs, hoes and shovels. Mordecai Pitt swayed from side to side, holding Lawton's pistol by the barrel. Jeremiah snatched up his discarded knife. Gwen had slumped back down on the step, staring at her victim's broken head, clutching her own fruitily bruised bosom.

Their fury and hate evaporated in a blink of an eye. The dragoons twitched, keeping an eye over their shoulders as the mad bitch in the blue gown held her trembling pistols steady.

'Put 'em down now, missy, there's no harm,' an older, toothless dragoon advised.

Bella compressed her pale lips. 'I've shot one bastard down already, I'm not scared to do it again,' she growled.

The dragoons swallowed, nodded ingratiatingly. 'No trouble, missy,' their aged spokesman said, lowering his pistol.

'Drop them. Drop your weapons, all of you,' Bella ordered. The dragoons exchanged glances.

'We'll not be butchered by country folk,' a younger, wild-eyed horseman called out.

'There'll be no butchery. Just get on your horses and get out.'

The toothless old-timer smiled maliciously. 'What, and niver come back?'

'I'm warning you,' Bella threatened.

Sensing the abrupt change of mood, the villagers raised their weapons, closing in on the compressed mob of dragoons.

'You come back when you've cooled down, and we'll sort it all out,' Bella said feebly.

The toothless dragoon snapped up his pistol. Bella

fired, catching him in the arm. The dragoon screamed and fired back, hitting her in the head. Mordecai snarled, crying with rage and shame and hate at once. He caught the wounded man by his coat and clubbed the old bastard to the ground. With a sudden yell of hatred the wronged villagers closed in on the paralysed dragoons, cracking skulls with shovels, shoving kitchen knives into kidneys. Jeremiah tackled one rider and his brother jumped on his chest, grabbing him by the hair and cracking his head into the hard-baked road. Three dragoons ran off down an alley, another fired his carbine straight in a woman's face before he was skewered on a pitchfork by her irate husband.

In another red second the street was cleared. The surviving dragoons climbed on their nags and galloped off to raise the alarm, leaving the stupefied citizens with a street full of bodies.

Bella lay spreadeagled in the road, a trail of blood leaking from her white forehead, her blue gown tossed up from around her long legs. Gwen Pitt hurried over, covered her mouth as she gazed down on the familiar waxy features. Her daughter Mary hurried out, frightened by the shouts and shots. She lifted her skirts and dashed over to help her mother as she bent down beside the pale victim, tugged her gown straight as if it was the least she could do.

Bella's hazel eyes were fluttering, the deep graze across her forehead running with shockingly bright blood. Gwen swooned, as if this precious liquor was ten thousand times purer than the red filth the dragoons had been pumped so full of.

'Bella? Mother ... she's never dead?' Mary cried, holding her stomach.

So they were when Sir Gilbert finally struck up the courage to ride into the embattled village, urging the snorting grey mare down the bloody street a few moments later.

PART FOUR

ON WASH COMMON

All were Englishmen, and pity it was that such courage should be spent in blood of each other.

Bulstrode Whitlock commenting on the
Battle of Newbury

BY

HAMPSTEAD PARK,

NEAR NEWBURY,
19 SEPTEMBER 1643

'I'll tell you what. By the time we get there every bleedin' billet in the town is going to be stuffed with those mounted monkeys,' sure-shot and veteran whiner Billy Butcher told the toiling company. Nobody could be bothered to argue with the snivelling sniper, they were all too busy with gloomy imaginings of their own.

'We'll be lucky to bed down in a pig's piss house, if you want to know.'

Mercer's weary footsloggers didn't seem to care where they slept. Many of them seemed to be shambling along with their eyes closed as it was. Bone-weary, soaked through, and hobbling on despite severely lacerated feet, the sorry company looked as if they would have the utmost difficulty fighting their way through a wet cheese, let alone the King's entire, unfought army.

'We won't have to fight now, will we? They must be miles behind,' Stephen Talbot called, lifting his string-bound shoes from the glutinous filth which ran in a stream of slurry along the sunken lane. The unkempt tracks seemed to have been deliberately tilted against them so the shuffling, cursing soldiers had to constantly contend with rills of steaming ox dung. The slippery, stinking ordure fouled their legs and tripped them up, coated every wheel with layers of toad-green slime. Lending a hand with the guns or bending a shoulder to a stuck cart inevitably distributed the filth to coats and breeches, hats and hair, transforming soldiers into so many shit-smeared scarecrows.

Despite the hellish hardships the Earl of Essex's army followed each atrocious track as if it was a direct route to paradise, stuck to the overgrown lanes as if they would perish if they dared set foot on the lush green meadows to either side of the reeking alleys. The fearful troops hurried along to join the press, regiment after regiment jamming itself into the apparent safety of the main road.

After running the gauntlet of Aldborne Chase, the Roundhead army preferred the snail's-pace sanctuary of the lanes to the easier going of the open fields. The battered, bloody, and increasingly anxious force split up like a slow tide running away out of an estuary, carving new gullies and channels as it trickled towards the east.

It had rained on and off all day, and the hedges and overhanging trees dripped cold water down scrawny necks. Guns went aground on bramble-coiled banks, carts tipped up on unseen obstacles. Every sack and sheet, every coat and hat was soaked, heavy with moisture. Reins and weapons were slippery in their cold crushed fists, every horse slick with rainwater and sweat.

'Ah, he's gone past us by now, I reckon,' John Jewell predicted, trailing his greasy pike through the slurry as if he was ploughing furrows for the men trudging behind.

'I don't know what yer moaning about,' Gillingfeather snarled, his tawny beard sparkled with dewy drops. 'The King's got to follow the same roads as we have! The great God who is the searcher of our souls won't lay good roads for that Antichrist!'

Some of the newer men exchanged glances, unsure

what to make of this bug-eyed fanatic who could sleep on
the edge of a razor and march all day on a mouthful of
dandelions. His outbursts about His Majesty King Charles
bordered on the hysterical, as if he had directed all the
misery of the horror march against his own true sovereign.

'We're on the best road for home, that's certain,'
Rodney Sark said, wiping his dripping nose. 'We can't be
far from my cousin's place near Newbury.'

'You and yer bloody cousins,' Billy Butcher moaned.
'You got moure bleedin' cousins than a sheep's got ticks!'

'We ain't got no sheep, thanks to that red-headed
candle-waster!'

Nicodemus Burke, the most completely bewildered and
utterly forlorn scout in the entire army, looked up miserably as the snarling soldiers cast about for something else
to whine about. How was he supposed to have kept an eye
on a hundred bloody sheep in the middle of a battle?

The damned creatures had proved to be the biggest
thorn in his side since he left Gloucester. First of all he
assured Captain Sparrow Layton's farm had been stripped
bare by the Royalists. The discovery of more than two
hundred sheep hidden at the bottom of the cliff made him
look like a lying Royalist spy at worst and a fool at best,
and certainly hadn't endeared him to his new colleagues.
There was more bad feeling when the triumphant regiment drove the flock into the camp that night, only to
have a hundred and fifty of the bleating buggers commandeered for other hungry units. The sneering soldiers
seemed to blame him for the decision! Most of the
surviving sheep stampeded on Aldborne Chase, dashing
off in all directions the moment the Royalists attacked.
What was he supposed to do, tie them up? Nail their feet
to the nearest tree? The Londoners were scared out of

their wits by the ferocity of the attack, and rounded on the poor boy as if he had personally plotted the whole thing. All in all, he felt about as wanted as the plague. He might just as well turn around and go straight home, he reflected bitterly. At least Gar Maynard had managed to find himself a pike, so he looked a little like a soldier. Poor Nicodemus trudged along with nothing in his hands but a switch, which he brought down with malicious intent on the clockwork hindquarters of an ox chained between the shafts of a wildly unsteady powder wagon. The precariously balanced load creaked and slid beneath a tightly bound tarpaulin, slick with rain. Woe betide him if one of the barrels fell off, that would be his fault too, no doubt.

'Cheer up, lad,' Master Jackson said, resting his pale hand on the boy's twitching shoulder. 'Not far now.'

'Not far now? Not far from what, is what I want to know,' Billy Butcher crowed, eavesdropping on their muttered exchange. 'Bloody purgatory, that's what.'

Colonel Nybb had ridden up and down the bedraggled, straggling lines of men since dawn, watching the shifty-eyed sharpers who dawdled near the woods or hung about at the back as they trailed through one fearful village after another. The regiment he had inherited from that treacherous reptile Morrison had shrunk to about a quarter of its original strength, with most of the Wiltshire men slipping away to their homes as they marched back from Gloucester. Hungry and dispirited by the lack of success outside the fanatically held city, they deserted by the dozen. The fact the King had counted on almost thirty thousand men outside the defiant outpost had not helped his cause when it was time to leave the town behind.

Hundreds of individuals looked at the vast host and imagined they would not be missed amongst such a throng. The fact that so many felt the same way reduced regiments to companies, companies to idle, moaning gangs of lily-livered scoundrels.

Nybb took long detours away from the jammed road, working his way over the fields to come back on the busy highway from the rear. He ran into small groups of gleeful deserters who thought themselves safely away from the coughing host. They stopped dead in panicked surprise when they found their various ways home blocked by their bandit of a commander on his snorting coal-black stallion. 'Guten tag, mineers, off for a stroll, eh?' he would ask, driving the fearful wretches back to the main body at pistol-point. Cully Oates and his new corporals Zach and Eli had also marched double the distance of the rest of the men, making their way along the hedgerows putting up the slinkers who had stayed too long at their ablutions.

'You've had long enough to shit a yard, you beef-witted bastards,' the veteran sergeant would snarl, escorting the miscreants back to the road with a series of brutal kicks. 'You must think I came down with the last shower of rain!'

Nybb pulled up his horse under an overhanging oak and glared at his dismal regiment as it shuffled and stumbled past. The least formidable unit he had ever had the misfortune to serve with.

'Hosen oder schleime,' the boar-tusked freebooter growled, 'what a set of shit-spined sacks!'

Cully Oates was puffing at his rain-tamped pipe, taking a breather while his young lieutenants scoured the hedges for more pigeon-hearted soldiers. 'Good Lord 'elp us if we got to stop the Crop'eads gettin' back a Lunnun with this lot,' the rusty-whiskered old stoat leered.

Captains Shea and Allington trudged along, halberds over their shoulders and hats pulled down over their sopping brows. They were muttering to each other in fearful undertones and didn't notice the murderous crew taking shelter under the tree.

'Keep up you two, yer men are slacking,' Nybb called. The rain-soaked officers jumped with surprise, nodded feebly. They doubled past, anxious to put as much distance between themselves and their despised leader. Sergeant Major Findlay marched along with his long fowling piece butt up against the wet weather. He was wearing ankle boots and leather gaiters, emblems of his previous profession as gamekeeper to the Ramsays, and seemed to be making light of the conditions. His small company strode behind him, cheerful enough despite the atrocious going. Nybb did a quick headcount and snorted into his rain-spangled beard.

'What, picking up stragglers along the way, mineer?' the colonel enquired.

Findlay looked up at the mounted bandit, tipped his hat brim to let a spout of water run off over the treacherous path. 'No. They're the same I brought from Gloucester,' the stone-eyed sharpshooter replied laconically.

Nybb slumped forward over his damp saddle to peer at the supercilious gamekeep, irritated as always by his manners. 'Not lost one, eh, Findlay?'

'Not one,' Findlay replied with a tiny flicker of a smile. 'Sir,' he added as an insolent afterthought. He marched on, his men hurrying along behind him, muskets upended as their sergeant had shown them. Nybb spat into the mulch beneath the tree, and muttered a series of hair-raising Polish oaths.

'I tell you, mineer, one day, me and him,' Nybb vowed.

Cully Oates closed one eye and watched the gamekeeper march on up the filthy lane.

'Ah, but he can shoot the knackers off a horsefly at a hundred yards,' the veteran reasoned, as the last bedraggled stragglers struggled up the slope and hurried on after their soaking wet colleagues.

'I'll be nearer the bastard than that,' Nybb growled.

'I'd rather have him this side than theirs, mind.'

'We'll see, mineer,' Nybb said icily. 'We'll see.'

The quartermasters, grooms, and light-fingered layabouts who generally kept themselves to themselves safe at the rear of the hopelessly entangled columns dashed on ahead for once, anxious to secure themselves or their masters the best quarters in Newbury. The worried residents eyed them suspiciously as they rode in on the Enborne road on their filthy horses, pointing and shouting and arguing loud enough to wake the dead. The Roundhead scroungers went from house to house chalking names on doors and crude directions on walls. Several opened their purses before the uncertain owners, loudly reassuring them that the approaching army would pay its way, as well as it might.

'We don't loot you, we'll sign chits for everything,' a red-checked, barrel-bellied quartermaster told the doubt-ful landlord of the Green Man.

'N'mind yer chits. I can't eat chits nor pay my grocer wi' 'em either,' the suspicious publican snorted. 'Hard cash, on the nose, or you can piss off same as the other crew.'

'Is that so, Uncle?'

Further debate on the engrossing issue of provisioning fifteen thousand half-starved soldiers was rudely interrupted by a flurry of pistol shots from the far end of the street. The Roundhead scouts looked up expecting to see some irate burgher letting fly at some overly impatient forager. Instead they found themselves face to face with a party of Cavaliers, galloping down on them with gleeful ferocity. The drop-jawed advance parties ran for their lives, dashing down alleys or throwing themselves into doorways as the King's horsemen thundered down the main street from the north, skewering the stragglers and shooting at the fugitives as they scrambled through windows or over gardens. Half a dozen held up their arms, holding nothing more threatening than a lump of chalk. In a moment the town changed colour, altered its allegiance with the breeze.

But most of the burghers greeted the Cavaliers with even less enthusiasm than they had the Roundheads. At least Essex's men made a pretence at paying for their keep. The King's men simply grabbed what they wanted and left them fuming.

The frightened survivors leaped on their quietly grazing horses and spurred back down the Enborne road to report the dreaded news. Rupert and all his cavalry had crossed the river and seized the town from under their noses. The Roundheads had lost the great race for Newbury.

In actual fact, Newbury had been seized by one small troop of horse, the hard-riding vanguard of Prince Rupert's veteran cavalry force. The Cavaliers made up in noise what they lacked in numbers, easily convincing the terrified Roundheads they were many thousand strong. The rest of the cavalry arrived by drips and drabs, worn out after their forced march south from Wantage. They formed up in a large field to the west of the town, the perilously extended ranks thickening slowly as troop after troop completed the exhausting journey and were directed through the streets to face the even slower moving enemy, who were massing away on the wooded slopes towards Hampstead Marshall.

By dusk, the first of the King's infantry had begun to trickle in to the town, joining their brothers in the waterlogged meadows beside the swiftly flowing River Kennet. They had marched sixteen miles that day, and still arrived before the toiling Roundheads, who had only managed to cover seven or eight miles from Hungerford.

Soaking wet and sore to the bone, the tardy Parliamentarian army had paid the price of its own lethargy. Now the King had blocked the London road they would have to fight through his whole army to get home.

King Charles, tickled by the excitement of the chase, spurred along with his officers packed in behind him, his cavalry unleashed like hounds on the scent. The entire officer corps seemed intoxicated, carried away by the sheer, primeval thrill of riding down their russet-coated quarry.

With his rapidly arriving army safely deploying to the west, the King retired to his quarters in Newbury to confer with his bone-weary but elated commanders. The Duke of Richmond, who had helped encourage the mournful monarch after the disappointments at Gloucester, was uncharacteristically enthusiastic about the imminent battle.

'Be assured, Your Majesty, this rebellion will be strangled by this time tomorrow night.'

'Essex will grovel like a dog.'

'How is it we beat him to the town? We marched double the distance this day!'

'That's easy enough, my lord, his men knew what awaited them. Hard battle and just punishment. A thief will not run to the assizes nor the hangman's rope!'

Lord Falkland glared at the red-faced crowd, sickened by their bloody boasting and malicious glee. They were like a bunch of schoolyard bullies waiting to pounce on some unsuspecting pupil. Earls and barons and generals alike gloating over the seemingly inevitable triumph. The thoughtful Secretary of State was not so sure of himself. For one thing, he dreaded the revenge such a bloodthirsty cabal would take on their revolted countrymen if they ever succeeded in gaining the victory they craved. They intended to slaughter as many of the rebels as possible on the morrow, and then march on to London to punish the rebel capital.

By God, it was an occasion for mournful reflection and sober consideration, not bottles of sack and bloody oaths. The miserable nobleman glanced up at the King, noted that His Majesty's eyes, downcast that morning, were now glittering with relish, reanimated by the thrill of the chase.

The King tugged at his red beard, buoyed up all over again by the enthusiastic predictions of his commanders. Falkland smiled feebly, clearly out of sorts after the day's excitements. He glanced over at his nephew, who was brooding over the heaped maps, tapping his balled fist against his jutting chin in distraction. King Charles held his hand up to quiet the feverish council, nodded at the towering figure of the Prince.

'Why now, my lord? Is our victory not as assured as our friends would have me believe?' he asked indulgently. Rupert glanced sideways at his uncle, shrugged his shoulders. The King frowned in mock surprise at his nephew's non-committal response.

''Twas you who urged the necessity of reaching the town before my lord of Essex,' his uncle reminded him gravely.

'So that we might fortify our position before him,' Rupert corrected him fiercely. 'We have blocked the road, Essex must either go through or abandon his march on London.'

The rosy-cheeked general officers sighed at the argumentative Prince's want of enthusiasm. They exchanged glances as the German tyrant built himself up into a familiar rage.

'We should avoid fighting at all costs. Manoeuvre, certainly. Put out patrols, assuredly, but the foot need time to recover before we rely on them again.'

'My men have marched going on ninety miles from Gloucester! They'll fight on the morrow or I'll know why,' one bloated blockhead announced in a rasping voice.

'My lord was all for an immediate attack on that city, I seem to recall. How is it he recommends such cautious counsels when we have that cuckold Essex at our mercy?'

Rupert glowered at the beady-eyed generals, staring straight through them with his usual supercilious scorn.

'That was a completely different situation. It is Essex who must move, not us. My cavalry captured enough food in the town to keep us going for a week. We have reinforcements, supplies, and more powder on the way.'

'But Essex will be reinforced if we sit here on our arses!' an irate earl snapped, forgetting his manners in front of his sovereign.

'Good. Let him collect every last man he drew out of Gloucester. Let him collect every man from every garrison along the way. He can't feed what he has now, let alone any more. We have more cavalry and more dragoons, we can harry his foragers and pen him up beside the river. The obvious course would be to dig the infantry in and let Essex come to us.'

'Dig in before those dogs? I'd rather be buried alive than face that shame!'

'I am surprised at you, sir, advocating such craven policies.'

Rupert ran his tongue over his teeth, swallowed his temper, and calmly addressed his uncle.

'Sir. We are missing near two thousand foot and six hundred horse. We are short of powder and match. To fight tomorrow would be to invite a bloody stalemate. If we hold them off, they will perish.'

Charles blinked rapidly, his glittering eyes dimmed by his nephew's pessimistic predictions.

'Surely sir, the f–f–fact Essex has m–m–marched like a sna–snail this day bears out the fact that his men have no stomach for this f–f–fight?' he stammered, disconcerted by the Prince's unwelcome reading of the strategic situation. The senior officers nodded in agreement, united against the upstart German. Why, they had been making war when he had been pissing his breeches!

'Essex wouldn't be here at all, my lord, if you had succeeded in holding his relief army from our backs!'

The glowering demon trembled with fury, picked his words from the churning bile in his throat. 'There was never any intention of holding him off. We sought to entice him into the open, here he is.'

'And you say don't fight!'

'I say let him fight, fight on ground of our choosing!'

'Aye, right here!' a choleric earl snorted, stamping his foot upon the boards.

'This country is no good to my cavalry!' the Prince

stormed. 'It's all enclosed about with hedges and ditches and Lord knows what else.'

'Well, if your horse won't fight, the foot will have to! Isn't that so, Astley?'

Sir Jacob Astley, veteran commander of all the King's infantry and notoriously silent around the council table, looked startled to be spoken to at all. He knitted his brows in consideration and thought for a moment. 'Ah,' he said wisely.

'There!'

Rupert rolled his eyes at the ceiling.

'Surely, Your Majesty,' Falkland interrupted, 'this is the time to send to Essex for negotiations. He lays at your mercy across the meadows there, his men willing him to come to the table.' The Secretary of State's heartfelt outburst immediately united the rest of the King's officers.

'What? Negotiate now we have brought the dogs to heel? Let them send to us, if they want to surrender!'

'Essex is the one who ought to be pleading for mercy, not us, my lord!'

'I am not saying we should not fight, I am saying . . .'

King Charles held his hand up, as if pained by his council's embittered disagreements.

'My lords, I think we are all agreed there is no suggestion the cavalry will not fight. And I must declare I see no advantage in going to the rebels cap in hand. My mind is made up, gentlemen. Tomorrow we will take arms to the earl. If he wishes to lay down his weapons and come to me for forgiveness, then, and only then, will we talk.'

WASH COMMON,

NEAR NEWBURY, DAWN,
20 SEPTEMBER 1643

S ome slept on despite the constant alarms and the odd, isolated shots as the musketeers cleared the damp debris from their dew-jewelled barrels. Others, bone-weary and raw-eyed with nervous exhaustion, hadn't slept a wink, squatting around the feeble embers of the previous night's watchfires as the impacted armies stretched their aching tendons and flexed their many shaded muscles. The sky was overcast, livid purple bruising running like dye across the distant horizons. Everything seemed drenched by the all-conquering moisture in the air. Horses whinnied gently at their steaming picket lines. Pikemen coughed and patted their pockets for their last treasured pipefuls of baccy. A lucky few who had managed to forage themselves some breakfast stoked up the cooking fires and maliciously fried hunks of bacon on the points of their blunted swords. They had used their side arms to cut firewood, rendering many of the blades unfit for anything but culinary applications.

Sparrow's cutlass, however, was as famously sharp as it had been the day he unwrapped it from its greased packing back on the *Conqueror*, in those bleak days before the siege of Bristol. The wicked weapon was normally issued to naval boarding parties, but he had found its menacing whistle somehow reassuring. He might not make a good swordsman, but he had hoped his blade would make most Royalists think twice about crossing swords with him. Sadly, it hadn't made them think any such thing. The Cavalier officer who damn near lopped his arm off back at Bristol hadn't been in the least impressed by the cumbersome weapon, clearly believing a gentleman would have discarded such heavy-handed ironmongery as unnecessarily crude.

Well, Sparrow didn't mind what they thought.

He ran his eye along the razor-edged weapon, and swung it around in the still dawn air, slicing the drifting mist into silky tatters. Most of his company had taken shelter beneath an overhanging hedge, their weapons leaning against the brambles and hawthorns like so many toothpicks arranged against a plate.

There! Thinking about food again! He'd long since demolished the last of his bread and cheese, and he was going hungry the same as the rest of them, tortured by the appetizing smells drifting along on the mist. The delicious aroma of frying bacon slid sensually under his nose. He quivered all over.

'Those bastard gun boys, I bet they were out foraging while we pushed their fucking culverins for 'em,' Billy Butcher called out vindictively, 'They could 'ave 'ad the decency to come and share,' he bawled, prompting the happy cooks in question to raise their loaded knives in familiar greeting.

'Same to you, yer bastards! The Shagpolls'll 'ave it out of you this morning, you wait and see!'

Sparrow snorted with derision, sheathed the dangerous blade with a flourish.

The whole hill seemed to be moving now, as if a termite mound had been disturbed by some particularly energetic bear. Sparrow could sense the tramping feet and creaking wheels through the cold soles of his boots, hear the clatter of equipment and jingle of harness from over the hedge as another cavalry regiment moved up towards the common. The bleary-eyed infantry made way for their brothers in arms, greeting the horsemen with the usual flurry of insults and observations.

'Stick around a while longer than ye did at Etch-Hill, boys, they don't pay yer all them wages just to look fancy, mind!'

'Up yours, Uncle!'

William looked up as a bedraggled knight on a sweating horse fell out of the trotting column and worked his way through the narrow gap in the hedge. The captain nodded a greeting as Colonel Fulke looked around the narrow enclosure, his white hair already teased and tufted by the breeze. He climbed down and steadied himself as Nicodemus ran over to hold his tired horse.

'Here you are. I've been up and down these damned lanes looking for your lot half the night,' the gallant old gentleman observed testily. Sparrow shrugged, stood aside as Fulke strode over towards the steep verge which separated their field from the next. The game old bird hauled himself up the crumbling earth bank and fished for his perspective glass. William leapt up beside him and peered towards the east. All he could see were more hedges, tiny patchwork fields of root vegetables or broader slopes of stubble and furrow. Odd units of infantry were forming up in every available space and seemed to be following the sunken lanes towards the south. He couldn't see any sign of the enemy.

'We're to be brigaded with the London Trained Bands,' Fulke commented as he studied the converging ropes of horse and knots of foot. 'Essex is planning to leapfrog the army south, one unit replacing the next until we're round them.'

William was not a gifted tactician, but a sleepy milkmaid could have picked out the glaring faults in such a grand design.

'Leapfrog around them? What are they going to do, wave us goodbye as we go?' Sparrow asked, forgetting his manners for a moment beside his tetchy commander.

Fulke lowered the glass and glowered, his lively eyes lit up by the dawn's feeble efforts. 'It's as sound a plan as you'll find,' he snapped. 'What else do you suggest, Captain Sparrow?'

William grinned. 'Well, I mean. Leapfrogging one unit after the other across three miles of enemy front?'

'I've seen the Swedes do it,' Fulke snapped.

'Never mind the Swedes, what about these turnips?' Sparrow breathed.

Fulke glared at him. 'These turnips will do as they're told, if you're there to steady them,' he said acidly.

Sparrow held his stare for a moment, watched Fulke's wrinkled features rearrange themselves into a boyish grin.

'Come on now, William, you've been through far worse than this,' he encouraged him. 'Steady heart, steady head, is what I always say.'

William stared over the heads of the confused congregations filing this way and that beneath the arched alleyways of lanes and thickets, caught the glimmer of steel on the misty hillside to his right. Fulke raised his glass and followed the movement, his lips moving silently, ranks and files of white whiskers rising and falling as he licked his pink gums.

'They're on the hill already. Skippon will hold them

423

there while we get the guns and baggage past, then he'll move on and we'll take their place. We'll remain in battle order until we're past them.'

Sparrow sighed heavily. 'And what are they going to do about it?'

'The enemy? Oh, the usual,' Fulke shrugged. He glanced at his hulking protégé through one beady eye. 'You're not going to encourage your men if you look as if you've just beshit yourself,' he scolded.

Sparrow made a noise in his throat. 'It's different now,' he explained lamely. 'I didn't know what I was about before, didn't have time to think about it.'

'You stay with them and they'll stay with you,' Fulke replied simply. He lowered his voice, leaned closer. 'I've been doing this since I was fourteen, lad. I watched the Dutch surrender Ostend to Spinola. Now he was a general,' Fulke reminisced fondly.

Sparrow was staring gloomily at the busy countryside beyond the crumbling bank. Never mind bloody Spinola! It was all right for him to go on about dying with your boots on, he was sixty years old! Sparrow had all his life ahead of him, and would rather look forward to dying in bed in sixty years' time than take a roundshot in the belly that morning. The shrewd colonel seemed to sense his thoughts, the doubts and worries congealing about his evaporating courage.

'Do you think I don't value my life every bit as highly as you value yours?' he asked, raising his eyebrows.

Sparrow smiled feebly. 'Of course not. Only a fool seeks death.'

'Then make sure he doesn't come across you today moping by some tree. I've seen men blown out of holes by mortar rounds while their friends advanced across open ground before them without suffering so much as a scratch!'

As if to punctuate Fulke's energetic advice a cannon boomed in the distance, followed closely by another. The rumbling retorts echoed back down the slopes, freezing the entire army in its mud-stricken tracks.

'Good old Skippon. What a stout old fellow he is,' Fulke grinned, tickled by the tiny barrage. Sparrow glared at the wooded hill, the gently rounded summit which commanded the long lane-dissected ridge and overlooked the broad heath beyond.

Wash Common, the locals called it.

Where the King's men were waiting for them.

If William Sparrow had possessed the wings of his tiny namesake he might have been able to fly towards the grey heavens and seek his invisible enemy for himself. Such a fantastic sight as would surely have sent him flying back the way he had come, along with every other sparrow and starling, blackbird and wren in the whole woebegone flock. Below them a complex network of intersecting tracks, no easier to follow than the swirls of skin on a man's palm.

The heavily wooded hedgerows were bordered by the brown course of the River Kennet to the north and the smaller, swifter Enborne stream to the south. The main road ran alongside the former, passing through the rolling parkland of Hampstead Marshall before running like a causeway along the water-meadows directly into the sprawling town of Newbury.

The Andover road ran away from Newbury to the south-west, creating a broad triangle at the centre of which was a low-backed horseshoe-shaped ridge. The ridge ran east to west, rising to a large, gently rounded eminence called Biggs Hill, and then turned away sharply towards the south. The broad plateau between the outflung arms of the long ridge was called Wash Common. The bare heath was criss-crossed in turns by smaller tracks. One, Dark Lane, ran from the Enborne road in the north to an exposed crossroads on the common. The second ran away west from the crossroads towards the equally deserted wilderness of Crockham Heath. A third track ran from the crossroads, up and over Biggs Hill and off towards the north – a lightly populated common scattered with small-holdings and goose droppings called Skinner's Green.

It was into this triangular arena that King Charles committed his army.

His men were up at dawn, filing out into dead-end fields and sunken lanes still heavy with dew and pale streamers of woodsmoke. The Royalist host filtered out into the complex enclosures and constricted fields to the west of Newbury, working their way forward along narrow cart tracks or splashing through waterlogged meadows along-side the busy, rain-swollen Kennet.

Four weak brigades of infantry soaked into the tightly compacted countryside like water into a sponge, hardly able to see each other let alone the enemy. The King's infantry eventually formed a rough skirmish line along the deeply sunken Dark Lane, while the majority of the horse continued on south to the drier, open expanse of Wash Common.

Hugo Telling was nodding in the saddle, bored by the monotonous and almost featureless expanse of common and the complete absence of any enemy forces. His small

troop made their way towards a cluster of red-brick buildings, the mossy tiled roofs reminding him of a scatter of
snails.

All he had been told of the day's impending events was
that the Earl of Essex would be coming that way with his
entire army, hoping to skirt around the inconveniently
held town and resume his march on London. Hugo
blinked rapidly to clear his bleary vision, and studied the
bare ridge ahead of them. The gentle slopes ran away
towards his left, where they reared up in a small conically
shaped hill, crowned with thickets and hawthorns. The
track they were following converged on the crossroads at
the foot of the hill, and the deserted red-brick farm
buildings just beyond.

'They'm 'aving a lay-in, seemingly,' Alexander Gull told
him, nodding at the deserted lanes and silent hedgerows
which ran like some broken-down steeplechase ahead of
them. Well, Hugo would be over the fence in one bound,
the rest of the King's massive host following along behind.
He glanced over his shoulder, noting with some satisfaction that Cornet Hazell had taken up station a few lengths
behind his skittish mare. The damned fop had shaved that
dawn, his pink chops glistening as he smiled and nodded.
Telling nodded back, showing his teeth. Just stay behind
me this day, you arrogant son of an Algerian whore, he
thought maliciously.

'No sign of 'em anywhere,' Gull suggested, lifting his
bulky body out of the saddle to peer at the featureless grey
horizon.

'Surely the Prince has sent somebody up to that hill
there,' Telling said, anxious as ever to promote his own
grasp of tactics. Gull regarded the silent mount for a
moment, settling back into his straining saddle.

'No doubt about it. We'll be able to see fer miles, once we gets up there.'

'Our orders are to watch the farm,' Telling replied laconically, glancing up at the sudden dull boom from over in the misty distance.

'What was—'

Telling's horse reared in fright as the dull boom gave way to a slow whistle and a final ear-splitting screech. He watched drop-jawed as a small black roundshot arced towards them, thankfully burying itself in the springy tussocks a hundred yards and more to their right. Telling squinted up at the deserted ridge, picking out a tell-tale puff of white smoke – on the top of the hill!

'They're shooting the wrong way,' he mumbled, gripping the mare's reins tightly as he leaned over to look back down his jittery troop. He saw dirty coats and scraps of colour, white faces and rusty helmets, the lowered nasal bars extinguishing features and preventing him from identifying individuals. Hazell shook out the troop colour as if he was inviting the enemy gunners to do their very worst.

'Unless tother lot got there first after all,' Gull said disbelievingly. ''Tain't like ole Rupert ter drop a bollock like that!'

Telling frowned, straightened the mare's head, and kicked it on towards the farm. He felt horribly exposed, crawling across the empty plain while the enemy took potshots at him. Thank God the second shot had landed fifty yards to the left of the first, heralding a sudden, sinister silence.

A silence as fragile and transient as the rapidly evaporating morning mist.

*

The damned height with its gullies and lanes and outcrops of face-slashing brambles reminded Nybb of that damned hill at Wittstock back in '36. He'd been defending the hilltop that day with a company of raw Saxon farm boys who had been pissing their breeches in fear despite the fact they had been cowering behind an improvised wagon burg, a great square of carts and wains, piled trunks and heaped straw.

If anything, this was worse. The converging tracks and overhanging hedges provided plenty of cover for the enemy musketeers, who jumped up and fired salvoes down the naked lanes, dropping the rabbit-hearted scoundrels one after another. Nybb ducked back down as a bullet whistled through the elder bush above his head, scattering bloody berries over him.

As far as the cursing colonel could make out the regiment had wandered into a complex ambush. Either that or the damned Roundheads hadn't straightened their lines properly. The noise was appalling, the air clouded with acrid musket smoke. He squatted beside the bank, staring at the pitiful remnants of his regiment, squatting on their heels in their narrow sanctuary while the leading company was being shot to bits by the gate.

Allington and Shea crouched down with them, swords gleaming in their trembling fists as they alternately raised their heads like silk-clad turkeys then buried them back between their shoulders. Nybb looked up, watched a perfect storm of bullets lash the empty air above the cowering regiment. Surely the bastards would run out of powder at any moment? He rolled over and crawled on his hands and knees along the earth bank, pausing every now and then to peek over the pockmarked obstacle. The field beyond was full of corpses, jammed where they had fallen in the vicious crossfire. Crossfire? For all Nybb knew it was Royalist bullets which had cut his advance company down to size.

He grinned maliciously, remembering how he'd ordered that insolent rogue Findlay to clear the fields either side of the sunken lane. Nybb paused by the gate, ordered a handful of wild-eyed pikemen out of his way, dashed over the scarred lane, and hurled himself full length through the narrow gate to the adjoining enclosure. Nybb prised himself up and squinted at the row of sullen musketeers taking cover behind the hedge. It was funny, in a way, that soldiers looked exactly the same whether you were halfway up a hill in Thuringia or traipsing over a sun-rasped Spanish sierra. They had the familiar pinched sooty faces and white staring eyes of rabbit-livered cannon fodder the world over.

Findlay was a little further on, stooping beneath a bruised elm, its white flesh exposed by the storm of shot and shell the buggers up top were throwing down at them. Nybb strode over and ducked behind the tree, eyeing his sneering sergeant major.

'How many d'you lose this time, mineer?' Nybb enquired, his thick black lips pulled back from his boar's tusk teeth.

Findlay reloaded his long fowling piece as if he was after the ducks back at Kilmersden Hall.

'About a dozen or so. They've got a body of pike around the next bend, and all their shot dispersed along the hedges both sides. There won't be any budging 'em.'

Nybb snorted, wiped his smoke-stung eyes on his filthy gauntlet. 'We'll have to go around 'em, then,' Nybb reflected. 'We'll hack through the hedge down there, look, and work our way along the gully, all ist klar?'

Findlay raised his pale eyes and studied the embattled field, gave a small, non-committal shrug. 'As you like. We'll cover you this time, though, eh?'

Nybb snorted with laughter, nodded his boar-tusked head. 'Right you are, mineer. I'll have Allington and Shea send 'em through to you.'

Findlay finished reloading his piece and looked up to see the bandit colonel double back through the gate into the adjoining field. He turned towards the hedge, swung his musket to his shoulder, and squinted down the long barrel. He could see a smudge of shouting faces away between the jagged branches, a swirling colour rising and falling in the narrow lane. He tipped the barrel to his left and squeezed the trigger.

The red colour dipped and fell away out of sight, back into the screaming chaos of the lane.

Nicodemus Burke hadn't even known the man's name. A thin-featured jabbering Londoner in a huge red coat with vast round sleeves, turned back with gold buttons. A pretty coat, which must have cost its swaggering wearer a fortune. The man had a small russet beard, thin and pointed so that it exaggerated his narrow features. The bullet had scudded across his temple and clicked off the ash pole of his colour, killing the surprised ensign in one astonished blink of an eye. The toppled colour folded up, the shaft splintering as the ensign in the red coat fell over his own sword. The hunchbacked pikemen shied away from their downed champion, their weapons clattering like a stag's antlers in the smoke-clogged passage between the overhanging branches. Nicodemus crawled forward through the muddy puddles, hurting his hands on the stony path.

He threw himself down beside the dead man as another flurry of bullets screamed through the trees, sending broken twigs and scored leaves fluttering down over the heaped dead. The red-headed youth reached out and grabbed the broken shaft, dragging the heavy colour towards him. He focused for a moment on the ensign's staring eyes, the bloodshot rims wide around the cold blue irises. He looked away quickly as a thin trail of blood ran down the man's thin nose and dripped into his tawny moustaches.

'Bring it back 'ere, boy,' the pikemen were yelling at him, retreating step by step up the bitterly contested lane. Jackson was in the front rank, peering out from beneath his old-fashioned morion helmet. He was beckoning the boy away with his great hamlike hand, waving the red-headed scout back to the rapidly diminishing pikeblock. Nicodemus crawled back a few yards, prised himself to his feet, and lifted the broken colour. He hurried towards the crushed ranks, which opened magically to let him through and then closed over again like a wall, like the great gate of some ancient city.

Only this was a city made of fustian and cotton, flesh and bone. Hairy skin and bruised muscles.

The Royalist sharpshooters had located their shallow sanctuary, shooed the huddled pikemen from their lair with a spiteful tempest of lead. Even the ricochets had claimed targets, clipped arms or clanged off helmets, leaving their horrified owners to run their twitching fingers over the scored steel.

Mercer's men had been thrown into a gap in the Roundhead line between the vanguard and Lord Robarts' brigade. The leapfrogging advance had succeeded in driving a few bored musketeers from Biggs Hill, and had

carried on down the other side of the slope opening a gap
between the leading regiments and those hurrying behind.
It was into this chasm that the first clumsy Royalist assaults
fell, long lines of foot probing the hedges and ditches
while the eager cavalry turned agitated caracoles in the
cramped fields, waiting for the all-important break-
through. There was no room to manoeuvre, no space to
form up for the charge, merely a series of tight turns and
hidden hollows from which the defenders kept up a
continual and effective fire.

Fulke galloped back down the crowded lane, cursing
soldiers leaping out of his way as he waved his notched
sword towards the noisy summit.

'Sparrow, get all your musketeers forward at the double!
They're in the enclosures!'

Sparrow peered up the overhanging lane, wondering
what enclosures he was talking about. Before Fulke could
elaborate Long Col dashed off with his men bent double
behind him, their powder charges clinking around their
elongated necks. The nervous pikemen bunched around
the bewildered captain, heads tilted against the terrible
racket echoing over the tumbled slopes.

'Well, don't stand there catching flies, man, get your
pikes up on that bend, don't let them push you out of it or
they'll bowl us all down!'

Fulke wrenched his plunging horse around and spurred
on down the confused line, bawling at his captains as if he
was a master and they were so many naughty schoolboys.

William hadn't seen anything like it. Battlefields weren't
supposed to look like this! Why, the Earl of Essex might as
well have deployed his army on Bristol's rooftops as in this
cock-eyed backwater! He had expected to watch great
blocks of troops moving majestically across the plain, spy

his enemy just as his enemy spied him. Instead they were blundering along these stranglehold alleys, brambles and branches twanging their pikes, their visibility reduced to a few yards in each direction.

The fiercely contested battle raged on, the armies trading one vicious blow for another in the blind lanes and squalid fields.

First blood went to Mercer's.

Long Col's musketeers caught an enemy regiment deploying into a bean field, and one quick volley dropped the first rank in its tracks. Before they could waft the smoke away they were fired on from the right flank by a smaller band of musketeers, pressing ahead along a steep-sided hedge.

By the time Sparrow led his nervously chattering pike-men up to the crest more enemy musketeers had fanned out behind the hedges and hawthorns, catching his men with a belly-raking broadside. They recoiled back down the track, taking cover in the sunken lane before the enemy enveloped them once again.

Sparrow clutched his halberd, feverishly rubbing burn-ing smuts from his face as the pikemen edged backwards, giving ground to their invisible enemy. The musketeers fell back across the littered field adjoining the lane, scrambling over the hedge to drop down beside their colleagues. Long Col had lost his hat, and a stray spark had singed the hair from around his right ear. He dabbed the blackened stubble in a puddle-soaked rag, wrinkling his nose against the sickening stench. The rest of them leaned into the earth walls, getting their breath back while they reloaded their smoking weapons. Sparrow ducked down and peered around the corner, the lane dipping down into the willow-lined hollow and then curving away out of sight around the bloody hill. The track was littered with bodies, discarded kit, and broken equipment. A holed drum rolled down the path, banging hollowly against arms and legs, opened skulls. A bullet kicked up a storm of grit six inches from his nose and he ducked back under cover. Long Col was crouched alongside, his musket laid over his knees.

'There's a body of 'em two fields over and another lot making their way behind a gully over the back of them willows,' he panted, his lips bright red against his sooty face. Sparrow bit his lips raw, feverishly imagining what they should do next.

'I'll work my way along the other side of this lane and get broadside to 'em as they creep up on you,' Long Col suggested. 'You keep them here at push o' pike.' Sparrow nodded before he had even considered the sergeant's plan. *You stay here* rang through his bewildered brain, something he could latch on to with confidence.

'I'll stay here,' he confirmed, squinting at the huddled musketeers as Long Col pointed up and down the littered alley. He leaned his musket against the bank and began to pull at the overhanging bushes, tearing great sodden lumps of earth out on tiny umbilical roots. The musketeers soon tore themselves a breach in the hedge, and hauled themselves through one by one, leaving the captain with his depleted pikemen.

Sparrow climbed to his aching feet, already exhausted by the morning's chaotic efforts. The wound in his arm throbbed like the devil, filling his bunched fist with pins and needles.

'Right, form up, tight as you can,' he croaked. The pikemen shuffled closer, the front rank peering over their shoulders as their colleagues packed in behind them.

Caleb was in the middle, his pike clutched easily in his pink fist, face blank beneath his rusting helmet. John Jewell was fifteen years older than the dumb orphan, but his buff-coated shoulder was a good few inches lower than the boy's. The new man Jackson completed the rank, standing at his ease as if they were going to a barn dance rather than a battle. Sparrow closed in next to Jewell, his halberd held across his chest. He glanced over his shoulder as he felt the weight of the men pressing in reassuringly behind him. Nicodemus clutched the broken colour, wedged between two ragged-arsed recruits who stared back at him as if he had grown an extra head.

'Hold tight. They can't get past us in the lane, so as long as you keep pushing, we'll hold 'em,' he yelled over another vicious flurry of shots. To his left this time, over towards the mournfully wafting willows.

'Here they come!' Jewell yelled excitedly. Sparrow looked round and saw the enemy pikeblock march purposefully around the corner. A great many-coated block of men beneath a clattering thicket of pike points. They had wedged their blue colour at the rear surrounded by a bodyguard of picked men in breastplates and tassets, skirts of riveted steel plates which protected the groin and thigh.

Sparrow swallowed, watched the enemy tramp down the slope into the hollow they had vacated, trample over the dead and wounded kicking the broken drum away. The front rank caught sight of the concealed Roundheads and broke into hoarse shouts, encouraging the men behind to push them on.

'Charge your pikes!' Sparrow belatedly remembered the command, tilted his head slightly as the front ranks raised their weapons to shoulder height, their right arm stretched out to counterbalance the deadly points.

'Advance!'

'Knock 'em hard, boys!'

'Flatten the bastards!'

Sparrow leaned back against the crush, stamping his boots into the mud to set the pace. They matched him stride for stride, until the ragged block moved like some carbuncled centipede down the slope towards the equally steady enemy pikes.

Sparrow could make out their faces now, broad stubbled jaws and staring eyes. Gaunt boys and whiskered veterans, pale eyed and dark eyed and bandaged and bearded. Teeth bared, shouted oaths, curses, and challenges. And in front of them, wickedly wavering spikes, jabbing for eyes and hearts and bellies and groin.

The two bodies slowed, the front men using their points to knock their opponents' aside. A fearful clatter of wood and grating steel. The momentum carried the front ranks towards one another, pike points piercing thighs and clanging on helmets. Jackson stumbled and sent his spear into the earth bank along their gladiatorial lane. Sparrow used all his terrified strength swinging the halberd from side to side, knocking the jabbing points aside. The unbalanced poles fell away, opening a sudden aisle between the contesting troops. Sparrow ducked down past the jabbing shafts, aiming the leaf-bladed halberd at the frightened boy in the middle of the enemy block. The youngster dropped his pike to cover his head, the sharp blade slashing across the backs of his hands. William kicked out at the screaming youth, who doubled up in pain as his comrades propelled him on into the screaming Roundheads. In another moment Sparrow was sandwiched between the bawling ranks, unable to do more than squirm and elbow his enemies. Both sets of pikemen gave a great mournful groan as the wind was knocked out of them by the rib-shattering impact. Neither side gave way.

They clutched their hopelessly ensnared spears and spat and kicked and cursed for all they were worth. The young Royalist was clutching his bloody hands, staring at Sparrow with tears pouring down his filthy cheeks. William couldn't even look away, held straight by the men pressing behind, so he was forced face to face with his desperate victim.

'I'm bleedin'! I'm bleedin'!' the terrified youngster screeched in his face.

'Shut your fucking noise,' a foxy-eyed veteran yelled, crushed up against him with his pikeshaft rolling out of his crushed fists.

'Push!' Sparrow yelled. 'Push 'em back!'

'We'll push you back, you rebel bastard!' a flaxen-haired scarecrow cursed, trying to reach over the press to grab William's helmet strap. He locked his fingers in the sweaty leather and yanked William's face into the buckled shoulder of the older man.

Sparrow's nose cracked into his breastplate buckle, splitting his lip. He tried to kick but he couldn't because there were so many men crowding together going nowhere. Caleb shouldered past, elbowing the older man in the face. The front ranks broke up and locked together like buff-coated jigsaws, sandwiching friend and foe alike. The flaxen-haired man's fingers writhed in front of William's bloody nose. He wrenched his neck as he lunged forward and bit down as hard as he could. His attacker yelped in pain and dragged his hand away.

'You Roundhead turd, I'll fucking skin you for that!'

'Ah, fuck yourself,' William spat, reduced to trading insults by the chaotic press.

They stayed locked together for twenty more bone-crunching, spit-faced, dead-legged minutes before the rear ranks eased off, and let the bloody front ranks wrestle themselves away from one another. There was a mad dash to retrieve weapons. Daggers flashed. Kicks connected with sweaty lice-ridden groins. Sparrow ducked back as the flaxen-haired pikeman came after him, his knife clutched in his bloody bitten hand. Caleb lurched forward, bringing the butt of Sparrow's discarded halberd down square on his forehead. The man's skull split, showering them with warm blood. Sparrow kicked him back over towards his reeling mates, who bent down to drag him off over the heaps of maimed men.

'Back to the corner,' Sparrow ordered, accepting his bloody halberd from his silent saviour. Caleb bent down and selected another pike, and trailed it back up the lane. It was about eight o'clock.

Colonel Tobias Fulke was waiting at the top of the lane, a fresh body of pikemen drawn up behind him. More musketeers had spread out on each bank, watching the adjoining fields for Royalist snipers. Sparrow eased his dirty hand down the back of his neck, rubbed the pulled muscles with an exhausted wince.

'Right, get your men to the rear for a rest,' Fulke ordered, bending down to look along the front rank of the pale-faced replacements. Sparrow stood aside as they marched down the lane, another flock of musketeers closing in behind them. The survivors threw themselves down wherever they could, panting with exhaustion and boiled red with sweat. Sparrow wiped his face, his gauntlet coming away slick with blood and snot. He sniffed carefully, winced at the flaring pain in his nostrils. His scarred forearm felt as if it was afire, the pink flesh torn once more by the hideous wrestling match in the lane. The firefight over the hedge seemed to die away for a moment, and he rolled to one side as his musketeers scrambled back through the breach in the wall. A dozen and more strangers and then Butcher and Gillingfeather, Rodney Sark without his hat, Stephen Talbot looking as if he had suffered a double hernia, and finally Long Col, singed and sooty and dripping with sweat.

What a filthy bloody crew they must look. Not even their own mothers would recognize them, torn and shredded like dogs that had baited a young bear. Long Col spat into the path, coughed hoarsely as he leaned back against the earth bank.

A bullet hissed through the breach and buried itself in the soft earth wall opposite, making them all jump. Butcher was already reloading, Long Col shaking his head in consternation.

'We couldn't budge 'em. They kept filtering around the flank while they kept us pinned down from the front. One of those bastards is a damned good shot and all,' Colston Muffet panted, wiping strings of pink spit from his pale lips.

'Yeah?' Butcher responded, throwing himself at the turf battlement and firing off a quick shot. There was an anguished yell from the tangle of thorns and willows over the field. 'There's more than one shooter on this hill, I tell yer,' he said, leaning away from the sudden salvo which kicked up the earth around the rough hole. Sparrow stepped to one side, and peered through the tangled roots and leaves at the hedge opposite. Heads and hats were bobbing up and down comically as the enemy musketeers kept up a lively fire.

'Christ Jesus, I've never seen anything like it,' Butcher complained, running his sleeve over his livid face. Gilling-feather reloaded carefully, lay down at the breach to pick a target. Sparrow heard the shot and saw another Royalist topple through the shattered elderberry bush opposite. He squinted to the right, saw a tall figure duck down behind a stile, lean his elongated musket on a worm-eaten post.

'Look out!'

The shot thumped into the bank, sending up a gout of dirt and chips. Sparrow slid back down the back, frowned, and peered back up again.

The bastard was waving at him!

'Sparrow!'

William froze, turned to his astonished musketeers. Butcher winked. 'One of 'em recognizes you, Captain,' he joked. 'Never forget a pretty face like yours.'

Sparrow scowled, peered through the undergrowth at the tall figure in the corner of the field. He had taken cover behind a shoulder of the earth bank, lifting his hat in some bizarre challenge. His fowling piece must have been damn near six feet long. Findlay! Poor old Sir Marmaduke Ramsay's hawk-eyed gamekeep!

'That you, Findlay?' Sparrow called over the shots and curses.

'Aye. Come out and show yourself! I thought I recognized your fat arse!'

Butcher grinned. 'Who is it?'

'An acquaintance,' Sparrow snarled. 'You still fighting other men's battles?' he roared over the tumult.

'I know who I serve and why, more's the pity you don't, William.'

'How's Bella?'

His company crowded round delightedly, astonished at

their captain's swaggering bravado – discussing some flirt-gill in the middle of hell itself!

'Come over here and I'll tell you! You should ask your friend Hugo! He's been nearer her than most lately. He's away on the common chasing up what's left of your cavalry, if you want to know,' Findlay bellowed back over the stricken field.

William bristled with anger at the mention of his detested rival. So it was like that, was it? 'Have you seen much of Mary?'

'Wouldn't you like to know!'

'Mary? It was bleedin' Bella a minute ago, by Christ, Will, you change your tune quick enough!' Billy Butcher laughed as he finished reloading his hot musket. He rolled towards the breach, squinting along the barrel towards the corner stile. He fired, the bullet demolishing a mouldy post.

Findlay's answering shot hit the smoking barrel, clanged off, and hit Rodney Sark in the throat. The astonished Londoner staggered back choking, dropping his musket and clutching his spurting neck. Butcher rolled over in alarm, swallowing the mouthful of bile which had risen into his throat at his astonishing escape. Sark collapsed into the trampled track, kicking like a slaughtered deer.

'Have to be sharper than that, my friends,' Findlay yelled maliciously, ducking down behind the bloody hedge out of sight.

The cavalry were penned into the furrowed field like cattle for the slaughter. They had worked their way through gaps in hedges and smashed gates, along sunken lanes and body-strewn gullies. The dwindling band of musketeers who had accompanied them had run out of powder and wandered off towards the rear, leaving them milling uncertainly at the bottom of the churned field. Sir John Byron, their red-eyed commander, walked his horse in tight circles, pointing furiously at the ragged gap in the hedge. Beyond the breach they could see a stand of pikes waving uncertainly, catching ragged streamers of smoke. There were no pioneers to tear a wider passage. The foot he could have thrown into the gap were dead or gone. The dragoons had long since spurred off to find easier passages over the damned hill.

It was Lord Falkland, the King's thoughtful Secretary of State, who broke the hateful deadlock. He had been sickened by the mindless slaughter and the bewildering butchery of his countrymen, and had volunteered to serve in Byron's command as a common trooper. He drew his sword, eyeing the miserable, leering gap as if it was Satan's black eyeball, opened wide to gloat on the carnage. In a moment he had spurred forward, urging his horse through the heavy clay towards the tantalizing gap. Byron's encouraged troopers pressed after him, shouting challenges and spurring their chargers bloody.

Falkland catapulted through the hedge and blinked at the stubbled enclosure ahead. The enemy were clustered about in the corner, feverishly dragging about a pair of small drakes. He swallowed, clenched his thighs, and spurred forward, just as the cannon fired. The last thing he saw was a bucketful of tiny black peas, superheated by a gust of fouled smoke. The blast tore him and his horse into bloody strips, hurling a troughload of smoking offal into the faces of his followers. His sword clattered into the hedge, where it was quickly retrieved by a Roundhead sniper.

Byron's blood-splattered men came on, several of the furious Cavaliers dismounting to tear at the narrow canyon between the enclosures. They hacked a passage and stood by while more riders plunged through the gap yelling and screaming, their cornet fluttering in the stiffening breeze.

The Roundheads had lined the hedge with musketeers and reloaded their guns. The galloping Cavaliers were cut to pieces by the stinging volley and double-loaded case-shot. Horses lost legs and ploughed into the furrows, blinded Royalists rode on clutching their empty sockets. Arms and legs flew around in the bloody hail, decorating the hedges and thumping against the few survivors packed into the breach.

While the shocked Cavaliers took cover, the Roundhead rearguards made off to the next field, abandoning Biggs Hill to the enemy.

It was about ten thirty.

BY
WASH COMMON FARM,

MIDMORNING

'Well done, boys. We take the 'ill and you go and fuckin' lose it!' A pale-faced ensign strode past the exhausted, powder-blasted survivors of Mercer's regiment, ordering his own grim-faced company back up the bloody slopes towards the smoke-crowned ridge. The Earl of Essex's regiment, already in the thick of the action for four hours, had been ordered back up the hill to reclaim the summit from the bewildered Royalist horse. With all their reserves already committed and the few foot available rapidly running out of ammunition, the King's worn-out Cavaliers could do little except round up the small haul of prisoners and try to drag off the Roundhead guns.

Colonel Tobias Fulke, his features burnt black by powder and glistening with crystallized sweat and hard-baked blood, turned his lurid eye on the sneering ensign.

'We held 'em long enough, you'll be fighting the few we left,' Fulke snarled.

The ensign snorted, shouldering his colour and traipsing off after his men.

Sparrow was leaning against a muddy bank, closing his streaming eyes to try to clear his smoke-clogged vision.

'Never mind them, boys. You broke their backs up there,' Fulke encouraged, raising his fist and waving it at their punch-drunk faces. 'You've done your bit, lads, don't worry.' They were too exhausted to respond, staring out at the littered fields as if they didn't know where they were – let alone why.

But if they expected to be left in peace for the rest of the day they were mistaken. A messenger on a bloody white horse spurred down the lane, shouting for their commander. Fulke, covered in filth and sharing a pipe of tobacco with Long Col, had to step out of the stinking ranks to attract his attention.

Sparrow stared at the petrified horse, its great apple eyes bulging between its foam-spattered mane. The beast's twitching rear looked as if it had been decorated by savages, a clear red handprint branded onto its shivering rump. Sparrow frowned, wiped his eyes. He was too worn out to think.

Fulke turned smartly and clapped his dirty hands together as the relieved scout wrenched his rearing horse around and spurred off down the lane.

'Orders from Skippon. We're to join the London Trained Bands and support the right flank.'

Right flank?

Right, left, forwards, and backwards, it was all one in this damned shithole. Sparrow fumed in obstinate silence.

'They're trying to get around us on Wash Common,' Fulke informed the nodding captain. 'Everybody else is up to their necks.'

Sparrow nodded dumbly, unable to register any emotion one way or the other. The muttering regiment picked up its weapons, shouldered its muskets, and formed up into ragged files. Nicodemus shook out the stump of the colour, singed and stained and ragged, the yellow circles – their cheesy emblems – looking as if they had indeed been

446

attacked by mice. He was cutting a dash now though, in his precious – though rather roomy – new coat. Billy Butcher had darted down the slope and retrieved the treasured garment from the dead ensign, still warm under the armpits from its unlucky former owner. Despite the generous cut of the sleeves, the fine red coat pulled across Butcher's broad shoulders, and he hadn't been able to make himself comfortable in it.

'I'll have it altered when I get back,' the sharpshooting dandy decided, handing the coat over to the dead ensign's young replacement. 'You wear it till we get back, and mind you're careful. But only till we get back, mind,' Butcher warned.

'Goar, can I, Billy?' Nicodemus snatched it from the frowning musketeer and hurled his wiry little frame into its generous folds. He was admiring himself in the dim reflection of a discarded cuirass when the orders came through to move on.

'Mercer's regiment, have a care!' Fulke yelled, game as ever despite the smoke and the stink and the fearful din. Sparrow shuffled along beside the silent troops, resigned to whatever hardships lay ahead.

It couldn't be any worse than they had endured that morning, could it?

The two armies had mutated into one great brawling mass of stumbling men and trundling equipment. Artists and engravers would present the greedy public with idealized diagrams, showing neat blocks of patient pikemen with the prescribed number of musketeers at each angle. Commanders would be pictured on prancing stallions at the head of their neatly arranged men, the fearful smoke and cannon shot would be limited to the outer margins, framing the precise detail of the action, the fanciful etiquette of war.

The real life and death struggles, the stinking panorama of the battle, would have required a whole fleet's worth of canvas and a reservoir of paint mixed bright and shocking. Bright visceral reds and bowel blues, hideous flashes of orange and yellow, burnt out and buried by wash after wash of black and white and every shade of grey as the smoke boiled up to cover it all, extinguish every individual tragedy and triumph.

The great turf triangle, the lacerated landscape between the Kennet and the Andover road, had sucked up thirty thousand men and ten thousand horses, swallowed almost a hundred guns of all calibres and more wagons and carts than could be conveniently counted. There was no front line, no vanguard or centre or rear, merely an immense multiply armed mass of struggling, cursing, bleeding, stamping, and spewing men. To the north, the lashing tail of the carnage had caught up the Blue Auxiliaries of the London Trained Band and hurled them into savage contact with the purple-coated King's guard.

The belly of the beast sprawled and squirmed along Dark Lane, enmeshing the rest of the King's foot with Robarts' and Skippon's hard-fighting Parliamentarians.

The terrible fire-breathing heads of the death-bringing beast writhed like hydras about Biggs Hill, stretching out to rip and tear the men impacted about the lower slopes, and the bloody red-brick farm.

The enemy had finally appeared to the east of Biggs Hill, a black and tan mass of men and horses under a hundred fluttering colours. The Royalist cavalry seemed drawn to the newcomers as if they were so many gaudy iron filings attracted to a magnet. Hugo Telling's troop, on the far left flank of the great chequerboard of troops, had to spur towards their right, overtaking slower units in their haste to charge the insolent Roundhead cavalry.

Hugo frowned as Cornet Hazell cantered alongside, giving him a supercilious grin as the troop colour flapped about his preposterous hat. Hugo's horse stumbled, and he fell forward over the clumsy beast's neck. Straightening himself with a flash of irritation, he concentrated on the ground ahead. The broad heath was studded with tussocks of tough grass and sudden swampy pits which could break a horse's leg like a dry twig. The troop cantered on, picking up speed as the enemy grew in front of them. The Royalist horse was compacted by eager squadrons converging from the flanks, disrupting the unity of the charge. Hugo crouched instinctively over his horse, his sword in his fist. Clods of earth and pebbles flew around their heads as the steaming, snorting troop accelerated into contact with the slower-moving enemy, cuirassiers in lacquered armour raising clumsy carbines, lighter horse resting their pistols on their forearms as they took careful aim.

'Charge!'

Trumpets blared and hoofs thundered, a thousand throats yelled challenges as Rupert's horse careered into the apparently unbreakable Roundhead wall.

The sudden flurry of shot pattered against the Cavaliers like a deadly hailstorm, puncturing straining horses and knocking riders out of their saddles. The horrific din was intensified by rearing, screaming horses and screeching wounded, thrown to the floor amongst the stamping hoofs and kicking legs. The Roundheads drew their swords, a bright flash of steel through the drifting powder smoke.

Telling's horse had careered to a halt, its front hoofs kicking up sodden turf as it recoiled from the chaotic press. Unbalanced, Hugo hardly had time to parry a staggering blow from a wiry enemy officer who spurred into their ranks like a sawn-off Roland, hacking about for all he was worth. Telling twisted in the saddle and thrust at a cuirassier; the armoured knight heard the vile clang of steel on steel but didn't even flinch at the swingeing blow. The man was grasping for his second pistol butt, standing proud of his saddle holster. Telling kicked his hand away and gave him another blow about the helmet. The cuirassier gave him a backhander in return, knocking Hugo half out of his saddle and ripping his cheek open. Gull spurred alongside, thrusting the fearsome fighter back in his own reinforced saddle. The Roundhead wrenched his pistol free and fired at point-blank range, the ball smashing into Gull's broad freckled face. Telling cursed with impotent fury and brought his sword down on the cuirassier's rearing horse. It was no time for gentlemanly cut and thrust when one's precious life was at stake. The blade cut into its rump, sending the agonized beast plunging off into another panic-stricken mob of interlocked riders. Gull had slumped over his saddle, moaning and retching incoherently but somehow conscious. His great sausage-fingered hands quivered like fat pullets against his blood-splattered chest.

Telling snatched up the man's bridle, wrenched his own horse about, and spurred away from the terrible fight. He noticed Cornet Hazell out of the corner of his eye holding the flag out of the reach of three grasping Roundheads. He cursed under his breath, checked his mare's frantic escape. Gull was holding his face with both hands, lolling about drunkenly in his blood-spattered saddle.

'Wait here, I'll come back for you,' he hissed, dropping Gull's reins and turning the frantic mare once more. He levelled his sword and charged into the fray, bumping Hazell's horse into its lighter opponents. The lucky impact dislodged one Roundhead from his saddle. Another lashed at his head but he ducked in time and skewered the man through the armpit. He lurched back screaming, kicking himself out of his own stirrups. Hazell clubbed the third man away with the butt of the lance. The rider checked his horse, pulled his pistol, and fired, the ill-aimed ball skidding off Hazell's burnished breastplate. Telling wrenched his own pistol free and fired back, wounding the rogue in the arm. The two broken bodies of horse pulled apart like mating snakes, trotting back to regroup and re-form.

Gull had toppled out of the saddle and was lying in the grass, his bloated body trampled bloody by a retreating troop of horse. His tightly bound buff coat bore a dozen scuffed marks where his dying carcass had been ridden over by the escaping horsemen. There was no recognizing the downed man's smashed features. Telling clenched his teeth and looked away, spurring off towards the town with the silenced cornet panting like a wet dog beside him.

'The first time I've seen them stand,' Hazell snarled, wiping his bloody mouth.

Telling rode on, trying to control his feverishly twitching limbs. Aye, the first time they'd stood. Somehow, it didn't seem a good omen.

*

The London brigade had already been shorn of three hundred and more musketeers, sent off to patch up the skirmish line along the edge of the heath. The constant, rolling percussions from the batteries on the smoke-clogged ridge had pummelled the remaining men so hard so that they seemed to be clutching their pikes to hold themselves upright. Sparrow thought his ears must have collapsed from the continual shocks, his chest heaving as if he was being beaten with rolled-up wet blankets. He had never heard anything like it, not even at the height of the storm back in Bristol. He opened his mouth and swallowed, but all he could make out was a dull rumble punctuated by the odd shout as Butcher or Gillingfeather yelled something into his face.

'Eh? What's that?' Sparrow bawled back.

Long Col pointed his black hand at the bloody ridge. 'I said, they're ours, otherwise they'd be blowing us all to hell by now!'

Sparrow nodded painfully. If the guns belonged to them that meant the Earl of Essex's brigade had managed to wrest the bloody summit back from its temporary owners. So why were they marching away from it? Ah, it was no good trying to make sense of battles. You might just as well plough with dogs as make out what the generals were up to.

William sighed and peered back down the line, hardly daring to imagine what had become of the rest of the regiment. All he could see was a hundred and fifty or so wild-eyed survivors clutching pikes, halberds, or blunt swords, hurrying along as if they were carrying sacks of coal on their aching backs. Apart from Long Col's diminishing squad of sharpshooters, they were completely lacking any organized firepower. Sparrow strode on, peering through the drifting smokes towards the open heath. By Christ, if they were caught in the flank now . . .

He felt stones grate beneath his mud-plastered boots, and realized the fearfully reduced regiment had reached the road.

'Close up, close up at the back!' he yelled back down the line, the few sergeants that were left relaying the orders to the punch-drunk rank and file. Up ahead were a thousand or so strangers from the London brigade wearing a bizarre mixture of civilian and soldier coats, leather aprons and newly issued buff coats. They hurried down the slope and out onto the common, as if they were eager to confront the thankfully invisible enemy.

A ragged rank of shell-shocked willows and broken-backed sedge marked the swirling course of the River Enborne. At least their right flank was safe, then, William mused, switching the bloody halberd from his sore right shoulder to the left.

The London brigade halted for a moment, officers dashing this way and that to restore some order to the packed ranks of pikemen. A squat little man with curly black hair and piggy brown eyes strode towards Mercer's ruffians, jabbing his thumb over his shoulder.

'Get your musketeers forward with mine,' the man yelled, his dumpy face puce with excited effort. Sparrow stared into the mist as Fulke hurried up from the rear and held on to his arm in exhaustion, coughing and spluttering before the perplexed officer.

'By Heaven. Is it you, Toby?'

'Aye. Lost my damned horse on the ridge. Where are they?' he panted.

Sir Phillip Skippon, veteran foot soldier and hero of the London troops, whom he had led since the beginning of the war, pointed back towards the east, as if his close-set eyes could penetrate the swirling banks of smoke and fumes which rode by like fog over a beach. The frightened soldiers squinted into the shell-racked darkness, the rolling, retching smokes punctuated by jagged red tongues of flame as hidden guns opened up from over towards the main road.

'I need your pikes to hold the flank, Toby. They're holding a hill a little way ahead, and there's few enough of the Red and Blue now.' The old warrior shook his greasy black wisps of hair. Fulke wiped his eyes, coughed into the grass, and slapped Sparrow on the back.

'Go on then, William, down by the water.'

Why to Christ was it always up to him?

Wounded soldiers from both armies found the river first.

They staggered or crawled down the stepped slopes, throwing themselves down on the crumbling banks to scoop up the precious water in their bloody powder-blackened hands. Swollen with rain, the Enborne ran like well-spiced soup between the sedge-banked margins, chittered and chattered over switchbacked rills of pebbles and moss-bearded rocks. Cavalry troopers in their great boots squatted in the muddy shallows, heads bent between their knees. Dozens of wounded laid themselves out in the grass, raising their hands for their share of the floodwater. Others had stripped off their sweat-soaked, blood-splattered shirts and were splashing their cuts and bruises with handfuls of water. Three miles to the north more wounded were wading into the Kennet, delighting in the chance to cool their parched throats and wash the stink and slime of battle from their pale faces. The riverbanks had become temporary oases to the scattered soldiers of both sides, relatively quiet back-waters where they could regain their breath, locate their scattered wits, and bind their cuts and scratches.

William hadn't hoped to hold the parched remnants of his regiment. His own mouth was as dry as chalk, his furry tongue cleaved to his teeth. He couldn't have held them back if he had wanted to. Delirious with thirst they broke out in ones and twos, and in a moment the entire band had dropped their weapons and dashed towards the merry stream, stampeding through the cowering wounded and leaping the bundled bodies of the dead.

Sparrow leaped in beside a scowling Royalist officer, standing in his shirt while a whiskery old retainer wound a length of ripped sleeve about his slashed forearm. The thin-faced officer watched disdainfully as Sparrow shoved the butt of his halberd into the soft mud, unpicked his greasy helmet straps, and eased the steel pot from his head. He bent down with a wince, filled the rusty kettle with floodwater, and took a giant swig before replacing the helmet on his throbbing skull.

The freezing water paralysed him for a moment, galvanizing his dulled muscles all over again. They shrieked and popped in protest.

'I wouldn't dwink too much, if I were you,' the officer sniffed. 'The men have been uwinating in the stweam a little further up,' he informed him, holding his arm out as his servant finished binding his wound and bent to pick up his ragged doublet from the bushes where he had thrown it.

Sparrow stood in the shallows, feeling the rushing water numb his filthy feet, and acknowledged the stranger's well-meaning advice with a tiny nod of his heavily stubbled jaw.

'A few pints of piss are the least of my worries,' he said,

clamping his hand over his ear to try and clear the peculiar vacuum from his head.

The Royalist waded to the bank and waited for his toiling servant to haul him out. 'What a wacket those guns are making,' the man called down, raising his elbows as his servant helped him on with his coat.

Sparrow hauled himself out onto the slippery bank, watching his foolish troopers splashing each other as if they were away on some summer picnic and not in the middle of one of the fiercest battles in English history.

'I must say, sir, your chaps have stuck to it like vewy devils this day,' the wounded Cavalier observed. 'Such a pity we're on opposing sides, don't you think? Ah, well! Good luck to you, sir!'

Sparrow shook his head, taken aback by the officer's generous greeting. Two minutes before they had been hacking chunks off one another, now they were standing about as if they had known one another all their lives.

'And to you, my lord,' Sparrow called, bewildered and amused at the same time.

'SPARROW!' William heard the familiar bellow over the excited shouts of his men. He turned to see Colonel Fulke striding along, energetically waving his fist at him. 'Whatever do you think you're playing at? Get those men out of there at once!'

Sparrow turned to the grinning Cavalier, raised his dripping helmet. 'Time to go.'

'Indeed.' The Royalist horseman turned on his heel and began to pick his way through the bloody meadow of wounded and dying men towards the battered troop drawn up beneath a stand of trembling willows.

Fulke's features were flushed black beneath his greasy mask. 'Exchanging pleasantries with the enemy while you are supposed to be holding the flank? Have you lost your mind?' the game old bird squawked.

Sparrow tugged the halberd from the riverbank, wiped the dripping butt against a dead man's breeches. 'I couldn't stop 'em, sir. They'll fight better now they've had a drink, sir,' Sparrow apologized.

Fulke frowned. 'Get 'em out of there at once! We're going forward!'

The bedraggled pikemen formed up in soaking-wet ranks, the more thoughtful soldiers securing refilled water bottles behind their backs.

'Stand straight in your ranks and files,' Fulke bawled, stalking up and down in front of them. 'Prepare to march!'

His orders were lost in a sudden, deafening crescendo of noise. Roundshot screamed overhead, tearing up great chunks of sodden turf and the leg from a latecomer who was hurrying towards the muddied river to satisfy his own raging thirst. Sparrow tightened his straps, took a grip on his halberd as the guns opened up once again. Great iron balls trailing streamers of flame and smoke tore through the abandoned willows and crashed into the river, sending the swimmers scurrying for the bulrushes along the far bank. Huge spouts of water drenched the unfortunate men who had not managed to haul their broken limbs away. It was almost comic, the way they ran for their lives.

'Mercer's regiment will advance, God and the Cause!'

'God and the Cause!' They strode over the trampled ground, fuming rags and abandoned equipment littering the smoke-wreathed common, forgotten bodies thrown into the nettle-filled ditches. Sparrow spied young Nicodemus, his blazing red hair sticking up in all directions from his egg-white head. He winked encouragingly at the brave youngster wrapped in his outsize jacket. Nicodemus smiled feebly back, the snapped colour clutched in his white-knuckled fists, just visible under his turned-back sleeves. Where had he gotten that coat?

'Charge your pikes!'

Sparrow heard the familiar woody clatter as the front three ranks raised their weapons to shoulder height. He glanced to his left, saw the hunchbacked musketeers double forward between the solid blocks of pikemen.

There was a sudden blinding flash and a whoosh of superheated sound.

Sparrow opened his eyes. The solid block to his immediate left had disintegrated as a culverin shot ploughed through their bellies. The front rank crumpled, torn in bloody chunks by the burning ball. The round bored through the astonished file, disembowelling every man before it landed in the trampled grass behind, slick and red with blood and tissue. The pikeblock shook apart like a timber-frame house in a tempest, the shocked survivors to either side staring white faced at the bloody heap of maimed men and splattered stomachs. They shoaled together like blood-splashed mackerel, striding on leaving seven dead men sprawled behind them.

'Close up! Close up!' The sergeants thumped and kicked the survivors closer, re-forming the ramshackle block once more.

Sparrow stared disbelievingly at the ferocious carnage, the bloody swath the ball had cut through the Londoners. His mouth was drier than ever, his limbs pulsing and trembling as if he'd stopped a ball as well as the poor bastards lying behind them. Stand straight in your files?

They were lying straight enough in theirs.

*

The smoke cleared for a moment, gathering up its horrible grey skirts and revealing the empty bluffs to the fearful crowd advancing along the river. They had imagined hordes of Cavaliers on stamping horses, great blocks of steel-clad pikemen and dense knots of well-armed musketeers. Instead, a gloomy green wilderness of wandering horses, hobbling wounded, and abandoned carts and wagons. The brigade hurried on up a steep slope and found itself on a small hillock beside the river, with a commanding view of the stricken common. The heath fell away in a series of broad shelves towards the winding stream. Beyond, empty slopes and a deserted road.

Sparrow tipped his helmet back, pointed towards the east.

'The road's empty!' he yelled, hardly daring to believe his own eyes. They had fought right through the King's army, they had opened the way to London! The city regiments gave a ragged cheer, the pikemen at the back craning their necks to peer over their comrades' shoulders.

'We've opened their flank!' he called to his broadly grinning, stupefied soldiers.

'Charge for horse on the left flank!' A sudden anguished scream went up from the regiments along the summit, passed from one unit to the other until the vile warning reached Sparrow's lonely outpost. He stepped out of the crowd and squinted back towards the north. The Red and Blue regiments were already forming shivering schilitrons, ragged squares of pikes into which the grateful musketeers had quickly taken cover. Sparrow couldn't believe it. The road was open this way and they were turning back on themselves! He was about to shout out their error when he caught a flicker of steel in the murk away to his left.

And then he saw them, riding out of the rolling fogs. A squadron of Royalist horse, trotting forward with swords drawn. Another appeared on their right and another to their left.

'Charge for horse!' The order was passed along the line from one fearful gang to the next. Mercer's men coagulated about the hilltop, a hundred pikemen in a lazy ring, stooping down with their right foot clamped over the butt of their pikes, the iron-shod points held at a forty-five-degree angle. Sparrow was about to take his place amongst the gloomy ranks when he paused, squinting over the bluffs towards the empty plain.

It wasn't empty any longer. Two regiments of Royalist foot had been hurried down the Andover road to block their advance, screened by another two regiments of horse.

'Infantry to the front!' Sparrow shrieked, pointing his halberd towards the mass of troops gathering over the slope. Fulke hurried up, blowing hard against the steeply rising ground.

'You numskull, William, we've trouble enough without . . .'

Sparrow pointed grimly to the east. Fulke followed his gaze. The old man seemed to wither, shrink down inside his armour like a turtle left out in a desert sun. His armoured shoulders slumped, his notched sword hanging limply from his black fist.

Infantry to the front to pin them on their ridge, cavalry to the flank to stop them running away, and a couple of culverins to blast them to pieces.

Fulke realized their dreadful predicament in a moment.

'Ah, fuck,' he sighed, unable to keep the bitter realization from undermining his cheerful resolve.

It was just after eleven thirty.

BY
BUNKER HILL,

NEAR NEWBURY,
EARLY AFTERNOON

The grey day wore slowly on, as if time itself had been dragged to a standstill by the vast expenditure of blood, sweat, and powder, artificially elongating the endless morning.

How could either army afford such a cruel butcher's bill? Where were the mills that had ground the powder to feed the melting cannons' smoky lips?

If anything, the heart-stopping thunder of the guns had increased rather than diminished, and the ragged, punch-drunk remnants of the London brigade were no longer able to distinguish one shot from another. The small hillock trembled beneath their aching feet, as if the sinews of the earth had taken a chill, as if nature herself trembled at the endlessly inventive work of man. At least one heavy culverin and a couple of smaller drakes had been dragged around to bombard their desperate outpost, half a mile from the main battle line in the very heart of the King's left flank. The improvised battery was being bombarded in turn by the Roundhead cannon which had been dragged on to Biggs Hill, from which they were dominating the smoke-scoured common.

The enemy attack seemed to be running to the same timetable as the crawling morning.

The Cavalier horse had massed to the left of the hill,

and seemed to be making their way around their position to cut the Londoners off from the embattled main body. The Royalist foot seemed to be wading forward through several feet of particularly sticky treacle. Their evident caution cheered the glum pikemen and the forlorn hope of musketeers which had been drawn up in front of them, warily watching out for the swirling squadrons of enemy horse in case they unleashed a surprise charge up the empty slopes.

William Sparrow watched Fulke stride down the nervous ranks towards their lonely outpost overlooking the all too tempting river. The colonel had sent a runner to fetch a helmet of water, with which he had scoured the worst of the filth from his pink face. His recent wash had turned his white beard into a badger's backside of ragged black and white stripes. His eyes, however, were still blazing with youthful ardour.

'Haven't they come on yet? I told Skippon we ought to charge the rogues ourselves!'

The weary captain nodded sullenly. 'They don't need to, with those guns blasting holes through us,' Sparrow replied gloomily. The closely packed pikemen had suffered several direct hits from the large enemy cannon over the heath. Some shots fell short, ploughing great furrows in the sodden turf. Others were aimed higher, ploughing bloody lanes through sodden men.

The terrified soldiers would have broken and run if it hadn't been for the cunningly deployed Cavalier horse. They had remained stubbornly out of range, as if they were daring the impudent Roundheads to try and make a run back to their own hard-held ridge. The enemy gun crew was taking between three and five minutes to reload their piece, anxious moments for the sooty pikemen to wonder where the next shot was going to fall.

Fulke shook his scrubbed head in grudging admiration.

'They've stood up to it better than I expected,' he said. 'Of course, the men know Skippon, they know he won't leave them in the lurch.'

Sparrow eyed the old buzzard, wondered if the colonel was suggesting he lacked the determination to do the same.

The horribly regular bombardment was enough to drive a saint mad. If the culverin wasn't bad enough the lighter guns fired before and after the bigger piece, sending smaller balls sailing towards the man-packed hillock. The drakes did less damage than their basilisk brother, but were no less alarming if you found yourself in the front row. Fulke doubled down the hill towards Long Col's musketeers, who had taken cover behind a couple of furze bushes as if the tangled undergrowth would deflect enemy bullets. William yawned, his aching body racked with nervous exhaustion. Despite the terrible threat from the culverin, some of the London men had squatted down on their heels or were leaning against their pikes, eyes closed to snatch a few moments' sleep in the constantly fluctuating noise from the north. Sparrow paced up and down the front of the block, nodding at the pinched faces beneath the rusty, shrapnel-streaked helmets.

He looked over his shoulder, noting the miserably slow progress of the enemy foot. They seemed to be taking two steps backward for every one forward. The cavalry had divided like some horrible marine anemone, troops of horsemen breaking away from the main body and trotting ever closer to the defiantly held hillock.

He caught the puff of smoke in the corner of his eye, and stood still, feeling the clamour and racket of a thousand hoofs vibrate through the sodden soil. The roundshot came for them like some overstuffed crow, its belly full of mangled men and well-pecked eyeballs. The round looked as if it could be plucked from its flaming trajectory, caught like a tennis ball in one hand. There was something hatefully anonymous about the twenty-pound iron globe, the spinning sphere which would gouge turf or crush skulls without preference. There was nothing he could do to get out of its dreadful way, nowhere he could hide without pushing his way through his quailing pikemen and sprinting away towards the impenetrable wall of smokes and flames in the rear. Some, separated from their mates and cowering at the back, had dropped their weapons and done just that, tearing off their coats as they went haring off across the littered common. Several sergeants had formed a rough skirmish line of their own to try and stop too many of their colleagues doing the same, although they were keeping a wary eye on those damned cavalry at the same time.

Sparrow closed his eyes and prayed, his blackened lips moving feverishly over his clenched teeth. He felt the searing blast of the ball as it whistled past him and hurtled into the unprotected bellies of the pikemen crushed in behind him. They too had followed the dreadful passage of the ball, and had tried to barge their way out of its hideous path. John Jewell had thrown down his pike and lain flat on the floor, the hissing round rocketing over his crying head and impacting with the dozing shoemaker who had been second in his file. The ball tore through his grumbling belly and crashed into the next man, tearing off his right arm and a bloody chunk from his shoulder, then careered on into the groin of the fourth. The maimed men collapsed in steaming heaps, their splattered entrails glistening on their neighbours' coats and helmets. An enormous groan of shock and relief rose from the fearfully packed survivors, who mended their ranks over the pitiful heap of slashed men. The shoemaker had died instantly, his football-sized wound cauterized by the searing passage of the ball. The second man was dying fast, his torn ribs protruding like white sticks from his smashed torso. His teeth were chattering as if he was freezing cold, his left hand clenching the bared shin of his catatonic neighbour. The fourth man was lying on his back, his pelvis and thighs pulverized by the smashing impact. He was shrieking in agony, thin brain-splintering wails which every deaf and dumb pikeman heard only too clearly over the constant throb of gun and musket.

Sparrow surveyed the carnage for a moment before the hateful rainbow was hidden behind their shuffling boots and trembling legs.

'St–stand straight in your ranks and files,' Sparrow yelled, unable to hear himself above the din. The hill shook beneath his boots, as if all of hell itself was about to erupt from the smoke-wreathed summit.

'Charge for horse!' The cry went up again, passed along the ridge by three hundred parched throats.

Sparrow elbowed his way back into the great compact mass of pikemen, peering down towards the left as the leading enemy squadrons took advantage of the confusion to launch a ferocious charge at the reeling brigade.

They ducked down low over their horses, screaming challenges at the forlorn hope of Roundhead musketeers. They endured the brief volley, the gleeful survivors galloping on past the fallen, closing in on the musketeers as they scuttled for the safety of the pikes. Fulke, Long Col, and the rest threw themselves under the thicket of spearpoints, rolling under the pikeshafts as if they were taking cover from a hailstorm. In another moment the trampled hillock where they had stood was overwhelmed by a tide of blue- and green- and red-coated horsemen, hats and feathers and flags and pennants fluttering in the tempestuous charge.

They swirled and snorted and stamped and reared, but could not break through the deadly points, jabbing at their horses and prodding their riders back in their sweat-sodden saddles. The Cavaliers screamed defiance, and the Londoners screamed back. The Cavaliers fired pistols while the cowering musketeers reloaded. Gillingfeather was kneeling in front of William, swinging his musket to and fro along the gaudy parade as he chose his target with vindictive precision. He fired. Through the sudden puff of smoke and sparks Sparrow saw a rider throw up his hands and hop up and down in his saddle as if he had been stung. In another moment he had lost his stirrups and slipped under the thundering hoofs. The bloodied squadron galloped past towards the river, found itself enmeshed in a meadow full of shrieking wounded and terror-stricken deserters, and picked their way back through the throng towards the reluctant foot coming up the slope.

'Musketeers to the front!' Long Col bawled, doubling forward to kneel beside the bloody-faced sacks which the Cavaliers had left behind them. His bewildered colleagues stumbled forward as if they were under some brain-numbing spell, going through their drill like so many automatons.

'Hold your fire,' Long Col warned.

The enemy commander had attempted to coordinate his attacks so that the foot impacted with the Parliamentarians the moment the cavalry cleared the hill, catching them disadvantagedly deployed for horse. The precious moment's delay had enabled the Londoners to send their musketeers forward once more. They fired a stinging volley straight at the undecided Royalist foot, who fell back leaving a flotsam of bodies and groaning wounded behind them.

The furious cavalry wheeled about and charged back up to their rescue, but the canny Roundheads had scuttled back to the defiant hedgehogs of pikemen, and they were driven off all over again.

'Charge your pikes!' The order rebounded down the bloody slope, reaching Sparrow's ringing ears a good minute after Skippon had given it.

'Charge pikes? Charge for horse he means,' the befuddled captain croaked, squinting through the ragged smokes towards the main body of the brigade. As he watched the massive thickets of spears flattened like the spines of a vast porcupine, some pointing forward, others towards the rear. Were the bastards coming in behind them? Sparrow screwed his head around in panic, but his dazed troops were packed in so close he couldn't see the back markers, let alone any renegade Royalists.

'Sparrow!' Fulke hurried down the littered slope, waving his fist at his sooty-faced captain. 'Didn't you hear the order? Charge your pikes!' The remaining pikemen obeyed their commander's instruction, bringing their notched and bloody spears to shoulder height. Fulke elbowed his way into the closely packed mob next to the scowling youngster.

'We're breaking out in four directions. We'll drive them off and regroup on the ridge,' the breathless old warrior rasped.

'Drive them back?' Sparrow yelled, outraged.

'Mercer's regiment prepare to march!'

'Which way?'

'Retreat, he means, the fucking old duffer.'

'Down the hill!'

'Which way?'

Sheer blind panic ate through the ragged regiment in a moment, transforming terrified but tenacious soldiers into a pack of wild-eyed fugitives. The Red and Blue regiments of the London Trained Band must have understood Skippon's order, must have trusted their popular commander to lead them safely through hell itself.

But Mercer's battered command, dog tired, blinded by smoke, hammered by the guns, and baffled by the conflicting orders, fell apart at once.

Some ran back down the slope towards the rear, others tried to sprint after the more compact bodies of the Blue regiment. A few sorry fools, completely flummoxed by the chaotic confusion, ran towards the enemy foot regiments which were still making their way up the slope to close them in. Sparrow grabbed one harebrained youngster by the scruff of the neck and dragged him around.

'That way! Down to the river!' he bawled at the milling musketeers. He gave the dazed youngster a boot up the arse, sent him running towards the water-meadows. Fulke swirled his sword above his head and sprinted off down the open slopes towards the Enborne, leading the stampede towards the murky brown waters. Nicodemus Burke was knocked aside by the terrified men, and fell to his hands and knees over the broken standard. Sparrow saw his bright mop of hair through the running men, and barged his way through to recover the trampled youngster. He hauled him up by his coat and pummelled him towards the river, charging along behind him as if he intended to launch the youngster into space.

'Regroup on the bank, wave the damned thing for all you're worth!' he bellowed at the crying boy. Sparrow shoved him forward, turned on his heels as the white-faced lemmings hurled themselves down the littered slope, changing direction like a shoal of mackerel charged by a hungry shark. Mercer's regiment had collapsed in the blink of an old man's eye, a brave battalion reduced to a hundred and fifty gibbering scarecrows by the punishing uncertainty of their plight.

But their brainless and completely unpredictable flight saved the survivors from certain extinction.

The advancing Royalists didn't know whether they were being charged by fanatics bent on immediate suicide or whether their sudden thrust had been timed to coincide with some invisible threat from their rear. A squadron of horse caught in the flank by a sudden crazed attack by the Red regiment had stampeded back towards the Andover road, throwing the right-hand Royalist foot regiment into immediate turmoil.

The panic which demolished Mercer's men spread like a plague down the hill, turning the King's rather reluctant infantry into weak-kneed children, huddling together like lambs in a wolf's den. The desperately demoralized Royalists flung themselves on the few unfortunates who stumbled their way, beating their dazed brains out in a frenzy of panic, before their furious officers managed to restore order.

By the time the Royalist foot regiments formed up once

more Mercer's survivors had fled down the hill and sprinted across the bloody meadows towards the gentle Enborne. The groaning wounded and wild-eyed idlers who were lurking beside the rustling sedge looked up to see a regiment of madmen bearing down on them. They hurled themselves into whatever cover they could find as the fugitives stampeded through the litter of bloody cast-off clothing and amputated limbs, and took running jumps into the swirling river.

Nicodemus was vibrating with terror, his fists clutching the bloody mud-soaked banner as he stumbled along over discarded helmets and dead men, his bulging eyes fixed on the placid meadows on the far bank. Nimbler and swifter than most of the terrorized survivors, he had accelerated through the panic-stricken mob and led the charge towards the water. They followed their red-headed mascot through the quivering bulrushes and into the shallows, throwing away their weapons and splashing their way towards the far bank. The whirling eddies waltzed around their red necks as they groped and kicked and thrust themselves through the rain-swollen stream.

'Halt!' Tobias Fulke, senseless with rage and chronically short of breath, fell to his knees before he reached the choked obstacle, retching into the grass as his tired old body was attacked by a fit of cramps. Odd individuals threw themselves down around the crooked colonel, Long Col jabbing the fleeing soldiers aside with the butt of his musket. Butcher careered past, ducked under Gillingfeather's outstretched arm, and dived into the river. Stephen Talbot was hurt in the thigh, and he limped past as best he could, ignoring their frantic bellowings. John Jewell ran for his life, ignoring everything but the bobbing flag on the far bank.

William Sparrow bent over and held his trembling knees, his raw lungs crushed into his constricted throat as he fought to get his breath.

'Hold them,' Fulke said weakly, prising himself to his shaking feet. Long Col threw his arm about the colonel's shoulder to hold him straight as his senseless soldiers dashed past and tried to leap the churned river. Dozens of Round-head wounded, convinced they were being massacred by the King's Irish butchers, hauled themselves to their feet and hurried towards the blocked stream. Desperately con-fused Royalists who were groaning under the willows joined the panic-stricken evacuation, equally convinced they were being attacked by raving Parliamentarians.

A tiny kernel of men coagulated about the colonel, but most simply fixed their sights on the broken colour and intended to chase it all the way home.

Nicodemus unwittingly focused the fugitives on himself. He dragged his feverishly trembling bones out on the far bank of the Enborne and threw himself down in the lush meadow, oblivious to everything but his own thumping heart. Dozens of others waded in, dragged their saturated bodies up the crumbling bank, and collapsed in grateful heaps. They neither knew nor cared where the enemy had got to or whether the never-ending nightmare on the far bank had reached some kind of conclusion.

Fulke's scrubbed cheeks ran with tears of mortification and shame as he eased himself straight to watch the rout, his tenderly nurtured regiment breaking up like a rock-shattered stained-glass window into so many useless shards. Sparrow stood beside him, dumbstruck. Long Col was holding his musket out to catch the last few stragglers, while Gillingfeather and a tiny core of hotheads reloaded their muskets, searching the bodies of the fallen for

471

powder and shot. William bent down and lifted an elegantly forged sword from beside a waxy-faced Royalist lord, his loyal servants struck down at his feet. He had lost the halberd in the mad dash down the hill.

'Get back over here!' Fulke called chokingly to his frantically fleeing regiment. 'Re-form on the bank,' he groaned, the notched blade falling from his fingers.

Driven beyond human endurance by the six-hour ordeal, the doddering old soldier collapsed to his knees. Long Col looked around frantically. Sparrow waved the last few men in from the corpse-littered meadow, and peered up at the hill.

The Royalist foot had finally galvanized themselves to occupy the bloody shell-scored summit, planting their pikes in the smeared and trampled entrails of the dead Londoners. The Trained Bands stuck together like one of Caesar's finest legions, forming a human testudo impervious to the sweeping, soaring Cavalier attacks. The dour pikemen traded thrust for thrust with the triumphant horsemen, holding them off as they inched across the hellish heath towards their own bloodily defended lines.

Rupert's squadrons rolled away and re-formed, turned and attacked again. But the stubborn squares marched on, ignoring feverish yells for them to lay down their arms.

At last, the bloody bone-weary cavalry gave up, turning their blown horses and trotting back towards their gunlines on the common. Many discovered wounds they hadn't even felt, bloody cuts and bruises where they had been stabbed with blunt pikes or hit by failing musket rounds. They sagged in their saddles like sacks of vegetables, unable to muster the last effort necessary to complete the rout of the stubborn Roundhead flank.

One troop took the longer way back, picking their way

along the bloody water-meadows beside the rushing river. They found friends and foes lying amongst the tussocks, squatting in the grass beneath the shell-shattered willows as a surgeon made his bloody way among them.

Hugo Telling had never seen so many maimed and wounded men, a good half of them smashed and torn by artillery rounds. He slumped in the saddle, his horse lame and winded, his sword arm numb from the elbow where he had been caught by a Roundhead pole-axe. Cornet Hazell, miraculously alive despite a dozen hair-raising scrapes, looked as if he had spent the morning in a pit full of starving terriers, his handsome doublet and breeches scored and rent, his hat gone, his golden curls caked with blood, soot, and sweat. The cornet he bore was no more than a piece of rag on a scored stick.

Hugo raised his befuddled head and squinted past the willows, watched a gaggle of soldiers carrying a white-haired old tramp off the field on a litter of broken pikes. As he watched the men boosted their champion onto their crooked shoulders and waded down the bank into the stream. Hugo stared, fascinated by this touching loyalty. The big man at the front seemed to be waving his arms about as if he was appealing to some set of pagan gods. Perhaps they meant to set fire to their hero and push him off like some Viking jarl? The man turned round and faced the funeral party.

Telling's moustache twitched.

It was William Sparrow. He would recognize his broad, stupid features anywhere. Up to his peasant arse in water with his enormous red mouth open as usual. His fists clenched about his greasy reins as he spied his old adversary, apparently fleeing across the river with a few hundred of his misguided comrades.

Telling brought his spurs into contact with the bloody, foam-flecked flanks of the mare, encouraged it to one final canter.

'Sparrow! Sparrow, you bastard!' he yelled, closing in on the astonished rescue party.

BY

THE RIVER ENBORNE,

NEAR NEWBURY,
LATE AFTERNOON

It was one of the many brutal ironies of the day that the man who had argued so long against giving battle should have fought so hard to bring it to a triumphant conclusion.

Prince Rupert had been everywhere at once, his diminishing squadrons spurring after their indestructible commander from one corner of the wrecked field to another. But although they had beaten their horses bloody and driven home their attacks into the very teeth of the Parliamentarian lines, the reeling Roundhead regiments did not break. The pikemen shuffled closer while the musketeers doubled forward and doubled back like some fire-spouting tide, galling the Cavaliers with endless volleys of shot. While the Royalist horse swirled and charged on Wash Common the powerful Parliamentarian infantry forces assaulted the thinly held centre, pushing back their outnumbered and outgunned counterparts and retaking some of the lanes and enclosures they had lost that morning. They had even managed to catch up with some of their captured equipment which the Royalists had been unable to drag away. Besides recovering a lost colour there were few achievements likely to cheer a unit more than retrieving its precious plundered guns.

Artillery had only played a minor role at the majority of

the battles fought so far, its potentially devastating effects all too frequently eclipsed by the sudden cavalry charge or the resolute work of the swarming musketeers. Guns were far too heavy and cumbersome to be dragged about in time with the flowing fortunes of the fighting.

But at Newbury artillery was king.

The Earl of Essex had set up a battery of his biggest guns on Biggs Hill, from which they could bombard the Royalist forces as they massed on the plain below. His smaller pieces had been distributed to the hard-fighting brigades deployed along the edge of the common, and the lighter drakes and robinets wreaked havoc on the men trapped in the narrow, sunken lanes. The King's men captured several of the light guns, and even turned some on their previous owners, but every time they resumed their plodding advance they would run into another blind alley dominated by another energetically handled cannon. Handfuls of musketeers decimated regiments. Snipers picked off the bawling officers as they tried to re-form their battered ranks.

The day ground on like some monstrous millstone, chewing up more and more men as the pointless, pitiless carnage continued unabated.

Prince Rupert had predicted that without adequate reserves of men and equipment the Royalist assaults would bog down in the horribly enclosed warren of fields and hedges. He had warned his uncle the resultant stalemate would harm the King's men more than it would the better supplied and more readily reinforced Parliamentarians.

But even as his own gloomy forecast was proving all too accurate the tireless Prince redoubled his own efforts to swing the battle in His Majesty's favour.

Trumpets blared, rounding up the scattered Cavaliers from all corners of the stricken field. His senior officers rode back and forth collecting their decimated squadrons, trotting back to a new assembly area just to the west of the Andover Road.

Cornet Benjamin Hazell saw the massive body of horsemen forming up over the far side of the smoke-shrouded common. From a distance the assembled squadrons looked like a child's jigsaw, the scattered pieces filling out a flank here, thickening the line there. Rupert had stationed himself forward, where he could watch for a gap in the enemy line. His kingfisher-coated flock of senior officers crowded about him on trembling chargers, their servants hurrying up with an infinitely precious water bottle or a half-gnawed chicken leg to take their masters' minds off the imminent resumption of the fighting.

Hazell had been about to suggest they ride back to join their general when Telling had spurred off as if he had attracted all the fiends of hell to him. The startled cornet squinted after him as the captain rode down the shallow slope towards the river, yelling incoherently at a party of escaping Roundhead wounded.

Where was the honour in slaughtering the sick?

'Captain Telling!' Hazell yelled, bewildered by his suicidal and ungentlemanly charge. Why, there must have been several hundred enemy troops in various states of unreadiness lounging about in the shallows, or lying beneath the shattered willows bleating for the bloody surgeons. Hazell pulled his horse up, the rest of the troop coming to a grateful halt on the abandoned ridge, still littered with the horribly maimed remains of two dozen and more Londoners. The cornet could hardly tear his eyes from the fascinating shambles, the intricate balloons of glistening innards, the slick grey pulp oozing from eggshell skulls.

'Enemy horse coming up behind!'

The frantic shout from the rear terminated Hazell's morbid examination of the dead. He twisted around in his saddle and saw a large body of Parliamentarian cavalry moving from the far corner of the enemy flank towards the main road, clearly intending to shield the severely battered London Trained Bands from further punishment.

One squadron had detached itself from the main body to pursue Telling's lonely troop along the furrowed water-meadow. Two more had peeled off to their right, swinging in towards the sorry outpost on the hill as if they meant to charge the reluctant Royalist force which had assumed occupation of the bloody summit.

'Captain Telling!' Hazell yelled, his ringing ears barely registering his own shout.

To hell with the fool! Let him fight his own battles off among the dead men. Hazell had business nearer at hand.

'Troop, left wheel!' he roared, turning in the saddle and directing them with the ragged point of his splintered lance. Forty bone-weary troopers on blown horses cantered over the shell-shocked ridge behind the sullen ranks of their foot. Hazell peered ahead, noting that the dastardly Roundhead intruders had directed their charge at Rupert's lonely outpost half a mile beyond the hill.

Hazell dug his spurs into the foam-splattered flanks of his coughing stallion, and hurried to Prince Rupert's rescue. He'd be knighted before the day was done.

Or he'd be damned.

*

The deadly dandies who attended the legendary Prince had not spotted the danger yet. Some had dismounted to stretch their aching legs, others were washing themselves off as best they could, splashing water over their sooty faces from the basins being held up by their nervous menservants. A few had taken the opportunity to slip behind the hedge and complete the day's ablutions, gratefully relieving their uncomfortably loosened bowels.

Rupert – who never seemed to have time for such mortal considerations – had fixed his spyglass on the smoke-wreathed summit of Biggs Hill, the height which had been so carelessly lost earlier in the day. A determined regiment of good men with a couple of guns should have been able to hold the hill against all comers. Indeed, a determined regiment of good men had held the height, but they wore Essex's colours, not his. The summit had been the hinge on which the entire battle had swung, and the enemy had snatched it from under his nose.

Rupert twitched with fury and lowered the glass from the battered hill.

And that was when he noticed the enemy squadron galloping down the slope at him, helmets buckled and swords drawn.

'To horse!' he yelled, dragging his panting charger around with one furious yank on its reins. He grabbed for his sword as the enemy cavalry bowled through the astonished command, knocking the dismounted men flying and emptying saddles on all sides. A wiry little officer on an immense bay steered his horse straight through the confused fight, ducking and dodging as the alerted Cavaliers lashed out at their yelling attackers. Before Rupert could draw his own weapons the undernourished intruder had raised himself out of his saddle and pointed his own firearm straight at the despised German's face. Rupert automatically closed his eyes against the fatal explosion.

Which never came.

He opened his eyes as the cursing officer hurled his useless pistol to the floor. Paralysed by his miraculous escape Rupert held on to his terrified horse as the little man trotted through the screaming mob. Cavaliers thrust pistols at the insolent raider, but the would-be assassin was clearly blessed with Rupert's luck, because he ducked through the bitter fray without so much as a scratch.

Cornet Hazell gave a scream of exultation as he led Telling's troop into the rear of the enemy squadron, coming to Rupert's rescue in the nick of time. He prodded one wild-eyed youngster from his horse and then reversed the point, jabbing the battered lance into another. The steel butt ricocheted from his breastplate and jammed between his helmet bars. Hazell wrenched the lance free with such force that the enemy rider fell over his own saddle and lay stunned in the trampled grass. An older veteran in an enormous russet sash spurred to his downed companion's rescue, bringing his sword down on the splintered cornet and knocking it out of Hazell's fist. The Roundhead barked with malicious delight and tugged his horse to a standstill, easily parrying Hazell's angry thrust.

'Let that colour alone, you damned hound!' the cornet cried, desperately hacking at the wizened old cut-throat. The veteran leaned back in his saddle, Hazell thrust too far and tipped forward, completely off balance. The Roundhead lifted his pistol and shot him in the face.

The wounded cornet yelped and choked at once, blood pouring into his smashed mouth as he slumped over the horse's gore-splattered mane. Another Roundhead dealt him a vicious backhander which knocked him out of his saddle. Hazell crashed to the floor and tore at his face, his bloody gauntlets locked around his agonized jaw. He sucked up air through his nostrils, spitting a sudden stream of blood and shining teeth into the turf. A rearing horse trod on his leg. He screamed, rolling himself over the splintered colour. Somebody fired a pistol into the grass beside his head and he curled up like a terrified child in a thunderstorm, clutching his ragged flag like a worry blanket. The bandy-legged old sweat had jumped out of his saddle, and was trying to pull the colour away from him as he held on to his struggling horse with his other hand. Blinded with his own blood, doubled up with agony, Hazell held on to the battered stick. The cursing Roundhead kicked him in the head, knocking him senseless, but the cornet's brave resistance had not gone unnoticed. The furious Cavaliers spurred into the attack, driving off the fresher Roundheads in a moment. The leering veteran thought better of his mission, leapt back on his horse, and ducked over its mane as he spurred off after his retreating troop.

Prince Rupert had recovered his temporarily scattered wits and trotted over to watch the rogues run. He glanced down at the gargling cornet, who was lying on his side with his arms and legs beating like a dreaming dog. The pistol ball had smashed into his mouth, turning his face into a bloody mask with a smoking black hole. His golden curls were splattered with blood and decorated with a glistening tiara of splintered teeth.

'Get that man to my coach,' Rupert snarled at an astonished aide. 'See that his wounds are dressed!'

'At once, your highness!' It didn't do to even look the towering demon in the eye when he was in a mood like that. The Prince scanned the poached faces of his rescuers, recognizing the sooty troopers belonged to his own mis-placed lifeguard.

'Where's Telling?' Rupert wondered aloud.

William Sparrow watched the rider spur down the littered slope towards his pitiful rearguard, eventually realizing the lone lunatic was shouting his name.

Telling. God's wounds, not now!

'Hurry. Get him over the river,' he bawled over his sooty shoulder. The terrified survivors of the debacle on the hill needed no further urging. They boosted the litter onto their shoulders and splashed out into the broiling brown river. One of Fulke's dirty fists flopped from his makeshift stretcher and dragged behind like a waxy white rudder as they waded away from the crumbling bank. They had improvised the litter from broken pikes lashed together with discarded belts and snapsack straps, and hauled the catatonic colonel on board the rickety contraption.

Gillingfeather wiped his beard on the back of his hand.

'That's it, they're all away. You go,' he urged the hulking captain, who was absent-mindedly swishing his looted sword from side to side. Sparrow watched the lone rider trot forward, lifting his pistol from the leather holster along his saddle. He didn't take his bloodshot eyes from the unwelcome intruder.

'Bugger off, then. This is between him and me,' he snarled.

Gillingfeather snorted with contempt at his melodra-matic observations. 'This is no schoolyard brawl, William,' he told his captain as if he was correcting him on some obscure point of scripture. 'Leave him,' he advised, pulling at Sparrow's arm.

The man towered over him, growling like a singed bear as the Cavalier came closer. Gillingfeather couldn't hear what the Papist rogue was shouting and didn't much care anyway. This was no place for punctilious points of honour. Chivalry and single combat were not part of the wiry agitator's code, nor William's for that matter.

The hairy musketeer bristled with annoyance, raised his musket and fired in one fluid movement. Telling's horse collapsed onto its knees, its foam-speckled snout crashing into the bloody turf. It keeled over with a sigh of agony, trapping the furious rider by his right leg.

'Now come back with the rest of us,' Gillingfeather called.

Sparrow pushed him back. 'You go, I told you, this is between him and me!'

'This is a field of battle!' Gillingfeather roared. 'Before God, you've no right to make time for your petty quarrels!' he panted hoarsely.

Sparrow was as transfixed by his maniacal stare as he was by Telling's foul-tempered plight across the field. The dead horse had pinioned his leg, trapping the ragged Cavalier against the bloody earth.

Sparrow shoved the musketeer away and strode forward, stepping over the bodies of the dead and the fearfully staring wounded of either side. Telling glared up at him, grasping for his snapped sword. The blade was trapped beneath his thigh, cutting through his sooty, singed breeches. The thin-faced youth was boiling with impotent anger, spluttering and cursing to himself as Sparrow stared down at him. 'Don't you ever give up?' he said at length.

Telling fumed and spluttered and looked away. His pale eyes flicked back towards his despised rival. 'Why don't you shoot me dead and have done with it?' he hissed back.

Sparrow felt so emptied of all emotion that his bludgeoned brain might have been cast in lead. He shook his head and blinked at his helpless rival as if he couldn't quite place the fiercely twitching features.

Hugo Telling. Apprentice Cavalier.

He tried to remember exactly what had started their terrible quarrel, what he had ever done to Telling that the fuming fool should have made such blood-curdling efforts to avenge. If it came to that, why were they chopping chunks off each other at all? Any of them? All day they had been at it, back and forth across this damned plain. Thirty thousand men and more indulging themselves in an orgy of incomprehensible violence in the name of a cause few of the fighters truly recognized as their own. Grandiose principles which had no more meaning for the average pikeman than for the birds and beasts cowering in the hedges.

It was beyond all his limited understanding.

It wasn't as if he and Telling had any particular religious or political quarrel – they just happened to have chosen different sides in the hateful struggle. He wondered what haphazard twist of fate had made him join the Parliamentarians, while the drooling idiot on the floor had felt himself duty bound to enlist with the King. He tried to think of all the reasons he ought to be despising the Cavalier; all the reasons he ought to loathe his chosen cause; all the reasons he was fighting at all.

He was fighting so that the country could break King Charles' reckless and outdated stranglehold on the country's political, clerical, and economic future. That was it. That was what he had picked up from people like Morrison, from the dour Scots cavalry officer McNabb, from the bristling brows of poor old Fulke.

His own beliefs – his own sense of place in God's great design – were rather more vague.

He sensed Parliament's quarrel was more righteous than the King's. The notion of blind obedience to a man who relied on unquestioning support from his vassals was clearly out of date. You couldn't run a prosperous and energetic nation on a whim, as if it was a ring of mud huts behind an impenetrable wattle stockade. The world was too big for such artificially limited horizons, even Sparrow saw that. The hotheads like Butcher and Gillingfeather were always blathering on about some form of republic, governed by wise and just and godly committees who would oversee every aspect of modern life.

Sparrow couldn't imagine such a thing. The only committees he had ever come across were time-wasting talking shops where decisions were treated like live grenades – to be passed to somebody else as soon as possible – and energetically denied if they had proved faulty. Those old barons had forced King John's hand at Runnymede, but Charles Stewart had clearly skipped that page in his history books, preferring to find ever more ancient examples on which to model his reign. He was merely a . . .

'Are you proposing to stand there all day, you bloody oaf?' Telling enquired, peering up from the steaming mantrap at his feet.

'Sparrow! Run the fiend through and come on, they're massing up the slope!' Gillingfeather yelled distractedly from the bank. William turned, watched the swollen mob of Mercer's regiment making their way, somewhat foolishly now, along the far bank. They seemed to have picked up

dozens of wounded men and an equal number of stragglers, and Long Col had somehow managed to form them
up behind the boy with the broken colour.

He sighed, paralysed with exhaustion. It was no good
trying to sort the rights from the wrongs of this damned
war when you had spent all day and half the previous night
fighting. The brain couldn't cope with such cunning
complexities. Causes and reasons and rebels and rogues.
He blinked them all away, stared down at the scowling
Cavalier.

'I could have killed you, outside Bristol that time,'
Sparrow snarled, sticking to the practicalities of the
damned war. 'And you keep coming after me as if I'd
butchered your own mother!'

'I wished you had killed me, when Prince Maurice took
my troop away from me!' Telling cried, bitter tears welling
out of his mortified eyes.

Sparrow felt what little anger he had managed to
enflame evaporate through the holed soles of his boots.
He glanced up at the ridge, the confusing running battle
between Stapleton's Roundhead horse and Rupert's furious squadrons boiling up again like an unwatched pot.
The grievous day didn't seem to be any nearer a conclusion than it had been at noon, or during the everlasting
morning, or that bloody dawn.

'Don't tell me you've forgotten the time you kicked my
horse and ran away into the woods, don't pretend it wasn't
you who wrote that lying pamphlet! *Royal Wool-Gatherer
Foiled*, remember?' Hugo growled, watching the scowling
oaf smirk to himself.

'You were the one who ambushed me, I didn't know
what you were going to do, did I, leaping out on a fellow
waving your bloody pistols about!'

'You were jealous I'd steal your sweetheart. You've never forgiven me for taking Bella from you!' Telling snorted.

'Taking Bella?' Sparrow crowed back. 'You haven't the balls to take Bella on, believe me!'

'No?' Telling enquired. 'I took her on a few times at Gloucester, I'll tell you that!' Telling redoubled his efforts to free his trapped leg as Sparrow swung the looted blade over the dead horse's twisted head.

'You're lying! If you took her on like you say you'll have found her birthmark!' Sparrow leered, unaccountably alarmed at such a suggestion. 'Where is it, then?' Sparrow demanded.

'She has a strawberry mark just below her right . . . ah, you filthy swineherd! Only a peasant like you would have dreamed of asking! You must have pawed her when she was no more than a child, either that or when she was too weak to thrust you off, you reeking dunghill!'

'I did not paw her,' Sparrow raged. 'She was no child when she lay with me, and she wasn't sick either, not till I left her anyway!' he insinuated.

Telling foamed at the mouth with fury at this hateful innuendo and tried to push the hideous weight of the dead horse from his deadened leg.

'Pull me out and fight like a man!' Telling raged. Sparrow watched him, mightily amused by his sudden loss of control. Not so cocky now, sir! He shrugged his shoulders to rub further salt into the Cavalier's all too obvious wounds.

'She's no sweetheart of mine any more, whatever you've dreamed up in your sticky imagination!' he said breezily.

Telling squinted up at the bearded brute, licking his pale lips in silent contemplation. 'No, you're right,' he said calmly. 'She's no sweetheart of yours. Bella and I are to be married the moment we're together again, what do you say to that, eh, Roundhead?'

Sparrow ran his filthy sleeve across his nose. 'I could stick you right now and she'd never know the difference,' Sparrow pointed out, leaning over the trapped youth with his boot on the dead horse and resting the elegant sword at Telling's taut throat. Hugo glared back, holding his fierce stare for a moment.

'William! Kill the hound and come on, they're coming back for him!' Gillingfeather implored from the middle of the river. Sparrow looked back down at his rival, struck dumb by sudden uncertainties.

In the heat of the battle, thrown into one another as they had been outside Stow, he would have gladly fought the bugger till the stars fell out of the sky. Now, now that he had the boastful bastard at his mercy, he had to keep reminding himself why they were quarrelling at all.

'Renounce any claim to Bella and I'll accept your surrender,' Telling suggested.

William laughed out loud. 'Surrender? I surrendered to your lot once before. Never again.' He glanced up the slope towards the forgotten battle. The Parliamentarian cavalry had been forced back once more, and Telling's friends were hurrying down the slope after their missing champion. Sparrow stepped back, eyeing the retreating rearguard over the far side of the river. All his friends. His only friends in the world, leaving him behind with the wounded and the prisoners. And the bloody King's men.

'That's it, run away with your misguided friends. Until the next time, Sparrow! I'll invite you to the wedding, if you like!' Telling seemed to be delighting in his own helplessness, goading William into finishing him off. Sparrow seethed with frustration. Why, he could run the bastard through and piss over his body, if he had the mind!

Only he didn't.

He shut the insinuating doubt away in the dank dungeon of his consciousness. This was no time for idle chitchat with a Royalist whoremonger like Telling.

'I told you, you're welcome to her,' he repeated, eyeing the squadron of horse thundering over the summit towards their bloody sanctuary beside the bulrushes.

'Found somebody more to your liking, eh? Or maybe more suitable to your status?' Telling sneered.

Sparrow felt his anger simmering up all over again. Kill him and have done with it, just like the ferociously practical Gillingfeather had suggested. 'Maybe I have, at that,' he replied through clenched teeth. He took another few steps back.

'Bella's maid . . . Mary Keziah.'

Sparrow clenched his fists. 'You're very well informed all of a sudden,' he said quickly, prickling with anxiety. 'Have you heard something of her?' He realized he shouldn't have asked the grinning ghoul but he hadn't been able to help himself.

Telling relaxed, smiling smugly at his discomfited opponent.

'Ah, what have I heard?' he wondered aloud.

'Another time, Telling,' Sparrow snarled, striding away from the trapped Cavalier towards the safety of the river.

The Royalist captain looked almost disappointed to have survived their antagonistic encounter. Perhaps he had been hurt by the fact Sparrow wasn't going to skewer him after all? That he had shown no real inclination to transform the scared boy into yet another brave martyr to King Charles' martyred cause?

He didn't have time. He had to go.

'Sparrow!' Telling shouted, agitated all over again. William halted on the crumbling bank, peered back over his shoulder. God, they were close now. He could see them dragging out their pistols to finish off the stumbling straggler.

'Sparrow . . . she's pregnant! Mary, I mean.'

The bank seemed to lurch under his feet, his boots setting off tiny avalanches of rich red earth.

Pregnant?

'The cook at Kilmersden Hall told me before I left for Gloucester. She was puking so much they sent her home!'

The bewildered Royalist cavalry spurred down the hill after the insolent Roundhead, apparently caught red-handed as he tried to plunder their downed captain. They screamed with rage as he suddenly turned and leapt out into the water away from them, a gaggle of musketeers forming a rough skirmish line on the far bank, alternately waving their weapons and urging their hero to hurry.

There was a flurry of badly aimed shots, but it was growing dark now and neither party felt like closing in for the kill at that late stage.

There was no point in dying now the day was done.

WASH COMMON,

NIGHTFALL

The armies had fought themselves to a standstill, the punch-drunk combatants unable to raise the strength to deal their opponent one final, knockout blow.

The guns banged and crashed and lit the night as if they were happy to go on firing for ever, even while most of their poor human masters had fallen aside in uncaring exhaustion. Their exultant fireballs streamed like earth-bound comets from one burning horizon to the other, illuminating clumps of shell-shocked survivors as they made their way back down the bloody shambles of the lanes or wandered over the corpse-strewn heath. The sudden flares also exposed hundreds of light-fingered looters, the pitiless ghouls who had appeared out of the hedgerows the moment the battle had abated, to go about their grim work like so many witches' familiars. They cackled and called to one another, flitting from one corpse to the other to relieve the fallen of swords, pistols, purse, and powder. Both sides mounted patrols to drive the soulless crows away, but as soon as the sentinels moved on to another corner of the wilderness the vultures would return, stripping the bodies naked and loading their loot onto handcarts and barrows.

As the evening wore on the Royalists' powder ran out,

and their cannon fell silent one by one. The King's last few tattered regiments of foot were clinging to their positions now, pressed back along the sunken lanes and butcher's-slab enclosures by the resurgent Parliamentarian infantry, who fired half a dozen volleys at every single sniper. They winkled the Royalist musketeers from their holes, cleared the ditches and lanes by the light of burning wagons and torched trees.

Rupert's horsemen stripped down to their shirts so that their friends would see them better in the murk, but their broken-hearted horses were beyond any further effort. The defiant Londoners who had held them off all day crouched down where they were, too tired to hide themselves behind the pockmarked hedges.

Henry Mercer's battered and bloody regiment picked up so many wounded and stragglers on the southern bank of the Enborne that it had swelled back up to its original strength. The scarecrow soldiers blundered back along the scarred bank, bawling out the watchword at the suspicious dragoons who shadowed their progress across the river. Nicodemus Burke, blinking like an owl in the dusk, stumbled along over his own leaden feet and waved the broken banner at the trigger-happy horsemen. He had completely forgotten the password although Colonel Fulke had taken care to repeat it to the regiment at prayers that dawn.

'It's Religion!' Long Col remembered. 'Religion!'

'Ah, you could have overheard that somewhere about! What's the idea coming up on our flank like that?'

'I'm Colston Muffet, Elder Sergeant to Mercer's regiment of foot, formerly in Merrick's,' the grey-haired veteran called, shuffling along beside Colonel Fulke's unlikely carriage.

'Mercer's, you say? Where's your commander?'

'Lying on this litter, we're not carryin' him for our health!' the musketeer shouted into the rapidly gathering murk. Thick banks of sedge and bulrush were silhouetted in the lurid glow from a hundred brushfires as the tortured heath burnt through the night.

The scattered flames illuminated the bewildered survivors as they drifted like shadows about the stricken field searching for lost comrades. Mercer's men, already soaked through by their unexpected evacuation over the water, were as blue with cold and racked with chills as many of the seriously wounded lying along the other bank. But they hadn't dared stay where they were, isolated on the wrong side of an enemy held river. They had spent the last weeks in constant fear of Rupert's cavalry, and maintained a grudging respect for his supernatural abilities despite the rapidly gathering night.

Everybody knew full well the demonic Prince could see just as well in the dark as he could in the day.

Hereward Gillingfeather squinted into the gloom, wafting away the curious cloud of mosquitoes which had finally dared to rise from the shimmering banks of sedge beside the gurgling river now that the shooting had died down.

He watched William Sparrow haul himself out of the floodwater like some particularly ragged Neptune, strips of silkweed draped over his saturated buff coat.

'Did you finish him?' the mischievous goblin enquired with pagan relish.

'I couldn't skewer him in cold blood, could I?' William snapped, distracted by the musketeer's unwelcome intrusion. He needed time to think, God knew!

Pregnant? How? When?

Well, the how was fairly obvious and the when was easy enough. That night before Roundway, when he had finally thrown the girl down in the stables. Always supposing the babe was his, of course. But he must be the father, Telling wouldn't have told him otherwise. Unless it had been the runt-faced Cavalier all the time, trying to goad him into remaining on the bank where he would have been cut down by his fancy friends!

'You left him there to fight another day? God's blood, William,' the musketeer fumed, 'if every man shows such misplaced mercy we'll be fighting them through the next century!'

Mary would be almost three months gone by now, and without a word from him since that bright night in the stable! He would have to write, write and tell her he was well, at least. But of course, Mary couldn't read! He groaned aloud as he stumbled along the bank, the wiry agitator pulling at his coat like a distempered dog.

'The King's more than enough idiots flocking to his colours without you sparing every man jack you come across!'

William stopped, stared at the bony ghoul with the wildly unkempt tangle of dirty brown hair. Christ's very own Soldier of Mercy, slavering for the blood of downed men.

'I must have killed a few today same as you have,' he snarled, 'but I'll not slaughter their wounded! Go back and finish him off yourself, if that's what you want!'

'Is he kin? Do you owe him at all?' Gillingfeather sneered back. 'If that had been William Sparrow lying there under that horse, do you think he would have spared you? Spared you for what, another voyage in the *Messalina?*'

'That was nothing to do with him! What are you suggesting, we kill all our prisoners to avenge ourselves on one damned madman?'

'I thought you'd chosen to do God's work with us,' Gillingfeather hissed into the night, his eyes burning in his sooty skull with undiluted fanaticism.

'God's work? By the bowels of all the saints, Gilly, if this is God's work I'd hate to see Satan's!'

He left the muttering madman behind, worked his way through the bleary-eyed stragglers to the head of the column. Captain Speedwell had turned up from somewhere with a handful of his pikemen, shaking his copper-curled head as if stupefied by the extraordinary day.

'I saw six men lying like so many cod upon one another,' the veteran said disbelievingly. 'All their heads struck off by the same ball.'

William shrugged, unimpressed by his colleague's shocked observations. God alone knew how many had perished in that vile triangle between the Kennet and the Andover road.

'Where did you get to?' Sparrow asked, glad to have shaken off Gillingfeather for the moment.

'We hid in a ditch at the bottom of the hill. The Royalists didn't seem keen on coming down the slope to us, and we ran for it as soon as it got dark,' the regiment's only other unwounded officer replied.

'How's the old man?' Sparrow shook his head.

'Overdone it a little, I didn't see him hit.'

The remains of Mercer's regiment came to a ragged halt beside a flooded ford, peering over the swirling brown water at the party of dragoons. Long Col was still trying to convince them the ragged strangers were friends not foes.

'Well, if you're on our side, how come you ended up over the other bank?'

'We got pushed over by Rupert's cavalry. We'd been brigaded with the London men,' Sparrow bawled, irritated by the dragoon's clownish questions. 'Now hold your fire, because we're coming across!'

'The London men are back behind us!' the dragoon warned.

'We got cut off before we could join them,' Sparrow replied, stepping down towards the freezing water.

'Hold it! Wait there while I call the major!'

'We've got a hundred and more wounded and we're all soaked through! They'll catch their deaths waiting for you to run to your damned major,' Sparrow roared. 'We're coming over whether you like it or not, you four-legged fornicators!' William waded into the deeper water, felt the chill river flowing about his vitals. Well, at least they'd worked once, he thought savagely.

'Stay where you are!'

'I said hold your fire, you fucking cross-eyed piss-drinking bloats! Do we look like bastard Cavaliers to you?'

The bleary-eyed dragoon, who had been in and out of the saddle since the previous evening without rest, lowered his musket with a bone-weary curse.

'Advance, friend,' he called, too exhausted to care which side the foul-mouthed intruders claimed to serve.

Never mind their flags and slogans and words of the day – they were men again now, survivors. For now, that was more than enough for most of them.

ACKNOWLEDGEMENTS

The one thing my research has shown me in the three years I have been writing this series is that I could have based each book solely on real-life events. The Civil Wars abound with larger-than-life characters, junior officers like Harcus who sadly did not survive to tell their tales. Thankfully, there are historians as keen on recording their inspiring details as I am in incorporating their brave deeds into my stories. As usual with The Shadow on the Crown series, the truth is stranger than the fiction: Chillingworth did design pseudo-medieval war engines to send against Gloucester's walls; a loyal goodwife did extinguish a mortar round with a bucket of water; and sadly, Harcus did indeed perish when his grenades went off during a sortie over the walls.

My thanks must go as always to the Sealed Knot. Attending various musters up and down the country immediately rekindles my enthusiasm – there's nothing like a good pike push to sort you out after a hard week at the word processor!

Many members have carried out far more detailed research into aspects of the period than I have, but have always been glad to share the fruits of their research with me over a pint or three. They will hopefully forgive me distilling years of painstaking reading into soundbites for the more general reader.

Typical of these incredibly clued-up gentlemen is Peter Minall, editor of our regimental newsletter and keen student of Civil War correspondence. Another is Stuart Peachey of the Stuart Press, whose fine set of pamphlets (including an excellent account of the siege of Gloucester) is available at Sealed Knot musters or from 117 Farleigh Road, Backwell, Bristol BS19 3PG. Stuart also organizes genuine seventeenth-century banquets for Sealed Knot regiments, one of which I was lucky enough to attend (only in the interests of research!). Another excellent book to look out for is *Gloucester and the Civil War* by Malcolm Atkin and Wayne Laughlin (Alan Sutton publishing) and the more general *Civil War in the Midlands* by Roy Sherwood (Alan Sutton). For those wanting a slightly more general view of the Civil Wars and a good idea of uniform, tactics and weapons, look out for Philip Haythornthwaite's *English Civil War* (Blandford Press). For the military minded who want the details on the many skirmishes and battles of the three Civil Wars, then Brigadier Peter Young and Richard Holmes' *The English Civil War* is essential reading. Peter Young's *Civil War England* (Longman Travellers Series) provides a pungent guide to the best battlefields and castles to visit, as well as thumbnail sketches of some of the lesser known combatants. C. V. Wedgwood's *The King's War* (Penguin) provides the full political and strategic overview of the conflict, and further details of the bloody struggles on the Continent can be found in her excellent *Thirty Years War* (University Press). Details of the efforts made by the Royalists to organize themselves in the Midlands can be found in Ronald Hutton's *The Royalist War Effort* (Longman). The Osprey Elite series on infantry and cavalry of the Civil Wars provides good background on uniforms and organization, as well as including sets of excellent illustrations by Angus McBride.

While I have endeavoured to make The Shadow on the Crown series as historically accurate as possible, there are inevitably occasions when a little journalistic licence is required. Please forgive any unintentional errors as to when and precisely where certain events took place.

Nicholas Carter, pikeman and pamphleteer.